FIRE HAWK

ALSO BY GEOFFREY ARCHER

Skydancer
Shadowhunter
Eagletrap
Scorpion Trail
Java Spider

FIRE HAWK

Geoffrey Archer

Published by Arrow Books in 1999

3 5 7 9 10 8 6 4 2

This novel is a work of fiction. Names and characters are the product of the author's imagination and any resemblance to actual persons, living or dead, is entirely coincidental.

First published in the United Kingdom in 1998 by Century

Arrow Books Limited
20 Vauxhall Bridge Road, London, SW1V 2SA

Random House Australia (Pty) Limited
20 Alfred Street, Milsons Point, Sydney,
New South Wales 2061, Australia

Random House New Zealand Limited
18 Poland Road, Glenfield
Auckland 10, New Zealand

Random House South Africa (Pty) Limited
Endulini, 5a Jubilee Road, Parktown 2193, South Africa

Random House UK Limited Reg. No 954009

A CIP catalogue record for this book
is available from the British Library

Papers used by Random House UK Limited
are natural, recyclable products made from wood grown in sustainable forests. The manufacturing processes conform to the environmental regulations of the country of origin

ISBN 0 09 927143 5

Typeset by Deltatype Limited, Birkenhead, Merseyside

Printed and bound in Germany by
Elsnerdruck, Berlin

Terrorism is perpetrated by individuals with a strong commitment to the causes in which they believe.

The widespread changes occurring within the last two decades have allowed international organised crime groups to become increasingly active worldwide.

Louis J. Freeh
Director, Federal Bureau of Investigation
28 January 1998

For Eva, Ali and James

Prologue

The Englishman was naked. His hands were tied and his eyes were blinded by a rancid hood. His terror was unspeakable. They'd hurt him dreadfully and would hurt him again, searching for the moment when he could take no more.

The unseen interrogator stood close, smelling of tobacco and cheap after-shave. There were salivary noises from his mouth. The Englishman sensed his eyes on his bruised body, choosing which part to work on first.

Sam Packer struggled to close his mind to what was about to happen. Tried instead to picture something far away from this hell he was in. His mind focused on a face – the face of the woman he'd entrusted with his life.

Then they clubbed him behind the knees and brought him down.

Three days earlier.
Baghdad, Iraq.

They'd been friends for a long time – the middle aged Iraqi and the man he was about to double-cross. His decision to betray the secret they shared had been blocked by fear until now. The others would kill him when they learned what he'd done. But if the loss of his own life saved the thousands that the Colonel planned to murder, it would not have been lost in vain.

He sat hunched in the rear of the new-smelling military saloon, heart thumping, sweat dripping inside his shirt. The car had left behind the dust and poverty of the souks, crossing the Tigris towards the administrative sector of Baghdad. His breathing hurt – from fear and from the bad chest that had forced his retirement from the army a year after the Kuwait war, where he had served under the same Colonel who would soon be ordering his death.

He would do it just as they'd told him to, handing over the letter with its cryptic warning. But he would do something else, something they couldn't suspect, whispering in the Englishman's ear a secret so shocking he would move mountains to get it to his masters.

The road widened to a broad avenue. Looming on the right was the Rashid Hotel where the foreigners stayed.

Haji Abbas clutched his knees. All along, they'd kept him on the fringes of the conspiracy. Little more than an extra pair of hands. A doubter, but one bound to the Colonel by a loyalty that had now been tested too far. His knowledge of the plan and his complicity in it had become a shame he could no longer bear. The men in the front of the car were also tense. Their loyalty to the Colonel was unswerving yet their lives too were on the line. The Major, black-haired and moustached like their president, and the broad-shouldered Lieutenant behind the wheel whom he hardly knew.

The hotel gate guard lifted the pole and the driver swung in to the right and parked. Stepping inside the hotel's grand entrance, the three men trod solemnly on the face of George Bush painted where visitors would walk on it. Beyond it and to one side, long-faced men from Iraq's impoverished middle-classes sat at tables selling heirlooms to the few foreigners who ventured here.

They knew the Englishman was in the hotel. The Colonel had checked a short while ago. Abbas made for the elevators. Room 217, he'd been told. A room booked in the spy's cover name Terry Malone. As Abbas approached the lifts the Major touched his arm.

'No,' he hissed. 'Over there.'

Abbas looked across the lobby. The Englishman was sitting on a settee with a newspaper in his hands. Grey trousers, white shirt and dark tie. The British spy had a strong, square face with a determined chin, thick, dark hair and steady eyes that registered all they saw. The gritty face of a military man. *Ex*-military, though still in his thirties. Navy.

Abbas crossed the polished floor, tugging the envelope from his jacket. The Englishman looked up. Fear flashed in his eyes like an animal sensing a trap. The Arab's hand shot forward with the letter, the back of his neck prickling from the gaze of the men who'd driven him here.

'For you, Mister Packer.'

Shock in the eyes then quick recovery. 'That's not my name. I'm Terry Malone.'

But Packer *was* his name. His real one.

'You read please.' Abbas spoke hoarsely, his throat dry. With the letter passed, his duty to his friends had been fulfilled.

'Wrong man, old boy,' Packer insisted. 'Malone's the name.'

Heart in his mouth, Abbas leaned forward for the unscripted act that would betray his Colonel. Trembling lips close to the Englishman's ear, he unburdened his conscience of its dreadful secret. Words that might yet save thousands from a dreadful fate, but which he knew would seal his own.

I

Wednesday, 25 September 1996
Odessa, Ukraine

It was a little after seven in the morning when the two black Mercedes SL500 limousines sped through the elegant, tree-lined boulevards of Odessa. The sleek machines swept past the grey-green edifice in vulitsya Evreyska that used to house the KGB headquarters, the cars' heavy-set occupants giving it barely a glance. They'd feared the place in the old days. Feared the authority it represented. But today in this much-changed land it was they who held the power.

Gliding past two rattling Volgas and a packed bus belching soot, the limousines turned left by the Shevchenko Park. Then, tyres drumming on the cobbles, they pounded down the long, straight avenue to the Memorial to the Great Patriotic War, its obelisk set between a V of trees like the needle on a gun sight.

In the first car, two bodyguards rode up front, silently respectful of the man behind them dressed in a dark grey Armani suit and an expensively tasteful silk tie. Vladimir Filipovich Grimov sat on the central squab, keeping his distance from the armoured side windows. His close-cropped hair had the stiffness of a brush and his dark eyes were out of line with each other because one was made of glass.

The cobbled avenue ended in a paved circle. Parking

was forbidden here, but these men had nothing to fear from the Militsia. The two Mercs pulled up a couple of metres apart in front of a red marble tablet engraved with the dates 1941–1945. Beyond lay a small flower bed bursting with red geraniums, and beyond that a narrow, well-trimmed lawn flanked by flagstones stretched two hundred metres down the slope to the monument itself.

The doors of the second car were the first to open. Four men in black got out and spread through the trees, looking for shadows that moved. But at this early hour there was no one else here, as Grimov had expected. He strode down the slope to the terrace where the obelisk stood, ignoring the eternal flame flickering at its foot. He wasn't a man who paid homage. The terrace was edged by a waist-high wall. Like a preacher in a pulpit, he gripped its rim and looked down. Below and to his left lay the ugly sprawl of the docks. Beyond the cranes, most of them idle, a breakwater reached into the Black Sea, a small, white lighthouse at its tip.

The morning was clear and bright. He searched for the pier where the vessel had been due to dock. He held out a hand and an aide pressed binoculars into it. He raised them to his eyes, adjusting focus for the good one until he could read the names of the vessels below. He smiled. The container ship had arrived. As an ex-military man, it pleased him when things ran to plan. He lowered the glasses and watched the containers being swung from the deck to the quay, taking pleasure in knowing that those huge, powerful cranes were in part working for him. There was just one rust-red container on that ship that concerned him. It was his box, although his name and that of his organisation could never be linked with it.

The vessel had come from Piraeus, picking up cargoes there that had been gathered from ports all over the eastern Mediterranean. His container had been shipped from Haifa, packed with cartons of Israeli fruit and vegetable juices that were well past their sell-by dates and had been bought for next to nothing. The great plan he'd evolved for his foreign clients was going to make him very rich indeed. Their motives concerned him not one jot. Responsibility for the gruesome deaths would be his clients', not his. The one thing that *did* concern him was the complexity of the plan. Too much scope for things to go wrong.

He began to run through in his mind what lay immediately ahead.

In a few hours, if all went to schedule, the container would be delivered to a warehouse. A customs officer would turn up, to be greeted by the warehouse manager, who knew him well. The two men would drink tea together in the site office and talk about football, the customs man quoting from the match report in the morning paper which he would leave folded on the table when they went back outside. In the yard they would break the Israeli customs seals on the forty-foot steel box and open the doors.

Both men would recoil from the stench erupting from inside. Naturally. Both would click their tongues at the sight of the bursting cartons. The warehouse manager would curse the Israelis for sending them such rubbish, giving vent to his deep-rooted anti-Semitism. The load would have to go back. No question. But first the customs official would want it fully unloaded, to check for hidden drugs. Once that was done, and the box was found to contain nothing but rotting juice, the two men would retire to the site office again for a shot of pepper vodka. The customs official would agree to return in a few days' time to reseal the container, once a ship had been found for its return to Israel. There'd be no need to inspect the foul-smelling contents again, he would say. Of course not. No need at all. Then, after another shot of Pertsovka, the customs officer would pocket his folded newspaper – heavier now there was an envelope inside it – and be on his way.

Usually it was stolen icons that slipped out of the country this way. What it was to be this time the customs man would neither know nor care.

Vladimir Filipovich Grimov brushed imagined dust from the sleeves of his Armani suit and cast a last glance down at the harbour. He sniffed the crisp morning air. He had a good feeling about this one. A confidence that, despite its complexity, the plan would work.

He turned away from the view, handed the binoculars to his aide and strode back up the slope towards the cars.

It had begun.

2

Saturday, 28 September
Baghdad

The dusty yard behind the old, three-storey imports warehouse in eastern Baghdad had been little used since 1991 when the UN cut Iraq off from the outside world. Just large enough for a small truck to enter through its dilapidated wooden gates, it was shielded from prying eyes by a high breeze-block wall.

A small pickup in the dark green of the Iraqi army stopped in the alley at the back, a canvas awning covering its load area. Its uniformed driver undid the heavy, new-looking padlock on the gates and swung them open. Then he reversed in until the closed tailboard of the pickup was just a metre from a small doorway into the building. He quickly shut the gates again, glancing furtively at the empty neighbouring blocks for signs that his arrival might have been observed.

Then he went inside.

A few minutes later a different man emerged from the warehouse, also dressed in the dark green of Iraq's armed forces. Dark-haired and with a moustache that was a copy of his much-feared president's, he had the bearing of a middle-ranking officer. He stood beside the truck and listened.

It was early morning still. In the maze of mean streets

behind the warehouse lived some of Baghdad's poorest. For them another miserable day was beginning. The officer heard a baby cry, children shouting and mothers jabbering in efforts to shut them up. Smoke with an acid bite drifted into the yard. Many families, he knew, had been reduced to cooking on fires fuelled by refuse.

He checked the windows of neighbouring buildings, then, as satisfied as he could be that he was not being watched, he unfastened the tarpaulin at the rear of the truck and lowered the tailboard.

A minute later the pickup's driver reappeared, his left hand gripping the pinioned arm of a prisoner hooded by a black bag with a small breathing hole cut in it. The captive, who wore a white shirt, grey trousers and no shoes, stumbled as if his feet had been cut by broken glass.

'Where am I going?' An English voice. Weak. 'Where are you taking me?'

'No speaking!'

'I want to know, damn you!' Stronger now.

Silently the officer with the moustache stepped forward and punched him in the stomach. The Englishman buckled. As they bundled him into the rear of the pickup, his damaged shins scraped the tailboard and he yelped with pain. Crouching beside the prisoner on the ribbed metal floor the guard sat the Englishman upright, then unlocked the cuffs that held his hands behind his back.

'Tch, tch,' he clucked. 'I told you, no questions. It is better for you.'

He saw blood seeping through the prisoner's trousers. It had been several days since the beatings, but shins took a long time to heal. On the floor of the pickup was a stretcher. He told the Englishman to lie on it.

'Look, what the hell is this? Where am I being taken?'

'You soon see,' the guard whispered, tying the man's arms to the poles. 'If you lucky this finish quick for you.'

The Englishman felt as if his heart had stopped. The bastards were going to kill him.

The green pickup wove though the narrow alleys of the market district, squeezing past dusty tinsmithies where shutters were being rolled up for the day's business. The driver braked frequently to avoid crushing boys balancing trays of tea. Pungent smells wafted in through the open window. The moustached officer sat silently beside the driver, glaring out of the window, revelling in the intimidating effect his green uniform had on those who saw it.

The vehicle's jolting on the rutted back alleys of Shaikh Omar turned the stretcher Sam Packer was lying on into a bed of nails. He was a strong, fit man, just under six feet tall, but a couple of weeks of being battered by what he'd assumed to be the Mukhabarat – the Iraqi secret police – had reduced his strength to a girl's. Above all else he wanted to see again. Since the day they'd grabbed him they'd removed the foul-smelling hood from his head just once, and then only for a desperate purpose. None of the training he'd been given upon joining the Intelligence Service six years earlier had prepared him for what they'd put him through. But he'd told them nothing of what they wanted to hear. To confess to being a spy meant the gallows, and death had no appeal for him. A terrible dread, however, told him that death was now to be his fate, confession or not.

It had been the middle of September when he'd arrived in Baghdad, but how many days had passed since then he had little idea. His visa application had given his employer as Entryline Exhibitions of Egham, Surrey. The job was genuine enough. So was the purpose of his visit: to survey arrangements for a trade fair the following year. But his second job was the one that mattered: listening out for hints of which European and Asian businessmen had plans to satisfy Iraq's appetite for arms once UN sanctions were lifted.

The moment of his entrapment was a scene he'd relived countless times as he lay on the stone floor of the latrine-like cell waiting to be beaten again. It had happened out of the blue. No inkling. Sitting in the lobby of the Rashid Hotel on his fourth evening in Iraq, he'd been glancing at a week-old *Herald Tribune* a German had passed on to him when a middle-aged Iraqi had approached. Small and scruffy, with pale, strangely dead eyes, the man was a creature he'd never seen before.

'*For you, Mister Packer.*'

It had been terrifying to hear his real name used, terrifying to hear it spoken by this stranger. The Iraqi had ignored his denials, leaning forward until his mouth was just inches from his ear. Then he'd begun to whisper, a warning that had taken Sam's breath away: '*Anthrax warheads – they have been taken outside Iraq and will soon be used.*'

Anthrax. Biological warfare. BW – the UN's living nightmare, the primary target now of its five-year-long inspection regime inside Iraq. *Will soon be used. . .* Where? And when? Before he could ask the man was gone.

His mind had cartwheeled. Was the warning true, or a trick? The man had known his name. Not Terry Malone, the name on his passport and the hotel register, but Packer. Sam Packer. And if they knew his real name, they knew he was a spy, and *they* must be Iraqi counter-intelligence. He'd felt caught in a spotlight. He'd scanned the lobby for watching eyes. The hotel was riddled with hidden cameras and microphones. *Someone* would have recorded the contact made with him. Slowly he'd stood up, slipping the envelope into the pocket of his jacket and making for the lifts.

Up in his bedroom, unmasked and a very long way

from home, he'd felt the first shiver of panic. He'd locked himself in the bathroom and hidden behind the shower curtain to avoid covert lenses. Inside the envelope he'd found a single sheet of lined note-paper. On it, two sentences of four words each.

Beware of Salah Khalil. He is Saddam's man.

The name had meant nothing to him. Two messages passed to him; one written, one verbal, one about a man, one about a plague. No obvious connection between the two.

He'd memorised the words on the note, then burned it, flushing the ash down the drain. Common sense had told him this was a trap – the Mukhabarat feeding him phoney intelligence in the hope of catching him passing it to London. Yet his guts had told him something else, that the messenger had been risking his neck to speak to him. That the man was in fear of his life. With no time in which to think, he'd concluded the warnings could be genuine, and since the danger from anthrax weapons was so great, the tip-off, however vague, had to be passed on fast. Direct communication with London was impossible. No phone was safe. But he'd remembered the German businessman who'd given him the newspaper, remembered he was heading home via Amman that evening.

He'd set to work fast, squatting on the loo seat and searching the newspaper for the crossword. Filling in blanks in its matrix, he'd scrawled K-H-A-L-I-L S-U-S-P-E-C-T and B-W A-T-T-A-C-K A-L-E-R-T – there'd been no time for code. Then he'd buried a phone number on the small ads page. Not the direct line for his controller at SIS – too risky if the German were to be stopped by the Mukhabarat – but a personal number, someone whose reaction to the message would be as instinctive as his.

Chrissie Kessler, his lover until three months ago.

Downstairs, the German had had the taxi door open when Sam found him.

'Your paper. You wanted it back,' he'd declared, willing the man to understand. In a whisper he'd added, 'Look inside. Later, not now. Ring the number on page six. It's London. Ask for Chrissie. Read her the crossword. Please.'

Not wavering for a moment, the German had climbed into the taxi and driven off.

Three minutes later, back in the hotel lobby, Packer had been arrested. The Mukhabarat had seen everything. A trap after all. Two men had hustled him to a car, one of them with shiny black hair and a Saddam moustache. And now, God knew how many days later, here he was, strapped to a stretcher in the back of some truck that smelled of piss, heading for whatever fate they'd decided on. He was helpless. On his own. They could do what they liked with him – and they would.

The bumping of the wheels that had been causing him such discomfort ended suddenly. The truck's tyres began humming on smooth tarmac. There was no more stopping for lights or crossroads. They were on some highway now. He forced himself to concentrate, to make an intelligent guess at what was happening. He knew what the pattern was. Foreigners arrested in the past had been interrogated in police cells, then moved after a farce of a trial to the main prison at Abu Ghraib, west of the city. Abu Ghraib. A place of misery and executions. His heart turned over again. Did they give prisoners fair warning when they were about to kill them, or did they just string them up?

In the days that had followed his arrest, the worst part for him had been the isolation. Not knowing what was happening or why. No comfort call from the Red Cross. No diplomatic visit from the Russians who looked after British interests in Baghdad. It was as if the outside world had forgotten he even existed. He knew that once caught, a spy must expect to be disowned by his own people, but the reality of it had been hard to stomach.

At first they'd questioned him without physical violence. His interrogator who'd spoken in a plummy English accent acquired, he guessed, at a British staff college several years back, had demanded he confess to spying and name his contacts. But he'd denied everything, maintaining he truly was Terry Malone, an exhibition contractor. Then after a couple of days the atmosphere had changed. They'd begun to rough him up. Instead of the catch-all about spying, the interrogator, whom he'd nicknamed 'Sandhurst', had posed a different question: what was it the middle-aged informant had whispered to him in the Rashid Hotel lobby?

The switch of question had thrown him. Why were they asking it if the informant had simply been acting on Mukhabarat orders – and he must have been, he'd reasoned, because he knew his real name. Only a counter-intelligence service could have broken his cover, and he had no clue how. He'd begun to wonder if the tip-off man had gone further than his Mukhabarat masters had intended and revealed a secret in that fear-laden whisper. He'd bluffed it out with his questioner, pretending the informant had simply exhorted him to read the letter then destroy it. The interrogator's response had been brutal. Concentrating first on the small of his back, the blows had knocked the air from his lungs. But he'd told them nothing. In later sessions they'd used sticks on his shins and glowing cigarettes on his chest. But he'd still said not a word about anthrax.

Between beatings they'd returned him to his cell and deprived him of sleep and nourishment. How often the cycle had been repeated he didn't know. He'd lost sense of time and place, floating on a cushion of pain, kept alive by his certainty that to admit anything at all would mean certain death. As his strength had faded, two questions had circled unanswered in his head. How the hell had the Iraqis broken his cover? And had they received his message in London – had Chrissie ever been given it and had she passed it on?

Confirmation that the thin-faced informant must have exceeded his instructions had arrived soon after. They'd been interrogating Packer again, punctuating their questions with blows to his feet. Then suddenly they'd stopped, dragging him to another room and whipping the hood off. Dangling in front of him was a corpse, naked like himself. The anthrax messenger had been suspended from a rope by hands bound behind his back. His arms were half wrenched from their sockets, his eyes were cataract white, his belly black from the beating that had ruptured his innards.

'This will happen to you, Packer,' Sandhurst had hissed from behind his head. 'Unless you tell me what he told you.'

Back in the interrogation room his captors had forgotten to replace the hood at first. For the first time since his arrest he could see his surroundings. The room was some sort of store, large and bare, its windows blacked-out with cardboard. And for the first time too he had seen the faces of his tormentors.

Sandhurst, he'd finally realised, was the creature with the Saddam moustache who'd arrested him at the Rashid, dressed now in a dark green uniform which bore no insignia. The guard who'd carried out the beatings on Sandhurst's orders had been the second man at the arrest.

And there'd been a third person in the room, a man whose presence he'd been unaware of until then. A commanding figure sitting a few feet away from the others, motionless and silent, eyeing him with a brooding intensity, his dog-like face leathery and lined, his hair and mournful moustache a distinguished sandy-grey. This was the man in charge. The man who controlled his fate.

For several seconds he'd felt the intensity of his gaze, the commanding presence. This sand-blasted figure was a veritable Saladin of a man. And it was him, this one, he'd decided, who was so desperate to discover what the messenger had whispered to him.

Suddenly the Labrador eyes had turned angry, the man's chisel chin jerking forward involuntarily. He'd shouted at his subordinates. He'd been seen by the prisoner and didn't want to be. The hood had been jammed back on.

Then, two days ago, Packer had had the feeling they were giving up, that he'd defeated them. Yesterday there'd been no interrogation session at all and they'd let him sleep out his exhaustion. At the end of the day they'd disconnected his arm from the heating pipe to which he'd been shackled, moved him from the stinking toilet of a cell whose vile, shit-caked confines he'd defined through touch on day one of his incarceration, then never again, and hosed him down with icy water. After that they'd let him eat something that tasted like food instead of sewage, and given him a room with a bed instead of a stone floor. He'd felt absurdly relieved. Almost euphoric.

This morning, however, when his guard told him he was being moved, his fear had returned. Something new was in store and they wouldn't say what. A show trial perhaps? Some travesty of a court process? A spy hearing for which there was only ever one sentence in Iraq?

It was hot in the back of the truck now. The tyres had hummed for what seemed like hours. If it was Abu Ghraib they were heading for, they should surely have arrived already. But if not Abu Ghraib, where else? The road they were on sounded smooth and felt straight. The only route from the capital that he knew personally was the motorway to Jordan. With no flights, all commercial visitors to Iraq had to take the ten-hour drive from Amman. But there were other main roads from Baghdad

– north, south and east. They could be taking him anywhere.

If you lucky this finish quick for you. At that moment the guard's words had only one meaning for him. Death. The noose over the head, the tightening at the throat, the floor dropping away. He ordered himself not to think about it.

From time to time during the past days he'd felt intense, bitter anger at his masters at SIS for failing to get him out of there. What were they doing in London? There'd been nothing from the world he knew. Not a word. And Chrissie – surely to God she would have moved heaven and earth for him.

From time to time, too, he'd ruminated on what madness it was that had made him want to be a spy in the first place. A thirst for excitement had been one motive, and as he lay there in his own filth in the bare cell it had seemed a damned stupid one. But there'd been more to it than that – a fundamental belief that the dissemblers of this world needed sorting out and that he should be one of those to do it. For now, however, the dissemblers had won. He was their prisoner.

Suddenly the truck slowed down, bumping onto the rough verge and coming to a juddering halt. The sun had turned the rear of the vehicle into an oven. Sam's throat felt parched. He heard the flap being unlaced and someone climbing into the back.

'What's going on?' He felt panicky again. 'What's happening?'

He imagined a pistol being put to his head. His arms were untied and he was jerked up into a sitting position.

'We have stopped to urinate, Packer. That is all.' Sandhurst's mellow tones. It surprised him the interrogator was still with him. 'We don't want you making a mess of our vehicle.'

Why was Sandhurst here? Interrogators weren't normally involved in transporting prisoners around the country.

'Then take this damn hood off so I can see what I'm doing.'

'You're not allowed to see. You're a *spy*, Packer.'

Gingerly, Sam felt for the edge of the platform and swung his legs over. When his feet hit the ground he yelped with pain. Hands gripped him and he was marched a few paces.

'This will do.' Sandhurst's voice again. 'You can do it here. What is it you call it in the Navy? Pumping ship?'

'Something like that.'

The Navy . . . *How* did this man know so much about him?

Packer fumbled with the unfamiliar buttons of the trousers given to him to wear that morning. Unable to see what he was doing, the flow didn't come easily. Behind him on the road he heard the swish of heavy vehicles passing, confirming they were on a main highway. And from the strength of the sun above he guessed it was midday or later. Must have dozed a little in the truck.

After he had buttoned up, the hands were back on his elbows, spinning him round and steering him to the truck.

'Look,' he protested gently, 'for the love of God, can't you tell me where we're going?'

'You'll find out soon enough,' Sandhurst snapped, shoving him against the tailboard so he could feel the ledge. 'Get in. There's some water in a bottle if you want it.'

'What about food? I've had nothing.'

'Oh, really? Haven't you heard?' Sandhurst mocked. 'There's a food shortage in Iraq. UN sanctions, you know.'

Sam eased his backside onto the tailboard and swung

his legs up. His shins burned horribly. He edged backwards until he found the stretcher again. A plastic water bottle was pressed into his hands. He unscrewed the top and raised the rim to his lips. The water was warm and unpleasant, but he drank gratefully. He heard breathing. His hearing, made more sensitive by his inability to see, told him it was the guard beside him rather than Sandhurst.

'What's going to happen to me?' he whispered. 'You can tell me.' Between the beatings this man had shown a degree of kindness to him in the past few days.

'Tch!'

Sam held out the bottle.

'No. You must drink more. You get dehydrate.'

He felt he'd had enough, but took several more swigs.

'Where are we going, friend? Tell me.'

'Tch, tch,' the Iraqi repeated, taking the bottle and pushing Sam down onto the stretcher. He retied his arms. 'You are spy. Soon finish for you.'

God! That word 'finish' was like a bell tolling.

'What d'you mean?'

'This night. All finish for you,' the guard whispered, then scurried away.

Tonight. Within hours. The ambiguity of the words tortured him. He tensed his arms, testing the strength of the ties. No chance of escape. He heard the canvas flaps being fastened, then the cab doors banging shut. The engine coughed back into life and they began to move again.

As the tyres picked up speed on the highway, his mind filled with the image of a face. The face of the woman whom he'd entrusted with his life. A face framed by silky chestnut hair and dominated by cool grey eyes.

Chrissie.

It had been a whim to put her phone number in the German's newspaper. An instinctive act, stemming from a belief that she still cared for him. She'd been Christine White when they first met, although she'd used a different surname as her cover. Christine Kessler now, the wife of a department head at MI6. Ironically it had been here in Iraq their affair had begun, six years ago. With Iraq's army massing on the border with Kuwait, Western intelligence had been short of agents in place. Newly transferred to the Intelligence Service from the Royal Navy, he'd been despatched to Baghdad as an extra on a trade mission. A few days later the Iraqi army had invaded Kuwait, and when the West threatened retaliation most foreigners in Iraq, including himself, had been rounded up as hostages.

He'd been told before his mission that there was another MI6 agent in Baghdad, but not her name. A woman whose cover job was with a British company running a construction contract. He knew that she'd been told about him too. At the hotel where most of the Britons were being held by the Iraqi security services, they'd identified one another through a process of elimination.

She'd attracted him instantly. Physically at least. From the crown of her red-brown hair to the immaculately pedicured toes peeping from a pair of slingback sandals, she'd oozed style and sensuality. Her character had grated at first – she'd tried to pull rank because she'd worked for the Intelligence Service longer than him. But the antipathy hadn't lasted. Thrown together by confinement to the hotel, their relationship had become close and equal.

But not intimate at first, not until the Iraqi announcement that the foreigners were to be used as human shields against American bombers. Then a change had come about in her. The fear spreading through the hostages that they would all be killed had gripped her with an irrational intensity. She'd kept her cool in public, but alone with him in the privacy of his room she'd gone to pieces. She'd shared his bed that night and he'd done what he'd wanted to do since first clapping eyes on her. The next day, when the hostages had been shipped off to be held at strategic targets, Sam had been separated from her. Only at Christmas when they were repatriated to Britain had they met again. Only then had she told him that she was engaged to be married. To Martin Kessler, a senior official at SIS.

He'd expected that to be the end of the matter – a sexual interlude in a moment of crisis – but the bond forged in Baghdad was not to be broken so easily. A few months after her wedding she'd contacted him again, inviting herself to his apartment one Sunday afternoon. Within minutes of walking through the door she'd told him her marriage had been a terrible mistake. That her husband lacked bedroom skills and seemed disinclined to acquire any.

She'd made no secret of the purpose of her visit. Her directness had disarmed him. He wasn't used to women declaring so openly that they wanted sex, particularly women who attracted him as much as Chrissie. Despite qualms about what he was getting into, he'd obliged her, because when she'd unbuttoned her shirt in his living room that Sunday afternoon, the reasons for doing so had seemed infinitely more appealing than those against. Their affair had lasted for over five years on and off, until three months ago, when she'd announced her 'final and irreversible' decision to commit herself to her husband. No good reason given. At least, none that had made sense to him.

The truck hit a pothole suddenly, shooting pain through his bruised back.

How stupid. How incredibly ill-judged, he realised now, to have sent his message to a woman who'd rejected him. Phoned through to the home she shared with the man he'd cuckolded, a man who could by definition be no friend of his, a man high up in MI6 who had the power to decide that a spy whose cover was blown in Iraq should be left to rot there.

'Stupid,' he mouthed to himself. 'Fucking stupid.'

Despair engulfed him. He was utterly alone – and he felt it.

It was hot in the back of the truck and getting hotter. He would have given anything for some more of that water, despite its unpleasant taste, but if the bottle was there, his pinioned arms were preventing him getting to it. An irresistible drowsiness began to creep over him.

When he came to, his head throbbed and he had no idea how much more time had passed. The truck had stopped. A cool draught of air blowing over him told him that the canvas flap had been lifted and it was night. How could he have slept so long? He tried to snap awake, but his mind was a fog. Suddenly it occurred to him that the water he'd drunk could have been drugged.

Minutes passed. He listened but heard nothing that would tell him where he was. Then through the rough fabric of the hood he saw a light being shone on him. Thick rubber soles thumped up onto the truck's steel floor. He had company. Someone who reeked of sweat. The sleeve of his shirt was pulled up, fingers tapping on his veins.

'What the fuck . . . ?'

Terror hit him. Sheer, blind terror.

'What're you doing?'

He strained at the ties binding him to the stretcher. A needle jabbed in and a flush of coolness spread up his arm.

'Oh no. *No!*'

Not like that. Not so soon. Not when he wasn't ready.

3

Amman, Jordan

The Airbus turbofans whimpered into silence and the dozen business-class passengers began to unclip their belts. Cabin staff delved into hanging spaces for jackets, their eyes betraying an eagerness to be rid of their passengers. It had been a long flight.

Towards the back of the cabin an English woman in her mid-thirties, whose red-brown hair fell in wisps across her forehead, had given the appearance of being asleep through most of the flight. Now she sat up straight and made a bleary-eyed check that nothing had fallen from her handbag. Then she stood up to extricate her small suitcase from the overhead locker.

'Let me.'

A steward reached up for her and lowered the bag to the floor.

'Thanks.'

She flashed him her warmest of looks and noted the interest in his eyes. At least one of them wasn't gay.

'Hope we'll see you again soon, Mrs Taylor.'

'Thank you. I hope so too.'

A stewardess held out a cream linen jacket for her.

'Thanks. I'm glad half of me won't look creased,' she said, brushing her lap in an attempt to smooth the wrinkles of the matching skirt. 'I'd have done better wearing jeans.' She slipped the jacket on. 'What did they say the temperature was outside?'

'Not sure, madam. Twenty-four Celsius, I think. But it'll drop at this time of year. Nights in Amman should be pleasantly cool at the end of September.'

The woman made liberal use of a perfume spray while the dark-suited, dapper little Arab, who'd been seated three rows in front of her smoking like a chimney during the flight, brushed past, heading for the exit. His face, she noticed, was still puckered with anger and disappointment at being expelled from Britain. She stepped quickly into the aisle to be right behind him, flinching at the acid whiff of his perspiration. The aircraft's main door was open but the stairs had yet to be wheeled into place. Beyond the galley in the crowded tourist section of the plane she saw passengers queuing impatiently to get off.

When the steps finally arrived, she stuck right behind the man she'd been shadowing as he descended to the tarmac. There was a fifty-metre walk to the terminal. She glanced up at its roof. Half-lit faces watching for relatives. She knew that among them would be professionals, Iraqis checking that the man whose return they'd demanded – the man in front of her – had truly arrived. But it was dark on the tarmac. Passengers hurrying from both ends of the plane were all around them now. Would the watchers spot him in the gloom? It was vital they did. Timing was critical.

As they neared the building they entered a small pool of brightness cast by a floodlight. She darted forward, touching the Arab on the arm. Then she stepped in front of him, forcing him to stop in the glare of the light.

'Excuse me. I'm so sorry, but I think I must have left my cigarette lighter on the plane.' She held a Silk Cut between her fingers. 'Could you possibly . . .'

Startled, the Arab began fumbling in his pocket. Then he stopped abruptly.

'But it's not permitted here.'

'Oh? Are you sure?'

'Quite sure.' His voice was irritable. 'They said on the aircraft. Not until the terminal.'

'Ah yes, of course. I'm sorry to have troubled you.'

The Arab hurried on again. But it had been long enough. If the Iraqis hadn't seen him by now then they couldn't have been looking.

In the over-chilled concourse of the Queen Alia International Airport she kept a few metres behind Salah Khalil as he followed the signs to passport control. What sort of reception would he be expecting, she wondered? None at all, probably, hoping it had merely been some whim of the British Home Office that had got his asylum application rejected. Yet she knew Khalil would be quaking in his boots, knowing as he did the obsessive, unforgiving nature of the people he'd run away from in Baghdad. The Jordanian capital Amman would be far too close to home for him. Far too easy a place for his enemies to find him in.

The information that the Secret Intelligence Service had gleaned on Khalil had been sparse. When he'd turned up in Britain six weeks ago hoping to buy asylum with titbits of information about the regime in Baghdad, his name had elicited few responses from the databases at Vauxhall Cross, or from those in Washington or Jerusalem. He'd claimed to be on the fringes of Saddam Hussein's inner circle, a cousin of someone related to the Iraqi leader by marriage. He'd maintained that the Mukhabarat had falsely accused him of embezzlement and his life was in danger. Enquiries with Iraqi exiles used by MI6 and the CIA as sounding boards had produced the suggestion that Khalil had in fact been the banker in a drug-smuggling operation run by one of Saddam's sons. There was a suspicion he'd run off with the takings.

The woman in the linen suit sensed heads turning as she walked into the crowded immigration hall. It had been happening that way for as much of her life as she could remember. As an only child she hadn't liked it at first, not wanting her neat prettiness to make her stand out from the crowd. But as a teenager, when her father's long absences from home had left her deprived of male attention, turning heads was a skill she'd learned to perfect. She was tall for a woman, about five nine, with a generous bust and a neat, almost boyish behind. Her lightly tanned skin, thin but sensuous lips and long, elegant nose gave her a natural attraction that she'd learned to exploit.

The man she was following headed for the middle line at passport control. She quickened her pace and overtook him just as they joined the queue. She turned to him and smiled, holding up the cigarette again. Still irritated, he dug in his pocket and produced a gold Dunhill lighter.

She pictured the scene beyond the arrivals doors. There would be many watchers there, some obvious, some not. First to make their move would be the Iraqis, making it clear to Khalil he had no option but to go with them. Watching to ensure it happened peacefully would be the Jordanian secret police, alerted by SIS to Khalil's presence on the flight from London. And finally there would be someone from the British Embassy, poised to call up the SIS officials out in the desert the moment Khalil was back in Iraqi hands.

There was a lot at stake in the coming hours. Plenty that could go wrong.

Part one of her mission – ensuring that Khalil made no trouble on the flight out and was spotted the moment he landed – was over.

Part two of her mission would not be so simple.

20.30 hrs
The Iraqi–Jordanian Border

There was a chill in the air. The bleak, boulder-strewn border between Jordan and Iraq was at an altitude of close on a thousand metres and at this time of year the desert soon lost the heat it had absorbed during the day. The sky was a black and moonless shroud, pricked by the glimmer of a billion stars.

Quentin Mowbray checked his watch again and stared down at the briefcase-sized satellite phone terminal with its flat antenna which he'd set up on the sand behind the long-wheelbase Land Rover. He willed it to ring. Behind him on the straight, bumpy road from the Jordanian capital, trucks stuffed with sacks of rice and wheat queued to have their papers processed so they could thunder on to a hungry Baghdad. The desert night air that should have smelled fresh was laced with the fumes of exhausts.

'This could be the one,' a soft voice murmured behind him.

Mowbray swung round. His number two, Simon Twiss, was leaning on the bonnet of the Land Rover peering down the road to Iraq through image-intensifying binoculars.

'May I?' Mowbray asked, reaching out.

He took the glasses and refocused them. On the far side of the sodium-lit no man's land between the border posts stood the blockhouses of the Iraqi police and customs. Parked beside them was a pickup of a type he knew to be used by the Iraqi army and police. A man in uniform stood in front of it, binoculars pressed to his own eyes. Watching them watching him. Then a grain lorry drove through, blocking Mowbray's field of vision for a moment.

The satphone trilled suddenly. Mowbray thrust the glasses back at Twiss and crouched to pick up the receiver.

'Yes?'

'He's here. Just going through immigration.' The voice of an excited second secretary from the embassy, on stakeout at Amman airport. 'His friends saw him on the tarmac. They're moving to the next phase. Any signs?'

'We think so. We're about to check. Ring again when he's through customs.'

'Will do.'

Mowbray replaced the receiver. 'This is where we get stuffed,' he murmured. He'd been against this deal. Too easy for the other side to cheat and leave egg all over some very important British faces.

'That chap in uniform is on the phone,' whispered Twiss excitedly, the binoculars jammed into his eye sockets. 'Bugger's even got the same kit as us!'

Mowbray snorted. The satphone was American-made. Supplying the Iraqi intelligence organisations with it was in breach of UN sanctions.

'Better go for it.'

Twiss swung up into the driving seat of the Land Rover and held up the walkie-talkie to show he had it. Mowbray turned to a Jordanian border guard.

'We're ready. If you please.'

The policeman stepped into the road to delay the next truck. No man's land would be kept empty for the next few minutes. It was in nobody's interests that there should be casual witnesses to this skulduggery.

The Land Rover's engine rattled into life and the vehicle pulled away. The Jordanian policeman chatted to the delayed truck driver to divert his attention, determinedly not looking at what was happening behind him. On this border across which countless illegal items had been smuggled into Iraq, turning a blind eye was second nature. The Land Rover drove fifty metres into no man's land and stopped. Through the glasses Mowbray watched the Iraqi pickup crawl forward to meet it. It also stopped and two men jumped down from the back. Mowbray's anxiety racked up a notch. Neither of the men resembled the description he'd been given of Packer. Then he saw something else.

'Fuck!'

A stretcher was being lifted from the back of the pickup.

'Fucking Ada!'

No one had said anything about a stretcher. Nothing about Packer being ill or injured. Or dead.

'Bastards!'

There was always *some* catch with the Iraqis, but Packer being a casualty was one he hadn't planned for. A total no-show – yes, he'd almost expected it. But not this. He had no doctor with him. Nearest usable medic five hours' drive away. And the embassy Land Rover was full of seats. Nowhere to lie a sick man down. Or to lay out a corpse.

Mowbray saw Twiss standing there in the gloom, hands on hips, puzzling over what to do as the uniformed Iraqis dumped the stretcher on the ground.

'Jesus Christ!'

He snatched up the short-range VHF handset lying next to the satphone.

'Is it him?' he hissed into it.

Mowbray saw Twiss crouch down and lean over the body.

'Affirmative.'

'Is he all right?'

'He's breathing.'

'What's wrong with him?'

'They won't say.'

The satphone trilled again. Mowbray's man at the airport.

'The Iraqis have just picked him up. Two of them. He looked pretty horrified to see them, I must say. Tried to turn back into the baggage hall, but some rather luscious woman blocked his way. Anyway, they've taken him off in a limo now. One of the heavies was busy on a mobile phone, so if they stick to the agreement you should see some action pretty soon.'

Mowbray shuddered at the way the airport watcher was talking so openly. He'd had to rope in a young third secretary from the consular department to help him complete the circle of watchers and signallers needed to ensure the swap happened.

'We have him,' he answered curtly. 'You'd better get back to the office.'

'Great.'

Cursing silently, Mowbray waited for three anxious minutes. The Iraqis seemed to be awaiting the final order to complete the hand-over. Then, suddenly, there was movement. Packer's body was lifted from the stretcher and humped into the back of the Rover like a sack of sand. Twiss got back behind the wheel and the Rover made a cautious turn.

'Good man,' Mowbray growled as Twiss drew along-side him. His junior's face was pinched with tension. 'Any injuries that you can see?'

'Legs look a bit messy. There's blood on his trousers.'

Mowbray looked into the back and saw the dark stains in the region of Packer's shins.

'Jesus bloody Christ,' he breathed.

He recognised Sam from the photo London had faxed him, but only just. A couple of weeks in the hands of Iraqi security had given a grey pallor to his pleasantly pugnacious face and put bags under his eyes, but the stubborn chin was unmistakable. The thick, dark hair looked greasy and uncombed. Mowbray prodded him gingerly but Packer lay motionless. The clothes he had on were twisted and ill-fitting, as if they'd belonged to someone else. His feet were bare. A suitcase had been slung into the luggage space at the back.

'Might be drugged, rather than ill,' murmured Twiss.

A Jordanian officer bustled from the guardhouse.

'Finished?' he asked, not looking in the vehicle.

'Yes. Yes, thanks.' Mowbray shook his hand and the policeman waved at his subordinate to re-open the road.

'He's certainly breathing easily enough,' Twiss continued, leaning over the body sprawled in the back. 'Sleeping like a bloody baby. No injury that I can see, apart from the legs. No fever. He's not hot or anything.'

'Okay. Strap him in somehow and let's get the hell out of here before some curious truckie begins to figure out what's going on.'

4

Sunday, 29 September, early a.m.
Amman

Sam was aware of being awake and of not wanting to be. His leaden limbs and thick head demanded more sleep. He had no idea where he was. A memory of the piss-smelling truck and a needle in the arm, then a vague recollection of a different vehicle. Of an endless journey in acute discomfort on an extremely bumpy road. Of retching on an empty stomach.

But now he felt soft bed-springs beneath his back and heard voices. He half-opened his eyes and saw two faces he didn't recognise. At least two. Could have been more. Might just have been one, multiplied by the kaleidoscope someone seemed to have lodged in his eyeballs. He blinked and twisted his head to get a clearer focus. It *was* two faces and he still didn't recognise them. But something in his head told him they were going to kill him. The needle in the arm was a mere preamble. A trial run. Maybe he was dead already.

He tried to swallow but his throat felt as dry as the Iraqi desert he remembered pissing on some time back. Then logic kicked in. He couldn't be dead, because surely when you're dead things like being thirsty don't happen any more.

One of the faces pressed closer. An Arab face,

scrutinising him like he was a laboratory rat. The injection . . . the Iraqis were using him as a guinea pig for their weapons trials . . . the fluid shot into his veins some vile chemical concoction . . . and now he was in some secret lab the bastards had kept hidden from the UN inspectors.

A hand reached towards him and a finger pushed his eyelids fully open one by one. From somewhere close he heard a gentle English voice ask, 'What was it d'you think?'

'Can't tell. Some barbiturate probably.' It was the Arab who'd answered.

'Sam . . .' Again, the English voice. But truly English this time. None of your phoney Sandhurst. 'Sam, you're okay. You're in Jordan. Can you hear me?'

He turned his head to focus on the face that was speaking his name. It was thin, lean and tanned, with straight fair hair, a beak of a nose and grey eyes that were observing him with a cool concern.

'Hello,' Packer croaked, his voice sounding as if it wasn't his.

'I'm Quentin Mowbray. Station officer in Amman. You're free, old man. We got you out.'

'Out?' Sam's mind wasn't registering.

'Out of Iraq. You're in Jordan.'

No. A trick. He couldn't risk believing this. But *Mowbray*. The name was right. Quentin Mowbray, station head in Amman.

'You're free, old man. Not a prisoner any more.' Mowbray spoke loudly, as if addressing a geriatric.

'It's true?' Sam croaked.

A wet wave of emotion threatened to overwhelm him, but he held it back. Don't let go. Names proved nothing. If the Iraqi Mukhabarat had known who he was, they'd surely know about Mowbray too. This room could well be in Iraq, his tormentors playing cruel games with him, wanting him to think he was among friends so he would open up and tell them at last what that dead messenger had whispered to him.

'How did I get here?' he asked, testing them. The haze was beginning to clear.

'They drugged you with something,' Mowbray hedged. He indicated the Arab and added, 'This man's a Jordanian doctor.' Then his eyes narrowed so Sam would understand to be careful about what he said in his presence. 'He wants to examine you.'

'Yes, my friend. If you don't mind.' The doctor's voice was flat and dispassionate. 'Do you have any pains?'

Who wouldn't have pains, after what you lot have done to me? Sam wanted to say, but he held his tongue, badly wanting to believe that he truly was free.

'Back's sore,' he answered carefully, 'and my shins feel as if they've been worked on with a potato peeler.'

'Of course. You've been seriously maltreated. But inside? Any internal pain?' The doctor prodded Sam's chest and stomach with the tips of his fingers. 'Does this hurt?'

'No.'

'Good. All right. Try to sit up, Mister Packer. I want you to drink some water.'

You and me both, thought Sam. Glancing from face to face, still searching for some definitive confirmation that what was happening was real, he let them lever him upright and reposition the pillows behind him. Then he reached out a hand for the glass being offered, but it slipped through his jelly-like fingers.

'Let me,' said the doctor, holding it against his lips.

Sam took a huge slug and choked, the water sticking to the sides of his throat.

'Slowly. Just a little,' the doctor urged.

Sam sipped more cautiously. This time the liquid descended, his body absorbing it like blotting paper.

He looked down at himself. Someone had undressed him, apart from white underpants that he didn't recognise as belonging to him. His bare chest was a rainbow of bruises and burns.

'Let me feel your back.' The doctor pushed gently in the region of his kidneys.

'Ouch!'

'Yes. Very tender, I think.'

'Fucking painful, actually.'

'Yes. It will be so for several days. There is serious bruising here.'

Sam looked beyond the two men, noticing rabbits on the wallpaper, furry toys heaped in a corner. A computer on a small desk. This was a child's bedroom.

'Where is this?' he asked.

'My place,' Mowbray explained. 'My home in Amman. Jenny, my daughter – it's her room, but she's away at school. In Somerset.'

'Where in Somerset?'

'Frome.'

The way Mowbray had answered straight away, the way everything in this room apart from the medic was so utterly English, Sam suddenly knew it was right. Knew that at last he could drop his guard.

'Chri–ist!' His mouth twitched. His eyes began to fill. 'Christ.' He gulped. 'Sorry . . .'

'Don't worry.' Mowbray took his hand and held it like he would a child's. 'Let it out, old man. You must've been through hell.'

Sam pulled his hand back. He disliked being touched in any personal way by men. He pressed both hands to his face to try to get its muscles under control.

'Well, I'll be buggered.' His face split into a smile. 'I

thought I was dead, you know that? Thought you'd all given up on me. I don't know whether to laugh or cry.'

'It's all right, old man,' Mowbray reassured him, new-mannishly. 'You can do both if you like.'

Suddenly Sam himself grabbed Mowbray's hand and shook it. Then he shook the doctor's too. 'Thank you. Thank you both,' he mouthed, lost for any other words.

Mowbray chuckled matily.

Sam looked around him again, blinking back tears and relishing the cosy normality of the room. Daylight glowed through a little curtained window and was brightening by the minute. No iron bars across it, no blindfolds or chains. And two faces with smiles on them. From somewhere outside he heard the wail of a muezzin. Dawn.

'Thank Christ!' he wheezed. 'I mean Allah,' he joked lamely.

Mowbray laughed with unnatural vigour. 'The first words of the hostage after his release!'

Sam frowned at the word 'hostage'. Was that what he'd been? He drank some more water, his brain building up revs.

'I can't begin to tell you how this feels.' He tried a grin. 'How did this . . . this *miracle* come about?'

Mowbray didn't answer, but turned to the doctor and asked, 'Will he be okay now?'

'Nothing obviously wrong with him, but he should have a proper examination. X-rays. He should rest for twenty-four hours. And in a day or two get someone to change those dressings I put on his legs.'

'Of course. He'll get a thorough check when he's back in London.'

Mowbray shook the doctor's hand and the Arab leaned towards Sam. 'You are most welcome in Jordan,' he breathed formally. Then he left. They heard his feet on the stairs and the front door closing.

They were alone now, and Sam saw the bonhomie

drain from Mowbray's eyes as he became a single-minded Six man again.

'Okay. Now we can talk,' Mowbray began. 'Just needed the quack to confirm you were still alive. And I have to tell you we weren't at all sure when we first clapped eyes on you.'

Sam leaned back against the propped up pillow and rested his head. He felt absurdly weak.

'You're not the only one,' he whispered. 'When that bloody needle went into my arm I thought I was on my way to Saint Peter.'

'Ah. So they *did* give you an injection.' Mowbray pulled up a pink-painted nursery chair, swung it round next to the bed and straddled it, clasping his hands together and resting his elbows on the back. 'Presumably did it so you wouldn't make trouble at the border if the thing went for a ball of chalk.'

'What thing? What happened? You're saying there was a deal?'

'A swap happened. You for that man Salah Khalil you sent the signal about.'

'*What?*' He'd thought Khalil a fiction. 'But swaps are Cold War stuff. Six doesn't work like that these days.'

'The chap had fled Baghdad,' Mowbray explained. 'With a load of Saddam's money, by the sound of it. Turned up in London offering his services and asking for asylum. We didn't like the look of him much anyway and when your warning came through that he was suspect, it sort of clinched it.'

'But London negotiated? With the Mukhabarat?' Sam was aghast.

'Wouldn't normally. But SIS wanted you out of there very badly. Just as badly as the Iraqis wanted Khalil back. Presumably now they've got him they'll blow his brains out.'

Sam stared at Mowbray. Was that what his arrest and torture had been about? All that horror just because the Iraqis needed a British hostage to swap for a thief? Not that simple. It couldn't be.

'Now look, there's not much time.' Mowbray spoke briskly. 'They're waiting in London. Waiting for the report of my debrief. I'll have to trot across to the embassy in a minute to send it. They desperately want to know what the other part of your message meant. "BW attack alert". Biological warfare, yes?'

'Yes. Anthrax. I'd been given a tip-off that anthrax warheads had been slipped out of Iraq. To be used in an attack.'

'Christ! Used where? And when?'

'That's the trouble. I don't know.' He saw Mowbray's face fall. 'A man came up to me in the hotel in Baghdad. An Iraqi. Scared witless. The bugger addressed me by my real name. They knew who I was, Quentin.'

'Yes. So we gathered.' Mowbray sucked in his cheeks. 'We'd better come back to that.'

'Not down to *me*, that one,' Sam insisted. 'Everything *I* did was watertight.'

'Of course,' Mowbray replied neutrally. 'Anyway, tell me about this man at the hotel.'

'He shoved a letter in my hand. When I opened it a few minutes later it contained the warning about Khalil, nothing else.'

'Nothing about anthrax?'

'Not in the note. The man whispered that warning.'

'What, exactly?'

'Anthrax warheads taken out of Iraq and soon to be used. Just that. Nothing more. Then he ran off.'

Sam felt giddy all of a sudden. He put his hands to his head.

'Drink some more water,' suggested Mowbray, holding up the glass for him. 'When did you last eat anything?'

'Don't remember. But I could certainly do with something.'

'Yes of course. Look, my wife's away in England, the maid doesn't come on a Sunday and I'm not much use in the culinary department,' he explained uncomfortably. 'But I could open a tin of fruit. Give you a bowl of cornflakes with it. Boil an egg if you like. Sorry, it's not exactly—'

'It's perfect,' Sam assured him.

Mowbray made to stand up, but Sam stopped him.

'But in a minute. Let me finish. That man in the hotel – he must have been a Mukhabarat stooge if the whole point of the game was to arrange a swap. The note he gave me, the warning to beware of Salah Khalil – it's obvious now that they *wanted* me to pass it up the line. To make London think Khalil was an agent of Saddam, not a defector, so we'd be keen to get rid of him.'

'That's pretty clear.'

'But the warning about the anthrax warheads – I'm sure that wasn't part of the Mukhabarat plan. For some reason – don't ask me why – the guy was operating on his own on that one.'

'You think? Makes little sense,' Mowbray countered. 'Why should a police stooge know anything about the Iraqi biological warfare programme?'

'I don't know. It doesn't make any sense, but I'm sure I'm right about this.'

'Why? Why so adamant?'

'Because the Mukhabarat tortured him too, Quentin. They were so bloody desperate to get him to reveal what he'd whispered to me that they beat him to death.'

'How d'you know that?'

'I saw the body.'

'Ah.' Mowbray frowned with concentration. 'But how do you know that's what they were trying to get out of him?'

'Because it's why they did *this*.' Sam pointed down to his bandaged shins. 'Trying to get me to reveal what the man said.'

'I see.' Mowbray became thoughtful. 'But they didn't succeed.'

'I think not. Not with me certainly. I tried to convince them that what the guy had whispered was of no consequence whatsoever.' He frowned. 'And I *must* have convinced them. If they'd thought I knew where and when the anthrax was to be used, then presumably they wouldn't have let me out.'

'You're assuming the security men who held you also knew about the plans for an anthrax attack?'

'Well . . . yes.'

Mowbray's elbows were still on the back of the nursery chair. He tapped his fingers together.

'Interesting. I'll think about that while I sort you something to eat.'

He got up. As he was leaving the room, Sam told him not to bother with the egg.

The more Packer thought about what had happened the more he realised how little he understood. But his mind was beginning to work again. The drug's after-effects were lifting fast.

Mowbray returned with a wooden tray. 'Best I can do in the circs,' he apologised.

'You've done me proud.' Seeing the bowl of tinned fruit salad reminded him of wardroom meals in the Navy. Not top of his food favourites, but this morning it tasted good.

'Going back to your theory,' Mowbray pressed him. 'What motive would the man have for telling you about the anthrax?'

'Because he wanted us to prevent the attack happening. Knew what was planned and didn't want the deaths on his conscience. That's a guess. I don't know.'

'A philanthropic act? Assuming rather a lot, aren't you?'

'Gut instinct, that's all.'

'I'm not sure they'll go for that in London,' Mowbray warned him. 'If the man was just a stooge for the security people, how on earth could he have access to top-secret info on the BW programme?'

'I don't know.'

There'd be long faces in London when he got home. Severe disappointment at the paucity of the intelligence he'd garnered.

'No,' Mowbray insisted. 'That informant *must* have been under orders to tell you about the anthrax as well as give you the letter. Extra bait to make us want to go for the deal.'

'Then why beat the shit out of him? And me.'

'I don't know.'

'What are you saying, Quentin? We're going to ignore the warning because we don't think it's true?'

'Not ignore, no. Don't worry. The prospect of anthrax being released in the London Underground or the New York subway is so horrific, *any* hint of an imminent threat's going to be taken extremely seriously. It's already been passed on to the Americans and the Israelis, for what it's worth.'

Sam rested against the pillows for a moment. He was thinking about Chrissie now. She hadn't let him down. But the logistics of his release still puzzled him.

'Who made the first move about getting me out?' he asked. 'Us or the Mukhabarat?'

'They did. But actually Sam, it wasn't the Mukh.' Mowbray's eyebrows bunched. 'Seems to have been some other security organisation that we haven't been able to identify yet. Saddam has plenty of them, as you know. To tell the truth we're not exactly sure who we've been dealing with.'

Sam stared in astonishment. 'What d'you mean?'

'Well, the first I knew about any of this was a phone call, out of the blue, from a man describing himself as Colonel Omar of Iraqi counter-intelligence — a cover name, I presumed. I mean, that alone was a shock. I *never* have direct contact with Saddam's security people. He said they'd arrested a British spy in Baghdad called Packer and that he would be tried and executed. Then he came straight out with the offer to swap you for Khalil. A quick deal with no publicity, he said. Told me he would ring again in a couple of days for a response. Now, I knew of your presence in Baghdad because London had briefed me, so I rang the Rashid Hotel and they confirmed that "Terry Malone" hadn't used his room for two nights.'

'But London agreed to the deal? Just like that?'

'No. They were highly suspicious. Didn't want to touch it. You see, it wasn't for another couple of days that your German friend remembered to phone your message through. Only after they got your cryptic warning about a BW attack did the Firm start taking things seriously.'

'I see.' What if the German had *never* remembered? Would he still be in Baghdad?

'Colonel Omar rang me every other day. Always on a satellite phone, judging by the echo. Wouldn't give me a number to call him back on. Odd man.' Mowbray's thin lips curved in a faint smile. 'Had the sort of plummy voice you'd expect in an officers' mess in Wiltshire.'

'Good God!' Sam sat up with a jolt. 'But that must've been Sandhurst. He was my interrogator.'

'Really?' Mowbray's eyes popped.

'And the same bloke was in charge of transporting me to the border.'

'Extraordinary. Sounds almost like a one-man operation,' Mowbray murmured, deeply perplexed. 'There *were* others I take it?'

'Three of them altogether that I was aware of, plus the messenger. Sandhurst and one other less senior man arrested me and worked me over in the interrogation room. The same two took me to the border. I was blindfolded, so there could have been others involved, but I don't think so.'

'And the third man?'

'Saw him for just a couple of minutes when they forgot to cover my eyes after they'd shown me what they'd done to the messenger. An older man. Greying hair and moustache. I got the clear impression he was in charge.'

'I see.' Mowbray stood up from the chair and crossed to the window, half-opening the curtains. A hazy dawn light had turned the flat-roofed Amman skyline into a mass of pink cubes. 'You say they knew from the start that you worked for SIS?' he checked, without turning his head. 'Could that just have been a good guess?'

'They knew my real name, Quentin. They'd need to be world champions at guessing to have worked that one out.'

Mowbray sat down again. He seemed to be puzzling over what to tell London.

'How did they break your cover, d'you think?' he asked with a casualness that wasn't entirely natural.

'I have no idea.' Sam fixed Mowbray in the eyes. 'But I'm determined to find out.'

'So is London,' Mowbray warned. 'There've been mutterings already that you might have let something slip over a drink or three.'

'They can mutter till their teeth fall out, it wasn't me,' Sam snapped.

'Yes, but in their minds the alternative's pretty frightening, you see. If the Iraqis knew about you because of some higher level security breach, then what other areas of SIS business might Saddam also have an inside track on?'

'Well, they'd better start looking,' Sam growled, sickened to be under suspicion from his own side after what he'd been through. He ran his fingers through his thick hair. He felt greasy and sweaty. Defiled.

Mowbray shifted uncomfortably. 'Look, will you be okay on your own for a couple of hours? I've got to go to the embassy to talk with London. If you want more to eat and drink, raid the fridge.'

'I'll be fine. By the way, what's the date? I've lost track of time.'

'Twenty-ninth of September. It's a Sunday. They had you for about ten days.'

And they were still beating the life out of him three days ago, while making final plans for the swap. He was right about the anthrax warning, he was sure of it. The messenger *hadn't* been ordered to tell him.

Suddenly Mowbray sat up dead straight and cocked his head like a heron listening for fish. He'd heard a car pull up outside. He stood up and peered through the window.

'Damn.' He made for the door. 'Excuse me a moment.'

Sam eased himself into a sitting position, realising he was still hungry. A plate of bacon and eggs and a mug of tea would do wonders. He began to look around for his clothes but couldn't see any.

He heard voices downstairs – Mowbray saying 'bad idea' and 'asked you not to come'. The second voice was little more than a murmur, but it sounded like a woman's.

A Mickey Mouse alarm clock beside the bed gave the time as 06.35. He heard feet on the stairs.

The door pushed open. He looked up.

'Hello, Sam.'

He gaped. The shock was electric.

'Christ!'

It was Chrissie, mannequin-cool in a cream linen suit.

5

Seeing her there in the doorway brought a lump to his throat and a stab of the old longing in his guts. But why was she here, this woman who'd walked into his life six years back, then walked out again three months ago? Surely SIS wouldn't have sent her?

'She's not staying long,' Mowbray insisted from behind her. 'I've told her you're in no state for social calls.'

I'll be the judge of that, thought Sam, wishing he had a shirt on to cover up the marks on his chest. The last thing he wanted was her feeling sorry for him.

Chrissie turned and waved Mowbray away.

'I'll be back from the embassy as soon as I can,' he announced, heading for the stairs.

'Officious prat,' Chrissie mouthed as they heard him descend them.

She pushed back the strands of hair that fell across her forehead, exposing the frown on her otherwise smooth brow. Her grey eyes registered shock as they took in the marks on Sam's chest. Being told he'd been maltreated was one thing, seeing the results quite another.

'God . . .' She covered her mouth with a hand. 'Oh you poor man. What have they done to you?'

Sam's mind was doing somersaults trying to work out why she was here. There'd be no simple reason. There never was with Chrissie.

'But this is outrageous,' she murmured, moving into

the room. Her eyes were angry now. She turned the pink-painted child's chair round and put it hard against the edge of the bed. She sat, gently taking hold of his hands. As she gaped at his scars, Sam's eyes lingered on her mouth – a mouth that had tasted every inch of him. 'They *burned* you.'

'You sound so surprised,' he mocked. 'They *do* that in Iraq.'

'Yes . . .' Her voice tailed away.

'Anyway, it looks worse than it is,' he assured her, uncomfortable at the fuss she was making. He tried to see beyond those cool eyes of hers for some small sign that she might have changed her mind again, that she'd come here to tell him she wanted him back. 'Good to see you,' he mouthed.

'You too.' She squeezed his hands, blinking back tears.

'How come you're here?' She didn't seem about to volunteer the information.

'They sent me on the plane with Salah Khalil. To make sure the hand-over went okay.'

Official visit then. Not personal.

'They gave me strict orders not to contact you of course,' she confided, 'but sod that. I had to check you were all right.' Her gaze kept returning to his scars. 'But you're not, are you? You're not all right.'

'I'm fine. A few scratches, that's all. I'll put on a shirt.'

'Oh, Sam. Don't be so damned *English*. They tortured you for God's sake.' She detached her hands from his and clasped them on her lap as if not entirely trusting them. 'Will you tell me about it?'

'No. I don't think that'd be much fun for either of us.'

She bit her lip. 'But are you okay – you know – inside?'

'Getting better every second.' He reached out and rested his hand on her knee.

She was a tactile woman with a body she'd always liked him to touch. Her legs were bare now. Always were in summer. Only in the winter had there been tights to remove. But touching something he couldn't have any more was a fool's game. He returned his hand to his lap.

'I really was about to get dressed,' he told her. 'Quentin said there's food in the fridge.'

'You must be starved.'

It felt odd being alone with Chrissie in a bedroom, now that the rules had changed. For five years a great deal of their time together had been spent lying down, and despite his present debilitated state and the impractical narrowness of the child's divan, it was hard to shut his mind to the idea that they could make love here. And she? What was *she* thinking? He couldn't tell. The old signals were muted.

'Clothes . . .' Chrissie jerked her eyes away from him. 'There's a suitcase in the corner. Is it yours?'

'Good heavens!' He hadn't noticed it before. 'Last time I saw that was in the Rashid Hotel.'

He pulled his knees up ready to swing his feet off the bed and Chrissie backed the chair away to give him room. As his soles took his weight on the floor, pain shot through his bandaged shins.

'Shit,' he winced, dropping back onto the edge of the bed.

'I saw that, you idiot!' She screwed up her face as if the pain were hers. 'You're far from all right. What did they do to you, Sam? What happened to your legs? Tell me.'

'Oh I don't know, they kept banging into things,' he answered facetiously. 'I'm told they'll heal.'

'The bastards.' Her frown was back. 'I simply don't understand. Why mess you about like that if all they wanted was a hostage to swap with Salah Khalil?'

'Perhaps they thought that I knew something. Something sensitive which I wasn't telling them.'

She sat beside him on the bed and slipped her arm round his waist as if to give him support.

'And did you?'

'Yes.'

'Was that what your message was about? Your message to me. The BW attack?'

Sam nodded.

'So, what was it exactly?' She rested her head against his shoulder and asked it in an offhand way as if her interest in the matter were only peripheral. 'What had you found out?'

About to reply, Sam checked himself. In their years together they'd sometimes blurred the service's rules on case confidentiality, but their relationship was different now. Different because she'd made it so.

'We can't talk about this, Chrissie, you know that.'

She detached herself from him. She'd understood the point he was making.

'No. You're right. I was just being curious. I mean, it *was* me you addressed the message to. And I *am* involved in the case. I mean, I'm here aren't I?'

'Yes.'

But *why* was she here? What did she want from him?

She thrust her chin forward. 'There is one thing you can tell me,' she said, more abrasively.

'Oh?'

'Yes. Why did you have to give my number to your courier? Why not one of the unlisted lines at Vauxhall Cross?'

He looked towards the window. The truth was he didn't fully know why. 'I only had a couple of minutes to think. It was in case the German got stopped. I thought it best not to give one of the official numbers. Yours just came into my head.'

Chrissie's look was sceptical. 'Just came into your head,' she repeated doubtfully. Then, lowering her voice, she continued. 'Martin took the call, you know. Not me. I was out.'

'Ah. How awkward for you.' There'd always been the risk of that.

She stood up from the bed and crossed to the window. She opened it and lit a cigarette, blowing the smoke outside.

'I was at the gym,' she told him over her shoulder. 'It was in the evening.' She sucked in a lungful of nicotine then expelled it into the cool morning air. 'Martin went ballistic when I got home. Thought the whole thing was a stunt. Some little billet-doux from you to me, in code.'

'Ah, yes.' He shivered at the thought that Kessler might have binned the message.

Chrissie had her back to him still. There was something he didn't want to ask but knew he had to.

'How *are* things with Martin?'

She turned slowly, then leaned against the window sill.

'I made my choice back in midsummer, Sam,' she said in a small voice. 'I'm sorry, but it was the right choice.'

There it was. Quite unequivocal.

'Ah. Well bully for you, then.'

He cast his mind back to the day in June when she'd asked him to meet her in the middle of Barnes Common. A meeting in the open for once, at which she'd said her husband had found out about their affair and had told her she had to choose. A brief and bitter encounter, witnessed from afar by curious dog-walkers and, Sam had discovered a few minutes later, by Martin Kessler himself, watching from a car.

He hadn't seen Chrissie since that day. Not until this morning.

Sam stood up again, trying to ignore the protests from his shins. He looked down at his suitcase. 'I shall now get dressed,' he announced determinedly.

Chrissie took a last puff on the cigarette then threw it out of the window. Pulling her mouth into a tight smile, she came towards him and slipped her arms round his waist. She touched her soft, tanned cheek to his, taking care not to press her body against his burns. She smelled of smoke and perfume. To him it was a sexual smell that was uniquely hers.

'Shall I tell you the truth, lover?' she whispered by his ear. 'It's been hell. Absolute bloody hell. I've missed you dreadfully. But—'

'You took the right decision,' he interjected. One that had never made sense to him after all her talk of divorcing Martin.

'Yes,' she breathed. 'As I told you, I *need* Martin, Sam. I don't want to but I do. And he needs me. And I've promised to be good. A promise I mean to keep.'

'Fine.' Couldn't be clearer.

He took her by the shoulders and edged her out of his way. He stared at the closed suitcase on the floor, wondering whether he was capable of bending down to open it without falling over. Chrissie saw his dilemma, crouched and unzipped the lid for him.

'They've folded everything so neatly,' she murmured. 'Such thoughtful jailers. D'you have any preference for a shirt?'

The concept of wearing his own clothes again gave him unexpected pleasure. Chrissie's fresh-washed smell, however, was a sharp reminder of his own pressing need for a clean-up.

'I think I'll take a shower first,' he told her.

'You can't.' She pointed at his shins. 'You'll get those dressings all wet. You could sit on the edge of a bath with your legs outside and do a sponge wash. I'll help you. D'you know where the bathroom is?'

'No. And I can manage thanks.' He didn't want her fiddling around with him when he was naked.

He opened the bedroom door. Mowbray's was a small, modern house with a narrow landing. He moved along it, touching the wall for support until he found the bathroom. Tiled in pink and white it had a small tub and a hand shower. He knew Chrissie was right behind him and he half-closed the door to keep her out. Some odd sense of propriety told him that if they weren't having sex any more she wasn't entitled to see his genitals. He slipped the white cotton pants down over the bandages on his shins, then tried to lift one leg while balancing on the other, but the pain became excruciating.

'Fuck!' He fell against the wall.

He heard the door swing open behind him. 'You half-wit,' Chrissie clucked. 'Let me help you.'

He perched on the edge of the bath as she'd suggested and allowed her to untangle the shorts from his ankles. He saw her shoot a searching glance at the hairy tangle of his groin, as if checking for damage.

'They didn't . . . ?'

'No.'

She remained crouched in front of him, looking up into his eyes.

'Good,' she mouthed, grinning in that silly way she'd often grinned when they were about to have sex.

But they weren't.

She stood up again. 'You're a lot thinner,' she told him.

'It's the diet I was on. Might write it up as a paperback and make my fortune.'

His weak joke made her smile. But then, she'd *always* laughed at his jokes, however feeble. 'You're looking good,' he added, even though he seemed to think her stomach wasn't quite as flat as it used to be. All those dinners out with her husband, no doubt. 'Nice suit.'

'It's Prada,' she answered, smoothing it down.

The label meant nothing to him, but he knew it would mean a lot to her. She'd always had expensive tastes in clothes.

He turned round and ran the bath water until it was warm.

'I wish you'd let me help,' she pleaded.

Twisting to reach the taps had caused a twinge in his kidneys. Every movement he made seemed to hurt.

'Well, all right.' Time he stopped being childish. 'Thanks.'

She took off her jacket and hung it on the hook on the door. Then she searched the cupboard over the basin and amongst bottles of baby oil and skin lotion found some shampoo. Wrapping a towel round her waist to protect her skirt from splashes, she wet his thick, dark hair with the hand shower and massaged the shampoo into it, her long fingers lovingly re-exploring the shape of his head as if recovering a half-lost memory. She worked the shampoo down to his neck and shoulders.

'You're so tense,' she breathed. 'Your neck muscles are like a statue's.'

'I can think of a nice way to loosen them,' he murmured, reaching up to hold her hand against his neck.

'Sam . . .'

With a snort of a laugh she took her hands away. Picking up the shower, she rinsed his head. Then she laid it in the bath and stood back.

'If you're going to be like that, I think I'd better leave it to you to wash the rest.'

She folded her arms and watched as he soaped the more intimate parts of his body. When he'd almost done, she took the sponge from him and dabbed at his back, biting her lip at the extent of the bruising she saw there. By the time the washing was complete, there was water all over the floor.

'I'll mop it up in a minute,' she told him.

She took a towel from the rail and draped it over his shoulders. Her hands hovered for a few moments. If he'd been facing her he would have seen the indecision in her eyes. Making up her mind, she pressed her body against his, hugging him from behind as tightly as she dared. Her mouth reached the level of his shoulders.

'I haven't half missed you,' she whispered, sighing.

Sam knew that nothing had really changed in her, mind and body still pulling in opposite directions. And the body had usually won. A woman who wanted it all, whatever the consequences. He knew then that he could persuade her if he tried. He knew it for a certainty. And why not? Why shouldn't they make love, even if it were for old time's sake.

'They'd written you off, lover.'

Her words sliced through his thoughts.

'Who had?'

'The Firm.'

He swallowed hard. He'd expected it – denying spies when they got into trouble was the name of the game – but to hear it confirmed that SIS had been ready to let him die was still shocking.

'They'd got the denials all prepared,' she continued softly, still clinging to him, 'for when the Iraqis paraded you in front of the press. You were dead meat, Sam.'

He didn't need to know this. So why was she telling him?

'And? What changed it?' he croaked. 'What swung it my way?'

She clung to him harder than ever, her chin hooked onto his collar bone.

'*I* changed it. I told Martin I'd divorce him if you died.'

Slowly he twisted round. He stared at her in astonishment. There was, he supposed, some daft female logic in what she'd just said.

'You'd divorce him if I was *dead*? But you weren't prepared to do it when I was living and breathing and wanting you to?'

She shrugged and looked down at the floor. It didn't make a lot of sense, but then what she felt seldom did.

'Well anyway,' he breathed, nonplussed. 'Thanks. Thanks for saving my life.' He began to dry himself.

She folded her arms as if feeling the need to get in control again.

'Well,' she added, deciding to make light of it, 'I suppose I did owe it to you, since you saved *my* life.'

He watched her fingering the long strands of hair that curved down to beneath her jaw line. They were dark and damp from being pressed against his wet shoulder.

'You kept me sane when Martin was driving me mad,' she explained. 'And you took the flak on the Kiev cockup.'

She was referring to a drugs investigation they'd both been involved in a year ago which had gone sour.

'And you took it pretty well when . . . when I had to give you up,' she concluded pointedly.

Well? She had no idea how *un*well he'd taken it.

'Ah, yes.'

Was that it? Was this the other reason she'd come here, he wondered cynically? To make sure he knew that it was *she* who'd saved his life? That she'd repaid all debts to him?

'But above all, Sam,' she added, noting the incredulity on his face, 'I couldn't let them kill you.'

'Thanks.'

'I mean, *could* I? You knew that. That's the *real* reason you gave my phone number to your pigeon.'

She was right of course. Their eyes locked. They had the measure of one another.

'There is one other thing I want to say,' she declared softly, looking down. 'Just for the record.'

'What?'

'All those things I said to you when we broke up – I meant them. All of them.'

Meant that despite deciding that from now on she had to be faithful to her husband, it was still Sam she really loved and always would.

He stopped himself from asking her again. She'd explained why she'd chosen Martin instead of him, even if it defied logic.

'Thanks a million, love.' He pulled open the bathroom door and stumbled back to the little bedroom with its rabbit wallpaper.

Chrissie followed a few minutes later, wiping up his wet footprints on the woodblock floor with the towel she'd used to mop up in the bathroom.

'I expect you'll need to be on your way,' Sam mouthed when he heard her come in behind him. He was halfway through dressing.

'That's all right. You said you were hungry. I'll cook you something.'

'No need,' he told her, still with his back towards her. 'I'm sure you've got other things to do.'

'Sam . . .' Her voice cracked as if he'd hurt her. 'I've got time. I don't need to be at the airport until midday. I'd rather be here with you.'

He completed the zipping of his trousers and turned round to find her standing very close to him. Her lips were slightly apart, her eyes half-closed. He disengaged his brain and let his arms take the decision, pulling her towards him. He touched his lips to hers and felt her breath tremble. Then he kissed her greedily like he used to, feeling her body mould to his as if it were a second skin. Her hips responded to his. He knew his wants were matched by hers. Pure chemistry, like always. Then, to his surprise she pushed him back.

'God I've missed your kisses,' she whispered, closing her eyes. 'Missed them terribly. But . . .' She shook her head as if wondering how she was going to win the fight going on inside her. 'But I really have promised to be good.' She turned away from him and moved towards the door. 'And now I'm going to make you some breakfast.' She glanced back with a mischievous smile. 'At least then I'll have satisfied *one* of your appetites.'

The kitchen was little larger than a galley, fitted out with neat lime-washed cupboards and a shiny marble work-top. He sat at the small plastic-covered table while she checked out the options.

'There's eggs and tomatoes,' she told him, her head in the fridge. 'Would an omelette suit?'

'Fine.'

As she opened and closed cupboards looking for a frying pan, Sam tried to recall the last time she'd cooked him a meal. She found a glass bowl, broke three eggs into it and beat them with a fork. Then she cut up some tomatoes while the rings heated up on the cooker. The smell of the cooking fired up his appetite. She put on a pan of water and found coffee and a filter.

It felt odd sitting here with her like this. Like being a proper couple, but not.

'Never seen you this domesticated before,' he remarked.

'That's because you were always so determined to use the limited time we spent together in other ways, my darling,' she riposted.

'I seem to remember that determination was mutual.'

'Well, I can hardly deny that. But there was another reason. I always had the distinct impression you didn't *like* me in your kitchen. Afraid I'd scratch the non-stick off your pans or something.'

'Nonsense.'

She served the omelette on a plate painted with flowers which looked Italian and hand-made.

'Got nice taste, Mrs Mowbray has,' Chrissie remarked.

She turned her head as if listening. 'Where is she, by the way?'

'In England. Their daughter's at school there.'

She sat down opposite him and watched him eat.

'This is good,' he told her.

He felt she was observing him. Like a doctor studying a patient – or an inquisitor working out what approach to take.

'How bad was Baghdad?'

He glanced up. Her face had an odd, bruised look, as if in some way she felt responsible for what had happened to him.

'It wasn't nice,' he answered.

'No. I've gathered that much. They interrogated you for a long time?'

'Yes.'

'What did they ask?'

He hesitated. She was approaching forbidden ground again. But he could tell her some of it.

'Well, a man approached me in the hotel. He whispered something to me. The interrogator wanted to know what it was.'

'And that "something" was to do with biological weapons?'

'Yes. The man mentioned anthrax.' No harm in telling her that.

'*Anthrax!*' Her alarm surprised him. 'But what exactly? He gave you details about an attack being planned?'

'Not details.'

'Well, what *did* he say then?'

'Chrissie . . . I can't go into this.'

She looked uncomfortable and began twisting the diamond and ruby ring on her wedding finger. 'No. No, of course you can't.'

Sam finished eating. He could see there was more she wanted to know.

'When they arrested you, I get the impression they knew who you were – is that right?'

'They knew precisely. They had my real name.'

She put a hand to her mouth. 'But how? Any ideas?'

'None whatsoever.'

She took in a deep breath. 'That must have been one hell of a shock.'

'Yes.'

'They'll go mad in London.'

'Undoubtedly.'

She was breathing faster than before, as if nervous for him. He watched the rise and fall of her breasts and noticed a couple of buttons had come undone on her blouse.

'And later,' she asked after a while, 'did it ever get so bad that you thought you might not—'

'Yes. I got pretty low,' he interrupted euphemistically. He wasn't going to tell her just *how* low he'd got in that stinking, shit-caked cell. Despair like that was shaming to look back on. Best not talked about. Best not even remembered.

'I'm so sorry.'

'Wasn't your doing, sweetheart,' he replied dismissively. He didn't want her pity.

'No. I know it wasn't. But I'm still sorry.'

They drank the coffee she'd made.

'I can't tell you how good that was,' Sam murmured, pushing away the plate. 'I feel almost human again.' He stroked his chin. 'Could do with a shave though.' Two days since a razor crossed his skin – or was it three?

She reached over and touched his hand. 'Won't you tell me about it? It might help to talk.'

'No.'

She took her hand back as if his refusal hurt. She

looked down at her long, slim fingers with their neat clear-lacquered nails. Her hair fell forward covering much of her face. She tossed it back but kept her eyes down. The set of her mouth conveyed a sadness which he'd seen before from time to time and never fully understood.

'Trespassers keep out,' she murmured.

'What d'you mean?'

'Sometimes you draw a circle round yourself, Sam. A circle nobody's allowed to cross.'

She stood up and moved his plate to the sink. He watched her as she rinsed it. She was right of course. He *did* treasure his personal space. He was far from sure he could ever share his life fully with a woman. But whatever the qualities such a woman would need to have, Chrissie had come closer than any other – because of how they'd been in bed, and because of how it felt just to *be* with her.

Watching her leaning forward at the sink, he couldn't stop himself thinking about what was underneath the neat skirt and blouse. He pictured her firm, round arse and slender thighs; the long, downy back. He looked at her hair and knew that beneath its chestnut layers there were cirrus-cloud wisps of a paler colour at the nape.

She finished at the sink and turned round. 'What are you thinking?'

'What I always think when I look at you,' he answered, smiling.

'Sam . . .' She came round behind his chair and put her arms round his neck. 'What am I going to do about you?'

'I could make a suggestion or two.'

For a short while she remained still, holding her breath. Then she let out a long sigh and stood up straight again, her hands moving to his shoulders.

'You're so tense,' she whispered. 'I can still feel those

knots.' Her thumbs kneaded gently at the base of his neck. 'I suppose I could . . .'

'What?'

'. . . give you a little massage. Purely therapeutic, you understand.' But the tremor in her voice told him it might be otherwise.

'Of course.'

'You've got great, hard lumps that need seeing to. Don't have to be a professional masseuse to feel them.'

Too right, thought Sam.

'You'd have to try to empty your mind, you know . . .'

'Meaning?'

It was a few seconds before she answered. 'Meaning you'd have to forget it's me.'

He swallowed. What was she on about?

'And how do I do that?'

'I don't know. That's for you to work out.'

He heard a rising excitement in her voice, as if caught up by some idea.

'Think of me as some professional therapist.' Her fingers worked away as she spoke. 'Hands touching you, but not *my* hands. Not *my* body . . .'

He closed his eyes and tried to put his brain in neutral. If she wanted it to be a game then a game it would be – just so long as she understood where it was heading.

Suddenly she stopped the movement of her hands. She slipped her arms round him again and kissed his neck. 'The masseuse says you'll have to get those clothes off, mister.'

'What are we doing, Chrissie?' he murmured.

'Chrissie? I'm not Chrissie, remember? Chrissie's the one who's made a promise to her husband.' She gave a little laugh. But a laugh with pain in it. 'How long do we have?'

'Quentin said a couple of hours . . .'

'. . . about an hour ago.'

'Yes.'
She kissed him on the top of his head.
'Then I don't think we should waste any of it.'

Back up in the child's bedroom, her mouth opened to him and he kissed her. He felt the press of her stomach against his and smoothed his hands down her back and over the curve of her behind. Then, after a few seconds, she pushed him gently away.
'No. Not like that. It's got to be my way.' She put a finger to his lips.
'Chrissie, for God's sake. Stop farting about.'
She made a clicking noise with her tongue and walked out along the landing to the bathroom, returning with a dry towel and a bottle of baby oil.
'For the massage,' she explained.
He narrowed his eyes.
'Trust me.'
She spread the towel on the bed and helped him to remove his polo shirt and trousers.
'God, those bruises,' she hissed, turning him round. 'I can't believe they did this to you.'
He lay on his front and she manoeuvred his arms until they were stretched out by his head. Then, using the oil as a lubricant, her hands kneaded at his knotted muscles with a skill that surprised him. As she worked her way down the sinews of his back, carefully avoiding the parts that had been beaten, he felt his body begin to relax for the first time in a long time.
'You're supposed to use aromatic oils for stress,' she murmured, trickling more oil onto his shoulder blades. 'Lavender, hyssop, that sort of thing.'
She smoothed the unction round the curving spars of his ribcage and along the sides of his muscular back as if moulding a pot on a wheel. A tenderness was taking over in her touch. Less therapeutic and more sensual. Her

breathing became shorter and uneven. Then, abruptly, the massaging stopped altogether, her hands holding on to the sides of his body as if drawing on its energy.

'Sam . . .' Her voice had become husky. 'It mustn't be *me*. You understand? Oh God,' she sighed, 'don't make me explain. Just tell me that you won't think of it as *me* here.'

'Chrissie . . .' he growled.

'Not *me*, Sam. Not Chrissie. Just say yes, lover.'

'Yes.'

Her hands left him and he heard her fingers fiddling with the buttons of her blouse. Then the snick of her bra strap disconnecting and the purr of the zip on her skirt. He began to turn over to look at her but suddenly her arms were alongside his, her breath warm against the back of his neck. He wanted to face her, to lock their mouths together and press his erection against her belly, but her weight held him where he was. He felt her bare nipples brush lightly against his shoulder blades, moving in loving circles against his oiled skin. In his mind he let himself drift back, pretending the break in their relationship had been a dream, a nightmare.

'Feeling your body like this . . .' she whispered, close to his ear.

He could feel her heart thudding against his ribs. He pulled one of her hands to his mouth and kissed it with the strength of a bite.

'Sam . . .'

Her voice sounded like a plea. But for what? To sate the hunger he knew would be as strong as his own by now, or a plea for him to take her back? He needed to know. To see the answer in her eyes. He tried to turn over, but the pain in his kidneys and her weight on him stopped him.

'Not yet, lover,' she insisted, breathlessly. 'You have to promise me something.'

'What?' he croaked. What now?

'That you won't look at me.' There was an edge of dread to her voice.

'This is getting stupid.'

'No. It *has* to be that way. It can't be *me*, Sam. I've told you that. *Please*. I need you to think of this as just some woman with you. *Any* woman. No identity. No past. No future . . .'

He understood at last. For all the time he'd known her she'd pretended things weren't what they were. And she was pretending still. If what they were about to do had no more meaning for him than if he were doing it with a whore, then it would be okay. Her promise to her husband would somehow remain intact.

No more meaning than with a whore. But no less either. And that would be enough for now.

'Okay,' he breathed. 'I'll keep my eyes closed.'

'No. Eyes closed is not enough.' Her voice had a tightness about it that he knew well. She wanted him inside her now. Wanted the rush of orgasmic blood that would blind her to all reality. 'I have to cover your eyes,' she told him.

A blindfold. Could she have suggested that if she'd known he'd spent the past ten days with a hood over his head? What game was this? What extraordinary game of self-delusion was she involved in?

'Whatever you say,' he mouthed.

She bent down to the floor and picked up the hand-towel she'd used to dry the splashes he'd made after his wash. Then she slipped it under his head and tied it behind his neck.

'Now, turn over,' she whispered.

As he rolled onto his back, he reached out for her shoulders but felt his hands pinned down onto the bed.

'Please,' she breathed. 'There's a massage underway here. I have to do your pectorals.'

Giving in reluctantly, he felt a trickle of oil on his sternum, then her hands spreading the liquid over his chest, avoiding with delicate care the blisters from the cigarette burns. Her fingers brushed against his nipples and circled them.

Deciding the time had come for him to take control, he reached a hand up to the back of her neck, forked his fingers through her hair and pulled her mouth down to his. As his tongue sought out hers, she breathed in sharply and squirmed against him. After a while she pulled back. He felt for her breasts, locating the bud-hard nipples, then raised his head and took one in his mouth. It had the sweet taste of the oil she'd used on his body.

'Oh shit,' she gasped, clasping his head to her. 'Oh *God* how I've missed you!'

Then she broke away again. He heard her get off the bed and remove her pants. He had an urge to rip off the blindfold and let his eyes gorge themselves on this body that he knew so well and loved so much. But he sensed that to do so would wreck their deal. He raised his hips and pushed off his own shorts. Feeling her weight back on the bed, he held his breath, anticipating her mouth on his erection. Instead he felt a trickle of oil.

'Jesus . . .' he croaked.

She spread the unction down his shaft.

'Now,' he insisted. 'For Christ's sake . . .'

As she straddled his legs, he reached between her thighs, exploring her own warm, wet readiness with his fingers, he pulled her towards him. She guided him in and, as he penetrated her body, she let out an anguished cry. She rocked her pelvis, slowly at first, then with an increasing vigour, emitting little mews of pleasure as she did so. Finally with a moan of ecstasy she gasped his name as he unburdened himself deep inside her. She shuddered with her own climax, then fell forward on his chest.

He held onto her with his fingers through her hair in that deliciously peaceful way she'd always loved. For a few seconds she lay very still as their pulses subsided. He felt her lips move against his shoulder and knew she was smiling. Then, stiffening as if hearing a noise, she lifted herself off him and stood up.

'Remember, still no peeking,' she told him.

He heard her pull tissues from a box on the child's dressing table to dry herself, then realised she was hurriedly putting clothes on over by the window. Enough of this bloody nonsense, he decided. He lifted the towel from his eyes. She had her pants on already and was pulling up her skirt, standing side on to him.

Then he saw.

Her stomach was indeed fuller than it used to be. So, he suspected, were her breasts. And this wasn't the sort of weight gain that came from dinners out with husbands.

She caught him looking and guiltily zipped up her skirt. Then she turned away from him, reaching behind her back to hook up her bra.

'How many weeks?' he asked, shocked.

'Don't know what you're talking about.'

For a moment or two she made as if she hadn't heard him properly. Then he saw her straighten up as if deciding she would after all have to face the confrontation she'd gone to such lengths to avoid. Her face was flushed when she turned, but her grey eyes were pewter-hard.

'Twelve,' she told him defiantly. She held his look. She knew what he was calculating. 'No,' she told him simply. 'It's Martin's. I'm quite sure of it.'

She *couldn't* be sure. Couldn't possibly be sure the baby wasn't his. He and she had made love more than once in the week before the break-up nearly three months ago.

'Chrissie love . . .'

Suddenly she jumped. There *was* a noise outside.

'Quentin's back,' she exclaimed, peering through the window. She hurried over to the bed, organising him. 'The towels . . . you'll have to stand up.' Her voice was brisk, devoid of all its softness.

She took the towel they'd been lying on and the one she'd used for his blindfold and hurried them back to the bathroom with the baby oil.

'I have to go now,' she told him, re-entering the room. 'I'll be late for my flight to Heathrow.'

'But, hang on a minute. We need to talk about this.'

'No. There's nothing to talk *about*. The baby's not yours, Sam.'

But the brimming of her eyes told him differently. For a moment he thought she would come to him, but she bit her lip and turned away, closing the door behind her.

He swung his legs to the floor. He heard voices downstairs. Urgent voices, as if Mowbray had returned from the embassy with information that had changed things.

Nothing to talk about, she'd said. Pretending again. Making things out to be not what they were. Numbly, Sam picked up his polo shirt and pulled it over his head, his body smelling of her sex.

Damn you, Chrissie, he thought. Damn you and whatever game you're at.

As he pulled on his trousers over the shin dressings he heard the front door go. He hobbled to the window and looked out. Mowbray was hustling Chrissie to his car. They drove off at speed.

He was alone in the house.

Chrissie was pregnant. And she'd conceived in June.

He looked round the little bedroom. Bunny wallpaper. Cuddly toys in the corner. How apt. How sickeningly bloody apt.

6

08.30 hrs
Bahrain

The Persian Gulf was new territory. Dean Burgess had never been further from the USA than Europe before. The body-clock of the tall, ectomorphic American was eight hours askew. His brain told him he should have been starting a night's sleep right now instead of lining up at the hotel buffet to fix breakfast. Ideally he would have left the States a day earlier to allow more time to adjust, but there'd been a small, or maybe not so small, domestic crisis to attend to before setting off for what was scheduled as a three-week field trip.

'Dean! Excellent. You made it!'

Burgess turned his thin face to see the lean figure of an elderly but fit Englishman loping towards him across the coffee shop. The man thrust out a hand, then seeing that Burgess's were fully occupied with a tray, he abandoned the attempt at a formal greeting.

'Hi, Andrew.' Burgess smiled weakly. 'Won't say good morning, because it sure doesn't feel like one!'

'Lousy flight?'

'No. Just five times as long as I'm used to. I'm a simple hometown American boy, remember?'

'You'll soon acclimatise.'

'Sure.' He bristled, sensing the guy was patronising him.

'Let me get a tray and I'll join you at a table.'

'Okay. I'll stake out a claim.'

Burgess chose a table with four unoccupied chairs, on the assumption that other members of the UN Special Commission would be joining them. The inspection team leader Andrew Hardcastle was the only one of the bunch that he'd met, albeit briefly. At thirty-four, Burgess guessed he was about half the age of the Englishman.

His secondment to UNSCOM had come out of the blue, following swiftly on his relocation to FBI headquarters in Washington on the staff of the Bureau's new Counter-Terrorism Center set up in the wake of the Oklahoma bombing. Burgess had been assigned as a special agent dealing with the threat from weapons of mass destruction. His knowledge of WMD was still low, however. The move from New York and the negative salute his wife Carole had given the upheaval had left little time in which to read himself in. Being assigned as note-taker to the head of the next UNSCOM team bound for Baghdad had been seen as the best schooling available on the production and concealment of biological weapons.

The team leader approached with his tray. Burgess had an antipathy to the British which he knew he would have to control. He wiped his mouth in case some of the fruit salad he was eating had got stuck to his small honey-coloured brush of a moustache.

'Suppose you've had about ten breakfasts in the past twenty-four hours,' Hardcastle remarked, sitting down opposite him. 'Airlines seem to think passengers are never happy unless they have food shoved down their throats all the time.'

'You're almost right, Andrew. Two breakfasts and

three main meals since I last saw a bed,' Burgess answered.

'Well, I'm afraid we can't promise an easy day today,' Hardcastle warned him. 'We go from here to the briefing, then it's a miserable three-hour ride in a Herc to a military airfield outside Baghdad – as you know, the civil airport's closed because of sanctions. But tonight you'll get a proper sleep. The hotel in Baghdad's perfectly comfortable.'

'Can't wait.'

Earlier that week the two men had met for just one hour when Hardcastle had been in New York for his mission briefing from the head of the UN Special Commission. The Englishman's childlike enthusiasm for the search for Iraq's biological weapons Burgess had found hard to interpret. The guy was either a latter-day Saint George who'd smelled the spore of the dragon and couldn't wait to see the red of its eyes, or a bumbling Don Quixote.

'You used to work on CBW in England, you said?' Burgess checked, still feeling his way with the acronyms.

'Yes. At Porton Down. They pensioned me off a couple of years back when I hit sixty. But retirement drove me barmy, so when the UN asked for specialists to help unravel the intricacies of Iraq's BW programme I leapt at the chance. It's been like a bloody great detective story. Huge fun. For an amateur of course,' he added hastily. 'Just another job of work for you professionals, I suppose.'

Phoney self-deprecation. Typically goddamn British, thought Burgess.

'No way. This is the most interesting thing I've done in a long while,' he replied flatly. 'And it sure makes a break from the organised crime beat I've been tramping for the past ten years.'

Hardcastle looked away, his small grey eyes focusing terrier-like on something across the room.

'Aha!' He raised his hand and waved it slightly, then smiled when he got a response. 'It's Martha,' he explained, pronouncing the *th* as a *t*. 'She's a veterinary officer from the Dutch army. Charming creature. And brilliant on anthrax. Aah! And here's Pierre.'

Burgess looked round to see a stocky, curly-haired man with the face of a Native American, dressed in a bright blue Hawaiian beach shirt with sunglasses pushed up onto his thick, wiry hair. He placed his tray on the table and shot out a hand.

'Pierre Latour.'

'Hi. I'm Dean Burgess.' He'd recognised Latour's accent as being from north of the Great Lakes.

'*Major* Latour,' Hardcastle added. 'Canadian Royal Mounted Police. He's our Mister Fixit. And does a good job of watching my back.'

'Glad to know you,' said Burgess.

'And Martha!' Hardcastle rose to his feet in a gentlemanly gesture of welcome as an ample blonde woman in her late forties joined them. Burgess stood up too and introduced himself.

'Major Cok,' she said shaking his hand. 'Good heavens, you're a tall man!' She peered up at his face with an exaggerated crick of the neck.

'Six-two,' Burgess confirmed.

'What is that, six *metres*?' she mocked.

'Feet 'n' inches,' he grinned. 'We're the Stone Age guys, remember? Metric's too modern for us.'

They sat again.

'Excellent!' Hardcastle grinned. 'All the most important members of the team gathered on one table!'

'Don't let the others hear you say that, Andy,' the Dutch woman cautioned. 'Some of the new ones seem a little sensitive. I was talking with them last night.'

'Won't last,' Hardcastle countered. 'The Iraqis' bluntness will soon knock the corners off them.'

They continued with their breakfasts, the chat centring on the idiosyncrasies of the minders who were routinely assigned to them in Baghdad. Burgess listened, feeling very much on the outside of their world. He tried to absorb some of their culture but his mind kept flipping back to the little clapboard house thirty miles north of Manhattan in Westchester County, where Carole and the kids would be sleeping soundly just now. A home that had recently lost its warmth for him.

Twenty minutes later the full UN inspection team gathered in the lobby and began to file out to a waiting motor-coach, a process involving a few seconds of intense outdoor heat before they were back in air-conditioning again.

Hardcastle took the seat next to Burgess at the front of the bus.

'Is Clinton going to make it back in?' he asked. The presidential election was due in a month's time. 'Saw him being interviewed on CNN while I was getting dressed this morning. Can the scandals be made to stick?'

'I guess it's a question of whether enough people want them to,' Burgess answered. 'The problem is, if they sink Clinton, what do they get instead?'

'Quite. Better the devil you know. Some people say the same about Saddam Hussein, of course.'

'All present and correct, Andrew.' The voice was Pierre Latour's and came from above them. He'd just walked backwards down the bus counting heads.

'Good. Let's go.'

The coach turned out of the grounds of the Holiday Inn and headed down a broad highway leading to the outskirts of the city. Behind Burgess and Hardcastle sat eighteen delegates from six countries.

'Most of the people in this team have been selected by their own governments,' Hardcastle confided. 'Most are high-grade scientists, but some have been selected for reasons I can't fathom. National politics and patronage, I suppose.'

The UN inspection teams had been set up after the expulsion of the Iraqi army from Kuwait in 1991 with the aim of ensuring that never again could Saddam Hussein get his hands on weapons of mass destruction. They'd been successful up to a point. Iraq's nuclear programme had been all but destroyed, huge arsenals of nerve gases and blister agents had been safely disposed of, and the teams and establishments involved in developing the toxins, viruses and bacteria suitable for biological weapons had been put under such close scrutiny as to make them virtually inoperable. The ones that were known about, anyway.

After about ten minutes the coach turned off the highway into a residential area, where the desert was studded with palatial residences surrounded by well-irrigated lawns. Each mansion was protected by fences or walls high enough to ensure the security and privacy of its oil-rich owner. The house where the coach pulled up had a crenellated roof reminiscent of a Crusader fortress.

A uniformed local policeman sitting in the shade of a palm tree leapt to his feet, peered in through the side window of the coach, then gave a signal for the heavy green-painted steel gate to be rolled aside so the bus could enter.

'Not bad,' murmured Dean Burgess, looking around at the palatial mansion. 'The UN owns this?'

'Rented on a long lease. We call this the Gateway,' Hardcastle explained. 'It's the threshold between the real world and the one ruled by Saddam where nothing is ever the way it seems.'

Burgess noted the antenna farm set up beside the house – an impressive array of satellite dishes.

'Everything's encrypted of course,' Hardcastle explained. 'We've got totally secure communications here. One-hundred-and-twenty-eight-bit PGP standard.'

'Who exactly runs this place?'

'The UN. But in practice it's the anglophone alliance. Americans, Brits, Canadians, New Zealanders and Australians. Or rather the intelligence professionals of those countries. We run it because we're about the only ones in the UN who fully trust each other,' Hardcastle added, pointedly.

And even that was relative, Burgess reflected. His own trust of the British intelligence record was limited.

Hardcastle stood up from his seat and turned to address the occupants of the bus. As he did so, the driver handed him a microphone.

'Ladies and gentlemen, if you could listen to me for a moment.'

Not much point for some of them, Burgess thought. He'd been told there were two Russians on board and a Japanese whose knowledge of English was almost non-existent.

'I'll be able to brief you in about fifteen minutes. There's a couple of things I need to do first. Major Latour will show you where everything is. We spend the morning here, briefing and practising some drills, then have a lunch snack before heading out to the airport for the flight at fourteen hundred. That's it really. See you in about fifteen minutes. There's some coffee if you want it, but maybe it's too soon after breakfast. Up to you.'

He gave the microphone back to the driver and bent close to Burgess's ear.

'Why don't you come with me,' he suggested. 'I think you'll find it rather interesting.'

Burgess perked up at the prospect of not having to make small talk with bowing Japanese biologists.

Inside the house Hardcastle marched purposefully through the magnificent entrance hall, the rubber soles of his lightweight hiking boots squeaking on the polished marble floor. The house reminded Burgess of the hotel they'd just left – glittering with gold and cut crystal. A broad corridor extended from the back of the hall, lined with doors. Hardcastle stopped outside one labelled Communications Center. He tapped a code on the keypad next to it, then opened the way to a spacious white-walled room whose windows had been panelled over. In the centre of the room several linked tables provided a surface for printers, scanners and computer terminals. Against one of the flank walls, banks of transmission equipment winked as encoded signals were bounced back and forth to UN headquarters in New York.

'Well hi! Good to see you again, Andrew!'

A strident-voiced, red-haired woman, her ample chest stretching the fabric of her yellow polo shirt, shook the Englishman vigorously by the hand.

'And who do we have here?'

Hardcastle introduced Burgess. The red-haired woman was a US Air Force lieutenant colonel from Nebraska. A second female in the room, oval-faced and less forceful, announced she was a British army captain on attachment from a listening post in Cyprus.

'You want to look at the material we have for you, Andrew?' the redhead asked, glancing uneasily at Burgess.

'It's all right,' Hardcastle told her. 'He's got all the clearances.'

'Okay. If you say so. And you have one message. To call London. A Mr Waddell. Want me to get him for you?'

'Ah. I'll leave that for a minute, perhaps.' Waddell was SIS. Wasn't sure Burgess should be around when he made that call. 'Let's see the material first.'

'Surely. I got a seat for you twos right here.'

The first of the files she placed in front of them contained overhead photographs taken by Keyhole KH11 satellites and the US Air Force U-2 spy plane which UNSCOM had at its disposal. Attached to each picture of buildings and other objects spotted in the desert was a small explanation of what it showed, as interpreted by the photo analysts in New York.

'They beam all this material in by satellite,' Hardcastle explained with a boyish grin. Burgess was reminded of a small kid showing off his Buzz Lightyear toys. 'Saw most of these shots in New York, but there's a couple of fresh ones. Look. This is the Haji Animal Feed factory, taken yesterday. As you know, we suspect the place may have had its "use" changed temporarily. They've got fermenters and stuff which we know about, but three weeks ago a U-2 spotted other kit being smuggled into the place in the middle of the night. Not positively identified, but we *think* we know what it was. I'll cover the details in my briefing.' He looked at the new pictures closely. 'Yes, well . . . All that these new ones show is that the place looks perfectly normal again.'

The second file detailed two other sites they were to inspect, one in Baghdad, the other in the desert about ninety kilometres to the west – a patch of ground showing signs of being recently dug over as if in preparation for the erection of a large building.

'The concern is they could be trying to bury something,' Hardcastle explained. 'Ah, yes! Now *this* is what I was waiting for.' He held up a list. 'All the top personnel at the Haji plant. Out of date, but better than nothing. It's come from some Norwegian supplier whose last deal with the Haji company was before sanctions, of course.'

He did a quick count. 'Oh God! Only nine names on it. There must be several hundred employed there.'

Burgess read over his shoulder.

'If they're top guys they'll probably still be there,' he suggested.

'Probably. Aha! *That's* interesting,' Hardcastle muttered, jabbing a finger at the page. 'This chap Shenassi, MD and Chief Scientific Officer. Got his BSc in Food Science at the University of Leeds in 1978. You know it's that sort of information that can make all the difference in tripping these buggers up.'

Burgess didn't quite see what he meant, but decided not to query it. His head was beginning to throb from the jet lag.

'Good. Excellent!' Hardcastle stood up again, looking at his watch. 'Better get the briefing under way before they start the slow hand clap. Thank you very much, ladies,' he called, heading for the door.

'Now Andy, you're not forgetting to call Mr Waddell?' the Lieutenant Colonel chided.

'Oh, yes,' Hardcastle faltered, snapping his fingers. 'I was forgetting. Dean, would you mind going on ahead and telling them I'll be another few minutes?'

'Sure thing.'

With Burgess out of the room, Hardcastle asked the English Captain to get SIS on the circuit.

'We'll have a jolly good try,' she replied, picking up the handset of an encrypted telephone and dialling.

At the headquarters of the Secret Intelligence Service in London it was a little after six in the morning.

'Hello.' The voice at the other end sounded deeper than Hardcastle expected. He remembered Waddell as being small.

'Hardcastle here.'

'Oh, excellent. Thanks for finding the time to call. Look, I know you must be in coiled spring mode by now, but there's some intelligence come our way that you should know about. It comes with a bit of a health warning, mind.'

An Ulsterman, Hardcastle remembered from the accent. Young, pushy and too fond of the jargon they taught on management courses.

'Go on.'

'The source was in Baghdad. It's not corroborated yet. We've got absolutely nothing else that matches it. And it could even be disinformation. But the line is that some anthrax warheads have been smuggled out of Iraq for imminent use.'

'Good Lord!'

'But as I said, we've no collateral. Just this one source who may have had any one of a dozen motives for peddling such a yarn. Anyway, there's nothing *you* can actually do about it, but I just thought you ought to know for background. In case it fits in with anything you pick up. Keep it to yourself please. We've told Washington and Tel Aviv, but treat it as info for us and the Americans only at this stage if you wouldn't mind.'

'Of course. But how alarming. If it's true it means UNSCOM's failed. All our efforts in vain.'

'Yes, well let's just hope it *isn't* true, Mr Hardcastle.'

'Quite.'

Hardcastle replaced the receiver and distractedly left the communications centre without another word to the women who ran it.

Dean Burgess was sitting in the briefing room in the first of four rows of plastic stacking chairs. Next to him was Major Martha Cok who'd been chattering to him solidly for the past five minutes. He'd been responding with monosyllables, his mind unable to quit thinking about the newspaper clipping his wife had inserted into his suitcase just before he left home and which he'd only discovered when opening it in the hotel that morning.

The clipping was a sign of her new attitude to him. His promotion within the Bureau had prompted Carole to take a stand about his performance as husband and father. Her complaint was common enough in his line of business – he was a 'workaholic who treated his wife and children like toys, to be taken out and played with only when the Bureau allowed'. And she was right. He wasn't proud of it and he knew his constant refrain of 'Please be patient, it's only for now' had long ago lost all credibility. The trouble was that Carole was refusing to move with the kids to DC.

The clipping from the *New York Post* was a further sign of her desperation to hold the family together and for him to change. The news feature had concerned Pledge for the Family, a right-wing Christian movement that was gathering strength across the States on a platform of male renewal and rededication to family values. Joining such a movement of what he dismissed as religious head-bangers was unimaginable for him, and the fact that Carole had thought he might was a mark of how far apart they'd drifted.

'Ah! Here is our great leader,' whispered Martha Cok.

Andrew Hardcastle had entered the briefing room. Burgess saw at once that something was up. As the Englishman stepped onto the raised dais, his mind seemed elsewhere. He put his hand on the projection equipment as if trying to steady himself.

'Good morning again, gentlemen – and ladies,' he began, absent-mindedly sifting through the material he would need to project. He looked up as if to check his brief opening words had been understood by those with poor English. 'I thought I would start with some background for those of you new to UNSCOM.'

He glanced down at Burgess, then at the rows behind him.

'First thing to stress is the *importance* of what we are doing. Be under no illusions, ladies and gentlemen. What we are dealing with in Baghdad is a regime that has refined the art of deception to a level almost unprecedented in the history of the world.' He paused for effect. 'And *our* problem is this: our inspections have certainly produced conclusive evidence that biological weapon agents have been produced in Iraq, but no signs of stockpiles of the agents themselves. Finding those weapons – and they *must* exist – is what this UNSCOM mission is all about.

'A quick reminder of the BW story so far. After the Gulf War, when the UN search for Iraq's weapons of mass destruction began, Saddam's men strenuously denied ever having had a serious biological weapons production programme. Chemical, yes. Mustard and nerve gases. But biological they denied. We didn't believe them of course, but couldn't find the evidence we needed. Then in 1995, you'll remember, we had a breakthrough.

'As you all know, one essential ingredient for producing large quantities of bacteria, viruses or toxins is growth medium. Well, in 1995 we discovered that suppliers in Britain and Switzerland had sold the Iraqis *thirty-nine* tonnes of the stuff back in 1988. Far more than they could possibly use legitimately in medical labs and so on. So we managed to acquire the delivery details from the companies concerned and then asked the Iraqis to account for these stocks.

'It took time. But eventually they did come up with an extraordinary tale of woe. Ten tonnes had been lost in riots, they said. Other stocks had been burned accidentally. And, would you believe it, some had even got lost falling off the back of a truck! They even produced a fistful of blatantly forged documents to back up their nonsensical fairy tales. Anyway, to cut a long story short, eleven tonnes of the medium was accounted for legitimately, but for the remaining twenty-eight tonnes they had no valid explanation of use.

'So in the end they did admit it. Yes, they *had* had a BW research programme, but had never weaponised the stuff. There were no piles of warheads and they'd destroyed all the stocks they'd produced.' Hardcastle raised a derisory eyebrow. 'They seemed to hope that would be enough to make the UN draw a line under the affair and ease up on sanctions. Well, my friends, they were nearly right. There *was* a move to abandon the inspections. But then came an amazing stroke of luck. Lieutenant General Hussein Kamel, a son-in-law of the president, fled to Jordan and admitted being a key figure in their biological weapons programme. Known as Project 324, it was based at Al Hakam, a sprawling site in the desert. He gave us a mass of documentary detail, including all the types of warheads they'd developed and tested and where they'd been stored. But then, you'll remember, Hussein Kamel made a fatal mistake. Saddam asked him to return to Iraq with a promise of safety. The idiot did so, and was dead within days.

'Anyway, the evidence he gave us meant we had 'em. Proof at last that everything they'd told us up until then was lies. We demolished Al Hakam with explosives a few months ago. And UNSCOM moved into a new phase, with more remote surveillance cameras set up in dozens of Iraqi labs and factories, the pictures live-linked back to the thirtieth floor of the UN building in New York. All these sites have a legitimate use of course – pharmaceutical plants, agricultural feed-stuff factories – but all have the capability also of being rapidly switched into BW production. But gentlemen – and ladies – despite those breakthroughs, despite the monitoring, we *still* haven't found any stocks of anthrax, botulinum toxin, aflatoxins or ricin, all of which, according to General Kamel, have been turned into weapons by the Iraqi regime.'

And, Burgess remembered from the initial brief when he'd taken up his new duties in Washington, just a few grams of the stuff fed into the ventilation system of a New York subway interchange could kill thousands within days. His jet lag was easing, his mind was focused. Hardcastle's enthusiasm had begun to get to him.

'Some of these pathogens and toxins deteriorate when stored,' the Englishman continued, 'but with the Iraqis finally admitting to producing some *eight thousand five hundred litres* of anthrax, we assume some of it's still around, hidden in places we haven't yet got to, like Saddam's own palaces.

'Now. Enough of history. Let's turn to this mission. Our primary target for inspection on day one is an animal feed factory. They produce single-cell protein concentrates for cattle using fermenters, freeze-dryers and milling equipment. All dual-use gear which without too much effort could be diverted into producing bacteria or toxins in huge volumes.'

He pointed to the far end of the room where a triple-glazed window looked out onto the antenna farm.

'Would someone mind closing the blind?'

As the room darkened, he clicked on the projector light. Under its lens he slipped the U-2 photo taken a fortnight earlier.

'About three weeks ago this thermal-imaging shot of the factory was taken by a UN aerial platform at about two in the morning Iraqi time. A Friday. The layout of the buildings is exactly as it was in previous photographs, but in this shot there is something extra visible. Have a look to one side of the main building.' He pointed it out with the red beam of a hand-held laser. 'What you see here is a truck – a four tonner, according to the photo analysts in New York. And –' The red beam moved a small distance to the left '– what you see *here* is some sizeable object apparently being moved from the truck into the building. Now, definition isn't exactly wonderful. We can't really tell what the object is from this view. But –' he replaced the photo with another one '– with a little computer enhancement, the object is substantially enlarged and actually takes on a shape.'

He turned to his audience to see if they'd recognised what it was. In the front row Dean Burgess shook his head. To him it was just a lump.

'One can't be absolutely certain, but to every expert who's studied it closely it looks like some piece of milling equipment. You see this cone shape? Could be a hopper. It's the sort of machine that could turn a cake of dried anthrax spores or botulinum toxin into a powder with grains between one and five microns in diameter. And that's exactly the size needed if the agent is to be weaponised effectively.'

'The milling machines already at the factory can't do that?' Burgess enquired.

'No. They produce a much coarser particle, which is quite unsuitable because it won't stay airborne for long.'

'And this *fabrik*,' the Dutch vet asked, 'it is in Baghdad?'

'Um, at this stage you don't need to know where the *factory* is, Martha.' He'd spoken more sharply than he'd meant. It had sounded like a rebuke, and the pointed correction of her English a trifle rude. 'It's the old need-to-know thing,' he went on, his voice softer. 'Preventing the Iraqis knowing where we'll pounce next is absolutely vital. If they *have* got something at this factory which they shouldn't have, they'll sure as hell move it somewhere else if they get the slightest hint we're coming.'

Burgess remembered that when he had met Hardcastle in New York a few days back, the Englishman had told him there *had* been leaks from within the multinational

UNSCOM teams and several inspections had been turned into a farce.

'Yes, okay,' Major Cok answered, 'but can you tell us perhaps if this feed *factory* has been inspected before?'

'Yes it was. A little while back. No hint of anything out of place at the time. We decided to install some remote cameras though, because of the potential dual use of the plant. All the relevant processing equipment is listed and tagged of course, so we'll know if anything's missing or been added.'

Hardcastle removed the photo from the projector and replaced it with a drawing of the layout of the factory made at the last inspection. He pointed out the main office block.

'We'll need to go through their files meticulously. The MD of the company has a BSc from a British university, so he's likely to be pretty organised in keeping notes of everything that goes on there.'

Burgess reacted and felt the Dutch woman doing the same. Hardcastle could be unconsciously arrogant at times, as if only *British*-educated scientists were capable of such thoroughness. For an audience like this he would do well to choose his words more carefully, Burgess decided.

The beam of the laser pointer moved across the plan.

'We believe that just *here* there's a small laboratory,' Hardcastle went on blithely. 'Normally used for test batches and so on. If they *have* been brewing something they shouldn't, it could well be in here that we find some trace of it. We'll need to check the lab from top to bottom. There'll be masks, gloves and gowns available for the team that does that. Then finally, over *here*, there's the freeze-drying plant. If they've used some of the equipment for lyophilising anthrax spores, they'll have a devil of a job cleaning it afterwards, so it's quite likely to be "broken down" or "waiting for spare parts" when we have a look around.'

He switched off the projector. 'Now, about our methods. Um, would you mind?' Hardcastle raised his eyebrows in the direction of the back row, indicating that the blinds could be opened again. 'Thank you so much. I think the most useful thing we could do next is for Pierre to organise you into four separate teams so we can do some role-playing to remind you of procedures. And it'll give newcomers an idea of what to expect from our hosts when we get on the ground. It's not always pleasant and the quicker you get used to that the better.

'Remember gentlemen – and ladies – this may at times seem like a game, but it's a deadly serious one. That's why we spend time preparing for it here, secure from eavesdroppers. Once in Iraq we'll be under scrutiny the whole time. Old hands know this, but it bears repeating: the Iraqi secret police will be listening to your every breath. Your hotel room is bugged, and so are many of the public rooms you may visit and restaurant tables. Our base – the Baghdad Monitoring and Verification Centre – that isn't safe either. Nor are the vehicles. Just assume that everything the Iraqis *can* bug, they will have done. So do not discuss anything confidential with one another unless you are in the open air, well away from anything that could contain a directional microphone.

'The time now is after ten-thirty. Our flight departs at fourteen hundred hours, with an ETA at Habbaniyah of sixteen-thirty. By the time we get to the hotel it'll be seven or eight in the evening. Just time for a meal and some sleep.'

Burgess nodded appreciatively.

'Then, at nine tomorrow morning we'll reveal to the Iraqis where we want to inspect. Remember the bottom line, ladies and gentlemen,' Hardcastle concluded. 'We're as certain as we can be that Saddam still possesses a couple of dozen ballistic missiles and a stockpile of mass destruction warheads. With those he could cause huge and horrific casualties in Israel, Saudi Arabia or Iran. Our job is to find them if we possibly can, but failing that, to keep up the pressure on Saddam so he never has the chance to bring 'em out and use 'em.'

A little under three hours later the motor-coach deposited the team outside a hangar on the military flight-line of Bahrain's Al Muharraq airport. The baggage was quickly unloaded onto a trolley for transportation to the aircraft. Each of the inspectors carried a small rucksack large enough to hold the personal kit needed to keep going for forty-eight hours in case the Iraqis played games with them on their arrival.

As Burgess got out he heard the deep-throat crackle of a jet. A Bahrain Air Force F-16 hurtled down the runway for the start of a training flight.

The afternoon heat was as fierce and dry as a sauna. They entered the hangar, grateful for its shade. Along the flank wall was a row of offices once used by aircraft maintenance teams with windows overlooking the hangar floor.

'Right. Now pay attention,' Hardcastle said, clasping his hands like a school-teacher. 'At the first window you'll be issued with UN hats and armbands, and a forty-eight-hour emergency ration pack. At the second you'll be given an envelope for all your personal stuff. Put everything in it that you won't be needing in Iraq, including your national passports. Anything that identifies who you are and where you come from, leave it here. In exchange you'll be issued with special UN documents. From now on you don't belong to any particular nation any more, just to the UN.'

Burgess collected the envelope with his name on and began emptying his pockets. Credit cards, FBI badge, personal diary and wallet. He began stuffing them all in, then stopped to take from the wallet the Polaroid of Carole and the kids, snapped in front of the tree last Christmas. He looked at it for a couple of seconds, wanting it with him. But nothing personal, Hardcastle had said. Nothing the Iraqis could use against him if things got unpleasant. He pushed it into the envelope and closed the seal.

When he'd finished, he found Hardcastle waiting for him. The Englishman took him to one side.

'Just to keep you informed,' Hardcastle breathed, his voice too low for anyone else to overhear. 'The British Secret Intelligence Service has picked up something that's rather alarming. Word is the Iraqis have managed to assemble some anthrax warheads in recent weeks and to smuggle them out of the country.'

'Shoot!'

'No word on when or where they're to be used. Can't even be certain the tip-off's true. Washington's been told of course, but just wanted *you* to know. Puts everything we're doing into context, don't you think?'

'Absolutely, Andrew,' he breathed.

Fifteen minutes later they sat strapped into the webbing seats lining the fuselage of a UN L-100 Hercules, on charter from a company in South Africa. Buckled firmly to the aircraft floor in front of them were pallets piled with the equipment and supplies they would need for their mission.

Dean Burgess felt the adrenalin buzz of an assignment under way. On the opposite side of the fuselage Hardcastle looked drawn and anxious. The Englishman hated flying, he'd confessed as they'd boarded. As the four big turbo-props spun up to their operating revs Burgess dug the foam plugs deeper into his ears. He closed his eyes and rested his head against the red nylon straps that supported the seats. He felt dog tired suddenly. The travel was catching up with him again.

His mind was still churning over what Hardcastle had whispered to him a few minutes ago – anthrax warheads already in place. Somewhere outside Iraq. Somewhere that might even be the United States of America . . .

Keeping him going up to now had been the childlike sense of adventure he always felt at the start of a new mission, but as his mind began to fog, that stimulus evaporated. In its place there emerged a dark foreboding, some premonition that what he was embarking on would have consequences far beyond anything he'd imagined.

As he began to doze, he had a nightmare vision of an imminent disaster with Carole and the kids in the midst of it, their faces turned his way, begging him to save them.

He shivered, because in his bones he sensed he was going to be powerless to help.

7

Monday, 30 September
The Port of Piraeus, Greece

A grey-blue pollution haze shrouded the dawn sun as the black-hulled, Gibraltar-registered container ship was eased from the jetty by two tugs. The vessel had been in the Greek port for a mere six hours, off-loading cargoes she'd brought from further west and hoisting on board others which had destinations to the east.

The great sack of the eastern Mediterranean is criss-crossed by a spider's web of shipping routes, at the centre of which lies Piraeus. Well-placed for the Med and the Aegean with its routes to the Black Sea, a quarter of the port's 'box traffic' consists of transshipments from one container line to another.

The thick, oily water of the inner harbour churned and frothed as the ship's screw began to turn. This modern, well-run vessel was a workhorse of the container business, shuttling relentlessly the length of the Mediterranean, transporting her sealed and invisible cargoes. The next port of call on her journey east was Limassol on the southern coast of Cyprus. Some twenty of the containers stacked on her deck were bound for that divided island, all of them loaded at Piraeus. Among them was a forty-footer transshipped from a vessel out of Ilychevsk in

Ukraine. The Single Administrative Document accompanying it gave the container's final destination as Haifa in Israel and its contents as defective fruit and vegetable juices being returned to their supplier.

The clasp locking the container's doors bore the seal of the Ukrainian customs in Odessa. The officer who'd applied the seal had not checked the container's repacked contents. A bribe had seen to that. If he *had* looked behind the single pallet of expanding Tetrapaks, he would have found a far more explosive cargo.

09.10 hrs
Baghdad

Overlooking the sweet-water canal in east Baghdad, a modern hotel served as the UN Special Commission's headquarters in Iraq. Its blue frontage was pierced by large porthole-like windows and the car park in front was crowded with white-painted vehicles, some of them armoured. Two Nissan Prairies and two Toyota Landcruisers lined up with their engines running to get the air-conditioning going. Most of the members of the newly arrived UN inspection team were already inside waiting for the start of their first outing.

Dean Burgess stood in the open with Andrew Hardcastle, trying not to be irritated by the mild chauvinism which had first shown itself the day before at the briefing in Bahrain. They watched their plain-clothes Iraqi security escorts digest the news of where the day's inspection was to be. Above the pale cotton slacks and shirts and the multi-pocketed fisherman's vests which both UN men wore, Burgess was sporting the blue baseball cap with the

UN logo he'd been issued with in Bahrain. It gave him a small feeling of authority in a situation where, for an American in particular, there was little such comfort to be had.

He had a clear head this morning after a good night's sleep helped by Temazepam. His unease about his marriage had been buried under the flood of impressions that arrival in Iraq had entailed. His only problem was the lingering culture shock. The hostility with which they'd been received on arrival last night at the Habbaniyah Military Air Base west of Baghdad had been as blatant as he'd expected. As far as the Iraqi military were concerned, the UNSCOM team were spies, whatever cloak of legality the outside world had given them.

The air base itself had been eerie and unpleasant. MiG-29s stood ostentatiously on the flight-line, proof of Iraq's surviving military strength despite America's best efforts to destroy it in 1991. The immigration process had been handled in a so-called executive lounge. Burgess had needed to use the bathroom after the flight but had nearly thought better of it when he saw the filthy, excreta-caked hole in the ground he would need to crouch over.

The bus ride into the capital with its ubiquitous portraits of the Iraqi leader had surprised him, although it shouldn't have. Despite knowing that the bridges and buildings bombed in the 1991 war had all been repaired, subconsciously he'd expected *some* sign of the billions of dollars' worth of damage inflicted on the country. Gleaming palaces, broad, well-surfaced highways – it just didn't fit.

Potemkin villages, Hardcastle had said. A good-looking frontage, but behind it poverty and hardship for the masses. Across the river in the eastern half of the city, he'd seen skinny street children hawking cigarette lighters and unemployed graduates trying to sell their textbooks at the kerb.

An hour ago they'd driven here to the Canal Hotel, home of the UN's Baghdad Monitoring and Verification Centre, from the nearby Al Hyatt where they were billeted. A tour of the BMVC had impressed him with well-equipped laboratories, and its crowded operations room with computer terminals that could call up pictures from remote cameras in over a hundred sensitive sites up and down the country.

'Come on, come on!' Hardcastle chivvied, glaring across the car park at the trio of army-green jeeps. The news that their destination for the day was to be the Haji protein factory seemed to have caused puzzlement. They should have set off immediately, but the half-dozen minders were propped against their vehicles while their leader busied himself on the radio.

'What's going on Andrew? How do you read this?' Burgess whispered.

'God knows. But one thing's sure. They'll be phoning the Haji plant to warn them we're coming.'

'Complete surprise must be pretty much impossible to achieve.'

'It can never be total,' Hardcastle acknowledged. 'But they'd need more than one hour's notice to remove all the evidence at the Haji factory if they *have* been up to no good there.'

'Are these guys Mukhabarat – the Ba'ath party intelligence?' Burgess checked. He liked to classify people. To give them labels.

'They never tell us who they are, but no, I think they're Amn al Aman. That's general security. Saddam has several parallel security organisations, each reporting to him and each keeping an eye on the others. Helps stop assassination attempts.'

'Neat.'

'Mr Hardcastle!'

His name had been shouted from the doorway of the hotel. The voice was antipodean.

They spun round. Burgess recognised the uniformed operations officer from New Zealand he'd met half an hour earlier.

'Message for you, Mr Hardcastle. Urgent!'

'Damn! Keep an eye on those minders, Dean. Don't let the buggers take off without me.'

'Sure thing.'

Hardcastle strode back into the hotel.

'It's from New York,' the New Zealand army captain told him. Where else? thought Hardcastle.

They entered the conference room which UNSCOM used as its operations centre, its walls papered with lists of equipment and personnel involved in Iraq's biological weapons programme. A couple of headquarters staff sat at work tables surrounded by papers, reference books and half-empty coffee mugs. The computers they tapped away at were notebooks whose liquid crystal displays didn't give out the radiation of desktop cathode ray screens, a radiation that could be read by Iraqi electronic monitoring devices set up in rooms nearby.

'Over here, Mr Hardcastle.' The New Zealander handed him a sealed envelope. 'Came on the secure fax link.'

'Secure' didn't mean too much here. The UN's signals from New York used a low-level encryption system that could be cracked within an hour by a good Iraqi technician with a Pentium PC.

'Thanks.' Hardcastle read the brief note, then grimaced. 'Bugger!' A change of mission. 'Damn, damn!' They'd just alerted the Iraqis to their interest in the Haji factory and now they weren't bloody going there. At least not today.

He re-read the fax.

New overhead imagery shows suspected building

materials and heavy plant at site known as Task Two. Urgent you change plan and inspect this site first.

Task Two. The patch of disturbed sand in the desert. Why not do both sites? Send half the team to the Haji place and half out to the wilderness. Why not? Because the Amn people would insist they hadn't the manpower to host both locations. Arrant nonsense of course, but it would provoke hours of prevarication.

'Right, then,' Hardcastle puffed, resigned to the change of plan. He showed the signal to the New Zealander. 'You need to know about this. I'll give you the co-ordinates.'

The UN was certain the monitoring centre itself was bugged, so they'd established the routine of passing critical information to one another in writing. Hardcastle jotted down a summary, together with the map reference.

Site is in middle of the desert. U-2 spotted sand disturbance a few days ago. Now think it's being built on. They could be putting up a building to conceal something interesting that's been buried there.

He swung the small pack from his back and unzipped the map pocket in the lid.

'I'll show you where on this.'

He unfolded one of the large-scale aviation charts which they used for navigating the desert around Baghdad.

'X marks the spot.'

'Got it,' said the New Zealander, marking up his own chart and writing down the exact co-ordinates.

'Miles from bloody anywhere, as you can see,' Hardcastle complained.

'And well beyond VHF I should think.'

The ops officer opened a ring-binder and checked his list of the communications masts used to link live pictures from the remote cameras and to extend their radio net.

'As I thought,' he confirmed. 'Nothing near it. It'll have to be the sat system.'

'Don't worry, I'll keep in touch. You'll confirm to New York that I'm switching tasks?'

'Of course, Mr Hardcastle. Happy hunting.'

Hardcastle stuffed the map back into his rucksack then swung it round onto his shoulders.

'Thanks.'

Out in the car park Burgess was glad to see the Englishman reappear, whatever his reservations about him. He felt very much the new kid on the block and his American accent had prompted an adverse response from the short, weasel-faced headman of the Iraqi security team. The man, identified to them only as Mustafa, now stood waiting in the shade of a large tree, the armpits of his striped shirt dark with sweat, his gross stomach straining at its buttons.

'Change of plan, I'm afraid,' Hardcastle grumbled, taking Burgess by the arm. 'We're heading for the desert. Better inform our guard dogs. Where's Mustafa?'

'Over there.'

They walked across the car park to the shade-giving tree, watched by the expressionless security man.

'Mustafa, we have a problem,' Hardcastle announced abruptly.

'We go now?'

'Yes. We'd like to leave immediately, but not to where I told you.'

The Iraqi's pinched face darkened.

'No Haji factory? They all ready for you there.'

You bet, Burgess mused.

'No. Not the Haji factory today. There's another site we want to see that's west of Baghdad. About ninety k's from here. In the desert.'

Mustafa glared suspiciously at Hardcastle's folded-up air chart.

'What other site? You have map reference? Co-ordinate?' he growled, hoisting up the trousers which had slipped under the weight of his belly.

'Of course.'

'Why you want to go there?' Mustafa bitched, making no attempt to conceal his annoyance.

'Just for a look.'

Hardcastle spread out his map and pointed at the general area of interest. The Iraqi squinted at it. Needs glasses, thought Burgess, and too vain to wear them.

'There is nothing in this place,' the Iraqi snapped dismissively. 'I know this area. Just desert. Maybe some goats.'

'Then you've no cause to be concerned, have you Mustafa?' Hardcastle purred.

'You have exact co-ordinate?' the Iraqi repeated, making no attempt to conceal the hatred in his hard, brown eyes.

'Yes. *I* have them. *You* don't need them.'

The security man bristled.

'We'll take the highway that leads to Habbaniyah,' Hardcastle continued firmly. '*I'll* tell you when to turn off. Just follow my directions, okay? Get a move on, shall we? The sooner we're there, the sooner we can come back again.'

'One moment . . .' The security man made to walk away with the map.

'Hang on. That's mine.' Hardcastle grabbed it back. 'Come on. Let's move it. I'll give you directions on the VHF when we get close.'

'One moment,' the Iraqi repeated, turning towards his own jeep which was almost blocking the car park exit. 'I have to check if is possible.'

'It *is* possible,' Hardcastle growled between clenched teeth. 'And don't you dare pretend otherwise, you little shit,' he added once the security man was out of earshot.

Burgess flinched at Hardcastle's high-handedness, suspecting that antagonising the minder would prove counterproductive.

'He's real scared,' Burgess breathed. 'Thinks we're onto something he doesn't know about.'

'Probably,' said Hardcastle, then shouted after the Iraqi, 'Five minutes, Mustafa. Five minutes, then we're setting off! Better tell the troops what's going on,' he added softly to Burgess. He strode over to the UN vehicles to warn his team of the switch to Task Two.

Burgess ambled to the front of the UN convoy and rested his backside against the wing of the leading four-wheel-drive. He watched the Iraqi minders huddle round their own map twenty yards away. They reminded him of a bunch of used car dealers plotting a mileage fraud.

It was nine-thirty in the morning and the last day of September, yet the sun was already blisteringly hot. He'd put on sunblock but was glad of the UN's baseball cap to give his fair skin some extra protection. He wore a long-sleeved, light-grey shirt – added to his bag by Carole in a moment of female practicality because it wouldn't show the dirt if he had to wear it for several days – and over it the fisherman's vest with pockets for his notebook, pens and a compass. Also some spare Hi-8 tapes for the camcorder he was to use to video all significant events. On his feet he wore a stout pair of Nikes.

Hardcastle joined him.

'I think they're about to play silly buggers,' he warned, leaning against the mudguard next to him. 'Time for some pressure. Get that camera out.'

Burgess opened his backpack and extracted the Sony. Hardcastle checked his watch.

'He's had his five minutes. Let's go prod him.'

Burgess folded out the viewer, pressed record and followed in Hardcastle's wake, the camera at chest height. As they approached, one of the minders produced his own camera and began videoing them. Mustafa emerged from his vehicle poker-faced.

'Ready, Mustafa?' Hardcastle asked, knowing what the answer would be.

'What you ask, it is not possible.'

'What d'you mean? We can go wherever we want. You know that.'

'National security . . .'

'Bollocks!'

'Yes. National security. Where you show me on the map it is a military training area.'

'Rubbish!' Hardcastle snorted. 'I know perfectly well where the training areas are and this isn't one of them. I demand you accompany us there. Immediately.'

'I'm sorry. It is Special Republican Guard training area. I have my orders.'

'And I have *mine*, Mustafa. I shall take the matter higher.' He turned on his heel. 'Bugger!' he whispered under his breath. 'They're such bloody time-wasters.'

Burgess switched off the camera.

'What now?' he asked, unsurprised that the Iraqi had responded to Hardcastle's aggression in the way he'd predicted.

'Well, we're in confrontation, so there's a procedure to follow. Official complaint to be lodged, all that sort of stuff. Load of nonsense.'

Back at his vehicle he reached for the VHF handset and told the ops room what was happening. 'Get the protests in right away,' he instructed the New Zealander. Clipping the microphone back in its holder, he put a hand to his mouth and stared across at the car park exit. 'Now, I wonder if we can't force the issue. Jump in, Dean. This could be quite a ride.'

The half-caste Canadian major was at the wheel. Hardcastle scribbled words on a notepad then held it up for Latour to read.

That gap between the Iraqi vehicles and the exit – think we can get through it?

The Canadian nodded.

'Okay.' Hardcastle grabbed the microphone again. 'Mike three, Charlie nine. Mike three, Charlie nine.'

The signal was code for 'wagons roll'. The three UN vehicles behind them shifted into gear. Latour let up the clutch and rolled towards the car park exit. The Iraqis had their heads down, talking on their radio.

'Okay. Foot down. Go, go, go!' Hardcastle hissed.

Latour slipped through the gap. He glanced left, saw a break in the traffic on the highway running parallel to the canal and pushed into it. Burgess twisted round to see whether the others had made it. The second UN Nissan swerved through the gap, then nothing.

'Shoot! They've blocked the two Landcruisers,' Burgess warned.

'You want me to stop?' asked Latour.

'No. Keep going. Steady speed.' Hardcastle squared up to the dashboard where he believed the Iraqi's microphone would be hidden. 'Under UN Resolution 687, they've no right to impede our inspection,' he declared combatively.

Burgess rolled his eyes. To him this sort of tactic was pointlessly provocative. He was distracted suddenly by two huge turquoise-coloured shells set well back from the road on their left, like halves of a coconut cleaved by a scimitar.

'Martyrs Memorial,' Hardcastle explained. 'Impressive, don't you think? So it damn well should be. It's Saddam's tribute to the hundreds of thousands he sent to die in his lunatic war against Iran.'

'Ha! Looks like we have company,' the Canadian chipped in, one eye on the mirror. He'd spotted a green jeep thundering up behind them.

Hardcastle grabbed the microphone. 'Sierra four, Sierra four. This is Golf. What's your situation, over?'

'Golf, Sierra four.' The voice was German and belonged to a demolition specialist from Mannheim in the third vehicle. 'They block us with two of their jeeps. We are still in the BMVC parking. Over.'

'Sierra four, have they said anything? Over.'

'No. But they are not happy. Boss man comes to see you, I think. Over.'

'Thanks. We see him. Out.'

The Iraqi jeep was closing fast, weaving through the traffic with its headlights ablaze.

'You want I do some Formula One?' Latour checked, ready to race.

'No. Let's see what he has to say when he catches up.'

A huge portrait of Saddam loomed up at the roadside then slipped behind them. The jeep pulled alongside, its warning lights flashing and its VHF whip aerial waving wildly. A security man pointed a pistol from a side window and flagged them down.

'So I stop, yes?' Latour checked, his voice heavy with irony.

'I think you'd better before they fine you for speeding.'

The two UN patrols slowed and stopped with the Iraqi jeep directly in front. Mustafa erupted from the door and came storming back along the kerb towards them followed by two of his dark-haired men.

'What you think you do?' he screamed as Hardcastle wound down the window. 'It not permitted that you go like that. You British, you think you still own Iraq. Mister Hardcastle, if you do not respect us, respect our laws, we will not have you in our country.'

'I'll respect you when you stick to the UN's rules, Mustafa,' Hardcastle retorted. 'Under Resolution 687 we can inspect any site we want. Without delay. All that nonsense about national security. It's rubbish, Mustafa. Rubbish!'

'You cannot go without escort,' Mustafa grimaced, exposing tobacco-stained teeth. 'And we need some clarifications. Show me your map, please.'

'Better still, I'll show you on yours, Mustafa,' Hardcastle countered, stepping from the cool of the vehicle into the scorching sunlight. 'Now let's be quick about this.'

'One moment,' said the Iraqi. 'Wait here.'

Mustafa walked back to his own vehicle and leaned inside, talking on the radio again. Eventually, after a couple of minutes, he returned clutching a military map.

'Now, show me.'

Hardcastle unfolded the chart and indicated a general location but with deliberate vagueness.

'We take the Habbaniyah road, then turn down the western side of the dry lake. Then when my GPS tells me –' he pointed to the satellite navigation handset clipped to the dashboard. '– we'll turn off and cut overland. You just follow me, okay?'

The Iraqi shook his head. 'This is not possible.'

'Yes it bloody well is!'

They glared at one another like deadlocked gladiators.

'Look, Mustafa . . .' Hardcastle softened suddenly. 'Maybe I have been a little brusque. I apologise. But we have our job to do. Let's string the convoy back together and move on. All right?'

'One moment. One moment please.' The security man stomped back to his jeep.

'Bloody hell!' hissed Hardcastle, slipping back into his seat and closing the door to keep the cool in.

Another five minutes passed, then the Iraqi jeep began to inch forward.

'What's happening?' Hardcastle flapped.

'It's okay,' Latour reassured him. 'Look behind.'

Fifty metres back down the road the other two UN

vehicles were driving towards them. The team was together again.

'At last. Let's go.'

Led by the security men's jeep, the UNSCOM convoy crossed the wide, brown river Tigris via the rebuilt Jumhuriya Bridge and progressed onto the Qadisiya Expressway heading west.

Nearly two hours later the GPS placed them 4.2 kilometres northeast of the Task Two grid reference. For thirty minutes they'd driven south on a dirt road along a strip of cultivated land watered by the Euphrates. Now, however, they were in undulating desert. In a small village of squat, flat-roofed houses the colour of the earth on which they stood, blue-eyed Bedouins in grubby dishdashas gaped at the unusual convoy, more used to seeing battered pickups loaded with goats or the daily bus that took the younger children to school. Burgess stared back in bemusement; before now he'd only seen sights like this on TV.

Then all life disappeared. A barren sweep of sand and stones reached to the horizon. The vast emptiness of the place brought home to Burgess the impossible nature of UNSCOM's task. In such a landscape it was only too easy to hide weapons of mass destruction. How had the photo reconnaissance guys picked up on this site? Pure chance?

'Any minute now there should be a good-sized wadi on your right,' Hardcastle told Latour, peering at his chart. 'That's if the wind hasn't filled it in.'

The Canadian slowed and glanced in the mirror. The Iraqi escort vehicle was directly behind, but the rest of the convoy was further back, obscured by dust kicked up by their wheels.

'Maybe here, you think?' the Canadian checked,

slowing to a crawl. A dry dip in the ground ran off to the right at ninety degrees to the track.

'Looks good. Anyway there's been nothing else that fits the chart.'

Hardcastle snatched up the VHF microphone to tell the others they were turning off.

Latour engaged four-wheel-drive and swung the machine to the right, gingerly testing the firmness of the sand. The wadi bed proved firm.

'How far along here?'

'One-point-one kilometres, according to this toy,' Hardcastle chirruped, straightening the aerial of the GPS handset to maximise the signal. He glanced back to check the convoy was following.

'All present and correct,' Burgess assured him from the rear seat. He'd noted the time they'd entered the wadi in the log, then shot some video, pointing the Hi-8 to the left and sweeping it round in a wide pan.

The ground in front rose gradually and the vehicle climbed at walking speed to ensure they didn't get bogged down.

Suddenly Burgess spotted something and pointed dead ahead.

'Wheel tracks.'

Latour stamped on the brake. The tread pattern was large, the mark of a large vehicle like an earth-mover. The machine had dipped into the wadi from one side and out the other.

'Left. Go left. Follow the tracks,' Hardcastle ordered. 'The GPS puts us three hundred metres north of our grid ref.'

Suddenly the green jeep with Mustafa inside swung out to pass them and climbed the shallow slope of the wadi's left bank. The guy had heard them, Burgess realised, the microphone in the dashboard transmitting direct to their jeep. Latour jammed into first and accelerated out of the ditch, sand and stones spattering from beneath the wheels. Beyond the wadi's ridge the plain stretched to a distant line of low hills. Thirty seconds later the tracks they were following ended in a swirl of disturbed sand at the centre of which stood Mustafa's jeep.

'We're there, gentlemen. Time for a leg stretch,' Hardcastle murmured.

Beyond the Iraqi jeep lay a stack of steel girders, cinder blocks and bags of cement sufficient to make a medium-sized barn. But no people.

'Maybe they're building a Holiday Inn,' Hardcastle mused.

Mustafa picked his way over to them, trying in vain to keep the sand out of his slip-on shoes. His face was smug. 'Why you come here, Mister Hardcastle?' There was even a glint of triumph in his eyes. 'There is nothing here of interest. Like I tell you.'

To Burgess the Iraqi's unconcern looked disconcertingly genuine. He suspected they were indeed on a wild goose chase.

'Nothing? What's this then? What are they building?' Hardcastle persisted.

The Iraqi shrugged. '*I* do not know. Why should I know? This is free country. Maybe someone build a house for chickens.'

'For flying pigs more like,' Hardcastle muttered.

'Nothing here. See?' Mustafa gloated. 'Have a good look.'

'I shall.'

Hardcastle marched forward. Next to the stack of building materials the ground had been dug over with a mechanical shovel, a rectangular area of disturbed sand some sixty feet long. The top had been smoothed over but only in part. Many of the stones visible were a different colour from those on the undisturbed ground nearby, as if churned up from a greater depth. Burgess took some shots.

'This stinks,' Hardcastle muttered, standing at the edge of the dug area. 'There's something under here.'

The rest of his team had caught up and were stretching stiffened limbs. He bunched his fingers over his head in a gather-round signal. When they'd assembled he checked they were beyond the hearing of their minders, then began.

'Right folks. This is it. Don't ask me what we're looking for because I simply don't know. All I can say is that I can't think of any *good* reason why somebody would want to erect a building in this Godforsaken place, and there's nobody around to tell us. Until three weeks ago this was just featureless desert, remember. Then overhead photography revealed the ground had been dug over. Another photograph taken yesterday showed they'd moved all this stuff here.' He waved a hand at the girders. 'My hunch is they've buried something and were about to cover the site with a building.'

Heads nodded in agreement.

'Could be SCUD components, or lab equipment carefully packaged so it can be recovered later.' He turned to the Canadian. 'Pierre, I suggest you divide us into teams and allocate sectors. Use the shovels from the jeeps, wear respirators and monitor continuously for CBW. Obviously we're not going to be able to dig deep without machines, particularly in this heat, but just see if you can find anything near the surface that would justify our suspicions. Be very careful of course. If there *is* anything interesting buried here it could be nasty. Better run over the site with the sniffers before we start, Pierre.'

Latour set to work with the nerve-agent detectors as the rest of the team donned light masks and prepared to dig. Mustafa's men watched with mild amusement at the prospect of so many of these intrusive foreigners melting in the glare of the midday sun.

Burgess videoed the scene, then he and Hardcastle measured out the site for the records and logged the building materials that had been dumped there.

'What does your detective's nose tell you about this place, Dean?' Hardcastle asked when they paused for a drink from their water bottles.

'That it makes no sense. But what I find most disconcerting is that Mustafa's men don't seem to give a shit that we're here. It's as if they *know* there's nothing to interest us under there.'

Hardcastle grimaced. 'I fear you may be right. But we have to be sure.'

'In which case the sooner we get some machines to help, the better,' Burgess told him, looking up at the glaring sun.

They heard an engine start up. One of the Iraqi jeeps headed back along the tyre tracks that had led them here.

'Where's that man off to?' Hardcastle wondered.

'Maybe *he'll* tell us.'

Mustafa was approaching them, his shirtfront now patchy with sweat. His expression had softened. He looked almost friendly.

'Sending off for some rations, Mustafa?' Hardcastle quipped.

The Iraqi smiled. 'I try to help you. So we don't waste so much time. I send someone to the village we pass through, to ask what this place is. Because *we* don't know. Really,' he confided. 'But soon we find out. Then we can all go back to Baghdad.'

'It's not that simple, Mustafa.'

The Iraqi held his smile for a moment, but with difficulty. Then his expression changed into that of a supplicant.

'Mister Hardcastle. Today is the birthday of my son,'

he pleaded softly. 'My wife, my other children – they will celebrate him this afternoon. I also would like to be there. We can finish here soon, yes?'

'Mustafa . . .' Hardcastle warned.

If this was a ploy the man's sincerity was worthy of Hollywood, thought Burgess.

'Mustafa, you know the UN cannot suspend its mandate for a birthday party,' Hardcastle replied dismissively. He pointed towards the broken ground. 'Something's been buried here and we need to know what. We require a mechanical digger from you.'

'Not possible.' Bruised by the rejection, the Arab had drawn in his cheeks and his face had set like stone.

'It's utterly possible,' Hardcastle insisted.

'Not possible. Here there is no digger.' He spread his arms to indicate the emptiness of the desert.

'There was one,' Hardcastle snapped, pointing at the tracks in the sand. 'Not long ago. Can't have got far. Maybe in the village where your man's gone.'

'Not possible.'

The security man turned on his heel and sidled like an angry crab back towards his vehicle. Then a shout from the direction of the area of dug earth stopped him in his tracks.

'Andrew! Over here.'

Pierre Latour was beckoning wildly. As they hurried towards him he pointed at his face mask to warn them to cover up. The three others who'd been digging with him were staring at the ground.

'Well, well,' breathed Hardcastle. 'Let's see what the cat's brought in.'

Mustafa walked with them, then fell back when they pulled on their masks. Burgess switched on the camera.

'Aha!' Sounds of triumph from beneath Hardcastle's mask. 'Just look at that! I knew it. I damn well knew it!'

Burgess zoomed in to where Latour pointed. There was

something sticking out of the sand. Something that looked at first like the blackened stump of a sapling. Then as the lens pulled focus he realised he was looking at the scorched hoof and bone of an animal's hind leg. The foreboding which had hit him on their departure from Bahrain came bombing back.

'Gentlemen,' growled Hardcastle portentously. 'Look around you. See any grazing land? Do you *heck*. There's only one reason anyone would bury a cow out here in the middle of nowhere. This benighted creature, gentlemen, was the victim of a biological weapons experiment.'

8

Midday
London

Sam Packer leaned against the window of the 767 looking down at the city he'd feared he might never see again. London's outline beneath the flight-path was dulled by a grey haze. He should have felt exultant to be nearly home, but instead he was troubled and uneasy.

The previous day, after Chrissie's abrupt departure from Mowbray's house in Amman, he'd slept long and fitfully in that narrow child's bed that still bore traces of her smell, helped by some strong painkillers the doctor had left. Then, in the evening, Mowbray had taken him to eat at a small Arab restaurant in the neighbourhood and given him the unsettling news that Salah Khalil, the Iraqi for whom he'd been swapped, had not after all been bundled back to Baghdad to receive his expected punishment from Saddam Hussein. Instead, the men who'd met him on arrival at Amman airport on Saturday night had hustled him onto a chartered Learjet the next morning and flown him to Cyprus. Mowbray had been tipped off by the Jordanian Mukhabarat. When he'd hurried Chrissie away from the house yesterday, it had been to take her to the airport for a midday flight to Larnaca.

The turn of events had alarmed Sam. Not only was the Khalil affair clearly more complex than SIS had thought, but it was Chrissie who was being sent into danger to check what the Iraqis were up to. Chrissie. Pregnant with a child he suspected was his.

Mowbray had had a simple explanation for the development.

'Cyprus means one thing and one thing only in a situation like this,' he'd told him. 'Money. The island's a beehive of offshore companies and dodgy banks. London's theory is that whatever accounts Khalil controlled on behalf of Saddam they were probably run from Cyprus. And now they're making him transfer the funds elsewhere. To an account Saddam can control more directly. We'll be warning the Central Bank of Cyprus of course. Telling them any large sums being moved by Khalil could be in contravention of UN sanctions.'

But why had they sent Chrissie?

'Simple. The Firm's been caught off watch. The Nicosia man's on leave. And she knows Khalil.'

The undercarriage clunked down as the gleaming curve of the Palm House in Kew Botanical Gardens passed beneath them, its glass burnished by a sudden shaft of sunlight penetrating the gloom. Beyond the gardens stretched dense suburban streets. All those people down there, he thought to himself. Easy pickings for some nutter with a biological weapon.

Anthrax. He knew little about the stuff, but the very word sent a chill through him. He pictured the scrawny face of the messenger in Baghdad, his milky, petrified eyes as he'd delivered his warning. Remembered the grotesque bloated corpse the monsters in Baghdad had reduced him to. A warning so cataclysmic and, he was convinced, so earnestly meant, yet one so vague in its detail the intelligence community could make little use of it.

The wind roared in the wheel struts as the plane made its final approach to Heathrow. There would be a car to meet him, Mowbray had said, to take him to a debrief, his controllers at SIS hoping he could inject some sense into what had happened.

The stewardess, who'd slipped him a few miniatures of whisky to take home with him when the bar closed, strapped herself hurriedly into the folding seat by the forward door. She gave him a tight, conspiratorial smile.

Sam eased the knees of his trousers. For the journey back to England he'd worn the lightweight grey business suit he'd had on at the time of his arrest and which he'd found neatly folded in his suitcase. The fabric kept snagging on the bandages round his shins, however. He was bruised and stiff still, but the sleep, the nourishment and a couple of drinks on the flight had set him to rights.

The wheels touched down. The seat belt dug into his bruised body. As the Boeing turned onto the taxi-way he unclipped the strap and gathered his belongings, including a newspaper the airline had provided. A report in it about the round-the-world sailing race he'd read with interest. He owned a half share in a sailing boat, kept on the south coast of England, which he hoped to spend some time on before winter set in.

Inside the terminal on the long walk to immigration and customs, the pains in his shins slowed him down. It was midday in London. The baggage came through unusually quickly, and once past customs he saw a line of dark-suited chauffeurs holding name boards.

'Mister Packer?' A murmured greeting and a light touch on his arm.

'Yes.' Sam recognised the man as an MI6 regular.

'We're in the car park, sir. Can I push the trolley for you?'

'Thanks.'

The vehicle was a three-year-old navy-blue Granada with a minicab aerial clipped to the boot lid. Sam slid into the rear and wedged himself in the corner as the machine descended to the exit and turned onto the road for London.

'Where are we going?' Sam asked.

The driver cleared his throat. 'Isleworth, Mr Packer.' He wound down the window slightly. 'Turned warm again. Going to be fine all week according to the forecast.'

'That's nice.'

Isleworth. A three-roomed flat above a launderette maintained by an SIS technical unit, its windows hung with faded net. He'd been there a couple of times, for debriefings after trips.

He began to focus on the man who would be waiting for him there. Duncan Waddell, a thirty-four-year-old Ulsterman, slight in build but with an aggressiveness to make up for it. Waddell had been his main point of contact with the Intelligence Service for the past couple of years, one of the young Turks of SIS, a new broom given rapid promotion after the clear-out of the old guard at Christmas 1992. Now running the Middle East desk in Martin Kessler's Global Risks department.

Sam himself was 'deep cover', operating in the field with an assumed identity and seldom crossing the threshold of SIS HQ at Vauxhall Cross. His instincts had been honed in the intelligence branch of the Royal Navy, his street wisdom acquired through six years of coming eyeball-close to his SIS targets. Waddell had been recruited straight from Cambridge, an inside man whose experience in the field had been limited to 'light cover' at embassies. In the past their different backgrounds had led to friction. Sam suspected it was about to do so again.

The car pulled up in a service road at the back of the parade of shops that included the launderette.

'You can leave your bag, sir. I'm to park up and wait to take you on somewhere else.'

'Fine. See you in a while, then.'

The entrance to the apartment was up a rusting fire-escape whose stair-treads clanged. The once-white back door bore a broken plastic number that had slewed sideways because of a missing screw. It was unlocked. Sam let himself into the kitchen.

'Ahaa. Good man. Sam! Welcome back, sir!' Waddell's sonorous voice resonated from the front room. Sam suspected that at some stage he'd had coaching to make it lower, to counter his lack of height.

The Ulsterman appeared in the kitchen doorway, dressed in a short-sleeved cream shirt and well-pressed fawn trousers. His arms spread wide in welcome. Several inches shorter than Sam, he had a clean-cut face and a brush of fair hair which was cropped like a teasel.

'Am I glad to see you back in one piece.' He clasped Sam's arms. 'Are you okay?'

'Never better.'

'Hardly that. Come on in.' Waddell went ahead, then stopped to let Sam go in front. 'You know, for a few moments in the last couple of weeks, you had us truly worried.'

'Me too.' Like on the previous day when he'd learned from Chrissie that this man now exuding such warm bonhomie had been ready to let him die.

'I'll bet. I'll bet. I must say you're looking better than I'd expected,' Waddell added.

The small, square living room was papered with a faded Regency stripe. From a wing-back chair on the far side an older man rose to his feet. Wearing a navy blazer his broad face had the steady, unyielding eyes of an inquisitor.

'This is Charles,' Waddell explained inadequately. 'He's come to listen in.'

'How d'you do,' said Charles.

Internal security, thought Sam.

'Didn't know whether they'd have fed you properly on

the plane, so we got some sandwiches in,' said Waddell, pointing to the low brass and glass coffee table set with two modest plates of food and a six-pack of sparkling fruit drinks.

The furnishing of the room was 1970s. Parker-Knoll chairs and a sofa with solid wooden arms. Sam flopped down onto it.

'Thoughtful of you, Duncan. But I've eaten.'

He straightened his legs to free the trouser fabric from the dressings on his shins.

Waddell noticed the awkwardness of the movement.

'It's the legs that are worst, is it?' he asked, clumsily. 'Mowbray gave us the doctor's report on you.'

'They're fine. I'm fine. Thanks.' He didn't want pleasantries. Wanted to know what they needed from him.

'To be on the safe side we've fixed for you to have a medical after we've finished our debrief here. At a private clinic in Wimbledon. You've got dressings on your legs that need changing – is that right?'

'Yes. But there's a pretty nurse at my local GP's who could do that for me,' Sam told him.

'No. I think not, old son. Best to keep it in house.' He gestured towards the sandwiches again. 'Are you sure you won't?'

'Quite.' They were egg mayonnaise and tuna, neither of which he liked.

Waddell passed a plate to the man called Charles, who took one of each.

'I'm going to tuck in too,' grunted Waddell. 'Shame to let them go to waste.' He took a small, neat bite, chewed it thoughtfully, then swallowed.

'Right, now. Let's start,' he announced, wiping hands on a paper napkin. 'You're an old hand, Sam. A pro. A man we all respect.' Deceptively warm words given an earnest tone by the Belfast growl, but Waddell's eyes were cold. 'And in the past few days you've been to hell and back. We appreciate that. But I have to be frank. There's a few aspects of this business that we're not entirely happy about.'

'Me neither, Duncan.'

'The bottom line is that what we've all just gone through should simply never have happened.'

'Dead right it shouldn't.'

Waddell clasped his hands like a church minister.

'But before we get into the business of how they broke your cover, let's look at the intelligence. This line you were fed about anthrax weapons being smuggled out of the country – I understand you think the warning was genuine.'

The implication being that Waddell did not.

'Yes.'

'We've communicated it to our friends in Washington and Jerusalem, of course,' Waddell assured him. 'But to be honest we do have serious doubts about it. You see, it simply doesn't make a lot of sense. Every reliable piece of information we have on Saddam points to him wanting sanctions lifted very badly indeed. So the last thing in the world he would do just now is mount some sort of BW attack in Israel or Saudi Arabia or America or wherever. We all know he's got the capability, but let's face it, it would be economic and political suicide.'

'Logically I'm sure you're right. Nonetheless I'm sure the warning was genuine,' Sam insisted.

'Well we'll have to part company on that. You see, we and the Americans believe that the whole business of your arrest had one purpose and one purpose only. For Saddam to get Khalil back and regain control of the bank accounts. Feeding you the anthrax line and then virtually making sure you communicated it to us – that was the hook, don't you see? To make us desperate to get you out in case you had more. To make us ready to deal over Khalil. And let's face it, it worked.'

Waddell looked down at his hands.

'If that's true, why the hell did they beat their own messenger to death?' Sam demanded angrily. 'And why bother to kick the shit out of me for day after day?'

'Just to make it convincing, I'm afraid,' Waddell answered soothingly. 'In the hope we would go on wasting huge amounts of manpower looking for corroboration of the anthrax story. They're like that you know. But in this case they're not going to succeed.'

'Too simple, Duncan. Too damn simple. Look, in my guts I bloody know that warning was genuine.'

He was getting angry and he told himself to cool it.

'In your *guts*,' Waddell answered sarcastically. 'Like in the Kiev affair? You had a gut feeling then, I seem to remember. No. It's facts we need, Sam, not judgements based on hunches. Particularly the hunches of someone who, if I may say so, has been through the mangle recently.'

Sam felt his face burning. 'What exactly d'you mean by that?'

Waddell pushed his tongue round the inside of his mouth to clear out particles of bread. 'Oh, just that being a prisoner in an Iraqi jail isn't exactly fun, that's all.'

But Sam knew that wasn't all.

'Look, you know what's *really* worrying us Sam,' Waddell reasoned. The man called Charles leaned forward. 'It's the very fundamental question of how on God's earth did those little shites in Baghdad know who you were?' His eyes were like spears and his face was turning a light shade of puce. 'How did they know who to grab, Sam? How did they know your real bloody name?'

Sam fought to control the red mist rising in his head.

They were accusing him. He'd just escaped from ten days of hell and the bastards were saying it was all his fault.

'I don't know, Duncan,' he intoned. 'Somebody must have told them.'

'Aye. Exactly.' Waddell leaned back, folding his arms.

'And might that somebody have been you?' Charles interjected, his pale eyes gleaming like polished glass.

'No it bloody wasn't.'

Sam was beginning to sweat. Not with fear that he might have let his guard drop, but with outrage at the unfairness of their accusations.

'A slip of the tongue, maybe,' Charles suggested insouciantly. 'Easily done, even for a hardened pro like yourself. An innocent remark let slip in a bar to someone you trust, overheard by a pro from the opposing team. On its own what you said might seem meaningless, but to him it's the final piece of a jigsaw you never even knew existed.'

Charles had a deceptively kindly look about him – like a country vet poised for a castration.

'No. No slips of the tongue, Charles. No cracks in my cover. They didn't find out from me.'

Waddell regarded him stonily.

'We've got to get to the bottom of this,' he fumed. 'Got to know how far you've been compromised. And more to the point, how far the Firm has.'

Sam swallowed. He'd suddenly realised what this was leading to. Unless he could convince them otherwise, they were going to drop him. A sudden end to his intelligence career – *and* to his so-called employment by Entryline Exhibitions. The MD of the company had *created* the job for MI6. They would put someone else in.

'I've some rather detailed questions I need to ask,' Charles announced, tight-lipped. 'I know you're still shaky after what you've been through, but the answers can't wait.'

Sam took a deep breath. 'Go for it, then.'

'Okay. Let's start at the beginning. And I *mean* the beginning. Nineteen ninety, when you left the Royal Navy and joined us – that was your first visit to Iraq, I think? Your first use of the Terry Malone cover. Cast your mind back, if you would. Whom did you meet from the Iraqi side?'

'Hell, that was six years ago,' Sam protested.

'Yes, but see what you can remember. Names, conversations, even casual ones. Let's see if we can crack this mystery, shall we? There's probably a simple explanation we've all overlooked.'

'Very well,' Sam shrugged. He began to list the people he could think of. Baghdad 1990. A turning point in his life in more ways than one.

'Christine Taylor – as she called herself – she was there too, wasn't she?' Charles prompted, as if reading his mind.

'Yes.'

'And in your debriefs after you'd been released with the rest of the hostages you both said you'd seen no evidence that the Iraqis had identified you as intelligence agents.'

'Correct. They'd have hung onto us if they had.'

'More than likely. But let's dig over that time in a little more detail, could we?'

With a razor-keen mind for detail, the security investigator took him through that visit. They talked for more than ten minutes until he was as knowledgeable about events as Sam was.

'And your relationship with Christine during this period,' Charles asked with beguiling innocence. 'How would you categorise it?'

'Very professional,' Sam replied, stony-faced. He noticed Waddell's eyes on him, wide with anticipation. They knew something, he realised. The question was how much. 'Once we'd identified one another, we collaborated and shared the workload. I put it all in my report at the time.'

'So you did. So you did.'

His affair with Chrissie had been secret. Secret until the end, he was convinced of that. But had Kessler now told the Firm?

'Let's move on.' Charles's eyes gave nothing away. 'Your next visit to Baghdad was the one you've just had, yes?'

'Yes.'

'With most of the intervening years spent in eastern Europe.'

'Correct.'

'And your cover remained intact throughout that time. As far as you know.'

'Exactly. As far as I know.'

It wasn't entirely true. The ex-KGB man in Kiev working for the Ukrainian SBU on the drug operation last year had known about him. But they'd been on the same side at the time and dragging that episode up would open a can of worms.

'So, let's turn to *this* Baghdad visit,' Charles continued.

Sam described the uneventful flight out to Amman, the journey to Baghdad in a GMC minibus, his chats with trade officials and businessmen from other countries that had produced a few meagre scraps of intelligence about potential post-sanctions arms deals. And he talked of the German who'd carried his message to the outside world.

'Did *he* know who you worked for?' asked Waddell.

'No. It was just one businessman helping another out. Happens all the time in places where you can't phone and there's no post.'

As he described the day of his arrest Sam felt himself being dissected by these men. There was something about Waddell that he both feared and despised. The man had gained a first at Cambridge, was magical with paper-work, and was a born conspirator. Above all, he had the power to put Sam on the dole. But he'd never got sand between his toes and believed gut feelings were to do with diarrhoea.

When he finished speaking, both men sat back to reflect. For a moment he thought he'd got through to them.

'You were there to hoover, wouldn't you say?' Waddell averred suddenly.

'I'm sorry?'

'Chatting in *bars*,' Waddell stressed. 'That was your main way to gather intelligence.'

'Well, yes. Iraq's not a country where people talk freely. Bars and restaurants are where I pick most stuff up. It's called *socialising*, Duncan.'

Waddell was a man with no known social life – a man, Chrissie had once told him, whose office juniors had awarded him the sobriquet of 'Robbie the Robot'.

'Easy enough to let something slip when you're *socialising*, wouldn't you say?' Waddell probed. 'When you've had a few. Without even knowing it, probably.'

'Easy for someone with a death wish, yes.'

'Or for someone who's a little too fond of the pop,' Waddell added, gloves off at last. 'No restrictions on drink in Baghdad for foreigners, I understand?'

'No restrictions if you can find the stuff. Heard of UN sanctions, Duncan? It has to be smuggled—'

'And even though you may not have a death wish, you did have reason to feel rather sorry for yourself on this trip. A reason perhaps to down a little more of the loose tongue juice than is strictly wise? Mmm?'

Sam froze. 'I don't know what you mean.' But he did.

'I mean that your long-running, adulterous relationship with Mrs Christine Kessler which began in Baghdad six years ago had come to an abrupt end, and you weren't exactly over the moon about it.'

Sam stared from one headquarters man to the other, his face reddening.

'It's common knowledge now,' Waddell stated, his lips pursed puritanically.

'My personal life and my work are not connected,' Sam protested lamely.

Waddell raised a derisory eyebrow and looked across at Charles.

'We have to dig, Sam,' the investigator intervened. 'There's been a very serious breach of security here. The PM's terrified the Iraqis will make capital of the whole affair and go public on how they penetrated British intelligence.'

'Well dig somewhere else, chum,' Sam remonstrated, rapidly losing control. 'Whatever the Iraqis knew, it didn't come from me.'

There was a moment's hiatus as they studied him wordlessly.

'Fine,' Charles continued eventually, brushing the lapel of his blazer. 'Let's move on then. Who arrested you?'

'He didn't give me his card.'

'But you thought it was the Mukhabarat?'

'It was security. I'd no way of knowing which bunch. They were official and they were nasty, that's all that mattered to me.'

'And you admitted to them that you were SIS?'

'No. I stuck to my cover story.'

'Gave them a few names, perhaps? Quentin Mowbray's, for example.'

'Come off it. What is this?'

'Suggested they should give Mowbray a call at the embassy in Amman so he could fix up a swap?'

'Did I *bollocks*! I can't believe you're coming out with this stuff.'

'I'm asking you, that's all.'

'And I'm *telling* you. No. I didn't give them anything.'

Charles sat rigidly in his chair scrutinising Sam without blinking. Waddell leaned forward and ripped open the cardboard of the drinks six-pack. He selected a can of lemon and indicated that Sam should take one too. But Packer shook his head. What he badly wanted at that moment was something far stronger.

'Och hell.' Suddenly Waddell smiled at him like an old friend. 'It's dreadful for us having to give you the third degree. Believe me, Sam, this hurts—'

'—you more than it hurts me.'

'Yes.'

'Don't be a cunt, Duncan.'

Waddell recoiled.

'Anyway, have you finished?' Sam stood up abruptly. 'Because if that's it, I've got things to see to at home.'

'Finished for now, yes.' Waddell remained seated, knowing he would be dwarfed if he stood. 'We've heard what you've said, old son. We'll need to talk with you again at some stage. But for now, you'd better take some time off.'

'Time off?' Sam's heart sank. Were they suspending him?

'You deserve a break after what you've been through. Entryline are in the picture. They're not expecting to hear from you for a week or two.'

'And then?'

'We'll see.' Waddell had the grace to look embarrassed. 'We'll talk about the future when the dust's settled.'

'Gardening leave. Is that what you're saying?'

Waddell shrugged. 'We just have to work out how this whole mess came about, Sam. You surely understand that?'

'Oh yes. I understand all right. My problem is I don't

trust you to look in the right place for the answers.' The words tumbled out before he could stop them.

Waddell glanced at Charles and smiled smugly. 'Don't underestimate the Service, Sam. I can assure you it's our job to know where to look.' He stood up. 'You can go now. The car's waiting outside. It'll take you to the clinic first. If they give the all clear then you can head off home. We'll contact you in a day or two. And you can always call me, remember. Maybe something else'll come to you. Some recollection of a little conversation over a jar that you might have overlooked.'

'Like fuck, Duncan. Like fuck it will.'

Charles reached out his hand. 'Good luck. And I'm truly sorry for having to put you through this.'

Waddell led him back through the kitchen towards the fire escape. He opened the back door for him.

'It's funny, you know . . .' He puckered his boyish brows as Sam brushed past him. 'I would never have guessed that Chrissie was your type.'

Sam restrained his urge to hit him.

'Have yourself a good rest, old man,' said Waddell. He went back inside and closed the door.

Sam stood on the top grating of the rusty staircase. Below was the waiting Granada. He was seething with anger, but also with dread. Because more potent than the shock of being disbelieved by the men inside the flat was his certainty that some vital trick was being missed. That by focusing on his broken cover, they were ignoring the real danger.

Somewhere in the world there was a lunatic on the loose. And he had a load of anthrax to play with.

9

His flat smelled musty, a dusty airlessness combined with kitchen odours. The apartment had been locked since he left England. Dumping his case on the parquet floor of the tiny hallway he stood still for a moment, letting the place envelop him. There'd been moments when he'd feared he would never stand here again. He bent down to pick up the weeks of bills and junk mail splayed across the doormat, turned to close the front door then clicked on the overhead lamp to boost the pale daylight spilling from the living room. On the walls of the hall hung a few old square-rigger prints unearthed years ago in a Plymouth junk shop, together with a silent bracket clock that had belonged to his father. It displayed the hour at which its spring had unwound several days ago.

The mental mauling he'd received at the debrief had left him bruised, as had the fresh prodding he'd just undergone at the hands of an MI6 doctor. Instead of lifting from him, his anger at what the Iraqis had done to him in Baghdad clung like varnish. The doctor had told him he should find someone to talk to, in order to get it out of his system. Inevitably he'd thought of Chrissie.

The medical man had checked him over with great thoroughness before confirming that no lasting physical harm should result from his maltreatment. The growth of new skin over his shins would show progress in days, he'd said, making the fresh dressings he'd put on redundant. The medic had been more concerned about post-traumatic stress. He'd offered counselling, but Sam insisted a few days' rest would see him right.

He was still in the hall. Hadn't moved a step further into the flat, because instead of feeling relieved at being home, he was experiencing a thudding emptiness. He walked into the living room and crossed to the sash windows that overlooked the river. But instead of taking in the view as he'd intended, he swung round, dogged by the feeling that someone else had been here while he was away.

Of course. They *would* have been. Charles's people, going through his things – hands down the sides of the sofa, a line by line check through the contents of his filing cabinet, and a readout of the hard disk on the Pentium PC.

'Bugger!'

He felt as violated by their treatment of him as by the beatings in Baghdad. He'd not deserved any of this. Life was being outrageously unjust. And he'd always railed against the unfairness of fate, ever since being deprived as a young child of the father he'd worshipped.

'Bollocks to them all.'

He unscrewed the security bolt on the centre sash then shoved it upwards to let in fresh air. Three floors below, a red bus droned past the front of the 1930s block. On the other side of the road a man exercised a black dog along the towpath. The tide was coming in, the water's surface ruffled by a contrary wind. Sam took a deep breath, hungry for the air that belonged to rivers, to their estuaries and to the sea. A smell of decay, but also of peace.

He turned his head to look down river, past the nature reserve of the old Barnes reservoirs. A pleasure craft cut through the water, bringing the last of the summer's tourists to Kew Gardens and Hampton Court. In the suburban maze to the right of the riverbank was where

Chrissie lived with her reconciled husband, the Kessler home only a few minutes' walk from his own. A neat coincidence of residential location which they'd shamelessly exploited for so bloody long . . .

Like his maltreatment in Baghdad, *she* was something else he needed to expunge from his mind. But how could he if it *was* his child she was carrying?

He turned away from the window. Chrissie had been rude about this flat, saying it reflected his years of institutionalisation in the Royal Navy. Sofa and armchairs in floral print. Pine green carpet. Built-in wall units, with a small hi-fi and TV set wedged among the paperbacks. Metal-framed prints of Turner seascapes. Not *bad* taste, she used to complain, more like no taste at all. She had a need to be surrounded by beautiful things, she'd told him, and marvelled at his ability to live without them.

For him the main trouble with this room was that he couldn't look at it without seeing her in it. She would appear without warning late at night after some spat with her husband and throw her arms round his neck, clinging to him like a drowning child. Jammed on the sofa like Siamese twins they would sit and drink wine while she unwound. Sometimes she would talk volumes, pouring out her troubles in a slalom ride of anger at her husband's stunted emotions and at her own stupidity for marrying him. Sometimes she would merely stare at the walls while he played Verdi on the CD, letting the demons fight their battles inside her.

But always her tension would eventually ebb. Then a smile as fragile as a mayfly would signal that she was ready for what she'd come for. Later, after they'd had their fill of each other in the bedroom and he'd drifted into post-coital slumber, she would dress again and leave him, descending the communal staircase as silently as she had climbed it to walk or drive the few hundred yards that would take her back to her husband.

And Martin had never known. That's what Chrissie had said. Her husband had never once suspected she was having an affair. Always imagined that when his wife disappeared late at night, not returning for hours, she was driving round in her car letting off steam or parked up somewhere smoking cigarette after cigarette until she calmed down enough to return to him. Never known the truth until this summer. And Martin Kessler was by profession a spymaster.

Sam walked back to the hall, picked up his bag and took it to the bedroom to unpack, putting his things away with a neatness bred by years spent in cabins too small to swing a cat in. Chrissie had teased him about his tidy ways, asking where he would stow a woman if one were ever to move in with him. His life was too ordered, she'd told him, too complete for a woman to be let in permanently.

He changed into jeans and a T-shirt and, resisting the temptation to sink a large scotch, perched in the galley-like kitchen and brewed some tea in a mug that bore the crest of the last ship he'd served in.

It was late afternoon. The doctor had suggested he do things that were normal and routine. Might drop into the pub later for a couple of pints and some inconsequential chatter, then pick up a takeaway at the local Tandoori before dosing himself with the sleeping pills the medic had prescribed and try for a night without bad dreams.

He began checking the food cupboard and the fridge, with the idea of a visit to the supermarket – anything for distraction. But Baghdad came winging back into his head. The beatings, the endless questions about the messenger's whispers, the sheer bloody terror of believing he would be killed . . .

'Hell!'

This wouldn't do. He needed to fill his head with something else. He got up from the kitchen stool, stomped into the living room and switched on the TV for the news.

It turned out the world had moved little since he'd last been in touch with it. On the other side of the Atlantic the US presidential election campaign was as lacklustre as ever. At home Conservative MPs were still fighting like rats in a sack, and in Israel Palestinians were protesting violently against new Jewish settlements on the West Bank.

Then Saddam Hussein's picture came on the screen. He turned up the sound. The voice-over reported the Iraqi leader launching a stinging verbal attack on Jerusalem and Washington over their 'betrayal of the Oslo accords'. A warning that a failure of Middle East peace could lead to global war.

A war waged with biological weapons. Was that what the madman planned?

A shiver ran through him. Anthrax weapons were out there and he was doing nothing to find them. But what could *he* do? Like the man strung up by his hands in the Baghdad prison, he was just a messenger. He'd done his duty. Passed on all he knew to his masters. Not his responsibility any more. The hard part was to stop thinking that it was.

What he needed was to wash his brain out. The whiff of the sea might do it. A few days on his boat with a stiff sailing breeze and some sun on his back. Why the hell not? They'd told him to take leave.

He looked at his watch. Not yet six. To learn where the sloop was moored, he would need to talk with his sailing partner who'd used her during his absence. And Tom Wallace wouldn't be back at his Chichester home for another fifteen minutes or so.

Bored by the TV news, Sam switched off and stood by

the window again looking at the river. Water was a balm for him. Always had been, from the moment his long dead father first taught him to sail.

He would need to let Waddell know that he was disappearing for a few days. It smarted just to think of the man. *In your guts. Like in the Kiev affair? It's facts we need, Sam, not judgements based on hunches.*

Kiev. A balls-up of mega proportions which he'd never got to the bottom of. A sting run jointly by the intelligence organisations of three nations which had turned into a farce. The operation to crush an international drugs ring had been triggered by information from the Ukrainian SBU – part of the former Soviet KGB. Ecstasy tablets produced in Ukraine had been flooding markets in Germany and Britain. The lab producing them had been located but they wanted to nail the distribution network too. According to sources in Germany and Ukraine a huge consignment of drugs was to be transported to western Europe hidden inside trucks carting display material back from a trade fair in Kiev. Conveniently, Entryline Exhibitions had had the contract for the British companies represented at the fair. Sam had been dispatched to Kiev as site manager.

Coincidentally, Chrissie had been there too, acting as backup for the new SIS resident at the British Embassy who'd only been in the post a few weeks. With a charm that could suck foxes from their holes, she'd assembled a contact list to die for during her career with the Foreign Office and SIS. One of those contacts was a man named Viktor Rybkin whom she'd met in Washington two years earlier. Rybkin was SBU, resident in the American capital then, but on his return to Kiev he had become SBU liaison officer on transnational crime. It was he who had been running the Kiev end of the ecstasy investigation.

On that occasion too Sam had used the Terry Malone pseudonym, but his real identity was known to Viktor

Rybkin. No reason not to be. In that operation they had been on the same side. He and Chrissie had kept at arm's length from one another to preserve the secrecy of their relationship, but one night at his hotel there had been a message to meet her outside a café on vulitsya Khreshchatyk, Kiev's tree-lined, lamp-lit main boulevard.

He'd arrived at the appointed hour but Chrissie hadn't. Instead, he'd watched coming towards him the burly shape of Viktor Rybkin.

'I want to show you the sights,' he'd grinned. The SBU man had a small scar on his cheek and a lopsided jaw. 'Chrissie said she'd fix for you to be here.' His English had a heavy American accent. 'Now we all got the same enemy – hoodlums, Mafiya – you should take a closer look at our ones.'

Rybkin had whisked him round the city by car, pointing out restaurants and clubs from where the gangs operated. There were more than six hundred Mafiya-style mobs active in Ukraine, he'd said.

'We call them Mafiya, but they are New Russian criminals,' he'd explained in smooth, educated English, 'not like the Italian families. Except in one way. They kill just as easy. Every week here in Kiev there are maybe five, maybe six murders, half of them contract killings.'

The tour had ended at a *banya*. In a well-equipped gym, tough, fit men in designer track-suits and Lycra hipsters sweated over the machines and downed imported energy drinks. All Mafiya, Rybkin had warned. They'd stripped off their own clothes to mingle with the naked bathers in the steam room. The Ukrainian's torso had been exceptionally hairy, Sam remembered, and his penis unusually small. 'But I use it well,' Rybkin had assured him.

They'd sat in an alcove and Rybkin, his voice muffled by the hiss of steam, had pointed out some of the kings of

Kiev's underworld, the tsars of the Ukrainian black economy.

'They know who I am, I know who they are. It's a game. We watch each other. What I'm telling them is that if they cross the line I shall know where to get them.'

Being exposed like that to men who might have been running the very drug ring they were trying to crush had felt like professional suicide. But it was the way they did things in Ukraine, Rybkin had assured him.

That same night, surveillance cameras he'd set up at the Kiev fair site had recorded 'drugs' being hidden in British and German trucks. He'd reported a good 'gut feeling' about it to London. But when the vehicles got home, no one had come for the hidden cargoes. Eventually, a police forensic team had examined the load and found it to be chalk. Ecstasy tablets from Kiev *had* turned up on the streets a few weeks later. They'd gone by another route.

In the SIS witch hunt that had followed, suspicion for the blowing of the operation had focused on Rybkin, but some had stuck to Sam. Chrissie had begged him to say nothing about her unwittingly setting him up for the visit to the *banya,* because if the powers that be knew about it, she'd be for the Star Chamber.

Bugger Waddell, digging all that up again. Bugger his suspicious little puritan mind.

The time had come for a proper drink, he decided. He took his mug back to the kitchen then poured a couple of fingers of whisky in a glass, topping it up with a little water from the tap. He gulped down a good slug.

There was a good chance Tom Wallace would be home by now. He grabbed the phone from the wall by the kitchen door and dialled. He'd known his sailing partner for fifteen years, ever since they studied at Dartmouth together. Tom had left the Navy three years after him, to take over an antique business started by his father.

The phone was answered on the third ring.

'Wallace, you dog!' Sam growled.

'Packer! Where've you been?'

'Some hell hole or other. The usual, you know . . .'

Wallace had a good idea that he did dodgy work for the government and never asked for details.

'Expected you back ages ago. *Backgammon*'s in bloody Cherbourg. Been there nearly three weeks. You were supposed to bring her back to the Hamble, you sod.'

'I know. I was away longer than expected.'

'Living it up at somebody else's expense no doubt.'

'No doubt.'

'The marina charges'll be horrendous by now. Take your gold card with you. You *are* going to get her, I take it? That *is* why you're ringing?' Wallace liked people to do what they'd agreed to do.

'Yes. I plan to get the ferry over as soon as I've got a crew sorted. I don't suppose you're free . . .'

'No. Can't leave the shop this week. But I'm sure you can whistle up some bint from your little black book.'

Tom Wallace had a vivid fantasy image of Sam's love life, mainly because he never told him about it except to say it was active and complicated. Wallace himself had been married for eleven years but was now divorced, with two daughters he seldom saw. He lived alone, making little effort to attract a new partner. From time to time he talked of getting a Thai bride by mail order.

'You'll need to keep an eye on the engine, Sam. Bit of a water leak when she's running. God knows where from. Pump the bilges every few hours and you'll be okay. Hope the boat's clean enough for you. Took a couple of friends from the trade over with me last time. One of them was sick everywhere.'

'Oh thanks a lot.'

'No prob. Washed it off the seat covers for you.'

'Very thoughtful.'

'She's in berth F7. In the main marina at Cherbourg. You've got keys haven't you? Not lost them?'

'No, Tom. I've got my keys.'

'Good. Where are you planning to go?'

'Don't know yet. I'll check the tides and work it out from that. Be back in the Hamble within the week I should think.'

'Nice. Hope the weather's good for you. Piddled with rain half the time we were there.'

Sam rang off. He felt better for having decided to go away. Now to find a crew. It wasn't that he couldn't manage the boat on his own – he'd often sailed solo – but he wanted company. Someone undemanding.

Chrissie had never sailed with him. She'd always worried there'd be some incident or other that would make their relationship public. *Not worth the risk, lover. Anyway, I'd be sea sick.* The only boat they'd been on together was a Thames skiff last summer, soon after she'd returned from a two-year stay in Washington with her husband. During her time in America she'd had a *really serious* go at making the marriage work, she'd told him. But without any notable success. They'd found a deserted stretch of water somewhere near Goring, tied the painter to a tree root then made up for lost time among the cow parsley.

Shit! They'd spent some good, stolen times together over the years. Later that same afternoon, he remembered, they'd rowed slowly past an isolated, half-timbered waterside cottage. *I want it*, she'd moaned. *A gingerbread house.* To be their love nest, she'd said. Somewhere to spend whole days and nights together instead of snatched hours in constant fear of discovery. It was then that he'd realised that despite the frailty of her marriage she had no intention of ending it. A husband *and* a lover was what she wanted.

There had been other women during his liaison with Chrissie, particularly during her time away in America. Some he'd slept with, others he'd dated for their company. But thinking about them now, none came to mind as a potential crew for the next few days. And most of the men he knew had steady jobs from which they could never escape on weekdays. He began to resign himself to going alone. The *Backgammon* was an eight-year-old Moody 31 with rigging lines that ran into the cockpit to make single-handed sailing easier.

He began to write a list of things to take. The boat was well-equipped. All he needed was clothes, a passport and some money. He pulled an almanac from the shelf in the living room to study the tide tables. He would listen to a shipping forecast and check the ferries. He was sure there was a daily sailing to Cherbourg at midday.

Pottering around the flat getting together the things he would require felt good. Normality. It was what he needed. And there'd still be time for a pint in the pub.

Then he pulled himself up short.

'This is insane,' he muttered to himself. 'There's a madman out there with a load of anthrax warheads – and I'm going bloody sailing!'

10

Tuesday, 1 October. Early morning.
Iraq – the Task Two site west of Baghdad

Dean Burgess's neck ached after a night wedged against the door of the Nissan in the least uncomfortable position he could devise. The atmosphere had become threatening overnight and this morning the inspection team had donned their UN blue hats and were keeping together in groups of no less than three.

The first event that had cranked up tension yesterday was the empty-handed return in late afternoon of the security man whom Mustafa had sent to the village they'd passed to try to discover what was being built at this bleak desert site. Mustafa had abused him for his failure, clipping him round the head, before closeting himself in his communications vehicle for a full twenty minutes.

When he'd emerged, he'd contrived a ludicrously artificial smile and, without a flicker of shame, announced that the building being constructed was a shelter for goats and that there had indeed been a few animal carcasses buried here earlier – victims of some unidentified sickness that had affected the villagers' beasts. And now, with that little matter settled to everyone's satisfaction, could they kindly call it a day and return to Baghdad before the sun went down?

Hardcastle's response had been curt. The site, he'd told Mustafa, was to be excavated fully. Every animal carcass they found would have to be thoroughly examined by his team, with samples being taken to the BMVC for further analysis.

Mustafa's artificial bonhomie had vanished as rapidly as it had appeared. Putting an angry hand over Burgess's camera lens he'd insulted the UN team's mothers, then accused Hardcastle of megalomania and obstructionism, threatening to lodge a protest about his behaviour with the UN in New York. Finally he'd stormed off, warning that if they didn't leave the area voluntarily they would be forced out by the Republican Guard who were training here the next day.

Undeterred, Hardcastle, who'd seen such tantrums many times before, had told his team to prepare for a stake-out. They'd re-parked the vehicles at dusk so the headlights could be shone onto the excavation site, then prepared for the night with food cooked on camping gas stoves. Pierre Latour had established a watch-keeping rota to ensure there'd be no nocturnal interference with the dig. Then, as the air temperature plummeted and the clear night sky became an explosion of stars, they'd locked themselves in their vehicles to snatch what sleep they could, propped against the windows and using their backpacks as pillows.

Unable to sleep initially, Burgess had watched Mustafa's men also preparing for the night, some huddled in their jeeps, others in a small tent. They were like the two armies at Agincourt, he'd thought, hunkering down before battle at dawn. And, like Henry V in the Shakespeare play, uncertainty over what lay ahead had turned his own thoughts to home.

Not because of the desire for an uxorial embrace, but because of his guilt at *not* wanting one. He got his highs in situations like this, poised on the rim of a major crime.

The anticipation of a sensational discovery gave a shot in the arm for his spirit which no quality time with wife and children could ever replace, however much he loved them. What he was feeling here confirmed everything Carole had thrown at him, of course. It *was* his job that occupied his mind ninety-nine point nine per cent of the time.

He hadn't the slightest idea what to do about the situation. But it hurt him to the quick to know that the way *he* wanted to lead his life was making Carole so deeply unhappy. And the kids? They were all over him when he *was* at home. Nine-year-old Patty with the same freckles her mother had had as a child and seven-year-old Dean Junior's serious, thoughtful eyes. No sign of them being disturbed by his frequent absences. No. It was Carole he had the problem with.

Some time after midnight, all thoughts of home had been burned from his brain by headlights piercing the blackness behind them. Two large military trucks loaded with uniformed soldiers had arrived to swell the ranks of the opposition. That was been the moment when Burgess's uneasiness about Hardcastle's manner with the Iraqis had turned to a grudging admiration. The Englishman had stood his ground like Churchill. Refused to speak to the newcomers. Refused to open the vehicle doors even when the guns came out. Eventually the soldiers had backed off. This morning, however, the military men were still there, a menacing presence, although with no apparent orders to remove the UN team.

The mechanical digger Hardcastle had asked for, together with a reluctant local labourer, had finally arrived at the desert site an hour after dawn. Burgess watched now as the machine, driven by a terrified Bedouin enveloped in protective suit and mask, unearthed a fourth animal carcass, a dog this time, which it dumped unceremoniously at the edge of the pit next to two cows and a goat. Major Martha Cok, the Dutch vet, had taken charge of the dig, ordering non-essential personnel to keep well away and upwind. The rest of the team had erected awnings to protect themselves from the sun while awaiting developments.

Burgess watched through binoculars. All of a sudden he saw that something different was happening. The vet had ordered the digger driver to halt his work, and was lifting her VHF handset to the side of her mask.

'Golf, this is Sierra Two.' Major Cok's voice, muffled by rubber.

'Sierra Two, go ahead. Golf over,' Hardcastle responded.

'I'm stopping the dig for half an hour in order to collect samples. Over.'

'Understood. D'you want some boxes brought over?'

'Yes. Two containers please. Sierra Two out.'

A Ghanaian biologist working as the vet's assistant strode over to their vehicle to kit himself up in a suit and mask so he could deliver the hermetically sealed sample cases to the area of suspected contamination.

'She'll remove parts of the innards of these beasts,' Hardcastle explained to Burgess. 'Bits of the lungs probably. We'll need to get them back to Baghdad pronto so they can give them a thorough analysis in the lab.'

Burgess looked across to where the Iraqi minders were standing, silent and watchful, in the shade of a canopy erected by the soldiers who'd arrived during the night.

'They sure look nervous as hell this morning,' he whispered.

'They certainly are,' Hardcastle concurred, his head covered with an oversized blue floppy hat that gave him the appearance of an eccentric archaeologist.

'But I can't figure out whether they're scared because they *know* what's buried down there, or because they *don't* know,' Burgess added.

'My thoughts precisely,' Hardcastle concurred. 'One thing I *am* certain of is that we're on to something.'

'No chance that village plague story could be true?' Burgess queried. 'Anthrax is endemic in cattle.'

'Oh, come on! You saw Mustafa's face last night,' Hardcastle spluttered. 'Not even *he* thought we'd swallow that load of old cobblers. No. My guess is he doesn't know what's down there because his superiors haven't seen fit to tell him.'

'But surely he'd have been told by now?' Burgess protested.

'Not necessarily. You see, Saddam may have split his weapons people into small cells. One group making the stuff, another testing it, with neither group knowing the identity of the other one. Like with his security people. There are several agencies as I told you yesterday, plus the Republican Guard and the *Special* Republican Guard – those, by the way, are the boys who showed up last night. Saddam tends to wheel them out when he's expecting trouble.'

'You reckon Saddam himself is being kept informed about what's going on here?'

'Nothing important happens in this country without his knowing about it. And my guess is, the reason these security people are so jumpy this morning is they're scared as hell we *will* find something incriminating here and they'll get the chop for failing to conceal it.'

They turned their glasses back towards the pit which had grown to an area some twenty metres by ten, scooped out to a depth of one or two metres. Sand and stones had been dumped in a mound to one side, with the animal carcasses laid out on the other. The mechanical digger stood idle in front of it, its driver huddled in the cab waiting for instructions, its jib as motionless as a stone giraffe.

Fifteen minutes later the vet and her assistant had

finished their incisions on the dead animals and carried the sample containers back towards their vehicle, stopping at a point some distance away where they'd left decontamination equipment. They sprayed a bleach solution over each other's protective suits and the boxes. Then they continued to their vehicle and locked the containers in a sealed cabinet.

'My God!' Martha Cok gasped as she finally joined Burgess and Hardcastle, pulling off her gloves and mask to reveal a bright red face dripping with perspiration. 'Working in such conditions . . . terrible. Terrible.'

'What can you tell us?' Hardcastle pressed.

'A little, only. It's too soon. But it's strange. The burning is quite superficial. Like they planned to destroy the cadavers by fire, then changed their minds and buried them instead. There's nothing visible that tells me what they died of. The carcasses are several days, maybe weeks dead.'

'And the deaths couldn't be natural?' Burgess checked.

'Most unlikely. I can tell you already that it wasn't cutaneous anthrax. That's the most common endemic type in cattle. No sign of the pustules and rings of blisters you get with that. The lung sections I've taken may show something when we do the full analysis at the BMVC. If the inside of the lungs is a mass of haemorrhages it could point to pulmonary anthrax or botulinum toxin. But confirmation of anthrax would come if we found live organisms in the tissue. We'll probably be able to work it out with the equipment we have at the BMVC.'

'How soon to get a definitive answer?' Hardcastle asked.

'By tomorrow morning, I hope,' she answered cautiously.

'Good,' Hardcastle whispered. 'The sooner the better.' He turned to Burgess and lifted one eyebrow.

Burgess remembered what Hardcastle had told him in Bahrain about the British SIS report of a weaponised biological device having been smuggled out of Iraq. If true, it was just conceivable that this patch of sand had been the weapon's proving ground and these animals the first of its many thousands of potential victims.

The digger had started work again under the watchful eye of Martha's Ghanaian assistant. As the spoil fell from the scoop, the cascade of debris was examined through binoculars by the weapons specialists on the UNSCOM team, searching for metal objects.

Suddenly the engine cut. Burgess looked up to see the digger driver jump down onto the sand and back away from the pit, jamming the mask to his face. He turned and ran towards the security men huddled under their canopy. The last of the dust stirred up by the machine swirled away like tumbleweed.

'Christ! Now what's he uncovered?' hissed Hardcastle. They pulled their masks on and hurried over to the pit.

'Not too close,' Martha warned. Unlike them she had on her full protective suit and went ahead towards the widening hole in the ground.

Burgess switched on the camera and swung it round in a wide pan. He spotted Mustafa and one of the green uniformed Special Republican Guards marching towards the excavation.

They reached the rim simultaneously. Martha Cok was down in the pit and raised an arm to warn them not to come closer.

'Heavens!' Hardcastle grunted. 'Oh Lord!'

Dean Burgess zoomed in to the half-buried creature the vet was standing next to. The camera pulled focus automatically. No cow, goat or dog this time. Although half obscured by sand, a swatch of red checked material was visible. Material that had once been a shirt. Inside it was the blackened, swollen torso of a man.

11

Late p.m.
Cyprus

Pier four of Limassol port was abuzz with activity. Flatbed trailers queued to take up position beneath one of the two huge hoists unloading forty-foot containers from the deck of the recently arrived Gibraltar-registered vessel. She'd been late docking because of bad weather near Rhodes and was due out again that same evening, heading back for Piraeus. The ship's crew were in a hurry to get the job done, as were the dock workers, truck drivers and customs men.

The container from Ilychevsk that was bound for Haifa and whose administrative document described its contents as defective fruit and vegetable juices was scheduled to break its journey here in Limassol for a couple of days, until another ship arrived to take it on the last part of its circuitous route back to Israel.

The container's papers had been processed without comment in the port office. Rather than pay for storage on one of the port's huge quays, the shipping agent handling the cargo had gone for a cheaper option, moving it to a bonded yard on the edge of Limassol town. It was a routine process that raised not a single eyebrow.

The truck carrying the container on its short journey to

the storage yard stopped at the exit gates. The driver handed in his pink release paper and the vehicle was waved through. The bonded warehouse was less than five minutes' drive away. Inside the secure compound a giant forklift raised the container from the flatbed trailer and carried it into the warehouse building itself, setting it down in an area well away from the rest of the transiting cargoes. The container was on its own, in splendid isolation – except for one other identically sized box which had arrived a few hours earlier from Haifa.

It was the end of the working day for the yard. No more cargoes due in or out until the following morning. The workforce gathered up their lunch-boxes and jackets and made for the gate. From now until dawn a night-watchman would be the only human presence at the yard. And if anyone were to ask him in the next few days about the duty period which lay ahead, he would report that nothing unusual had occurred.

Seventy kilometres to the east of this Limassol container yard a much-delayed charter flight from Odessa landed at Larnaca airport with a full manifest of Ukrainian tourists on board, all of them frustrated and annoyed by the late start to their long-anticipated vacation. They filed through passport control to the baggage hall, grumbling that they should have been here six hours ago and that it would be dark before they reached their hotels and apartments.

Four men pushed their way through the throng waiting by the carousels, each carrying holdalls containing all they would need for their short time on the island. The men, who had the demeanour of skilled manual workers, were travelling as a group but took care not to make it look that way as they passed through the customs barrier into the arrivals hall.

Once outside in the open they stopped to get their

bearings, then one by one crossed the service road to the car park as they'd been instructed to do. The man waiting to meet them was heavy-set and had a scar on his left cheek. He stood beside the Toyota minibus he'd rented in Limassol, waiting for the men to find him.

'This is a bad situation,' he cursed as they piled into the vehicle. 'An hour ago they told me the flight had been postponed until tomorrow. I shit myself, I tell you.'

He swung himself into the driving seat and propelled the vehicle towards the exit and on to the road for Limassol.

'You have tonight, understand? Just tonight. Everything has to be finished by morning. Clear?'

'You have the equipment ready?' one of the men asked.

'Of course we do.'

'Then we'll do what we can, *tovarich*. Just keep off our backs, okay?'

'I'll keep off your backs all right. But I advise you not to fail me.'

'Fuck off, *tovarich*. We won't fail.'

12

The same evening
Cherbourg, France

The warm hue of the hardwood cabin fittings and the firm bulk of the foam-filled seat squabs in *Backgammon*'s cramped interior fitted Sam like a womb. He was *meant* to be on a sailing boat. This was his element. From the moment he'd slid back the hatch and breathed in the resinous smell from below, he'd known this escape to Normandy was a good idea.

He sat now with his knees wedged under the cabin table enjoying the food they'd rustled up from stores Tom Wallace had left in the locker beneath the bunk. Tinned curry, peas and boil-in-the-bag rice. Sitting opposite him was a man some twenty years older than himself.

'Cheers, Nat,' he said raising his glass of Côtes du Rhône. 'Good to have you aboard.'

'Bloody good of *you* to give an old sailor an airing,' the man replied bibulously.

Nat Gibbon was *not* an old sailor, but had spent years trying to look like one. He wore a moth-eaten Guernsey sweater and a sun-faded yachting cap. The ruddy face and watery eyes were natural, but the blue bags and boating shoes were what he put on when going to Sam's local riverside pub in Barnes. And it was there that he'd found him yesterday evening.

Gibbon was a regular occupant of the stool at one end of the bar. Sam had often chatted with him about sailing, Nat claiming to have spent a year crewing on board a charter yacht in the Caribbean. Sam had some doubts about the story, but no firm evidence it wasn't true. When they set sail tomorrow, the man's experience or lack of it would become instantly obvious.

His decision to invite Nat along had been very much an afterthought. He'd gone for a quick pint last night before bed. Still feeling dead tired after his ordeal, he'd become increasingly conscious of the pain in his back and legs whenever he moved and realised that a second pair of hands on board to do some of the heavy work might be wise.

Gibbon had leapt at the chance.

The man was a writer of sorts. Screenplays for television had been his forte. But the programmes he mentioned when asked about his career seemed to have been aired more than a decade ago. He talked darkly of having been in the big money once, but from what Sam could tell, all he did now was spend it on drink.

The drive down to the Hamble that morning had been mostly conducted in silence. Neither man had been talkative, each a little shy of the other without the hubbub of the pub to cocoon them. Indeed, one reason Sam thought Gibbon a suitable companion for the next few days was that he *never* talked much. He also showed little interest in other people's lives. For much of his time in the bar Nat would sit on his own, staring rheumy-eyed through the windows that overlooked the river, smiling occasionally at the regulars.

They'd left the car in the marina car park to have it waiting for them when they sailed the boat back to the Hamble, then they'd slung their gear into a minicab for the twenty-minute ride to the cross-channel terminal at Portsmouth.

Once in Cherbourg and on board the *Backgammon,*

they'd opened up the hatches to freshen the boat and Sam had shown Nat the forepeak cabin where he could sleep. To his relief, Gibbon did seem at home in a yacht. They'd checked fuel and water levels, then Sam had run the engine to charge the batteries and chill the fridge. The water leak Tom Wallace had told him about hadn't been hard to trace. A hose beginning to split, which he'd done a temporary fix on with tape and a tightening of the jubilee clip which secured it. It irked him that Tom was so useless with things mechanical.

Now it was nine in the evening.

Sam finished eating and pushed his plate away. The wine bottle was almost empty, Gibbon having gulped down the larger part of its contents. Sam had the feeling he was expecting to tackle another, but he himself would soon be ready to get his head down.

'What's the plan tomorrow, skipper?' Nat asked, a trifle uneasily.

Sam suspected the sailing his companion had done in the past had had more to do with sun and alcohol than handling a boat in strong winds and heavy seas.

'There's a nice force five forecast and I'm taking you down the Alderney Race.'

'Oh God, what's that?' Gibbon reached for the bottle again, forgetting it was empty.

'If we clear this stuff away, I'll show you.'

'Oh. Right.'

They moved the plates to the sink, then Sam turned to the navigator's table, picking up the chart for the Channel Islands and a Macmillan *Almanac*. As he spread them on the table he noticed Gibbon's hands shaking.

'Now . . .' Sam indicated where they were on the chart. 'The waters around here are hellishly tidal. Not only a big rise and fall but the tides create strong currents which have a mind all of their own. Particularly now we're at Springs.' He opened the almanac at the page showing

Channel Island tidal streams. 'Yes. At about the time we'll be going down through the gap between Cap de la Hague and Alderney, the water rips south-west at over seven knots.'

'Bloody hell,' Gibbon gulped. 'Hope you know what you're doing with this tub. I mean I'll pull on the sheets and all that, but I'm a bit rusty on the finer points.'

'Don't worry. I've handled her alone in a force eight before now. Just do as I say and we'll be fine.'

'No problem. Just give me orders.'

'Tomorrow the wind should be from the north, so wind and tide will be behind us. We'll be zipping along at around fourteen knots. If you get wind *against* tide doing the race is impossible.'

'And why exactly are we taking this particular route?' Gibbon queried, his tone suggesting it was a daft idea.

'Because with the conditions as they are tomorrow it's the only course that makes sense. We'll need to be away from here by six, up at half-five for a bite of breakfast. Should easily make Sark by lunch-time. There's a nice little bay halfway down the eastern side that's sheltered from the northerlies. With luck the water might even be warm enough to swim in.'

'No chance. I prefer looking at the sea from above.'

Sam turned to the sink and began washing up the plates. Nat condescended to dry.

'Got any more of that plonk?' he asked when they were finished. 'It was slipping down rather nicely.'

'Try in the locker in the middle of the table.'

'Splendid.'

Sam decided to join him in a glass before turning in.

'Can't remember what it is you do for a living, skipper,' Gibbon asked after a silence had dragged on for a while.

'Exhibitions. Setting them up at overseas trade fairs.'

'Oh. Interesting?'

‘At times.’

‘You just back from somewhere?’

‘Jordan. But didn’t get to see much. Just the inside of buildings mostly.’

It was what he always said when friends asked. Tended to deter further questions.

‘I went to Jordan once,’ Gibbon ruminated. ‘Remember *The Adventurers*? A thirteen-weeker back in the eighties. I did three of the scripts. Bloody hot and the place was full of Arabs.’ He chuckled at his little witticism.

‘Still is,’ Sam answered.

He drained his glass and said he was going to bed.

‘What are you like at early mornings?’

‘No idea, skipper,’ Gibbon chuckled, holding a brim-full glass. ‘Never tried one.’

Sam had forgotten to snub the halyards. During the night the wind got up, setting off a relentless pinging of taut rope against alloy mast.

In the quarter-berth cabin Sam turned restlessly, deeply asleep. Suddenly his body began to twitch and tremble, a vivid nightmare flashing though his brain. In his dream he was in darkness, clawing up a slope to escape the shit-filled whirlpool in the centre of his cell. He sensed someone there, someone watching but not helping. His nails broke on the concrete and his shins burned as some unseen force dragged him back towards the pit. He was naked, the poisonous filth in which he lay leaching into his body through his open wounds.

There was something banging. A rhythmic tapping against metal, like the radiator pipe he’d been chained to. Then he was on his feet, running, his breath sawing in his ears. Running and getting nowhere. And still close by, watching and not helping, was that same someone . . . He knew who it was now. Knew it from her smell.

Suddenly something jammed against his gullet, hard and rough like a rope, stopping him in his tracks, stopping his breath. His arms flailed. He knew it was the end. Knew, too, he wasn't ready for it. Why wouldn't she help him, this creature whose scent was so comforting? He twisted his head to see her, this woman he knew so well. He pleaded with his eyes. Pleaded for his life.

Sorry, she mouthed. *I'm so very sorry.*

Then the beatings began again. His back, his head. He knew her and yet there she stood doing nothing. Just watching him die. He filled his lungs and screamed her name.

'*Chrisssiiiee!*'

Suddenly he was awake. He sat up and banged his head. A coffin! They'd put him in a damned coffin but he wasn't dead.

'Shi-it!'

His shins felt as if they'd been scraped with a rasp. Then it came to him. This wasn't a coffin at all. He was on *Backgammon*. He reached out and pushed. The cabin door swung open.

Suddenly a light clicked on in the main cabin, startling him. He'd forgotten he had company. He shielded his eyes and looked across the saloon. Gibbon stood by the door to the forward cabin, bare-chested but struggling into his baggy blue trousers.

'Whatsup?'

Sam didn't answer. In his head he still saw Chrissie, her grey smudges of eyes full of a regret which he somehow knew she didn't feel.

'Bloody hell!' Gibbon pointed. 'What've you done to your legs?'

Sam looked down. The dressings on his shins were hanging off and scarlet with blood.

'Shit!'

He stood there confused, unable to move. He blinked at Nat.

'Don't know what happened there,' he mumbled. 'I'm okay. Really. Look, sorry about this. You go back to bed.'

'Dreaming, was it? You put the fear of God into me with that scream.'

'Sorry.'

Sam hobbled to the bunk next to the saloon table and sat down, still staring at his shins. He looked at the clock above the chart table. Nearly half-past four in the morning. The chill of the nightmare was still with him.

'I'd do something about those legs if I were you,' Gibbon suggested helpfully. He'd found his shirt and was buttoning it up.

'I will. You go back to bed.'

'Fat chance. Wide awake now. What you need is some water. Clean yourself up a bit.'

Realising Gibbon had no intention of helping him, Sam stood up again and opened the locker beneath the sink. He found a fresh pack of J cloths and a plastic bowl which he half-filled from the tap. He dabbed at his shins and eased off the saturated dressings. Must have banged them against something in his sleep.

'Best let the air get at them,' Gibbon suggested, showing no interest in how the injuries had been acquired. He squeezed past to get to the galley. 'Fancy a cup of tea?'

'Yes.'

Sam finished dabbing at his legs, then stared blankly through the hatch at the lightening sky visible through the gap they'd left open for ventilation.

Hell, he thought. Nightmares he could do without. And why that one? Chrissie *hadn't* left him to rot. She'd saved his life.

And was probably carrying a part of it inside her.

13

Wednesday, 2 October, 08.45 hrs
Baghdad Monitoring and Verification Centre, Iraq

Dean Burgess stood in front of one of the split-screen computer terminals watching a technician hop between the outputs of the hundreds of remote cameras that were live-linked back to the BMVC operations room.

'How the heck do you keep track of all this stuff?' he asked, baffled by the plethora of images.

'The computer helps,' the technician explained. 'The system alerts us whenever there's a change in the image. *Then* we take a look at it. The pictures are all time-lapse recorded.'

'Oh yeah. Sure,' shrugged Burgess. Should have thought of that himself. Always a reluctant member of the silicon generation. He turned away from the screens.

The startling discovery of a man's body yesterday morning had brought UNSCOM's excavation of the desert site to an abrupt halt. The red-bereted Special Republican Guard had taken control of the site and ejected the inspection team from it, accusing them of interfering with a grave.

That action had convinced Burgess that something very odd indeed was going on. The Special Republican Guard had direct lines to the President, he reasoned; if this burial ground in the desert *was* connected to the biological weapons programme, then surely the presence of a human corpse among the animal carcasses would have been known to the Guards. So why not *prevent* the inspectors finding such a damning piece of evidence by stopping the dig earlier? Why wait until the stiff came to light? In his own mind it argued for the site being connected with some local mishap rather than anything of international interest.

Burgess had argued the point with Hardcastle, who'd told him in a tone which he'd found unnecessarily dismissive that he was overlooking the muddle factor and the paranoia factor. What they in the West would call a normal cascading of information from the administration downwards simply didn't apply in Iraq.

The inspectors had returned to Baghdad angry and frustrated, praying that the tissue samples which Martha Cok had taken from the lungs of a cow and a goat and hermetically sealed in two specimen boxes would provide the evidence they needed. A lab technician had been working on them overnight.

Burgess drifted over to a corner of the room where there was a small refrigerator. On top of it an electric kettle fought for space with packs of coffee, tea and whitener. He picked it up to check there was water in it, then clicked the switch and put a spoon of Maxwell House into a plastic cup.

Despite Hardcastle's words of caution, the conclusion Burgess had drawn from yesterday's events was that the Iraqi security people had *not* known what was buried in the desert, and therefore the men at the top hadn't either. His expectation of what would emerge from the analysis of the animal samples was low, therefore. He suspected that the cause of the creatures' death would prove to be something rather less dramatic than pulmonary anthrax or poisoning by botulinum toxin.

'Do me a coffee too, would you?' Hardcastle had appeared beside him. 'Frustrating, this hanging around.'
'Like waiting for fish to bite in a swimming pool.'
For Burgess the wait had had the added disadvantage of setting him thinking about Carole again. Just before leaving home in the Hudson River Valley to catch the flights to Europe and Bahrain she'd told him he was on notice. That if he didn't buck up and become a proper husband and father again, they'd be heading for divorce. The injustice which he perceived in the situation had gotten his investigative mind scouring through their ten years of marriage trying to find the point where it went sour.

They'd begun dating at sixteen as high-school sweethearts, kept the romance going through college, then married a couple of months after graduation. To the best of his knowledge he was the only man she'd ever had sex with, and, apart from a couple of misguided and embarrassing one-night stands, she was the only woman he himself had had. The church had played a big part in their lives both as kids and in the early years of their marriage, but in the past couple of years Carole had mostly taken Patty and Dean Jr to the Sunday service on her own.

Their sexual relationship had all but ceased in recent months and he knew it was his fault. When he'd been around at a suitable time to initiate it, he'd wanted it so bad it had been over almost as soon as it began, leaving her wound up and dissatisfied; whenever she'd tried to get things started he was usually too preoccupied to perform.

The whole framework of their relationship was going to have to change if they were to get their balance back, she'd told him. And she was right – if the marriage was to survive as anything more than an umbrella for the kids to grow up under, they would need somehow to find space and time for each other. But the way she seemed to think it could be achieved was for him a non-runner. Pledge for the Family, the renewal movement she was pressing him to join, aimed 'to get America's pops back into the pews'. Even if he went along with that, he knew the fundamental problem would remain. The job was demanding more from him than ever before and he had no inclination to change it.

'Ah, at last,' Hardcastle breathed, clutching the coffee Burgess had made for him. 'News!'

Martha Cok had entered the room. After hours in the lab she looked weary but triumphant.

'Well?' Hardcastle demanded, hungry for the confirmation he needed.

'Here,' she replied, handing him a sheet of paper.

Hardcastle read her note and smiled with satisfaction. 'Excellent, Martha. Excellent.' Then he passed it to Burgess.

Cause of death of the cow and goat examined on site and at BMVC lab – internal haemorrhaging due to inhalation of anthrax spores. Live organisms were found in the lung tissue. Animals had almost certainly been used in an experiment to test biological weapons material.

'Excellent,' Hardcastle repeated, burning with excitement. 'We'll nail Saddam to the wall with this one.'

Burgess swallowed hard. He'd judged it wrong. Totally wrong. But the key question in his head remained. Who among the Iraqi hierarchy had known about it?

He detected a new glint in Hardcastle's eyes. St George had his dragon in sight.

The Englishman briefed the operations officer to send the lab results in an encrypted signal to New York where it was the middle of the night, then stalked out to the car park like a hunting dog, pausing in the centre of the tarmac as if sniffing the wind. He spun round on his heel, looking first at the six UN vehicles lined up for departure, then across at the single Iraqi escort vehicle waiting by the exit.

'Strange. Mustafa's men aren't exactly out in strength this morning,' he murmured to Burgess under his breath.

'Guess that means they've gone over the Haji factory with a fine-tooth comb and are confident we won't find anything of interest there. They have had forty-eight hours to check the place over.'

Hardcastle raised an eyebrow.

'You think they're wrong to believe it's clean?' Burgess queried.

'I was born an optimist,' the Englishman answered flippantly. 'That's all.'

But it wasn't all. Burgess could see that Hardcastle was fired up by something much stronger than optimism.

'You believe this is connected with what your SIS picked up?' he checked. 'The warheads that are supposed to have been moved out of Iraq?'

The Englishman stared at him for a few seconds, not wanting to commit himself.

'Well, the timing could be right, couldn't it?'

'Sure. So you think the Haji factory could be the place where this particular batch of spores was produced?'

Hardcastle's eyes widened like marbles.

'Well, it's the timing again, isn't it?' he nodded sombrely. 'Everything happening about three weeks ago – the equipment smuggled into the Haji factory in the middle of the night, the fatalities in the desert.'

Burgess saw a flaw in the argument.

'But why should they need to *test* the stuff after perfecting all their weapon systems at Al Hakam years ago?'

'That's puzzling, I agree. One explanation is that there's something different about this particular weapon.'

'Such as?'

'That the way the anthrax spores are to be released involves a method they hadn't tried before.'

'A terrorist weapon, you mean?'

'Precisely. In the past we've always assumed Saddam would use anthrax in one of his SCUDs lobbed at Tel Aviv or Riyadh. The explosive warhead technology for that particular missile was certainly perfected before the Gulf War. No more testing needed.'

'But for a terrorist attack don't they just spray the stuff into the ventilation shaft of a government building or the subway?' Burgess countered.

'It's not quite that simple. The spray technology has to be right. Nozzle size for liquids, particle size if it's a dry powder. And that's maybe what they had to check out in the desert.'

'Particle size? You talked about that in Bahrain. The grains have to be five microns.'

'Between one and five microns in diameter. Smaller than one micron and the particles of spores or toxin get sucked into the lungs of the intended victims and then exhaled, doing no damage; bigger than five microns and they get trapped in the phlegm of the upper respiratory tract where they're relatively harmless. Only when they're between one and five microns do they penetrate to the alveoli – those are the terminal air sacs of the lungs – which is where they need to be if they're to do their worst.'

'I follow. But this particle size, it's tough to produce? What's the technology they need?'

'The first part of the process is quite easy. The toxins or pathogens can be brewed up in a growth medium in a relatively simple laboratory – like the Haji single-cell protein plant where they have self-sterilising fermenters and centrifuges. They'd need a freeze-dryer to turn the fermented liquid into a concentrated dry cake of lethal agent. But it's after that that the critical part comes.

Milling the solid into a powder of the right size. Every suitable milling machine that we know about in Iraq has a UN tag on it or a camera watching over it. That's why the object the U-2 photographed being smuggled into the Haji factory is of special interest. It's quite possible they had a machine somewhere we hadn't managed to tag, or else sneaked a new one into the country. And they chose the Haji plant to set it up in, for the very reason that our fixed cameras were there. They calculated we would be so confident about the place we wouldn't be giving it an extra look.'

'Neat idea. But there's no way that particular machine is still going to be there.'

'No. We won't find the machine, that's for certain, but we might find something else.'

From the corner of his eye Burgess saw movement behind Hardcastle's back.

'Watch out. Here comes ya ol' buddy.'

Hardcastle turned.

'Ah, Mustafa. Good morning to you.'

'Where you go today? Haji factory?'

'Wouldn't you be surprised if I said no, Mustafa?' Hardcastle teased.

The Iraqi's eyes became beads of glass.

'You ready now?'

'Pretty well.'

Mustafa turned on his heel and headed for his jeep.

Fifteen minutes later they were on the northern outskirts of Baghdad, cutting through a different part of the city from yesterday. No broad avenues lined by palaces and monuments this time, but grubby, potholed roads strung with a cat's cradle of overhead power and phone wires and dotted with shops and businesses that seemed unused to customers. Traffic was light. Dilapidated trucks and an overladen bus or two. Very few private cars, but the occasional orange and white taxi. The only new-looking vehicles belonged to the police.

'God knows how they smuggle them in,' Hardcastle murmured. 'Strictly forbidden under UN sanctions. But you can see where Saddam spends his money. Palaces for himself and new kit for his security men instead of aspirins and anaesthetics for his hospitals.'

Most people were on foot, unable to afford any transport. A tide of dusty humanity, most of them in need of a good meal.

'There is real hardship in this country,' Hardcastle continued, twisting round from the front seat. 'UN sanctions hurt both the poor and what used to be the professional classes. The statistics for child mortality are horrific. Poor diet, poor sanitation, lack of medicine.' He pointed to a large poster of Saddam Hussein smiling down at them from a billboard on a street corner. 'While that man and his friends live very nicely, of course.'

'There's no justice,' Burgess mumbled, uncomfortable at being a part of the system helping to cause such hardship.

They reached an interchange. Signposts in English and Arabic pointed ahead to the towns of Samarra and Mosul. There'd been a nerve-gas factory at Samarra, Burgess recalled, bombed in the 1991 war, and nuclear research sites near Mosul. Huge programmes for weapons of mass destruction employing tens of thousands of scientists. An industry for domination, not self-defence. And the man who'd felt the need for it was still in charge, still chasing the same dreams in greater secrecy than ever before.

The Haji Animal Feed factory loomed up on their right, a block of long pre-fabricated buildings set back some fifty metres from the road and ringed by a high fence. Beyond the buildings stretched an open landscape of sandy-brown earth dotted with fig and eucalyptus trees, and the remains of a crop of maize.

Led by the Iraqi jeep, the UN convoy turned into the compound. By now well prepared for the visit, the firm's managers were lined up outside the entrance to greet the inspectors, their faces nervous but confident. Stepping forward from the line, a man whose scalp was as bald and domed as an egg introduced himself as the general manager, Youssef Haydar. A contrary gust of wind blew aside the greased flap with which he endeavoured to conceal his baldness. It stuck out at the side now like a broken wing.

'I am very sorry, but Doctor Shenassi is not able to be here today,' Haydar explained in good English having announced he was the 'responsible' at the plant. 'His mother is sick and he must visit her. It is a pity you couldn't come two days ago. He was here then.'

Hardcastle checked the name Haydar against the list he'd been provided with at the Gateway in Bahrain. It gave his title as production manager.

As they began their tour Burgess's heart sank. Nothing, it seemed, had been left to chance. They inspected halls filled with stainless steel cylinders, attended by regimented staff in white coats who greeted their progress with curiosity and lightly suppressed annoyance. They were shown the small, unnaturally tidy laboratory used for batch production where there was a fourteen-litre fermenter vessel that might so easily have been employed a few weeks earlier to brew up an initial seed stock of *Bacillus anthracis*. They checked the tags on all the dual-use equipment against the numbers on their lists, to ensure none of the equipment had been moved. And they monitored the correct operation of the camera fixed above the plant's milling machines that would have surely picked up any misuse.

At each new sign that the place had been thoroughly

sanitised for their visit, Burgess's heart sank a little lower. There was nothing out of place. No sign of the extra machinery that had been smuggled in here one dark night three weeks ago. As they completed the tour and returned to the car park, Hardcastle looked depressed but determined. He gathered his team around him well away from the minders who were watching them from the shaded entrance to the administration building. They looked like sheep waiting to see if the dogs were fed up enough to leave their flock alone.

'This is a bust, so far,' Hardcastle sighed. 'Nothing out of place and all the staff I've spoken to deny all knowledge of additional equipment being set up here three weeks ago.' He looked to Burgess for help. 'What d'you think, Dean? You've been scrutinising faces through your zoom lens – d'you think they're lying?'

'Hard to say,' Burgess hedged. 'If they are deceiving us, they're darn good at it. How many people have we talked to? Thirty? Forty?'

'Something like that.'

'In a witness group that large, there's usually *some* character who gives the game away.'

'Except perhaps when they realise that to let anything slip will result in an excruciating death for themselves and their entire extended family,' Hardcastle growled, gritting his teeth. 'Look. The one thing about which there is no doubt whatsoever is that in the early hours of the morning of Thursday the twelfth of September some heavy piece of equipment was delivered here. And the fact that the head man Doctor Shenassi is absent today is to my mind distinctly suspicious.'

'I agree with that,' Burgess said.

Suddenly his eye was caught by movement in a wide window on the upper floor of the administration block. Two women were watching them studiedly, as if they'd been told to do so. When they saw that he'd noticed them they moved back from the glass.

'So we go for the documents next, yes?' Burgess ventured.

'Exactly. We'll split into two search groups, one linguist to each group. One takes the ground floor, the other upstairs. Dean and I will provide oversight. Every filing cabinet, every cupboard and desk drawer needs to be opened and searched. Every single document you can find – receipts, invoices, correspondence with suppliers, the lot – I want it all bundled up and brought down to the admin vehicle here.' He pointed to the large armoured personnel carrier that had accompanied them from the BMVC. 'We'll photocopy most of it and examine it in detail later.'

The administration building was small and on two storeys. The ground floor housed a large general accounting office, a smaller one for health and safety monitoring and a couple of rooms for managers. On the level above was Dr Shenassi's office and several others including a department of general administration with four staff.

General Manager Haydar, who'd so efficiently conducted them round the plant's technical areas, seemed more reluctant about letting them into the offices.

'There is nothing there which is relevant to your enquiries,' he insisted, the flap of hair now stuck firmly back across his shiny scalp.

'We'll decide that,' stated Hardcastle.

Realising further protest was pointless Haydar delegated two of his staff to escort the search teams; one upstairs, one into the main accounts office. Hardcastle and Burgess hovered in the small entrance lobby under the suspicious gaze of Mustafa.

'Why you come here, when you already have cameras here?' the security man asked, frowning with puzzled curiosity.

'To look at things the cameras cannot see,' Hardcastle retorted dismissively.

At the foot of the stairs an elderly doorman with a wizened face and milky grey eyes sat behind a small table. He eyed them as if wanting to speak, but held back because of the presence of the security official.

'Good morning,' Burgess said to him encouragingly.

'Good morning sahr!'

The old man got smartly to his feet and saluted. Then in gentle English and in one breath he announced that he was the security man and company dogsbody and that he'd served as a boy soldier when the Iraqi army was officered by the British.

'Oh really? You must've seen a lot of changes over the years,' Burgess chatted.

'Yes sahr.'

'Security man, you say?' Burgess checked. 'Does that mean you have to know about everything that comes in and out of this place?'

'Oh, yes sahr.' The man gave a little twist of his leathery neck as he answered, his eyes darting towards Mustafa to see if it was safe to speak. 'Everything that they deliver and send away.'

'And you keep a record? A log book?' Hardcastle chipped in.

Lips tight with suppressed pride the old fellow produced a ledger from his drawer and opened it for them to see.

'Even something that arrives in the middle of the night?' Burgess pressed, unable to read the Arabic script. 'Would that be in here too?'

The security man shot them a scornful look. 'Six o'clock, sir,' he assured them. 'Factory close for deliveries after six in the evening. Nothing come here in the night.'

'Never? Not even in the middle of September?'

The man closed his ledger and put it away. The

specificity of the question had unnerved him. He sealed his lips.

Suddenly the door to the general accounting office banged open and one of the Russian inspectors who'd been gathering documents staggered out with a blue plastic bin-liner filled with papers. Pursued by the dome-headed general manager who was protesting volubly, he pushed past Mustafa and out into the car park where the APC equipped with copiers and scanners was waiting. The manager held his arms wide in exasperation. Mustafa led him back into the accounts office.

Hardcastle beckoned to Burgess and took to the stairs. 'While there's a diversion,' he whispered. 'Let's go and see how the other lot are doing.'

On either side of the first-floor corridor they found four small offices, including the one normally occupied by the absent managing director Dr Shenassi. Burgess tried the door, but it was locked. From an office opposite where two inspectors were picking through the contents of a filing cabinet a matronly woman dressed in a white lab coat bustled forth gabbling in Arabic and interposed herself between Hardcastle and the door to Shenassi's office.

'You speak any English?' Hardcastle enquired.

'No.' Then she continued to berate him in Arabic, pushing him away from the door.

'They claim they have no key for that door,' the German demolition specialist announced, pushing past with a sack of papers for checking.

'A likely story,' Hardcastle mouthed.

The search seemed to be progressing, and the staff up here looked to be more junior than in the accounts office downstairs, so they returned to the ground floor.

'We've no idea what he looks like, this Shenassi guy?' Burgess checked, his suspicions mounting by the second.

'No. We don't have a photo.'

'So if he was here some place, keeping his head down, like in that office of his upstairs, we wouldn't have any way of knowing it was him even if we broke the door down.'

'Correct.'

'He could even be in the accounts office posing as a clerk.'

'Well, yes.'

'Then maybe we should ask to see everybody's ID,' Burgess suggested. 'Every *male* member of staff, that is.'

'Not a bad idea.'

Shouts erupted from inside the accounts office. One of the voices belonged to the UN's interpreter. The old soldier sat as motionless as a sculpture behind his small table, as if taught by experience that in unpredictable situations even a minor facial movement was potentially dangerous.

Suddenly, from the accounts office a bespectacled man with hair that was flecked with grey emerged in a state of agitation and hurried up the stairs. He wore a well-pressed pale blue shirt and dark trousers and carried an air of authority about him. Burgess and Hardcastle exchanged glances, both of a similar mind. Burgess scooted up the stairs after him.

'What's that man's name?' Hardcastle asked the security officer. The old soldier stared back, mute. 'His name?' Hardcastle repeated. 'Who is he?'

The wizened face turned slowly towards the open door of the accounts office. Hardcastle followed his look. Mustafa was standing there stony-faced.

Suddenly the front door to the building banged open. A British Intelligence Corps officer serving as an Arabic speaker at the BMVC, who'd been examining papers taken from the accounts office, burst in holding a single A4 page. Attached to it was a yellow Post-It note on which he'd written the words, *This memo is to the staff telling them the plant will be closed for four days for maintenance. The dates in question were the 12th to the 16th of September.*

'Aah,' breathed Hardcastle. 'Thank you *very* much, my friend.'

No wonder nobody knew about a machine being delivered here in the middle of the night. The entire staff had been given four days off. Enough time to produce all the finely milled anthrax spores they could need for a weapon and for the place to be thoroughly cleaned again.

Burgess thundered down the stairs to report that the man in the blue shirt had gone into Shenassi's office.

Suddenly the phone rang on the desk in the lobby. The elderly security man answered it, then sat up straighter as if the call was from a boss. He growled an acknowledgement in Arabic then replaced the receiver. He got up quickly and came straight up to Hardcastle, avoiding his eye and grabbing his arm.

'Please. Please, sir.'

He tried to push Hardcastle towards the ground floor accounts office but the tall Englishman wasn't having it.

'Get your hands off me, my man,' Hardcastle snapped, shaking him off.

'Please. Please you must come, sahr. There is problem.' The elderly man turned to Burgess in the hope he'd be more amenable. 'Please, sahr, we must hurry.' He kept his eyes down as if afraid of revealing his deception.

Burgess caught Hardcastle's eye, pointed up the stairs and mouthed *Shenassi*. Hardcastle understood the game that was being played.

'All right my friend,' he said to the doorman as if softening, 'let's see what your problem is.'

'Thank you sahr. Thank you.'

They allowed the old man to usher them into the main

accounts office and close the door behind them. He stood next to it, holding the handle.

'So?' Hardcastle said to him gently, watching the Russians sift through papers unmolested by the accountants. 'Where's this problem of yours? You'd better go and ask someone, hadn't you?'

After a moment's embarrassed hesitation, the security man's face became a picture of discomfort.

'Right,' Hardcastle said to Burgess.

They pushed past the guard and back through the door into the lobby just as the man with the grey-flecked hair and blue shirt reached the foot of the stairs. He had a jacket on now and carried a thin see-through folder with a few sheets of paper in it.

Hardcastle blocked his path.

'Ah, Doctor Shenassi! How nice to see you again,' he announced, smiling broadly. From the startled reaction he knew Burgess had guessed right. 'Last time we met was Leeds wasn't it? You were doing your degree there. When was that now . . . end of the seventies?'

Shenassi's jaw dropped, deceived and winded by the bluff. Burgess stood next to Hardcastle, making it impossible for the Haji MD to squeeze past and escape.

'Er, I don't quite—'

'I'm Andrew Hardcastle. You remember . . . I was lecturing in biology. How very nice to see you again. And I'm sorry we're putting you to all this trouble. Good of you all to co-operate so well with the UN.'

'I . . . my mother . . .' he protested feebly.

'Oh yes. Poorly, I hear. So sorry. You'll be on your way to see her no doubt. Tell you what, we're having to check all documents, so would you mind?'

He latched a hand onto Shenassi's folder, but the doctor wasn't letting go.

'Only need a quick glance, just to be sure, then we won't trouble you further.' He gave a sudden sharp pull which Shenassi had not expected. To Hardcastle's astonishment the folder was in his hands. He whipped round and headed for the car park. 'Won't be a moment.'

Burgess blocked Shenassi's panicky attempt to follow.

'It's good you're here, Doctor, because I've a couple of questions I'd like to ask.'

'Questions, questions. We already answer them.'

'But not satisfactorily, Doctor Shenassi. That's the problem.'

'I can tell you nothing more.'

'Well, *I* think you can. You see something happened three weeks ago, which you know about even if most of your staff don't because they were on vacation.' He saw Shenassi's face grow paler. 'A milling machine? You remember it now? Delivered here at night. Why was that, Doctor Shenassi?'

'I don't know what you talk about.'

They were no longer alone in the lobby. Mustafa had appeared with two minders, one of them armed with a camera. Damn, thought Burgess. Should be doing that too.

Shenassi seemed to stagger, as if about to faint.

'Hey, why don't we sit down?' Burgess pointed to the chair abandoned by the security man. He switched on his own Hi-8, set the lens wide and held it at shoulder height. But Shenassi made a dive for the door, babbling in Arabic while scrabbling in one of the side pockets of his jacket as if searching for a cigarette.

'I don't advise that you leave, sir,' said Burgess firmly, blocking his path again but realising that if push came to shove there was little he could do to stop him. 'The UN needs answers about that milling machine, Doctor Shenassi. What was it used for and where is it now?'

Shenassi fell silent as if fear had petrified him. But it wasn't fear of the UN, Burgess realised suddenly. What Shenassi was scared of were the two officials from his own country's security service whose faces had darkened alarmingly.

Abruptly, Mustafa ordered a stop to the filming by his own cameraman and they hustled the doctor outside.

'Now hold it there,' Burgess protested vainly, trying to follow.

Mustafa pushed him back with the flat of his hand, his dark eyes angry and confused.

'Now look, I got questions to ask this guy,' Burgess snapped. 'You got no right to take him away.'

Shenassi was being hustled over to Mustafa's Land-cruiser. He put a hand up to his mouth as if holding back vomit.

'Soon,' Mustafa told Burgess tensely. 'Soon maybe you can talk with him. Wait here please.'

As Mustafa hurried away, Hardcastle came bustling over from the UN vehicles.

'Nobbled him, have they?' the Englishman panted. 'Not bloody surprised. We've cracked it Dean! Bloody cracked it! One of those papers he was carrying – you won't believe it. A complete list of what they would need to produce ten kilos of anthrax!'

'My God!'

'It's all there. Growth medium, nutrient, pharmaceutical grade distilled water, sodium hypochlorite for cleaning up afterwards.'

'All that was written down?' Burgess asked incredulously. 'The guy's crazy.'

'No. Not crazy. Just a meticulous scientist who can't break a lifetime's habit of making records of his work. And the sooner we talk to him the better.'

They turned towards the Iraqi Landcruiser.

'Jesus!' Hardcastle exploded. 'What are they doing to the bugger?'

Dr Shenassi lay slumped across the hood of the vehicle

as if he'd been beaten senseless. The two minders were trying to lift him to his feet but he buckled in their arms.

'They've hit him, the bastards,' hissed Hardcastle. 'Come on!'

They strode across the tarmac.

'Or maybe he was so shit scared he had a heart attack,' Burgess croaked.

Mustafa saw their approach.

'No!' he yelled, holding up a hand.

The two Iraqis lowered Dr Shenassi to the ground and crouched beside him.

'He's having convulsions,' Hardcastle whispered. 'Bloody hell! Do we have a medic on the team?'

They quickly thought through the list of those with them.

'No we don't,' said Burgess, sadly. 'Martha would be the one but she's back at the monitoring centre.'

Mustafa stood up and hurled himself inside the Landcruiser to get on the radio. He began shouting in Arabic. Shenassi was lying absolutely still now. The second minder who'd been crouched beside him stood up, hands on hips as if totally perplexed by the situation.

'This looks bad,' Burgess warned. 'Real bad.'

'Do you think they could be pretending?' suggested Hardcastle. 'Wouldn't put it past them. They'll try any trick when they're cornered.'

'Doesn't look to me like they're faking it,' murmured Burgess, 'but maybe we ought to take a closer look.'

As they moved in, the security man standing over Shenassi swung round, his face puffy with shock and anger.

'Let me see him,' Hardcastle said forcefully, crouching down and grabbing Shenassi's wrist. 'I've had medical training.'

A first-aid course twenty years ago. He felt for a pulse and couldn't find one, but he was out of practice.

'He's turning blue for God's sake,' Hardcastle exclaimed. 'Is somebody calling an ambulance?'

Shenassi was breathing, but feebly and erratically.

'What happened exactly?' Burgess asked the security minder.

'He sick,' the Iraqi answered stonily.

'Yeah I can see that. But pretty sudden, huh?'

'Yes. He just go sick.'

Hardcastle turned his face up towards them. 'It *could* be a heart attack, you know.' He'd flattened his fingers against Shenassi's neck and found the carotid artery. 'Pulse is all over the place.' He stood up again. There was nothing he could do.

'Doctor coming,' the minder explained, pointing towards Mustafa shouting into the radio in the Landcruiser.

Burgess dropped to his knees and bent his head over Shenassi's face, realising the statistical chances of this being heart failure were remote in the extreme.

'Doctor Shenassi? Can you hear me?'

The man's eyes were open, but staring blindly into the air. He gave no sign of responding.

'What happened, Doctor Shenassi, can you tell us? Do you have a chest pain?'

Again, no response.

Suddenly Burgess sniffed, frowned and pulled back sharply. He stood up and pulled Hardcastle to one side.

'That's definitely no heart attack,' he whispered when they'd got beyond earshot.

'What then?'

'Hydrocyanic acid. Cyanide.'

'*What?*'

'Must have had a capsule of the stuff in his pocket and bitten into it a few minutes ago. Inhaled the vapours. The smell on his breath – bitter almonds. Unmistakable.'

'Funny. I didn't smell anything at all.'

'Only thirty per cent of people can. The ability to smell it is hereditary and I happen to have it.'

Hardcastle blanched. 'He took poison? Because of us? Because we caught him out?'

'Looks that way.'

'How appalling.'

They looked back at the scene by the Landcruiser. Mustafa was now out of the vehicle, standing beside the driver's door, hands on hips, glaring down at the motionless body of the scientist, his face flushed and baffled. He was totally perplexed, Burgess realised suddenly. Totally and utterly. Mustafa hadn't the slightest idea what Shenassi had been up to here at the Haji factory. Just like the day before in the desert, when the discovery of the human corpse had come as a complete shock to him. The multi-layered Iraqi state security system with Saddam at its top seemed for some reason to be out of the loop.

'No,' Burgess announced suddenly.

'What d'you mean, *no*?'

'It wasn't because of *us* he took the cyanide.'

Hardcastle's face puckered with puzzlement.

'It was because of *them*,' Burgess explained, indicating the security men.

'Scared what Saddam would do to him for letting the cat out of the bag, you mean?'

'No. Not even that,' Burgess insisted. 'No, Andrew. What Doctor Shenassi was doing here – my guess is that President Saddam Hussein knew nothing about it. Nothing about it whatsoever.'

'Impossible,' snapped Hardcastle. 'You simply don't know this place, Dean.'

14

Mid-morning
Cyprus

The bonded warehouse on the outskirts of Limassol hummed with activity. Three large container ships were due into the port that day and the yard had cargoes to be delivered to each of them. Most of the containers in question, both twenty feet and forty feet in length, were piled up in the open. Huge forklifts trundled between the stacks, shifting and shuffling boxes to get at the ones they wanted, then dumping them onto the flatbed trailer trucks which sped out of the yard, belching black exhaust on their way to the port just five minutes away.

Inside the warehouse – used by customers who requested extra security for their transiting consignments – the floor space to one side that had been left empty except for two solitary containers placed side by side was now occupied by just one. The container from Israel with a destination to the west had already been moved from its space earlier that morning, transported to the docks for loading onto a ship sailing for Algeciras at midday. The administrative documents accompanying it said the box contained printing machines.

The container from Ilychevsk in Ukraine, which had arrived here yesterday afternoon via Piraeus and was bound for Haifa, sat waiting for the ship that would take it on the final part of its journey. The seal on its door clasps marked with the identifying numbers provided by Odessa customs was firmly in place. Anyone reading the paperwork describing its contents as rotting fruit and vegetable juices might have been forgiven for treating it with the respect due to a smoking bomb.

The twenty-two workers at the bonded yard were all Greek-Cypriots. To them this was just another day of not too strenuous work under a pleasantly warm late summer sun. None of them was aware of the frenetic activity that had gone on inside the warehouse during the night while they'd been in their beds, work of great technical skill that had been completed just minutes before their arrival for work this morning, work carried out by a gang of men speaking a different language from their own.

None was aware of that, nor of how pivotal their place of employment was to be in the fulfilment of a plot that was gradually coming together, a plot to commit mass murder.

15

13.15 hrs
Sark, Channel Islands

Point Robert, the north-east corner of Sark, was on their starboard beam about a mile distant. As planned, the current had swept *Backgammon*'s sleek white hull through the Alderney Race at an exhilarating lick. They'd be at the anchorage for lunch.

Sam wore shorts to let the sun and salt air dry the scabs on his legs. The pleasures of the day had flaked away the stresses of the past weeks like dry onion skins.

Nat was proving perfectly adequate at the tasks of a crew. The white-knuckle ride of the race had even brought a smile to his lips. He'd managed the helm while Sam moved forward to take in a reef when the wind got up a mile south of Alderney.

'Beer, skipper?'

Nat emerged at the head of the companionway steps clutching two cans.

'About bloody time,' Sam grinned, reaching for one of them.

He ripped it open and drank a good draught. Then he gave a routine glance all round the horizon to check no other boats were close to them. He felt a pang of guilt suddenly. The foam-flecked sea, the clear azure sky – this was *too* perfect. He felt he hadn't earned it yet. Still that feeling of unfinished business to attend to and he was neglecting it.

Nat leaned back against the side of the cockpit, watching a couple of small fishing boats work the submerged rocks to their left.

'That's what I should have been,' he murmured. 'A bloody fisherman.'

'Hard life,' Sam cautioned.

'Never! Not those fellers. Deep-sea trawlermen yes, but those little boats just pop out when they feel like it. Bloody sight easier than playing God with people's lives like I did.'

'What d'you mean?' Sam frowned, wondering if there was a side to Gibbon he didn't know about.

'It's what a writer does, chum. Creates people then destroys them. I've fathered more human beings than Atatürk.'

Sam smiled. It was a harmless conceit. He knew so little about this man, but that was the way he wanted it to be.

He was beginning to feel hungry. He'd bought a bag of supplies before leaving home yesterday. Bread, cheese and tomatoes. The high cliffs of Sark were drawing closer. They'd be in the bay before long and could drop anchor. He noticed suddenly that Gibbon was scrutinising him.

'You certainly know your way around on a boat,' Nat conceded grudgingly. 'Sailed all your life have you?'

A flock of gannets swooped across their bows and dived, profiting from the fishermen's work.

'I was brought up in Portsmouth. My dad was in submarines. They had dinghies at the base at Gosport. When he came home from a patrol he would always take me out. He loved to sail. I think it was being cooped up in metal tubes for so long.'

'Still alive, is he?'

'No. Died when I was eleven.'

Gibbon puffed out through pursed lips. 'Never know how long you're going to get, do you?'

'No.'

And for Sam, death had come frighteningly close in recent days.

'But you went on sailing. After?'

'Yes. His mates in the Navy, you know – others with kids – they sort of took me on. Because they knew I was keen. And I think they felt sorry for me being stuck at home with a mother who never went out.'

He stopped himself there. He'd revealed enough. Didn't want to encourage more questions.

A short while later they rounded the headland that provided shelter from the northerlies for the cove known as Terrible Bay.

'I think we'll have that jib furled,' Sam announced.

'Right-ho, cap'n.'

Gibbon eased off the sheet and pulled on the furling line while Sam started the engine, tightened the topping lift and turned into wind.

'Happy to gather in the mainsail?' he asked.

'No probs.'

'Sail ties are in the rack behind the chart table.'

Nat slid below to get them, then clambered onto the coach-roof to release the halyard. The sail slid smoothly down the mast and Gibbon gathered it in like an old hand.

'Can you handle the anchor?' Sam shouted when the sail was secure. It was heavy and awkward.

'So long as you tell me when to drop it.'

He conned the boat round a second headland. Ahead lay a cove guarded by outcrops of rock, where the magically blue water ended some three hundred metres away in a steeply sloping shingle beach.

The chain clanked as Nat lifted the hook onto its

roller. The sea bed was coming up fast as they neared the shore. Eyeing the depth gauge repeater mounted on the cabin bulkhead Sam eased off the power and looked ahead for the paler patches of water which told of a sandy bottom that would be good holding ground. There was one other boat in the bay, a large powerboat made of sleek plastic. On its spacious quarterdeck faces turned from a lunch-table to monitor their approach.

'Getting shallow,' Nat shouted over his shoulder. 'There's rocks here.'

Seven metres of water beneath the keel, the gauge told him. Nothing to worry about.

'We'll drop anchor there.' He pointed to a circle of pale blue on their starboard bow and gave a touch on the tiller. 'I'll tell you when.'

He eased the throttle into neutral and at five and a half metres' depth shouted for the hook to be dropped. The chain rattled like a machine-gun.

'Easy,' he yelled, pushing the gear in reverse so the chain wouldn't pile up on the bottom.

Neutral again. He hurried forward to check the anchor line was securely tied.

'Had me worried for a moment,' Nat muttered. 'Thought you were going to put us on the beach.'

They made their way back to the cockpit then peeled off the weatherproof tops and leggings that had protected them from spray in the stronger winds of the open sea. In the cove around them a light breeze ruffled the surface of the water but caused no swell.

Nat went below. He passed up another beer first, then plates of bread, cheese and salad. Sam set them out on the small, varnished table which he'd unfolded in the centre of the cockpit.

'Very civilised,' Nat said, joining him.

The boat was anchored in an amphitheatre of rock and vegetation. Seagull cries echoed from the cliffs to their left. Small waves slapped gently against the hull. To their right a long, thin ruff of foam rustled against the stones of the beach.

Sam felt nagged by doubts again. The fear of being out of touch. There was a gnawing in his guts that wasn't just hunger, a sense that something was wrong. He began to think he should ring in.

'Think I might inflate the dinghy after lunch and row to the beach,' he mumbled, his mouth full of cheese. 'Interested in a run ashore?'

Gibbon looked up and caught sight of a tiny figure walking along a cliff path.

'No thanks. I get a bit of vertigo. Perfectly happy sitting here with a beer enjoying the view.'

Sam heard the faint strains of music coming from the large motor cruiser sharing their anchorage. Its fat hull rocked gently in a swell created by the wake of some distant ship which had passed the island long before. A lone figure stood on the quarterdeck, holding what looked like a radio. The sound of the Greenwich pips floated across the water. He glanced at his watch. Two o'clock. Of course. There'd be a news bulletin.

He dived below, needing to be certain that the anthrax attack the middle-aged Iraqi had warned about had not already happened.

The radio was built into a panel next to the log above the chart table.

'Just want to hear the headlines,' he shouted up to the cockpit.

'Personally, I'd rather not know,' mused Nat.

The set was kept tuned to Radio Four. The newsreader's voice boomed out. Sam lowered the volume to a more comfortable level.

'*As the American presidential election campaign gathers pace, a new allegation has been made about sexual harassment . . .*'

'Why do they think we care?' Nat moaned through the hatchway.

'In the House of Commons this afternoon a row is expected to break . . .'

Sam began to relax again. Nothing had happened. If the anthrax had been used it would be the lead story.

'A British woman has been murdered in Cyprus.'

A chill went through him. He leaned towards the loudspeaker.

'Her partially clothed body was found on a beach, said a police spokesman in Nicosia. The circumstances of the death are unclear, but it's believed the woman had been visiting Cyprus on business and was staying at a Limassol hotel. She has been named by the Cyprus authorities as Mrs Christine Taylor . . .'

Sam couldn't move. He felt as if his heart had stopped.

'A Foreign Office spokesperson told the BBC that Mrs Taylor's husband has been traced and informed of the tragedy. The couple had no children.'

His jaw dropped in horror and disbelief. Taylor. Chrissie's cover name.

His head filled with white noise, the newsreader's voice fading to a burble.

The man on the radio had just said Chrissie was *dead* . . . It couldn't be . . . it *mustn't* be . . . Taylor. A common enough name. And Christine – common too . . . He sank down onto the navigator's seat.

Chrissie was *dead*? He mouthed the word, trying to make it have meaning. But he couldn't connect with it. All he knew was that *he* was here, bobbing about on his fucking boat and of no damned use to her, when a few days ago *she* had saved his life.

It wasn't real to him. He needed to check if it were true, and check fast. Stupidly he'd not brought his mobile with him. He imagined them at Vauxhall Cross, headless chickens closing stable doors, preparing denials, getting an investigation under way.

An investigation *he* should be involved in.

'Shit!'

He knew there was a call box on Sark, but to inflate the dinghy and climb the cliff path would take an hour. He could be three quarters of the way to Guernsey by then, where the island had not only phones, but an airport.

'Nat,' he called up into the cockpit. 'Get the anchor up. Change of plan.'

'Eh?' Gibbon sounded startled. 'Oh, all right... What, *now*?'

'Yes.'

Sam climbed up the companionway. Gibbon saw the grim, shell-shocked expression on his face and scuttled forward to the bows without a word.

Don't ask, Sam said to himself trembling. Just don't bloody ask.

16

Thursday, 3 October, late afternoon
Cyprus

It was refusing to sink in. Chrissie's murder was fact, yet in Sam's mind it wasn't registering. As he pushed through bemused crowds of Russian holidaymakers in the baggage hall at Larnaca airport he half expected to begin to feel the impact of her death more strongly now he'd arrived on the island where it had happened. But the cotton wool that seemed to be filling his head didn't budge.

Two flights from the former Soviet Union had landed just ahead of the service from London. In the five years since he'd last been to the island, Cyprus had become a playground for Russia's new rich, a safe haven for their cash. Some of those around him were middle-aged package tourists in dowdy greys and browns, but many were younger, dressed in designer suits and carrying hand-tooled briefcases with gold-plated locks which he imagined to be stuffed with banknotes.

Dressed in jeans, cotton sports shirt and a navy-blue fleece, Sam headed for the green lane, his only luggage a holdall which he swung up onto his shoulder. The customs officials gave him less than half a glance, then the opaque glass doors slid back exposing a sea of tour agents wearing bright jackets and fixed smiles. His hazel eyes scanned the faces. Some illogical part of him expected Chrissie to be waiting, her face split by that grin of hers, announcing there'd been some crazy mix-up and she wasn't dead after all. He turned away from the faces and looked for the rental desks where a car was booked under the name of Terry Malone.

When he'd returned to London late yesterday afternoon, Duncan Waddell had been waiting for him above the launderette at Isleworth. He'd quickly briefed him on what they knew, which was little. Chrissie had filed just one report from Cyprus, on the Monday evening, saying she'd successfully picked up Khalil's trail. She'd given them the name of a lawyer he'd visited and said Khalil, clearly under duress, was being accompanied wherever he went by the two men who'd met him at Amman airport on Saturday night. SIS had checked out the lawyer in question and found he was one of many in Cyprus who made a fat living representing offshore companies.

Then in the early hours of Wednesday morning the British High Commission in Nicosia had called with the dreadful news that her body had been found in a car park near the beach in Limassol, cause of death not established, but clearly not natural.

'The Cyprus police checked out what she'd been doing and began to suspect that Christine worked for *us*,' Waddell had lamented. 'Unusually sharp of them. We've denied it of course, and will continue to do so. The Cypriots are very touchy about us working covertly on their territory. As you know, our station man at the High Commission was on leave – it's why we sent her there in the first place. We've sent Quentin Mowbray in from Amman to hold the reins. He's in Nicosia now, keeping a watchful eye on the High Commission's liaison with the Cypriot police. But he's under normal diplomatic cover, so his hands are pretty much tied. That's why we want *you* out there in Cyprus. By the way, Martin Kessler is particularly keen it's you who goes.'

Waddell had looked flummoxed when he'd said the last sentence. Sam had shared his surprise.

'Thinks your recent experience in Iraq might give you some vital insight into Chrissie's death,' he'd added in explanation.

Waddell had hurried the rest of his brief, explaining that Chrissie had been working under the cover of a debt-collecting agency. The High Commission had told the Cyprus authorities she was investigating an Iraqi named Salah Khalil, travelling on a Jordanian passport, who'd used fake credit cards in London to run up huge debts at hotels. Although still suspicious that it was MI6 who'd been running her, the Cyprus police were co-operating in playing down the affair, telling the press they believed she'd got into bad company in the bar of her hotel one night.

'You know the stuff,' Waddell had said, 'married woman away from home, fancies a fling, gets a little carried away on cheap brandy and cola. If they can persuade the press to swallow that tosh we'll be only too delighted. What *we're* assuming is she found out something significant about Khalil's activities in Cyprus but got too close to the flame. We need you to tell us what that something was, Sam. And fast.'

He'd handed over a small photograph of Khalil taken in London. Cyprus police were trying to find him, he'd said, but the man had checked out of his hotel on Tuesday evening with his two companions. The Cypriot lawyer he'd visited was pleading client confidentiality and refusing to answer questions, but the Cyprus Central Bank which had registration details of all offshore companies was being pressured to come up with a business name and account number.

'Then we can get at the big CHIPS computers to try

and trace the money which Khalil was presumably shifting,' Waddell had added.

'CHIPS?'

'Clearing Houses International Payments System. A lot of the banks use it for big money transfers. GCHQ monitors the satellites they use for shifting cash electronically.'

'And where do we *think* that money was going?'

'Into some other account more directly under the control of Saddam Hussein. Where else?'

Sam steered his rented red Toyota out of the airport and onto the road north. To his left stretched a bleak salt lake, its surface a yellow-grey crust that stank of decay. A flock of waders picked at the edges of it. To his right lay the suburbs of Larnaca, a straggle of three-bed houses with solar water heaters on their roofs and satellite dishes in the gardens.

As he turned west onto the road for Limassol, he thought about Martin Kessler. Had it sunk in with *him* yet?

The Deputy Head of Global Risks at SIS had been a constancy in his life for the past five years, entrenched at the other end of the rope in his tug-of-war over Chrissie. Yet he'd never met the man face to face, his point of contact with the Firm being Duncan Waddell. Almost all of what he knew about Kessler had come from Chrissie – late forties, a memory for detail on a par with a Cray computer, boarding school from the age of seven, emotionally stunted, a man who might have been actively homosexual if he'd allowed himself any choice in the matter. That she should bind herself emotionally to such a man in preference to him still stuck in his throat. A decision that would now remain a mystery for ever.

Kessler. He'd particularly wanted *Sam* to be sent to Cyprus because his recent experience in Iraq might give him some vital insight, Waddell had said. To rub his nose in it more likely, Sam had decided. To make damned sure he became as intimate with her in death as he had been with her in life.

He knew there was a voyeuristically manipulative side to Kessler – Chrissie had told him. The man took satisfaction in spoiling other people's pleasure when *he* wasn't getting any. Sam had experienced something of it for himself. In the moments after Chrissie had cut him loose in the centre of Barnes Common and he'd spotted Kessler watching his moment of eclipse, there'd been a look of triumph on his face. The eyes behind the round, smeary spectacles had been gloating.

He was out of Larnaca town now, the road cutting through a dry, sandy landscape, its verges punctuated by dusty fig trees and straggly mimosa long past the flowering season. In the far distance a range of hills was taking on the purple-pink hues of dusk.

Sam's eyes kept flicking to the left, looking out for the bar where he was to meet Quentin Mowbray. Soon he spotted the yellow painted sign that said OK Corral and slowed right down before swinging the car onto the square of compressed rubble serving as a parking lot. A terrace at the front of the squat, log-cabin-style building was sheltered from the lowering sun by lengths of rush matting and set with chairs and tables, at one of which sat Mowbray.

The only customer for now, he raised a hand in greeting but didn't stand up. Sam parked the car and locked it, a habit bred from living in a metropolis. Mowbray wore a pale, short-sleeved shirt and grey trousers.

'Hello, Quentin.'

Sam sat down opposite him.

'Hadn't expected to see you again so soon,' Mowbray mumbled uncomfortably. 'Sorry it's under such dreadful circs.'

'Yes.'

Mowbray signalled to a white-shirted waiter who'd emerged from the café at the sound of Sam's car.

'What would you like?'

'A Keo beer,' said Sam.

'Two,' ordered Mowbray.

The waiter took away his empty coffee cup.

'How are you feeling?' Mowbray enquired, with concern. 'All your Baghdad bruises . . .'

'Better. The pain's more mental now,' Sam admitted. 'Been here long?' he asked, turning the conversation away from himself.

'Twenty minutes. It's a faster run from Nicosia than I expected.' Mowbray took a sugar lump from the bowl on the table and toyed with it. 'This is a really bad business, Sam. Must have been a terrible shock for you.'

'Hasn't sunk in. But I'm not out here because I was a friend of hers,' he added defensively.

'God no. I know that.' Mowbray clasped his hands together, as if deciding from now on to restrict his words to business. 'Look, I need to warn you to be very careful about how you operate here. The Cypriots are desperately sensitive. Murdered foreigners are bad news, both for tourism and for the offshore activities which keep this country afloat. When anything goes wrong which might reflect badly on them, their instinct is to conceal and ignore rather than to investigate.'

'I understand all that.' Sam didn't need lectures. 'Have you picked up anything more about Khalil's movements here?'

Mowbray deferred his answer as the waiter appeared with their beers. He paid for them immediately.

'Khalil and his minders seem to have disappeared. Once we'd told the police Chrissie was looking for him because she was in the debt collection business, they naturally wanted to interview them about her death. But too late. They'd gone. And the other problem is that the Central Bank hasn't released details of any offshore companies Khalil might have been involved with. The bank protects its foreign clients' confidentiality pretty fiercely, insisting on clear evidence of financial wrong-doing before being ready to co-operate with the forces of law. London's still working on that, telling them Khalil may have been using his businesses here to circumvent UN sanctions.'

He paused, searching Sam's face for some evidence of what state he was really in behind the mask.

'Shall I tell you what's known about Chrissie?'

Sam swallowed. 'Yes. I think you'd better.'

'Well, as you know, she came over from Amman on Sunday evening. Checked into the Mondiale Hotel in Limassol. Five stars.'

'Nothing but the best,' Sam murmured. Chrissie had always enjoyed spending money, particularly other people's.

'She got lucky,' Mowbray told him. 'Initially anyway. Khalil and his escorts were staying in the Mondiale too.'

'Ah. Handy.'

'So, on Monday she tailed him to the office of a Limassol lawyer specialising in—'

'Offshore businesses. Yes, I know. Waddell told me. What happened then?'

Mowbray sighed. 'Well, that's the trouble. We don't really know. She phoned the lawyer's name through to London in the evening, then dined in the hotel restaurant alone. The head waiter confirmed that to the police and the meal for one was on her unpaid bill, which *I* settled. But what she did on Tuesday is something of a mystery. The police say she was seen in the hotel in the evening, drinking with a couple of high rollers. They suspect she went with them to some casino or other, but haven't identified the men or the place.'

'Could those high rollers have been the Iraqis?'
'You tell me. All we know is her bed wasn't slept in Tuesday night. Then, on Wednesday, at about five in the morning, she – her corpse – was found by a police patrol checking for stolen cars in a car park by the waterfront.'
'Where?' Sam croaked, wincing at the word 'corpse'. 'Where exactly was this?'
Mowbray unfolded a map of Limassol and spread it on the table.
'Here,' he pointed. 'Bang in the centre of the main promenade. The buildings overlooking it are mostly offices – empty during the night.'
'Shit . . .' breathed Sam. It was getting to him now. Mowbray's matter-of-factness was bringing it home. 'Where is she – her body?'
'At the Limassol morgue. The autopsy this morning was incomplete. Something unclear still about the way she died. Choking apparently, but no sign of pressure on the throat or anything. Just some bruises on her body and stress marks on the wrists and ankles suggesting she'd been tied up at some stage. So they were doing more tests. But we're moving her tomorrow hopefully. Back to the UK on the RAF Herc that shuttles to Lyneham every Friday. A funeral's being set up for Saturday. A private one. Just family, I'm told. Martin Kessler wants it over with quickly before the media realise the body's even left the island.'
'I'd like to see her.' The words slipped out.
'Yes, I imagined you would. Best if you wait until she's moved to the RAF base at Akrotiri. I've passed your cover name to a Squadron Leader Banks. Give him a ring first.' He wrote the number down on a page from a notebook.
'Don't the police have any witnesses?' Sam asked in exasperation. '*Somebody* must have seen something.'
'Well they may have by now, but they've not told us.'

Mowbray leaned back in the chair and folded his arms. 'The man in charge is an Anoteros Ypastinomos – a chief inspector to you and me – but he's no ball of fire. Got where he is through family connections. Father was an EOKA folk-hero in the nineteen-fifties. Killed a couple of British soldiers during the independence struggle but was never nailed for it. The son isn't much keener on the British than the father was. Not exactly making waves for us. But he's the High Commission's problem, not yours. For what it's worth I'll be getting an update tonight. I'll ring you later. Where are you staying?'

'I'll try the Mondiale,' Sam answered automatically.

'Of course.'

Mowbray lifted an eyebrow. Then he leaned forward again, placing his elbows on the table. A hand went to his mouth and he nibbled unconsciously at a nail as if debating how to phrase the next part of what he had to say.

'There's something else you ought to know, but don't for heaven's sake jump to any conclusions on this one. There's no proof of any connection.'

'Connection? With what?'

'With Khalil's visit to Cyprus.'

'You're talking riddles.'

'Sorry. There . . . there's been a report from the UN Special Commission in Baghdad.'

'Anthrax!'

'Well, yes, actually. They've found evidence the Iraqis *have* been producing biological weapons grade material in the past few weeks. The man in charge of the production committed suicide when they exposed him.'

'Did he!' He felt a certain satisfaction at what Mowbray was telling him, vindication of his belief that the message whispered to him in Baghdad *was* genuine. He leaned forward. 'Tell me more.'

'UNSCOM have had a team in Iraq for the past few

days. They're pulling out this afternoon. The Iraqis have withdrawn all co-operation.'

'But what exactly have they got?'

'Look, it's only the sort of evidence they always knew they *would* find one day.'

'Quentin!'

'No, Sam. Just because some unidentified man in Baghdad whispered a warning to you about anthrax weapons being smuggled out of the country does not mean there's a link. All this proves is the Iraqis are still experimenting with the stuff despite all their denials. It'll slap on the head any chance of UN sanctions being lifted in the near future, so it's of major political significance. But what UNSCOM has *not* uncovered is any evidence the Iraqis were planning to use the stuff. And when we're talking about biological weapons capabilities, it's *intentions* that matter more than anything else.'

Sam held his breath. He wasn't hearing Mowbray's words any more. In his head the links were clear, creating a conspiracy theory that was frightening in its potential.

'There could be a link,' he began.

'No evidence, Sam,' Mowbray insisted. 'No evidence.'

'Let's just play with a scenario.'

Mowbray shrugged uncomfortably.

'Let's imagine the anthrax production the UN uncovered *was* for warheads that have already been sneaked out of Iraq. And let's imagine also that the people who imprisoned me in Baghdad are directly involved in the scheme to use the warheads.'

'That's stretching credibility. They were just security men as far as we know.'

'But Quentin, their direct involvement is the only way I can explain why they were so damned desperate for me not to have found out about the anthrax.'

'It's not the way London sees it.'

'Bugger London. Look, suppose I'm right. Now,

getting anthrax out of the country would be no great problem considering the leakiness of the Jordan border. The hard bit is to get the weapon to the right target at the right time for maximum effect. And for that they might need money. A lot of it. So *that* could be why Khalil was brought to Cyprus. For them to use the cash stashed away in the accounts he controlled in order to buy whatever help they needed to carry out the attack.'

'Hypothetical speculation,' said Mowbray dismissively.

'Sure, but plausible. Now, follow that on. Chrissie turns up suddenly. She gets too close. Learns something that could wreck the Iraqis' whole scheme. Learns perhaps how the money was to be spent. So they kill her.'

Mowbray pursed his lips and blew out. 'I have to tell you that the feeling in London is that the money Khalil was brought here to free up was for something much more probable, namely to finance another palace for Saddam Hussein.' He flattened his hands together and touched them against his lips. His grey eyes had lost their certainty, however.

Sam downed the rest of his beer. The instinct that he was right and the great minds in London were wrong was powering him forward like a Californian surf.

'Facts, old man,' Mowbray growled at him. 'We *must* deal in facts and not suppositions.'

'Okay. Hang around and I'll bring you some.' Sam stood up, refolding the map Mowbray had spread on the table. 'I can have this?'

'Sure. But where are you going so suddenly?'

'Wherever it was Chrissie went.'

The Limassol highway skirted the foothills of the Troodos mountains, its two-lane dual carriageway almost free of traffic. Pulling down the blind to protect his eyes from the last of the crimson sun, Sam glanced right towards the purple heights of Mount Olympus which would be capped by snow in a matter of weeks. As the car dipped over a ridge, Limassol's hotels and apartment blocks appeared ahead, a hazy holiday and business conurbation which stood ugly and square against the leaching red of the horizon.

Junction 21 was signposted and Sam dropped his speed. The Mondiale Hotel was on the beach well short of the town itself. He turned left, then left again onto the old coast road. The entrance was down a winding drive lined with flower-beds and bungalows. The parking areas were mostly full, but he found a space, then took his bag into the spacious lobby.

It was a hotel of a type he was well familiar with, making its living from conference facilities. And there was a business group resident at the moment, he noted, judging by the clusters of young people in crisp shirts and neatly pressed blouses standing around, their chests decked with name badges.

After his 'Terry Malone' credit card had been swiped for the bill he took the lift to the third floor. No sea views available, they'd told him, and seemed surprised that he didn't care. He dumped his holdall on the double bed, then peered from the window down into the car park. It was after six by now and visiting businessmen who'd had dealings in Limassol during the day were returning to their five-star roost.

He closed the heavy beige curtains, unzipped the holdall and pulled out his wash-bag. He took a quick shower, then ran a battery shaver over his chin and dressed in dark grey trousers and the light check jacket that didn't crease which he always travelled with. Then, looking like any other businessman dressed for whatever the night might bring, he took the lift to the ground floor and sauntered into the lobby, racking his brains to think how Chrissie would have set about her task here four days earlier.

He heard a babble of bright young voices from the far side of the wide lounge. A long, narrow bar overlooking the pool and closed off with a crimson rope was crammed with conference delegates in dark suits and cocktail dresses, all animated, all still wearing their name labels. Tupperware reps, Sam guessed, although they could have been Mormons for all he knew. He strolled over to take a closer look and collided with someone heading in the same direction.

'Sorry! *So* sorry.' A young woman with straight blonde hair tied in a short pony tail whose otherwise appealing face was dulled by a receding chin, grabbed at his arm to steady herself. 'So *terribly* sorry. Wasn't looking where I was going.'

Something told Sam the collision hadn't been entirely accidental.

'My fault entirely,' he answered courteously. She had a trim, tidy figure encased in a low-cut black dress. 'Are you all right?'

'Yes of course. You going to the reception?' She shot a glance at his lapel. 'Oh no. No badge.'

'Wish I was,' he beamed, mind on autopilot.

'Well . . .'

It was all she said. Her eyebrows fluttered a couple of times as if to suggest that it wouldn't be hard to gate-crash, but he didn't react.

'Well, have a good evening anyway.'

'Yes. You too.'

He watched her disappear into the throng beyond the crimson rope, then turned to take in the expanse of the lobby.

How would Chrissie have stalked Khalil? Once she'd made the happy discovery that he was resident here, would she have just waited for the Iraqis to come down from their rooms? Waited where? On one of the velvet sofas in the lobby? A stool in the bar? And when Khalil appeared, how had she observed him? There were two ways to watch a mark. Unseen from a distance or right up close. Getting close was Chrissie's style.

Sam continued his slow perambulation of the lobby, deciding his eventual destination would be the still-empty cocktail bar tucked round a corner beyond the reception desk. Suddenly his eye was caught by a pin-board set up on an easel to one side of the main entrance. Photographs. He crossed over to look. Pictures taken at some gathering earlier in the week, each with a number. A notice said prints could be ordered at the reception desk.

Then he saw the date. Tuesday – the night Chrissie had disappeared. His pulse quickened.

The prints were standard six by fours, about twenty-five in number. A mix of faces in the shots. Some dark and heavy with Cypriot features, others quintessentially English. And a few that looked more Middle Eastern.

He pulled from his jacket pocket the small photo of Salah Khalil that Waddell had given him and began to scan the prints for any sign of him, or of Chrissie. He began at the top left corner of the board and worked systematically. Jolly faces with smiles like open zips, snapped in the bar and the lounge. Some revellers faced away from the camera, some were obscured by others. He became distracted by the varying states of inebriation displayed. A few weren't drunk at all – prim faces, hands clutching glasses of juice. Others seemed bent on flushing away inhibitions with heavy doses of spirits.

He reached the bottom right corner. There'd been no sign of Chrissie and no face that looked like Khalil's. Then he remembered it was on Tuesday that the Iraqis had checked out – Khalil *couldn't* have been here. He was about to look through the set again in case Chrissie was somewhere in the background of the shots, when a woman's voice cut in from behind him.

'Looks fun.'

Sam spun round. It was the blonde girl with the receding chin and the compact body. She stood a foot away, smirking at him.

'Were you there? That party,' she elaborated, lifting her mildly embarrassed face towards the photos. 'I wondered if you were in one of the pictures.' She laughed a little nervously, covering her jaw with a hand as if to conceal its inadequacies.

'No,' he replied. 'Not me. Just looking to see if I could spot any friends. You?'

'No. Only arrived yesterday.'

She beamed a smile, then waited as if to say *This is the second time I've made a move on you mister. Now it's your turn.*

Sam stared back like a dummy. He didn't want this distraction.

Confronted with his blank response, she decided to plunge in again anyway.

'Look, I was wondering . . . You see, some of us from the company are making our escape from the do over there.' She flicked a glance back towards the bar she'd just left, and her pony tail swished and bounced. 'Bit of a yawn really and the chief exec's about to make a speech which is really, *really* going to kill it stone dead. So we're taking off for a bite to eat somewhere, then a club. And we're short of one bloke.'

Sam looked past her and saw a couple standing a safe distance away trying to conceal their embarrassment at her forwardness by staring through the glass doors into the hotel drive.

'And, um, since you seemed to be on your own,' she concluded, in so deep now that she couldn't turn back, 'and you looked friendly . . .'

She coloured even further and laughed again, the hand darting to her mouth once more.

Sam beamed. 'Now, normally that's the sort of invitation I wouldn't dream of refusing. Unfortunately, there's somebody I have to meet this evening.'

'Oh. Pity.' She flattened her lips to conceal her disappointment. Her eyes showed she thought he was giving her the brush off. 'Ah well . . . just thought I'd give you a try.'

'Thanks. Normally, as I say . . .'

She began to move back to her friends.

'Maybe I can make it later,' he called after her.

Daft. There wouldn't be any *later*. Not for that sort of thing anyway.

'Club's called the Paradiso,' she called back over her shoulder, pushing at the swing door. 'And I'm Sophie.'

Then she was gone.

He turned back towards the board of prints. There was one in particular that had intrigued him at the first look. Two men and one woman at a table, she with her back to the lens, one man beside her, the other opposite, facing the camera. The man was leaning in towards the woman, one hand resting on hers, the other clutching a highball of ice and some dark spirit. A face built round a wide, leathery mouth in which the top front teeth sparkled with silver. He had close-cropped, wiry hair and wore a black roll-neck shirt and white jacket. The pebble-hard eyes weren't quite in line. One of them might have been glass. The tense set of the woman's shoulders suggested the man's advances weren't entirely welcome.

Metal teeth. There was only one place in the world where Sam had seen dentistry like that – the former Soviet Union.

The man had the looks of a Mafiya hood from central casting. Here to launder money, no doubt, some of which he was spending on a hooker by the look of it. Quite classy for a tart, the woman was. He couldn't see her face, but she had shiny, chestnut-brown hair. Gold earrings. Wearing a cream jacket that could have been linen.

Suddenly he felt the ground open.

'Oh my God,' he croaked.

Cream – linen – jacket. Jacket and matching skirt. The outfit Chrissie had been wearing in Amman. The suit from Prada she'd been so damned proud of. The shining hair, the shoulders tightly hunched – yes, she *did* that when she was tense.

'Shit!'

It *was* Chrissie.

Photographed on the night she was murdered.

17

His moistening eyes bored into the photo, unconsciously trying to draw her essence from the picture as if sucking moisture from a grain of wheat. He flicked a fingernail under the pin holding it to the board. He needed to have this picture like he'd needed *her* on Sunday in Amman. But more than that, it was the key to her death. He secreted it in the inside pocket of his jacket, turned to check no one had seen him do so, then, stifling his emotions, crossed the lobby to a corner seat where he could study it.

Did the police have a copy of this? he wondered. Had they identified the high roller who had his hand on hers? And the second male in the group, sitting on Chrissie's right also back to camera – also Russian? Why? *Why* had she been with these characters?

Sam studied the body language. The second man wore a green jacket and sat all square and straight, as if keeping his face from the camera had been his intention. Not a freckle showing. Same with Chrissie. Both of them squaring their shoulders to the lens to ensure their features weren't captured on film. Interesting.

He tried to work out where they'd been sitting. Beyond the group was a darker area where the camera's flash had hardly reached. About half a dozen bodies there, some seated, some standing by the bar counter. One man on his own looking towards the table where Chrissie sat, his face no more than a shadow.

Sam stood up again and moved towards the cocktail bar, easily locating the table in question, now occupied by a couple who weren't speaking to one another. He approached the counter and perched on a stool.

'A beer,' Sam ordered from the slim, crinkly-haired barman.

'Tuborg Export?'

'Keo, if you have it.'

The barman ducked down to the refrigerated cabinet, then plonked the bottle and a glass on the varnished mahogany bar top.

'Nice bar,' Sam commented chattily. 'Worked here a long time?'

'Me? Too long, sir.'

The man laughed and wiped the counter with a cloth. Then he nudged a bowl of crisps so that it slid along the varnish under its own momentum, stopping precisely in front of Sam.

'Neat,' Sam mouthed.

'But next month – finish,' the barman continued, ignoring his compliment.

'Really? Where are you going?'

'London, sir. Piccadilly.'

'Same hotel group?'

'Yessir. Better pay and more tips.' He flashed his straight, white teeth.

'But your regulars here – they'll miss you, I expect.'

'Of course.' He took it as a statement of the obvious rather than a tribute.

'Or perhaps you don't have regulars. Being a hotel.'

'Oh yes. Many regulars. This very smart place. Smartest in Limassol. Many rich people who live here, they come for drinks in the evening.'

'But I don't suppose you ever get to know them. I mean, their names.'

'Sometimes. Depends. They give me good tip, I take an interest in their name.'

'I see.' Sam took the photo from his pocket. 'Maybe you can help me then. There's a man I'm trying to contact.' He pointed to the face in the photo.

'You police?' the barman asked, not looking at the picture.

'Good heavens no. I did some business with him once but can't remember his name, that's all.'

'Because police, you see they already been here ask questions.'

'About *him*?'

'Sure. Because of Mrs Taylor. You know? She the Englishwoman who was killed. She stay here, in this hotel. Sat just over there.' He pointed to the table where the silent couple sat. 'I remember her, because she beautiful woman.'

'Haven't heard much about it,' Sam said, trying to sound just mildly curious. 'What happened?'

'Yesterday they find the body. Dressed in skirt but no pants, you know?' The barman leaned forward meaningfully, dark eyes concentrating on Sam. 'Police they look for the men she was with here, but me, I think maybe British soldiers do it. Often they drink too much at night-club, then become like animals. And take drugs.' He flicked a hand in the air to show that such people were beneath his contempt.

Sam swallowed hard. 'Why? Why d'you think it was soldiers?'

'Because I don't like them,' the barman answered, moving away to deal with another customer. Two Greek-speaking women also arrived at the bar and quickly monopolised his attention.

Sam looked down at the photo. It wasn't soldiers who'd killed her. He sensed that in his hand he held a picture of the men who had.

Eventually the barman finished serving and began polishing glasses.

'My friend,' Sam called to him.

'Yes, sir.' He checked to see if Sam's glass was empty.

'Do you know this man's name?'

He held out the print, but the barman ignored it and picked up the towel again.

'I don't know. Maybe. I don't know if I can help . . .'

Sam took a Cyprus ten-pound note from his pocket and laid it flat on the counter next to the print.

'Okay. I have another look.'

The barman covered the money with his hand and slipped it into his pocket. He took the photo to the cash register so he could look at it under a better light.

'He been here many times,' he announced.

'Yes?'

'Yeah. He's the one the police want to find. But they *never*,' he added contemptuously.

'What d'you mean?'

'Our police not very clever. They ask his name, but we don't know it. Nobody know it.'

Thanks for taking my money anyway, thought Sam.

'He's Russian, I think, so anyway, name is impossible to pronounce.' The barman screwed up his face. 'He always like that.' He tapped the photo with a finger. 'Drink very much and always with different girl. Prostitute, you know? Romania, Bulgaria – pffh. Normally we don't serve such women. But when they with *him* . . .' He raised his shoulders in despair. 'Manager say I must serve. Because he spend lot of money in bar and restaurant. Always cash – so they don't even get his name from credit card slip,' he confided.

'He wasn't a guest in the hotel?'

'No. He just come here for drink and restaurant. Many Russians have apartment in Limassol. They come here for few days then go back to Russia, you understand why?'

'Money.'

'Of course. Sometime one Russian he live with three or four dirty girls, you know? Live off them like pimp. But this man I think is different. I think he very rich. Maybe he have big villa here. You see them – many, many big, big houses. On the roads to Troodos.'

'Has he been here again, since Tuesday?'

'No. Maybe we don't see him ever again here because he know the police look for him now. In Limassol there are other place, many restaurant, many club where Russians go.'

'Any in particular? If I wanted to try to find him tonight, where should I look?'

The barman scowled as if it would be a waste of an evening. 'If I was him I go back to Russia by now. But you can try Paradiso Club,' he said. 'But later on. Ten, eleven o'clock maybe. They have girls there who dance in your face, you know?' He cupped hands in front of his chest to denote the dancers were topless. 'What you call it what they wear? I work in south France one time. They call it cache-sex. You know what I mean?'

'I know,' Sam nodded.

'You put fifty pounds in – in wherever you find some place to put it,' he smirked, 'then after the show maybe she go with you. S'long you don't mind get sick after,' he warned. 'Many these girls have HIV. And make sure you don't bring back here to Mondiale. Because night manager he not let her in.'

'Don't worry. Thanks.'

'But I don't tell you any of this. Understand me? Because I don't trust that man. He could do anything, you know?'

The barman snapped to attention as another customer

arrived. Sam pocketed the photograph, finished his beer and headed for the elevators.

Back in his room he placed the photograph under a desk lamp. He stood staring at it for a full half minute. Then he backed off, crossing to the window. He looked down into the car park wondering if he was deluding himself. It was all assumptions. Two and two make five. There was no proof this was Chrissie's killer.

The central question was *why*. Why when she was in Cyprus to observe three Iraqis had she let her attention be diverted by a Russian? There was one reason, of course. The only one that made sense the more he thought of it. The reason was that her investigation of the activities of Salah Khalil had led her to the Russian. Khalil and this man in the photo had done business together. But what sort? A contract to supply gold-plated toilet bowls for Saddam Hussein's latest palace? Or something more sinister. Something like the technical and logistical assistance the Iraqis needed to ensure their anthrax weapon reached its target.

Or was he letting his imagination run crazy?

He picked up the phone and dialled room service. When the number answered he ordered a club sandwich and a beer.

Just two days ago, Chrissie had been here in this hotel. In this very room for all he knew. He closed his eyes, trying to feel her presence, but there was nothing. Just an emptiness inside him.

The phone rang. He half expected it to be room service saying there was a problem.

'Sam?' Mowbray's voice.

'Yes.'

'I've got something for you. Perhaps you could ring me from a call box?'

'Sure. You're in the office?'

'I will be in half an hour.'

'Fine.'

He rang off, his heart jumping. Mowbray had sounded low.

The door bell chimed. He let in the waiter, scribbled his signature on the bill and gave the man a pound.

Twenty-nine minutes later he stopped the red Toyota next to a call box outside a pizza restaurant a couple of kilometres along the coast road into Limassol. Mowbray answered immediately on his direct line.

'There's been a development from the police,' he announced without preamble. 'I told you they'd come up with some trick to avoid a proper investigation.'

'What, for God's sake?'

There was a pause at the other end of the line.

'I'll be blunt. Chrissie had had sex with someone, Sam. Some time around the time of her death. There was, you know, semen in her.'

Sam bit his lip. His mind flashed, remembering the feel of her body on him last Sunday.

'The police doing DNA tests on it?' he asked, trying to sound matter-of-fact.

'I don't know. The man at the High Commission here didn't ask. Look, the police pathologist insists there's no sign of brute force being used. On the relevant parts of her body, I mean.'

Sam closed his eyes.

'No bruising, no contusions,' Mowbray continued, as if treading on eggshells. 'No sign of forced entry.'

'Hang on. What d'you mean no signs of force? Didn't you tell me earlier there were bruises on the body and marks on her wrists and ankles as if she'd been tied up?'

'Ye-es.'

'Well?'

'They're saying they believe that could have been voluntary. Part of the er, part of what they were doing.'

Sam held the phone away from his ear. He took in a deep breath, then spoke firmly into the mouthpiece.

'No, Quentin. That's simply not on.' Chrissie wasn't into S&M.

'Well, it's what they're saying. She was seen in the hotel earlier that evening with some heavy drinkers they haven't been able to identify. The bottom line is that they think she was having a wild night on the town which just went wrong.'

'*Just?* She ended up half naked in a car park, for Christ's sake!'

'They're putting that down to panic on the part of the man, or men, she was with. They think she might have been, you know.' Mowbray sighed, acutely uncomfortable in such territory. 'Well, that they were actually *doing* it when she had the seizure.'

'What *seizure*? What the hell are you talking about?'

'Because of the nuts she'd eaten. Peanuts. Apparently she had an acute allergy.'

'*Peanuts?* Oh my God,' Sam mouthed, remembering things that Chrissie had told him years ago.

'They found bits of nut in her stomach and mouth. That and vodka. She'd not eaten anything else. The police pathologist's theory is that she realised she'd drunk far too much and when things started to go a bit further than she meant she grabbed the only food available to try to blunt the effects of the booze.'

'That's insane.'

'Anaphylactic shock. There's no question of any doubt about cause of death apparently. They're claiming it was an accident, Sam. Just a dreadful, horrific accident.'

18

The main beach road through Limassol had a depressing end of season feel to it. Against a backdrop of dark, empty tower blocks, a dribble of late holidaymakers in pale fawns and greys defied the autumn chill, searching restaurant menu boards for novelty in a cuisine that was all too standardised.

Sam aimed the car towards the centre of town, weighed down by the unfolding horror of Chrissie's demise. Accidental death was nonsense and he'd told Mowbray so. There was no way she would have touched a peanut, however drunk she might have been. To do so would be suicide for her and she'd known it only too well. If there were peanuts in her stomach it was because somebody else had pushed them down her throat. Someone who knew that to do so would kill her.

Since the phone call with Mowbray, Sam had struggled to shut out the personal in what was happening. The details of Chrissie's death would bury him if he let them.

He had another reason for not allowing his thoughts free rein. There was a quality in Chrissie he'd never wanted to acknowledge, a ruthlessness that could take her past the bounds of normal human restraint. To get what she wanted she would use every asset she had. If it was information she'd been after from the Russian on Tuesday night and had been using her body to extract it from him, then it wouldn't have been the first time she'd resorted to that.

He shook his head like a dog.

It was approaching nine. Too early in the evening for the Paradiso Club. He drove into the downtown area, past fish restaurants half-obscured by parked-up Suzukis and BMWs. He turned by the floodlit medieval castle, passed a winery and the old port, and headed down the promenade to where Chrissie's body had been found.

There was a quiet prosperity about Limassol. Young, dark-haired men in jeans and leather jackets perched with their leggy, lipsticked girls on chromed scooters outside bars and fast-food restaurants. Mopeds and small four-wheel-drives zipped about like flies round a fish market.

He pulled into a car park and checked Mowbray's map to ensure he'd identified the right one. He switched off and opened the door. The place was less than half full and most of it was in deep darkness, the only illumination coming from street lamps on the promenade a short distance away. He sat there listening – for what he didn't know. He sniffed the air. Salt and decay; the sea was just beyond a narrow stretch of park. No other smell. He realised that subconsciously he'd been expecting one – a trace of her smoke-tainted perfume.

Had she *died* here, in this bleak rectangle of cracking tarmac, he wondered analytically? Probably not. Anaphylactic shock acted quickly. She'd have died in whatever place it was they'd forced the peanuts into her.

He tried to feel the reality of it but couldn't. Still couldn't believe in his heart of hearts that she didn't exist any more.

He became practical again, looking about him. As Mowbray had said, the buildings along the promenade that overlooked this place were offices. No one to see a body being dragged from the back of a car in the small hours of the morning.

The body of a woman in an early stage of pregnancy.

'Fuck!'

He got back into the car and switched on. This was not a place for him to be.

The Paradiso throbbed to a disco beat that hurt his ears. He'd never liked night-clubs, particularly this kind where sex was offered with the finesse of a cocktail with a sparkler stuck in it.

The ten pounds he'd paid on the door entitled him to one free drink. He selected a small unoccupied table close to the exit and was confronted by a broad-hipped waitress in black fishnet tights and a clinging top in see-through black chiffon. Her unfettered breasts beneath the tissue reminded him of steamed puddings topped with raisins.

'Just a beer,' he said, giving her his drinks coupon.

'Jus' one?' she asked, checking him out and glancing at the empty chair beside him. 'You all 'lone tonight?'

'My boyfriend's joining me later,' he replied stonily.

She pursed her bright-red lips and shimmied away in rhythm to the music.

The walls of the club, which had the size and shape of a large garage, were painted black. Tall, artificial palm trees marked the corners of a woodblock floor on which a handful of couples danced under the UV lights. On the dimly lit stage at the far end of the room a bilingual DJ sat behind a bank of equipment, almost fellating the microphone through which he announced the tracks.

It was just after ten. Thirty or so tables in the place, fewer than half occupied. In a club that might hold two or three hundred, a quick tot-up suggested less than fifty customers in so far, most of them men in groups of three or four. Sam slid low in the chrome-framed chair hoping to avoid being seen by the blonde pony-tailed woman from the hotel who'd said she would be here. Another check suggested she and her friends hadn't arrived yet. No sign of the man in the photo either.

The waitress returned with the beer.

'Anythin' else you wan', you jus' call me okay?' she grinned cheesily, shouting above the noise of the music. 'My name Ellie. I your waitress for the evening. You want anything, you tell me and I fix. We got great dancers tonight. I send one over for you later?'

'Any of them fellers?' he asked insouciantly.

'No,' she laughed, not convinced he was serious. 'But sexy girls. You never try girls?'

He beckoned her closer.

'Where you from, Ellie? How long you work here?'

'I come Nicosia. An' I work here jus' few month,' she explained, bending over him on the off chance that a closer examination of her chest might arouse some cash-generating interest.

'Oh, right. Only a few months. You see I'm looking for someone. Friend of mine. Comes here a lot, I think. But if you've only been working here a short time . . .'

'Wass he look like? He gay boy?'

'No. I don't think so. Rather the opposite. Can I show you a photo?'

'If you want.'

One corner of the print was bent over now from being pushed in and out of his pocket. He pointed at the face in the middle. She bent forward, then recoiled sharply. She stood up abruptly, shaking her head.

'No. Never see him.'

She scowled and turned smartly away. The face in the photo meant trouble and she didn't want any of it. She hurried off in search of another table to deal with.

'Bet your mum doesn't know you work here,' Sam murmured, putting the photo back in his jacket.

So he *was* in the right place to find this man – if he was still in Cyprus. This *killer*. He would need to be careful. He sipped at his beer. The club was filling up. Half a dozen lads with heavy shoulders and short haircuts barged in, beady eyes on the search for mischief. They had 'British squaddie' written all over them. Materialising from the shadows, a couple of girls wearing leather skirts of pelmet length homed in, scenting business but not appearing to relish it.

More customers arrived in a steady stream, mostly men. He locked his eyes onto each new face, scanning it for the features in the photograph, features now fixed in his mind like a scar. No sign of the man, but all of a sudden the blonde called Sophie walked in. Still accompanied by her two work colleagues, the girl from the hotel was no longer without a partner, clinging to the arm of a dark-haired smoothie in a navy blazer. There'd be a BMW outside, Sam guessed. Or maybe a Ferrari. Proof, were it ever needed, that persistence pays off.

The girl, however, was looking around as if the man she'd caught wasn't quite the sort of fish she'd been after. She spotted Sam. The diminutive lower jaw dropped an inch, merging with her stalk of a neck. She managed an embarrassed smile, then nudged her friends, who turned to look. Sam waved but stayed put.

She broke away from her new-found partner and crossed to his table.

'You made it!' she shouted, her voice straining to beat the music. 'Didn't think you would.'

'So I see,' Sam grinned.

'Oh come on, don't be like that,' she laughed.

'Anyway, you're no longer short of a bloke.'

'That's um, that's Nico.' She shrugged as if saying she didn't really know him. 'Bumped into him at a bar we've just been in. Look, won't you join us anyway?' she suggested, colouring.

'Don't worry about it. I'm looking out for someone. A chap who's supposed to come here a lot.'

He could see she didn't believe him and was convinced he'd really come here because of her.

'Amazing coincidence meeting Nico,' she explained uncomfortably, 'because we sort of know him. He chaired a seminar this afternoon. About lettings. We're travel trade, you see.'

'Ah, yes.'

'And you?'

'Trade fairs. Exhibitions.'

'Interesting.'

'Sometimes.'

'Well . . .'

'You go back to your friends,' he suggested. 'I'll pop over in a minute.'

'Great. Thanks for being so understanding.'

'No problem.'

The blonde pony tail jerked and danced as she looked round to see where her party had got to.

'Name's Terry, by the way,' he added, before she moved away. He held out his hand.

'I like the name Terry,' she commented. Her handshake was on the limp side. 'See you in a minute then.'

She crinkled her face as if saying she'd much rather be spending the evening with *him* than Nico. Another flash of a smile and she was gone.

Sam watched her trim figure cross towards the bar, weaving between the tables with deliberate slowness. Nice enough girl, he thought. And keen for it. There'd been a few like her that he'd scored with over the years. But relationships like that could never become close. When the woman started asking questions he would finish it, before she began to suspect what he really did for a living. That was why it had lasted with Chrissie. No need for secrecy with her. *One* of the reasons it had lasted . . .

He drained his beer glass. The bosomy waitress was nowhere to be seen. Out of the corner of an eye he saw one of the whores who'd targeted the soldiers a few minutes ago heading his way. She stopped by his table, one hand on the back of the second chair.

'Hello.' Her green eyes, black-ringed with mascara were cold and unsmiling. 'Like to buy me a drink?'

'No.'

A hooker rejected by a squad of randy soldiers couldn't have much going for her. The girl twisted her mouth in annoyance.

He stood up and moved to the bar. The crowd by the counter was three deep. He edged along the throng as if looking for a way through, but in reality was checking faces again. Still nothing. This was pointless. The Russian had probably left the country like the Mondiale barman had said.

Sophie, in the midst of the crush and pretending to her companion that she was interested in what he was saying, caught his eye suddenly and beamed broadly.

Sam pushed towards her.

'Get you a drink?' he shouted, still a couple of bodies away.

'Brandy and coke would be ace.'

'And your friends?'

She held up four fingers and grimaced.

'We're all on the same.'

Sam spotted a gap to his right and elbowed to the counter. The barman was serving someone at the far end. Sam held out a banknote to draw his attention. To his left and right the other customers were mostly in their twenties and thirties, mostly not Cypriot. The barman acknowledged his presence and headed his way, stopping briefly to collect used glasses and dunk them in a sink. Sam glanced to his right again. There was an older man standing a couple of metres distant. Late forties, he guessed. The same sort of age as the Russian in the photo. On his own. Seemed a little preoccupied. And there was something familiar about the face . . .

'Yes, sir?'

Sam looked at the barman, but his mind still saw the man to his right.

'Yes . . .'

He shot a glance sideways again. The scar on the cheek shaped like the letter Y – yes. He'd seen it before. That lopsided jaw too. He knew this man. But where the hell from?

The barman tapped the counter. 'Sir? What you want to drink?'

'Er . . .' Sam stared back as if paralysed. 'Four er . . .'

That face. He knew that damned face. And the man was wearing a green jacket for God's sake, like the creature who'd been sitting with his back to the camera next to Chrissie in the photo.

Jesus! He knew who it was.

He whipped his eyes right again, but the other man had seen him too. He banged his glass on the counter and pushed off the bar stool, startled.

'Hey . . .' Sam croaked. 'Viktor!'

Viktor Rybkin. Last seen in a gangster-filled steam-bath in Kiev a year ago.

'Four what, sir?' the barman demanded, increasingly irritated.

'Nothing,' mouthed Sam, turning away, his muscles tensing. 'Sorry . . .'

Rybkin was shoving away from the bar, jolting elbows, spilling drinks, then propelling himself across the dance square. The lights of an emergency door glowed on the far side.

'Shit!'

Sam barged through the crowd after him, knocking glasses, crushing toes, his eyes locked on the green jacket slipping away beneath the amber smear of the exit sign. The door banged shut before he could reach it. He thumped on the bar and pushed. It opened a hand's breadth then stopped, blocked by something. He threw his weight against it but the object wouldn't budge. Cursing, he spun round and barged his way back through the club, aiming for the main exit.

'Terry!' Sophie's voice, screeching as he passed the bar.

Ignoring her he ran past the cash desk in the lobby, and through the main door. Outside, a clutch of elderly tourists was timidly examining tease shots of the dancers in a display panel.

He stopped on the paving. The narrow lane was a turning off Ayiou Andhreou, Limassol's main street. Disorientated in the jumble of low-rise shops and flats, he tried to work out the location of the emergency exit Rybkin had used. It had to be in a parallel alley. He began to run.

Twenty paces to the main drag. He heard the heavy clunk of a car door shutting. As he emerged into Ayiou Andhreou, headlights blazed on dead ahead. A large, pale-coloured saloon parked on the far side began to jerk back and forth, frantically nudging the vehicles that were wedging it in. Sam darted towards it. The side window was down and the driver was Viktor Rybkin.

'Viktor!' he yelled.

The tinted-glass window of the old-gold Lexus slid shut. With a final wrench of the wheel and a nudge of bumpers Rybkin broke free from the parking slot and accelerated away.

'Shit!'

Where the hell had he left his own car? He snorted; it was one of the vehicles the Lexus had been shunting. He fumbled for the key and stabbed it at the door-lock, then threw himself behind the wheel and started up.

The Lexus was well out of sight by now, but he shot after it anyway. The road was narrow and one way. A crossroads stopped him. Left, right, straight on? Hadn't a clue. He'd lost the bastard.

'Jees-us!' he hissed.

Viktor Rybkin – ex-KGB, now of the Ukrainian SBU security service. A man Chrissie had called a 'good friend' during the drugs fiasco in Kiev a year ago. A man she'd trusted and he hadn't. And Rybkin had been with her two days ago, on the night she was murdered. *And*, Sam remembered suddenly from their conversation in Kiev a year ago, Rybkin knew about Chrissie's peanut allergy. They'd been in a bar together and she'd told him.

A taxi hooted him from behind.

'Which way? Where the fuck are you, Viktor?' he yelled.

He chose right, towards the coast road, guessing that if Rybkin had been running back to wherever he was staying in Limassol, then it would be somewhere near the sea. At the coastal promenade he hung a left towards where most of the hotels and apartments were. Eyes raking the kerbs of the palm-lined promenade, he cruised slowly, looking for the Lexus.

He drove for a couple of kilometres but there was no sign of the car. Worse than looking for a needle in a haystack. Pointless him driving around all night. He pulled up to think, parking outside a prestigious-looking apartment block. He debated whether he should get the police involved, but remembered Mowbray's derogatory comments. And anyway, the manhunt he was engaged in was personal. And becoming more so by the minute.

But could he be wrong? Was he chasing a phantom? Was it some other man in a green jacket Chrissie had been with? He clicked the vanity light and pulled out the photo. Nothing of the man's face was visible in the picture – just his back square on to the camera. But a broad back. The build was right. And the age, the hair – yes. Rybkin. He was bloody sure of it now.

But *why* Rybkin? What the hell was a senior officer in the Ukrainian SBU doing in Cyprus? He could be on the trail of Mafiya money being laundered here. Which would put a different perspective on things, he realised.

Suddenly it occurred to him that his whole scenario of what had happened on Tuesday night could be wrong. Maybe there was no link between the men Chrissie had been with and the Iraqis. Maybe the money being unleashed by Salah Khalil *was* to finance a palace rather than an anthrax attack. Maybe the whole anthrax business *was* a phantasm – just a hook, as London suspected. Chrissie *could* have met Rybkin here purely by chance. Could have been having a drink with him and the man with the silver teeth for social reasons – not unfeasible in this age of collaboration between former enemies. It *could* just have been a night out that went tragically wrong as the police suspected.

Yet she hadn't reported in on Tuesday. So totally unlike her. Chrissie was punctilious professionally.

No. There were too many oddities for there to be simple answers to any of this.

Suddenly he sat bolt upright. A car had popped up from a ramp in front of him, the exit from an underground car park. It turned on to the promenade and pulled away fast.

A Lexus. Colour – old gold.

19

The lexus drove fast, taking the ring road through the anonymous spread of functional architecture that was northern Limassol. To right and left showrooms for motorcycles and swimming-pools blazed with lights. Real-estate companies glowed with neon, some signs in Cyrillic script in recognition of where the customers for their villa developments were coming from.

Traffic lights slowed the aggressively driven Lexus and Sam was grateful for them. His clapped-out, hired Toyota had the performance of a camel. He couldn't be certain this was the same Lexus that had shot off outside the Paradiso Club; he'd failed to note its registration and the darkened glass of the car in front made it impossible to see the driver. But there couldn't be many such cars in Limassol.

The Lexus sped away again. At the next set of lights, which were at green, it slid into the right lane, the turning for the Troodos mountains. Sam slipped through after it just as the lights turned red.

The road out of the city was like a wide canyon. Flats and offices towered above each side, gradually petering out the further he drove. As the road gradient steepened, the Lexus pulled away. The more Sam put his foot down, the more the Toyota's engine misfired.

'Shit!'

He had a dread feeling he was on a wild goose chase, a conviction that it was some crazy Cypriot in the Lexus returning to his wife in the hills after a bunk-up with the mistress down town.

Tail lights blazed as the gold car slowed for a roundabout. The Toyota's dashboard clock said eleven-thirty. Foot hard down, he did his best to narrow the gap, but the limousine sped away on the far side of the roundabout and on up the road that led to the Troodos mountains. He would lose the bugger at this rate.

A full moon cast a silver glow across the spread of dark hills to Limassol's north, hills speckled by the lights of villas. The Troodos road wove between them, the tail lamps of the Lexus disappearing and reappearing in the bends, getting ever more distant.

Sam hugged the verge, telling himself he would give it another ten minutes. Suddenly, rounding a corner, the tail lights were closer. Much closer and swinging sharply right. He stamped on the brakes. The other car's headlamps swept across a roadside billboard, then began to climb. Sam slowed right down. As he passed the sign, his own lights picked out the words Golden View Estates.

He drove on a short distance then turned the car round in a yard selling ceramics. Heading back he saw a cone of light snaking up the hillside to his left. It had to be the Lexus – there'd been no other car on the road.

He doused his own lights. The skein of moonlight was bright enough to show up the white kerbstones lining the access road up to the building plots. He wound down the window.

The Lexus was out of sight by now. Sam drove faster, eyes flicking between the road and the hill above. The tarmac branched suddenly. He stopped. Along the spur to the right, dark outlines of houses under construction stood out against the sky. But no car. He continued up the hill, keeping the engine revs low. At the next spur he stopped again. More dark shells of villas-to-be. A brief flicker of red – tail lights being extinguished – told him he was there. He killed the engine, listening, imagining the other man doing the same. The hunter and the hunted. But which was he? He had an eerie sensation of being drawn into a trap.

He let the car roll backwards a few metres until an earth mound blocked the view from the spur. He listened again, holding his breath. A car door clunked, a solid, prestigious sound.

He got out of the Toyota and began walking quickly up the spur, using whatever cover he could find. The construction site was a mess. Cement mixers, diggers and the shells of uncompleted houses to left and right. He moved from one object to the next, staring into the darkness ahead, trying to identify shapes which the moonlight only hinted at. He still couldn't make out the Lexus. His heart raced, his breath roared in his ears. He had an unnerving fixation that his progress was being followed through the night sight of a sniper's rifle.

Suddenly, up ahead, he detected a faint red dot winking at him. It reminded him of the red-eye light on a flash-camera. He crouched down, grimacing as the scabs on his shins cracked like dry leaves. He watched the light for a few seconds before realising it was the alarm on the dashboard of a car. He stood again and crept forward. Soon the outline of the vehicle became clear. Behind it stood a sizeable villa, complete with roof, but no light inside.

Why would anyone visit a building site in the middle of the night other than to hide? He felt certain now that it *was* Viktor Rybkin.

Ten metres from the Lexus, he heard the clink of its catalytic converter cooling. He inched forward and crouched by the bumper, his shins protesting again. He listened once more, his eyes on the villa. The mansion commanded the edge of the hill like a mini-palace. The view would indeed be golden from here when the sun went down.

Behind the left-hand downstairs window of the house he suddenly saw a pinprick of fire, then nothing. Then the fire again, and nothing once more. A cigarette. His eyes better attuned to the darkness by now, the house took on a clearer shape. A central entrance porch supported by columns had window bays to each side of it. A cinder drive had been laid, still cluttered with building materials. He paced forward silently, then crouched by some breeze blocks. Again the pinprick of red through the left-hand bay – at the rear of the house, as if the smoker was on a terrace.

He crept to the corner of the building, then moved gingerly towards the back, painfully aware of his vulnerability. At the end of the side wall he put his head round.

The man was just an arm's length away from him. Sam held his breath. Suddenly a lighter flame flicked on. For a couple of seconds it illuminated a face. A familiar face with a scar.

He jerked his head back. Suppose Rybkin was armed? He himself had no weapons at all. Not so much as a boy scout's whistle. As he inched back trying to think of his next move, his foot trod on a piece of tile that cracked like a pistol shot. There was a sharp intake of breath from the terrace.

He stood stock still for what felt like several minutes, hardly daring to breathe. He was on the point of deciding to make a dash for the road when a thin beam of light pierced the gloom from the front corner of the house, followed a split-second later by a muffled thwack.

Jesus!

He was being shot at. A silenced pistol. The torch beam had picked out a stack of roof tiles three paces away. He ducked behind it, his heart exploding through his ribs. Another thwack sent chips of terracotta zinging around his ears. He threw himself on the ground, grunting with pain as his shins hit something hard.

'Viktor,' he yelled, pressing his face to the earth. 'It's Sam Packer, you idiot. Remember me?'

Silence, apart from the rasp of heavy breathing. He thought it was the other man's, then realised it was his own.

'Sam Packer! Well I'll be damned. So it *was* you at the Paradiso.' The voice was a growl, the accent half New York, half Moscow.

'Shouldn't have run off like that, Viktor. We could have had a nice drink together. And a talk about old times.'

'Seeing you there was a surprise, Sam. And in our line of business surprises are not often welcome. Now, come out so I can see your face.'

To do so might be suicide, but he had little choice.

'Okay, but put that fucking gun down.'

'Just come out. And watch your language,' the Ukrainian barked.

Sam stood up carefully and brushed himself down. His shins felt sticky as if they were bleeding again. He stepped into the beam of the torch, half expecting the thump of a bullet in the chest.

'You know, I thought you were a thief,' Rybkin pretended. 'This country's full of them, and most of them come from Russia.' He laughed, but hollowly.

Sam shielded his eyes from the torch.

'You've lost weight since we last met,' Rybkin remarked, shining the light at his waist.

'Been on a crash diet,' Sam retorted, suspecting Rybkin knew about Baghdad. Chrissie could have told him.

Rybkin moved closer, keeping the light in Sam's eyes and the pistol with its neat silencer pointed at his midriff. 'You took a big risk following me, you know. I could have killed you just now.'

'Like the way your friend killed Chrissie? Or . . . or was it *you* who did that?' The words had come out of their own accord.

'Tch, tch.' Rybkin let out a long sigh. 'That's why you've come, yes?'

'Why else? And take that bloody light out of my eyes.'

Rybkin pointedly left the beam where it was to remind him who was in charge.

'Turn around. Put up your hands.'

'Now that's not very friendly, Viktor.'

'Just do it.'

Slowly and fearfully Sam obliged. Rybkin felt his armpits and trouser waistband for a weapon, then patted his jacket and ran a hand down each leg, outside and in.

'You've got a luvverly touch, darling,' Sam lisped, trying to defuse the situation.

'Okay. Enough of your shit.' Rybkin lowered the beam and stuffed the gun into his belt. 'Come inside the house. But don't be dumb my friend. You go in front where I can see.'

Sam picked his way through the builders' debris to the porch and entered the hall.

'To the left,' Rybkin ordered, the torch revealing rough plastered walls with electric cables protruding and an internal arch with its door not yet hung. Beyond was the large room Sam had looked through from outside. The floor was bare concrete. In the middle stood two wooden chairs and a small trestle table. On it was a bottle of vodka and two glasses. 'Sit please. *Now* we will have a drink together.'

There was a candle on the table, stuck to its rough surface with melted wax. Rybkin lit it with his cigarette lighter. Then he sat opposite Sam and filled the glasses.

'*Budmo!*' said Rybkin, raising his.

'Absent friends,' murmured Sam.

The vodka was warm. They drained their glasses in

one. Rybkin refilled them. As he did so Sam noticed the hand clasping the bottle had the end digit of one thumb missing. The Ukrainian had changed out of his green jacket and was dressed now in a blouson windproof with its zip half undone. A patterned sweater showed underneath. The flickering candlelight exaggerated the crookedness of his jaw and his unreadable brown eyes watched with a wary concern.

This was the man who'd known about Chrissie's peanut allergy. So had *he* chosen the method by which she should be killed?

'Why did you do it?' Sam growled, plunging straight in again. 'Why did you kill Chrissie?'

'I?' Rybkin protested, his voice pained. 'You must not say such a thing. You don't believe that?'

'You were with her the night she died.'

The Ukrainian's jaw set as hard as stone.

'No games, Viktor. What happened? To start with, you can tell me why you're in Cyprus.'

Rybkin didn't answer immediately. Sam guessed he was trying to assess how much he knew so as to decide how much truth he would need to offer up to season the soufflé of lies he was concocting. Behind his back the glass doors to the terrace were open. Outside, a bat swooped and looped, its squeak on the limits of their hearing. In the far distance Limassol glowed and flickered like a distant conflagration.

'You know,' Rybkin began, his voice thoughtful and slow, 'you and me, we are the same. We do the same job. So we understand each other. Yes?'

'Don't give me that guff. What are you doing here?'

'Look, my friend, there are things that happen in this world that people like us have to know about, yes? To know, but maybe do nothing about. We are policemen but we are not policemen. You understand?'

'No, I don't. Tell me why you're here and what happened with Chrissie.'

Rybkin sucked in air.

'You see . . .' His voice when he spoke again began high like a falsetto and swooped deeper as the words emerged. 'Some of my countrymen, they . . . Well, it is my job to know if they are doing things that are not exactly legal, yes? I told you that in Kiev. So when they come to Cyprus for *biznis*, then it is good that I come too.'

The answer was absurdly inadequate. Sam fixed him with a steely look.

'And you visit their half-built homes in the middle of the night—'

'Sometimes it's nice to be alone, my friend. That's why I came here. And I like the view.'

'Or perhaps this particular little palace belongs to you?' Sam mocked, spreading his arms.

'Of course not,' Rybkin replied carefully. 'It belongs to one of those men that I speak about.'

'The man who was also with Chrissie on Tuesday night. The man who killed her,' Sam persisted.

Rybkin looked uneasy. 'The other man who was with Chrissie,' he acknowledged simply.

'Go on.'

'What can I say to you, when you think you know everything already?'

'Don't play with me, Viktor. What happened on Tuesday? How come you were all having a cosy drink together, then a few hours later Chrissie gets murdered?'

Rybkin sucked in air again. 'I will tell you the truth. I don't *know* what happened later. I wasn't there.'

He held up his glass. Sam shook his head, leaving his own full glass on the table. This man was lying to him. Pretending he wasn't responsible.

'No more vodka. You can drink alone.'

'A pity. You see, in my culture it is impolite to refuse.'

Rybkin shrugged. He tossed back the drink, smacked the glass down on the table, sat back in the chair, and tucked his thumbs into his belt.

'All right. I will tell you everything I know. I met Christine completely by chance at the Mondiale when I went there with a colleague for a drink. Big surprise. You can imagine. For her and for me. Well, of course I introduce Christine to my colleague. Then we have a drink together to celebrate this happy coincidence, but it soon becomes clear to me that it's not *my* company that Chrissie is interested in. You get me?' he asked pointedly.

Sam didn't answer, convinced this was bullshit.

'I could see that she and my colleague had things they wanted to do together. Alone. You understand me?' His eyes were like lasers. A faint, manipulative smile flickered. 'Of course you do. You know her appetite pretty good. Or you used to. Quite strong and healthy, huh?'

Sam bunched his fists on his lap and kept his mouth firmly closed.

'I tell you, my friend, they were sniffing each other like dog and bitch. You never saw anything like it.'

Sam tried to shut his mind to what he was feeling.

'I warned her Sam. I did tell her to take care.' His eyes crinkled with contrived concern. 'You see, I liked Chrissie. I liked her very much. We go back years, she and me. So when my colleague left us for a couple of minutes to go to the john, I took my chance and warned her that he was real hard case. I told her to watch out because he was a guy who didn't believe in rules. "No limits", that's what I told her.'

Sam faltered. Maybe there was some truth in what Rybkin was saying. He fought back thoughts about what 'no limits' might have meant in the context of what happened later.

'Who is he, your *colleague*? What's his name?' he snapped.

'I can't tell you. It's confidential information. You know that,' Rybkin whispered, refilling his glass and adding a drop to Sam's so the liquid reached the rim. 'Come on.' He raised the vodka. 'Let's drink to Chrissie, God rest her soul.'

Sam held his look for a few moments, wanting to believe that beneath the veneer of crocodile concern there might be an ounce or two of sincerity in this man whom Chrissie had considered a friend. He picked up his glass.

'Chrissie,' he whispered, then drank.

'You know, this beautiful island can be a dangerous place, my friend,' Rybkin whispered, his words full of an understated menace.

'Particularly with men like your *colleague* running around,' Sam answered gratingly. 'What is he? *Biznisman*? Mafiya? And what about you? What's your relationship with him? You work against him, or with him?'

He was remembering the *banya* in Kiev.

Rybkin's face set like granite. He rubbed his scar.

'You see, you damned English, you always have a problem understanding my country. You think everywhere in the world they play cricket. The same rules that you have. Fifteen men on one side, fifteen on the other. And virtue always wins.'

'Eleven.'

'What?'

'*Eleven* men in a cricket team,' Sam corrected.

'You see? You just proved it. You expect me to know these things,' Rybkin smirked. 'But look, you know my point, Sam. In my country virtue does not get its reward. No person can be on any *one* side. No person can be what you Anglo-Saxons call straight. We are different from you because to survive we *have* to cheat. All of us. In the countries of the former Soviet Union it is our way of life. It's the way we've always lived. And now more so than ever. Under socialism there was a kind of fairness, but not today, not any more. You know this Sam – you been to my country. People cannot live on what they are paid.'

His broad shoulders lifted as if to say that surely the whole world understood this by now.

'In my country, if you're sick, the doctor is there for you *free*. Oh sure. But if you want him to make you *better*, if you want medicine or surgery then you have to put money in his hands. Because the guy's got to eat somehow. Same with school-teachers. Your children will be taught for nothing. Free education is your right in Ukraine. *But*, to pass your grades, to get a certificate when you leave, then you got to pay. You got to give your teacher money so she can eat too. It's normal now for us. You understand?'

It was a given for Rybkin. A fact. A statement of the obvious.

'And you?' Sam snapped, his chin jutting. 'You get *your* payoffs from the criminals you're supposed to be fighting?'

Rybkin shrugged again. 'I showed you in Kiev how it is. These New Russians, they have many businesses. Some are criminal, some are not. But because in Ukraine we have crazy laws and a crazy tax system, even normal businesses have to cheat. 'So, you ask about me? I guess I'm kind of like a street priest to these guys. I mix with them so I understand their lives. I can't stop them sinning, nobody can, but I can tell them when they go too far. Being there among them, I'm like a warning that if they step too far out of line, the big judgement *will* come for them.'

'And like a priest you hold out your hand and the sinners put coins in it,' Sam mocked. 'Only in your case it's folding money.'

Rybkin's jaw set firm. 'I have to live, my friend.'

'By taking dollars from arseholes like the one that murdered Chrissie.'

'Believe me, I feel terrible about it. I introduced her to him for God's sake. How d'you think that makes me feel? Look, when I next find that guy I'm really going to let him have it.'

Rybkin's pretence at innocence was now nauseatingly transparent. Sam narrowed his eyes.

'Your colleague, this *guy* you're going to sort out. Why did he come to Cyprus?'

Rybkin's cheek twitched. 'He has investments here,' he said quickly, waving a hand around to indicate that the villa was one of them. 'They need attention from time to time – like indoor plants. That's all. Nothing else.'

'And he paid you to come to Cyprus with him? So you could help him water his plants?'

Rybkin's face pulled into a guilty smile. 'Well, it's kind of a free vacation for me. That's all.'

'Always take a gun on your hols, do you?' Sam goaded.

'When you are a KGB man for many years, you collect a lot of enemies,' Rybkin sighed.

That at least would be true, thought Sam.

'And these days they are all allowed passports,' Rybkin added ruefully.

'Where is he now, your *colleague*?'

'He had to return to Ukraine yesterday. Urgent business.'

'The business of avoiding a police inquiry into how the woman he went to bed with on Tuesday night ended up dead, yes?' He'd intended the words to come out cold, but they were tinged with bitterness.

'As I explained to you before, my friend,' Rybkin repeated, 'I don't know.'

'And I don't believe you, Viktor,' Sam snapped, his

eyes like knives. 'You knew about her lethal allergy. *You* decided how she should die. You were *there.*'

'Look, my friend,' Rybkin retorted, 'you may have a clever brain, but your heart is weak. How many years was it you let this woman play games with you?'

'Fuck off.' The man was side-tracking.

'No. Not fuck off. You have a weak heart with women and that means bad judgement all round. Believe me. And Chrissie too, she had bad judgement.'

'What d'you mean?'

For just a moment Rybkin seemed poised to tell him something, then decided against it.

'Bad judgement about how far it was safe to go,' he explained cryptically. 'I warned her about him – I told you that. And she ignored my warning, that's all.' He leaned forward, his elbows on his knees. 'And my friend, let me give *you* some advice. Because I like you, understand? I like you just as I liked Chrissie. And the advice is this. Don't try to find the man who killed her. His affairs do not concern you. Not you or your SIS. Just to ask questions about him will be dangerous for you.'

He swung his arm across his body as if drawing a line under the whole affair.

Questions. Had Chrissie died because she'd asked too many?

A hint of a breeze from the terrace set the candle flickering. In the guttering light Rybkin had the look of an evil god. He stood up and closed the doors, shooting the bolts at top and bottom.

'You talked with Chrissie,' Sam stated.

'Of course.'

'What about?'

The Ukrainian eyed him with an expression that contained a hint of pity.

'Look. On Tuesday she was drinking more than she should. I ask her why she drinks so much. She told me she was sad because a love affair had just ended. I ask if the lover had been you and she is surprised. Because I guessed it in Kiev last year, you see. Not great detective work. You were both pretending too hard.'

'Really,' he remarked flatly.

'She told me she thought you still loved her. Is it true?'

'It's irrelevant.'

'No. Not irrelevant. Look. Here's some more advice. It's better for you that you forget her. The more questions you ask about her, the more you will hear things you don't like.'

Sam blinked. 'What d'you mean?'

Rybkin's shoulders heaved again. 'I mean like how one moment she tells me she is sad about breaking up with you, and then the next she throws herself at my colleague. What sort of woman is that?'

Rybkin was deliberately stirring it now, Sam realised. He decided to throw a pebble into the water.

'Did she mention Iraq to you?'

The Ukrainian looked startled, but recovered quickly.

'No. Why? What about Iraq?'

An impenetrable mask clicked into place, one perfected through decades of Cold War deception.

'Never mind,' Sam answered. Rybkin's sensitivity to the question was enough.

The two men stared at each other across the flimsy table, each trying to read the other's mind. Suddenly Rybkin stood up and pulled the gun from his belt.

'And now my friend, we are going to say goodbye,' he announced abruptly.

Sam's stomach balled. The gun was being pointed at his chest.

Rybkin laughed. 'You think I'm going to shoot you?' He laughed again. 'You're wrong my friend. This time I just want to be sure you don't follow me. Understand? So, wait here five minutes after I've gone, please. But if I see you coming after me I *will* shoot, and this time I'll shoot to kill.' He started backing towards the open doorway. 'The front door – please close it when you leave. Because of the thieves I told you about. Just pull it shut. And I repeat, don't move from here until I am long gone.'

'What's going on?' Sam protested, his voice heavy with irony. 'A minute ago we were friends drinking vodka and now you're running out on me again.'

'Well, I apologise for leaving so suddenly but I have another appointment.' He paused. 'Look, I told you I like you Sam, yes? But I think it best that we don't meet again, if that's okay by you.'

He was in the hallway now.

'Suits me, Viktor,' Sam grunted. 'But do one thing for me will you? Take a message from me to whoever killed Chrissie. Tell him he's going to pay, okay? Just that. That he's going to pay.'

Rybkin's shoulders sagged. 'No Sam. I will not pass such a message. Because you are still a friend. And too many of my friends have been killed already.'

The front door clicked shut. Rybkin's feet crunched up the cinders to the Lexus. Sam leapt for the hall. When he heard the engine roar into life, he inched the door open. As the tail lights sped down the road, he sprinted after them, ducking for cover behind the construction plant. The limousine turned left towards the valley, its lights disappearing behind the bank of earth where the Toyota was parked.

'Fuck!'

The lights hadn't emerged from the other side. He heard a dull phut phut, followed by a hiss.

'Bastard!'

Rybkin had blown his tyres. A few seconds later the Lexus reappeared and accelerated down the hill.

Sam cursed again. He'd lost this round. But there would be another, he decided, and very soon.

He sprinted behind the mound to check the damage to his car. Both front tyres totally flat. It would take an hour to walk back to Limassol.

He returned to the villa to fortify himself with another shot of vodka and to satisfy his curiosity about the place. He downed a slug, then unstuck the candle from the wooden table. Across the hall from the main room was a smaller one – bare concrete floor and unplastered breeze-block walls. Behind that, a kitchen and a third room. All bare, all empty. He wanted to check upstairs but discovered that the staircase had yet to be installed in the house.

He returned to the main room and refixed the candle to the table. Then he unbolted the doors to the terrace and opened them, stepping onto a balcony three metres deep with a wrought-iron railing protecting its edge. Beyond it the ground sloped steeply downwards, the full moon casting silver reflections on the distant sea.

Why had Rybkin come up here this evening? Not for the view, that was for sure. To hide. Seeing Sam in the Paradiso had put the fear of God into him. And now? He'd be on his way out of Cyprus if he had any sense.

Sam stepped backwards to re-enter the house. Something crunched under his foot. He bent down and found that whatever it was had become pinned to the sole of his shoe. He felt underneath the rubber and pulled it away.

'My God,' he croaked when he saw what it was.

He strode back inside to check it in the light of the candle. In the palm of his hand lay a gold ear stud with a pearl centre.

'Shit.'

He remembered all those hours he'd spent choosing them.

One of a pair he'd given to Chrissie two years ago.

20

Friday, 4 October, 02.30 hrs

By the time the taxi deposited Sam at the entrance to the silently sleeping Mondiale Hotel nearly two hours later, he'd concluded that Chrissie's last terrified moments must have been spent in the concrete ghost town he'd just come from. A perfect location for a murder – no one around to hear her screams as they forced down her throat something that was a snack to most people, but which she knew would kill her.

And Rybkin *had* been there, he felt sure of it. The man had lied to him from start to finish. He hadn't been in Cyprus to monitor the progress of transnational crime, but to play a part in it.

Sam had walked for twenty minutes along the road to Limassol before a car had stopped to give him a lift. A couple of elderly British ex-pats heading for an early check-in at the cruise terminal and a five-day jolly to Egypt had dropped him outside a cab office on their way through the almost deserted town centre.

'Here, sir.' The cab driver gave Sam the receipt he would need to keep the SIS expenses department off his back. 'My number's on the card. Any time.' The man drove off.

When the sound of the engine had gone, Sam still hadn't moved. From behind the hotel he could hear the hiss of surf on shingle. He felt a light breeze blowing off the water, a mild wind from Africa. He filled his nostrils with smells of the sea and of the damp greenery of the beds lining the driveway to the hotel.

He'd phoned Mowbray from a call box in town, telling him what he'd learned about Chrissie's death. They'd agreed Rybkin was probably on his way out of the country by now, the 'other appointment' he'd talked of being with a check-in counter at Larnaca airport. Mowbray was alerting the Cyprus police to try to get him stopped.

Sam's limbs felt leaden, his heart encased in stone. Drawn so much closer now to Chrissie's death, the reality of it was biting hard. Since leaving that villa on the hillside he'd gone over in his mind the conversation with Rybkin. The fact that it had ended the moment he'd mentioned Iraq could not have been coincidental. He believed now that his original speculation had been right, that Chrissie had died because she'd uncovered a link between the Ukrainians and the Iraqis. A link they couldn't afford to let her report. He had no proof of this, as Mowbray had yet again reminded him, and no evidence of what the deal might have been.

For the umpteenth time he took from his pocket the photo snapped in the hotel bar. Some deep gut instinct told him there was another clue in it that he hadn't yet found. Holding it towards the light coming from the hotel entrance he looked at it again, searching for this thing that he might have missed. He shook his head. Only faces. Those that could be seen and those that couldn't.

He moved inside the entrance lobby where the light was brighter to study it more closely. Three figures only at the table in the picture: Chrissie, Rybkin and the other Ukrainian. A little way behind the table, beyond the range of the flash, figures stood at the bar, none of them more than a shadow. A couple of faces were turned towards the camera, one a man who appeared to be staring at Chrissie. Nothing unusual in that. Men had often stared at her. But if no stone was to be left unturned in trying to prove his suspicions, then these shadowy, indistinct faces should also be scrutinised more closely. A job for the forensic specialists, not for him, the photo analysts back in London, who with their computers could extract detail from the direst of murk. He would call Waddell and alert them to be ready for the picture when he got back to England later in the day.

He knew he should try to get some sleep now, but knew too he wouldn't be able to. The hotel felt claustrophobic. If he went to his room he would only brood. He needed air. He pushed back outside through the swing doors and turned left onto a winding path that ran through gardens to the back of the hotel and to a set of stone steps leading to the beach. The whispering of the surf grew stronger as he walked and he knew it was at the water's edge that he wanted to be. It was always at the bad times in his life that the soothing power of the sea drew him most strongly.

At the bottom of the steps the beach was soft sand, but as he approached the water it became stonier. The surf had pushed the shingle into a long, low ridge. He stood on it watching the sea's phosphorescent sparkle. With the sky now overcast the only light on the beach was what spilled from security lights in the hotel's garden. He took a few deep breaths to oxygenate his blood, then slid towards the gentle breakers, stones skittering beneath his feet.

He stared at the ripples as they sparkled forward, stopping just short of his feet. But instead of the sea comforting him, this time it seemed to heighten his sense of loss. He fished in his jacket pocket for the ear stud he'd found at the villa, and as he turned it over in his fingers

Chrissie's face filled his mind. He began to feel what she must have felt: excitement at uncovering, as he believed she had, the Iraqis' connection with the Ukrainians; the thin-ice thrill of danger as she used her old friendship with Viktor Rybkin to try to unmask the deal; then the cold, panicky fear as the ice gave way beneath her. And Sam knew what happened with Chrissie when a situation slipped from her control. He remembered her terror in Baghdad when they'd first met in 1990, remembered watching her disintegrate when she believed they were all about to die.

Then he thought of how she'd been in Amman, her hunger for pleasure and her need to have him wanting her still. He shook his head like a dog. Being out here in the dark with his memories was not such a good idea. He turned back towards the hotel.

Suddenly he saw that he was not alone. A solitary figure sat on the top of the shingle bank a little further along, silhouetted against the light from the hotel. Sam dropped to a crouch, fearing irrationally that it was Rybkin. But the figure sat motionless and benign; a woman, he thought, hugging her knees like a child. He began to move up the bank, his feet scrabbling against the slipping shingle.

At the top he stopped and looked again. She had fair hair hanging to her shoulders and was staring out to sea. So far as he could tell she hadn't noticed him.

Suddenly he realised who it was and moved closer.

'Sophie?'

The woman jerked with fright and stared round at him, straining to see.

'Wha . . . whozat?'

'It's Terry.'

'Oh. You.' A pause, then she turned her face to the sea again. ''Lo.'

He crunched over to where she sat, a picture of despondency.

'You all right?'

'No.'

His fault? he wondered. The result of his abrupt disappearance from the Paradiso?

'Look, sorry about the drinks. Suddenly saw someone I had to talk to.'

'Yeah, yeah. You're a heap o' shit. You all are.' She choked on the words. 'Whyn't you just piss off?'

He couldn't tell whether she'd been crying or was just drunk.

'Look, I said I'm sorry,' he repeated, trying to convince himself it was all right to leave her to her misery. Then he decided he'd better make sure she hadn't been harmed in some way.

He flopped down beside her.

'Did something nasty happen to you?' he asked gently.

'Na-asty? No way,' she spluttered almost laughing. 'Nuffing ever does. Tha's the trouble.'

Pissed as a fart, he decided.

'So, the bloke you were with . . .'

'Into a pumpkin. At midnight. Went home to his wife and sprog.'

'Which wasn't what you'd had in mind.'

She gave a gust of a sigh, her breath reeking of brandy.

'Look. Din't wan' a relashunship with him or anything like that,' she slurred. 'Din't pertickely like him. Jus' wan'ed a *shag*. Thas all. Not much to ask izit? You blokes are s'posed to wan' it all the bloody time.' She punched him feebly on the shoulder. 'So wha's wrong with *me*, eh? Why don't *I* get my share?'

He saw tears glinting on her cheekbones and put his arm round her shoulder. He decided to give her a couple of minutes and then be on his way. 'You will, sweetheart. There's a bloke out there who's for you, you'll see.'

'Huh. Anyway, I don't feel like it anymore, so gerroff.' She twisted away from him. 'Lost my libeediboo. So don' bloody try anything. Awright?'

'I won't. Have no fear.' He stood up. 'Look, I'm going inside. I'll give you a hand if you want. But I'm going in now. So if you're not coming, it's goodnight. Okay?'

'Hang on, hang on. Don' be like that.' She grabbed his arm and tried to pull him back down. Then she groaned as if in great pain.

'What's the matter?' Perhaps she *had* been assaulted.

'Wha's the time?' she queried miserably. 'Jus' remembered something . . .'

'About ten to three.'

'Oh gawd!'

'What?'

'Got to do a pres'tation in the morning. Morning? Christ! It's bloody morning already. I'll get the sack, I will.'

'You'll be all right. Drink loads of water, get some sleep, and down some paracetamol when you wake up. Be as right as rain.'

'No, no!' she howled. 'You don' understand. I've got to *do* the pres'tation. Like tonight.'

'You mean *prepare* it?'

'Yes,' she answered forlornly.

'That's a presentation I'd quite like to watch!'

'You *mean* bastard!' she howled.

Suddenly he thought of something. The presentation would surely be done on a computer.

'You've got the kit for this somewhere?' he asked tentatively. 'A PC?'

'Course. In my room. It's got more hardware in it than s-lilicon valley. PC, scanner, printer, the lot.'

'And software for playing around with photos?'

'Oh yeah. The lot. Done a course on it.'

'Brilliant. Come on then. I'll give you a hand if you like. It won't take you long. The sooner you start . . .'

She didn't move.

'I think I'm goin' to be sick . . .' She pitched forward and retched.

'Christ,' Sam breathed, suppressing his revulsion. Somehow he was going to have to sober her up a bit.

Ten minutes later he'd got Sophie to her room on the floor below his own, a room with the same striped wallpaper and faded Monet print. Clothes which she'd worn earlier in the day were strewn untidily across the double bed. He sat in front of her table-full of computer equipment while she threw up again, in the bathroom this time.

She emerged eventually, her face pinched and blotchy, her lank hair clinging to her small head like a beggar's. She perched on the edge of the bed, trembling.

'G-got to sleep,' she stuttered. Suddenly her eyes closed and she tipped sideways onto the mattress with the grace of a ballerina, tucking her legs into a foetal position.

'No, luvvy, you can't,' Sam cajoled, springing to his feet. 'You can't sleep yet, Soph. Sorry. You've got work to do.' He crossed to the bed and shook her gently. 'Look, I'll help you. Switch all this kit on and show me what it does.'

'No. I jus' wanna sleep.'

He grabbed her by the shoulders and pulled her upright. She stared gormlessly up at him like a beached fish. 'Come on.' He put his hands under the sticky armpits of her little black dress and lifted her to her feet.

'Gawd, I'm goin' to be sick again,' she wheezed.

'No you're not.'

He sat her down at the chair in front of the laptop and found the power switch to boot up the machine. Sophie began to retch, but dryly, covering her mouth with her hands. Sam found a waste bin and dropped it at her feet.

'Just in case, right? Now take in some deep breaths.'

'Sorry,' she whispered between gulps. 'Disgusting, aren't I?'

'No. Not disgusting. You just drank too much. Happens to us all.'

As she continued the deep breathing he went to the bathroom and returned with a glass of tap water.

'No.' She pushed it away. 'Tastes foul. There's some fizzy stuff in the minibar. It's what I usually have when I get like this.'

The screen in front of her was displaying the Windows desktop. Her hand swallowed the mouse as naturally as if it were an extension of her arm. She clicked on the icon for the presentations software.

Sam filled a glass from a bottle of mineral water and held out a packet of cheese biscuits. 'If you can nibble a few of these it'll help.'

She forced herself to smile. 'Thanks. You're being kind. Can't imagine why.'

'Pure self-interest,' Sam breathed, pulling across the chair from the dressing table and sitting beside her. 'Always wanted to know what you can do with pictures on a PC.'

She was beginning to nod off again, but he nudged her and she loaded a photo from file. A picture of the Mondiale Hotel.

'Well, well . . . recognise that?'

'Not half. Can you go close in on part of it? The doorway, for instance.'

She drew a box round the entrance porch then clicked on 'expand'. It filled the frame.

'Can you make it lighter, so we can see detail on the faces behind the window?'

'Course. Do anything. Even age someone fifty years if I want.'

She clicked and tinkered until a face that had been obscured by shadow was now much clearer.

'Amazing. With my PC at home I don't know much more than how to switch it on,' he told her disingenuously. 'Hey, tell you what. There's a photo I took from the board in the hall – can you scan it in for me?'

'Look, if I'm ever goin' to get this pres'tation sorted . . .'

'Won't take a minute.'

He placed the photo face down on the scanner glass. Her hand twitched across the mouse pad. Soon the picture was filling the screen.

'Who are these people?' she asked, mildly curious. Then she pursed her lips and pressed at her stomach as if suffering from cramps.

'No idea,' Sam lied. The faces by the bar were the ones he was interested in – still dark and unidentifiable.

'Oh hell!' Sophie rose unsteadily, both hands clasped to her stomach. She scuttled to the bathroom and banged shut the door.

Sam transferred to her chair and gripped the mouse, ignoring the explosions from the loo. He'd watched carefully what she'd done before. He boxed round the face of the man by the bar who was looking at Chrissie and expanded it to fill the screen. Still just a dark smudge, except he could now make out a pale moustache. The face had a mournful look. Something about it that was familiar, but he couldn't be sure it hadn't just *become* familiar by working on it.

He clicked on the drop-down image enhancement menu and played with the sliders for contrast and brightness. From the bathroom behind him there came a muffled sob. Slowly, using software tools to sharpen and highlight, the definable features of a man's face began to emerge from the blob on the screen.

'I don't believe . . .'

It was a face he now recognised. The oddly dog-like looks, the mournful droop of the moustache, the unflinching Labrador eyes – it was in the store room in Baghdad that he'd seen them before. The man he'd called Saladin who'd watched his interrogation in silence. The man to whom the others deferred. A creature for whom only one thing had seemed to matter – that the message whispered to Sam in the foyer of the Rashid Hotel had been harmless. That even if it had warned of the anthrax attack it had *not* revealed its date and location.

Sam let out a low whistle.

And Saladin had been *here,* in this very hotel on Tuesday night, watching with apparent disquiet as two Ukrainians downed booze and shot their mouths off with an English woman. Why should he be so concerned? Because the Ukrainians were men he'd done business with?

'Yes!' he hissed. There was no other explanation that made sense. Here was the link they'd been looking for. A tenuous, unverifiable one, but a link nonetheless.

The bathroom door banged open and Sophie emerged, wrapped just in a towel. She pitched forward onto the bed and closed her eyes as if she never expected to open them again.

Sam clicked the mouse and a colour close-up of Saladin rolled out of the printer.

21

06.15 hrs
Limassol

The bonded container yard on the western side of Limassol had come to life at six a.m. when a lone forklift driver arrived for work. Within minutes of him greeting the night security man, hanging up his leather jacket in the site office and climbing behind the wheel of his machine, the main gates had slid open to admit the trailer truck that had come to take away the container bound for Israel.

The forklift drove into the warehouse and lifted the Haifa-bound box from its position of isolation on one side of the shed. To the driver it was just a box, forty feet long and eight feet wide, with a weight of several thousand kilos. There was no need to know where it had come from, nor to enquire what it contained. His employer paid him well, with an unspoken understanding never to let his curiosity get the better of him.

The container that had arrived here from Ilychevsk near Odessa three days ago emerged now through the wide opening of the warehouse doors, raised high by the forklift like a mantis at prayer. With a precision born of years of practice the driver lowered it gently and accurately onto the locating lugs of the transporter's flatbed.

The truck driver collected the container's shipping papers from the site office, then with a final inspection of the trailer to ensure the load was secure, he swung up into the cab and drove out of the gates. At this hour of the morning he expected no delay at the port. There'd be a glance at his papers at the customs barrier, then straight onto the quay and the berth where the ship for Haifa was waiting. At noon the container with its unpleasant cargo would be on its way to its final destination.

There had been no need for Viktor Rybkin to be here in person to watch this final stage of the Cyprus operation. To do so would have risked drawing attention to himself. And there was nothing he could achieve in person here that money hadn't already secured for the organisation. Nowhere in the world were there business-men who couldn't be bought.

It would have been impossible anyway for Rybkin to be here. His flight to Odessa had just lifted off the runway at Larnaca. The Ukrainian passport he'd been travelling on had been issued in a false name. The grumpy policeman who'd made a special inspection of the departing passengers' documents on instructions from his chief in Limassol had not given him a second look.

09.15 hrs

The RAF flight carrying Chrissie's coffin back to England was due off the ground at midday, but to satisfy the RAF's procedures Sam needed to be at Akrotiri an hour earlier, Mowbray had told him. He was on his way already however, by taxi, well ahead of time, because he had something important to do at the air base before the flight. The car took the ring road north of Limassol, heading west.

Mowbray had driven down from Nicosia at dawn. Over bacon and eggs in Sam's hotel room, his parrot-grey eyes had examined Sam's photographic evidence with solemn concentration. Then, choosing his words with care, he'd admitted that it did give *some* weight to the idea that if an Iraqi group *was* preparing a biological weapons attack, then it *could* be being helped along the way by criminal elements from Ukraine.

Mowbray had put both the original photograph and the computer-enhanced print of Saladin into his briefcase so that he could transmit them to London as soon as he got back to Nicosia. Then Sam had handed over Chrissie's ear stud, but Mowbray suggested he put it with the rest of her possessions which he would find at the RAF base.

He'd surprised Sam by saying he wasn't intending to pass on any of what he'd just learned to the Cypriot police. 'To be frank, their "accidental death after a night out" explanation suits us well, Sam. Amazingly the press seem to be prepared not to speculate on the exact circs of Mrs *Taylor*'s demise, out of consideration for her family back in England.' Mrs *Kessler*'s funeral would take place tomorrow, he'd added. Quick and quiet before some scoop-hungry hack made a connection.

As soon as Mowbray had left, Sam had phoned the car hire company to tell them where to find the crippled Toyota. Then he'd gone downstairs to pay his bill. While waiting at the front desk, he'd noticed the travel trade reps filing into the conference room for their morning session. He'd kept an eye out for Sophie, but had seen no sign of her. Feeling guilty about not checking how she was this morning, he'd taken a quick peek into the room.

She'd been sitting on a podium at the front watching the delegates take their seats, with her laptop PC beside her. For someone who'd done a good impression of a rag-doll a few hours earlier, she'd looked remarkably fresh. Though pale, her blonde hair had shone. Dressed in a crisp, pale-blue two piece suit she was attractive again.

She'd caught sight of him standing in the doorway and blushed, covering her face with her hands to signal her shame. Then she'd removed them and smiled. She'd seen he was carrying a bag and gave a sad little wave, then touched her fingers to her lips.

The taxi left Limassol town behind it, cutting through estates of citrus. Five miles further on at the tip of the Akrotiri peninsula, the gates of the RAF base loomed ahead, the skyline beyond them scarred with antenna masts.

In a few minutes' time he would be confronted by Chrissie's corpse. He wondered how he would cope when the moment came, faced with such visible, tangible proof of her death. Also at the back of his mind were Rybkin's words, his cryptic warning that the more he asked about Chrissie the less he would like.

The taxi stopped in a visitors' bay by the gates to the base and Sam called into the guardroom, giving his name as Terry Malone. A clerk phoned through to Squadron Leader Banks. It was ten-fifteen. Five minutes later a grey Vauxhall Astra sped up to collect him. Banks was a short, slightly built officer in a uniform that had seen better days. And he was in a hurry.

'Expected you twenty minutes ago,' he declared, accelerating away with Sam beside him. 'Not much time for you to view the body now. A couple of minutes at the most. Needs to be packed up for the flight.'

'But that doesn't take off for another hour and a half,' Sam protested, annoyed at having his wrist slapped by an Air Force man. In the Navy they'd called them crabs.

'Cypriot customs, Mr Malone. Anything unusual and they make a right meal of it.' Banks cleared his throat uncomfortably at his unfortunate choice of words. 'Here we are. The base hospital.'

He stopped the car outside the low, modern building and led the way inside and down an ether-smelling corridor.

'In here.'

Banks pushed open a door labelled with a NATO numerical code and introduced him to a youngish ginger-haired Scotsman in a white coat.

'This is the MO. He'll show you Mrs Taylor's body. I'll come back in ten to pick you up again.'

'Thanks.'

'You okay Mr Malone?' the medical officer asked, noticing his pallor.

'Yes.' He steadied himself. 'Thank you.'

'Take no notice of busy-busy Banks,' the MO confided, leading him through a pair of rubber swing doors. 'There's no great rush. Take your time. The Squadron Leader's a bit of a wanker, between you and me. The RAF's admin ranks are full of them.'

'I know. I used to be in the Navy.'

The Scot stopped for a moment, looking at him quizzically.

'That's interesting.' Sam didn't understand why, particularly. 'And er . . . you're a relative of the deceased?' he asked curiously.

'No. Just a friend.'

'A *friend.*' The MO narrowed his eyes conspiratorially, as if using the word in its euphemistic form. 'Tell me something. Do I deduce from the fact that the RAF is repatriating Mrs Taylor's body that she was of rather more significance to HMG than an ordinary business-woman would be?'

'I . . .' Sam was thrown by the directness of the question.

'I apologise for being blunt. People are where I come from.'

'Look, I can't tell you what you should deduce,' Sam answered obscurely.

'No. Of course not. Perhaps I could put another question to you. And, believe me I *do* have a reason for asking.'

'Go on.'

'Is your interest in seeing the body just personal? Or *professional* as well?'

Sam answered with a nod.

'Fine. Just so as we understand one another.'

The doctor pushed through a second set of swing doors, holding them open. They were now in the antechamber to a small operating theatre. Sinks and autoclaves to one side, shelves of sterilised instruments on the other. And in the middle of the floor, a steel trolley.

On it lay Chrissie, her body covered with a sheet, but her face exposed.

Sam faltered. She was so yellow already, her cheeks so hollow, her hair so lank. He stood stock still, half looking for some movement – the flutter of an eyelid or a tremor of the lips.

After a few moments her absolute stillness began to calm him. He could see no sign of suffering here. Whatever agony she'd gone through had left no lasting mark on her.

He was aware of the MO watching him closely.

'You know the circumstances of her death?' the doctor asked.

'Some of them.'

'The police pathologist called it accidental.'

'Yes.'

'But I assume she knew she was allergic to peanuts?'

'Of course.'

'Then she wouldn't have touched the things, would she? So it couldn't possibly have been an accident.'

'No.'

'I see.'

The MO folded his arms. His opinion of the local police pathologist had just been confirmed.

'It would have been over quite quickly,' he went on, comfortingly. 'Anaphylactic shock sets in within minutes. There'd have been a bronchospasm. She would have fought for breath for a bit then her blood pressure would have dropped dramatically. A matter of minutes before unconsciousness – and then death.'

'I see. Thanks.'

The clinical description had helped. Sam kept thinking how still she was, and how *gone*. No feeling of her presence, nothing of the spirit which had inhabited this body.

'Forgive my asking something else, but it *is* important,' the MO ventured. 'Were you . . . ?'

'What?'

'Were you intimate with the deceased?'

'I don't see that that's anything to do—'

'Forgive me, but it is. You see there's a mark. On the body. There's no mention of it in the Cypriot autopsy report.'

'A mark?'

'Yes. Now, I don't know if it has any bearing on the circumstances of her death or not. But somebody connected with the case ought to know about it. What worried me was that the body would go straight to the undertakers back in England and nobody in authority would ever see it.'

Sam narrowed his eyes. 'What sort of mark?'

'A tattoo.'

Sam felt a shiver down his back.

'It's on the lower abdominal area. The reason I asked

whether you and she had been intimates was that if the answer was yes you would presumably already know about it. Should I show you?'

'I think you'd better,' Sam breathed, his heart thudding.

The MO lifted the sheet at a point midway along the body. There was a smell of surgical spirit and something sourer.

'Did you know she was pregnant?' the MO asked.

'Yes,' replied Sam, biting his lip.

He looked down at the narrow hips whose contours he knew so well. Next to the compact bush of light-brown hair a small blue globe about two centimetres across had been etched into the soft yellow of her belly just below her bikini line. The design was complete with equator, lines of longitude and some unrecognisable land mass in red. Beneath it was the letter B.

Sam stared dumb-founded. He'd never seen it before. The tattoo was like a brand. A company logo.

'I thought you ought to see it,' the doctor whispered.

'Yes. You were right.'

He felt transfixed. He knew every handbreadth of her skin and this mark was new. Tattoos were in fashion – a butterfly on a shoulder blade, a swallow on an ankle – but why a mark like a product label, hidden where only a surgeon or a lover would find it?

Viktor Rybkin's warning rumbled in his head. *It's better for you that you forget her.*

He looked at her peaceful, innocent face once more. A waxwork face. He had the weird feeling that this wasn't Chrissie lying here at all. Some other woman. Someone he didn't know. Like she'd pretended to be on that narrow child's bed in Amman. Keeping him blind so he wouldn't see the brand mark on her groin.

22

07.45 hrs
Magerov, Southern Ukraine

Major Mikhail Pushkin watched his wife prepare breakfast for himself and their daughter, his face pinched by a night of little sleep. He was dressed in freshly pressed uniform trousers and a crisp pale-green shirt.

The kitchen of their sixth-floor, two-room army flat was just long enough to accommodate the sink, the cooker and a small fridge, its width barely allowing space for the three of them to squeeze round the small table where they ate. At one end, a window overlooked the well-used children's playground wedged between the two bleak blocks of officers' apartments. At the other, a door opened into a narrow corridor which connected with the small box-room where their daughter slept, and a slightly larger space that served as their living room and as a bedroom for Mikhail and Lena. A tiny bathroom with rust stains on the tub and many of its wall tiles missing completed the sparse accommodation which, despite its deficiencies, they were fortunate to have. Thousands of Ukrainian officers were still homeless following the splitting up of the Red Army five years earlier into independent Russian and Ukrainian forces.

Mikhail Pushkin was a short, sinewy man with neatly trimmed dark hair and the sort of well-chiselled, honest face that Stalin's artists used as the model for their revolutionary heroes. He had little stomach for food this morning. The past eight days had made a nightmare of his life, torturing him with anxiety, guilt and anger. Today, unknown to Lena, he was primed to do something he would never have considered just a week ago – going over the head of his commanding officer.

Opposite him sat ten-year-old Nadya, chattering about her school-friends while her mother cooked. The curd cheese which was their breakfast staple had started to go off, so Lena was mixing it with a beaten egg and some sugar, then pressing it into pancakes and coating it in flour to fry as *syrniki.*

Lena had a pale, oval face. Naturally pretty like most Ukrainian women, her neat mouth was bracketed by lines of sadness, etched there by the misery which had dogged so many Ukrainians' lives in the years since independence. Salaries unpaid and devalued by inflation, a national economy in free-fall, the former bread-basket of the Soviet Union had crumbled into a nation of paupers.

Pushkin observed his wife at work. Lena had kept her figure as the years had passed. As he watched her twist between the stove and the table he remembered uncomfortably that just the sight of her leaning forward in a close-fitting skirt used to get him aroused. But a back-room posting in a bankrupt army had become bromide for him, in the same way that depression about the way they lived had for her. He couldn't remember the last time they'd made love.

The flat was cold. Autumn was biting but the communal heating had not yet been turned on. In the room where they lived and slept, condensation had smeared the windows that morning as he'd looked out onto the grid of roads and buildings making up the Magerov Depot of the 39th Supply Regiment. Here in the kitchen the air was steamy from the kettle, boiled first for their breakfast tea and now to provide drinking water for the day.

'Here, love.'

Lena placed a plate of *syrniki* in front of him, her bird-like voice little more than a breath. She handed him an open jar of runny jam made from pears picked at her parents' dacha last autumn, then turned back to the stove and shovelled fritters onto a plate for her daughter.

'And you?' Pushkin asked, knowing what she'd say.

'Later. I'll have something later.' She hovered over them as they began to eat, sipping at a mug of tea.

The crisis of duty and conscience that had taken hold of Major Pushkin had mushroomed to a point where he now feared for his own life. It had begun with a normal enough act for him – the routine checking of a request from an artillery regiment for spare parts that looked somewhat irregular. But with that simple act of dutiful vigilance he'd lifted the lid on a crime against the state. And by doing so he'd inadvertently caused a tragic death which he knew to be murder.

The 39th Supply Regiment for which he was the second-in-command had taken control of Magerov in 1992 after the relocation of the tactical bomber squadrons that had been based there as part of the Soviet Naval Air Force. The huge hangars formerly used by the Tu-22s had been converted into stores for a broad range of non-explosive military hardware. Magerov now served as a central spares depot for the four corps in the Odessa District of the Army of independent Ukraine.

The spares request that had caught his eye had been a large one: eight pages of part numbers, all stamped and countersigned by the quartermaster of an artillery regiment that was armed with multiple rocket launchers. The parts were for a small reconnaissance drone known as VR-6 or, more colloquially, Yastreyo, which was used as an airborne camera platform to spy out targets for the regiment's long-range rocket batteries. There was no logistical problem with the order; the computerised inventory system showed a fair stock of everything that was being asked for. Most military training in Ukraine had ground to a halt for lack of fuel, so the VR-6s were seldom flown and the spares in question had been gathering dust on the shelves.

The aspect of the order that had caused Pushkin to investigate was its extraordinary completeness. It wasn't just spare wings or a replacement nose cone that the 166th Rocket Regiment had ordered, but an *entire* set of parts. Every single item that was needed to assemble a brand-new, fully operational, turbine-powered pilotless plane, complete with launch rails and rocket booster. The only items not included were the drone's photographic equipment.

His first guess was that the 166th were trying it on. That they'd destroyed a drone in a training accident and had their request for a replacement refused by the Odessa Military District on grounds of cost. He'd suspected some opportunist gunner CO was simply trying to side-step headquarters by obtaining a new drone in kit form.

Pushkin had referred the matter to his own commanding officer, a man he'd known and trusted for many years. But instead of advising him to return the paperwork to the Rocket Regiment for verification – the reaction he'd expected – Colonel Komarov had ordered him to process the spares request without further delay.

It was then that his crisis of conscience had begun. He knew that his suspicions merited further investigation, yet to do anything about it meant disobeying a senior officer, something outlawed by the principles instilled in him by his five formative years at the Kievskoye Military Aviation Engineering school.

His dilemma had been compounded by the fact that

Colonel Komarov was a friend as well as his CO. Eight years earlier they'd served in Germany together. Of equal rank then, and still so four years ago when religion had returned to fashion in Ukraine, Komarov had become Nadya's godfather. With that honour a *kym* had been established between the two men, a personal bond that gave them the closeness of brothers.

In Pushkin's battle with his conscience, loyalty to his commander had won. He'd stifled his concerns about the legitimacy of the spares order and pressed on with preparing the goods for delivery. A telephone call purportedly from the 166th had asked him to provide transport because their own trucks were unserviceable. The drone components had filled a Ural eight-tonner. At an arranged hour an officer and two soldiers from the receiving regiment had arrived in a jeep to escort the load to its destination near the Moldavian border, one hundred kilometres away.

That had been Friday, exactly a week ago. It should have been an end to the matter, but hadn't been. Later that afternoon the empty truck had returned much earlier than Pushkin would have expected after a two-hundred-kilometre round trip. His curiosity aroused, he'd telephoned the quartermaster of the Rocket Regiment to check the delivery had been made correctly.

The brief, uncomfortable conversation which had followed had shaken him to the core. The 166th Rocket Regiment, he was told in no uncertain terms, had not placed any order whatsoever for spare parts for their VR-6 reconnaissance drones.

'Goodbye papa. I love you.'

Nadya kissed him on the cheek, her coat on and her schoolbag in her hand.

'Goodbye my darling. Be good to your teachers.'

He always said that. Some subconscious hope that the

child being well-behaved would mean that a box or two of surplus fruit from Lena's parents' dacha would satisfy the teachers at exam time rather than the money he didn't have.

Lena saw her daughter off to the bus which took the officers' children to the village school, then came back into the kitchen and sat down opposite her husband. Pushkin saw from her eyes what she wanted to talk about, but he couldn't. Not this morning. Not when he was secretly on his way to see the General and his insides were burning up with fear of what the outcome might be.

Last night, after Nadya had gone to sleep, Lena had talked to him at length. Starting with her familiar moan about how hard it was to survive on his army pay, she'd insisted that he let her get a job. She had one already, part-time at the nursery school – a highly suitable role for the wife of an officer who still nurtured hopes of making the rank of colonel – but the wages were pitiful. The job she'd talked about was in an office in Odessa.

She'd told him of her visit to Odessa earlier that same day. She'd taken the twenty-minute ride south on the electric train in order to shop in the huge farmers' food market where competition made the prices keen. But before plunging into the maze of stalls she'd been unable to resist a stroll through Odessa's tree-lined streets to peer into the handful of glittery boutiques where *biznis-men* bought their women skimpy dresses for more money than an army major earned in a year.

'You want *that*, woman?' Pushkin had asked her angrily. 'You want to throw money away like those criminals and their whores?'

'No. Not like them. We'd think of better things to spend it on. But Misha, is this *it*?' There'd been a crack in her voice. Her small hand had swept round the room and its meagre contents. 'Are you saying *this* is all there is for us?'

Two single beds used as sofas during the day. An old rug from her mother's house spread on the wall to cover the cracks in the plaster. The twenty-year-old sewing machine with which she stitched her daughter's clothes. A cassette player and a small TV on a shiny veneered wall unit. A few books.

'Is this the best we can *ever* have, Misha?' There'd been tears in her eyes. 'Tell me!'

He hadn't replied. Hadn't dared to, because the answer was 'yes'. He saw no hope of being able to provide them with more.

Seizing on his silence, she'd pressed home her bid to make their lives better, telling him of the small word-processed note she'd spotted in Odessa, stuck to the door of a fine nineteenth-century mansion now used as offices.

'Good wages for a woman ready for any sort of work, it said.'

He knew what that meant. *Bez Kompleksov* was what they wrote in the ads. Women sought 'without complexes'.

'I went inside.'

He'd felt shocked that she should even have considered it, and afraid.

'It was import–export. Beautiful office. Computers. Italian chairs.'

'New Russians,' he'd retorted disparagingly.

'So what? They pay good money. We'd eat *meat* more often, Misha. And Nadya could have clothes which hadn't been made by the clumsy fingers of her mother.'

Pushkin, however, was a man stiffened by the codes of honour and loyalty that Russian officers had held dear since the tsars. To him, the new businessmen with their Mercedes and BMW cars, their Ralph Lauren shirts and their mobile phones were thieves and traitors, creatures who smuggled their ill-gotten profits abroad and betrayed the needs of their countrymen. Parasites, as responsible for the decline of his newly independent nation as the corrupt and incompetent politicians who filled the parliament in Kiev.

'They offered me the job,' Lena had whispered, cutting through his thoughts, her pretty eyes sparkling at the thought of connecting with a life she'd glimpsed so tantalisingly on satellite TV. 'They said they'd teach me computer with Windows 95 and Microsoft Office.'

'Impossible, Lena. Such places are not for the wife of an officer.'

Lena had turned away from him to hide her anger.

'You're a dinosaur, Misha. You live in the past. Think of *us*,' she'd pleaded. 'Think of Nadya and me – not just of your own precious position in society.'

The last word had cut deep. Society was upside down now. People like him, people who used to be revered – the military, the intellectuals, the artists – all now at the bottom of the heap. Below the poverty line. Society's new leaders were the nouveaux riches, the get-rich-quick criminals who'd sold their country's assets to line their pockets. The thieves had taken over the prison.

'This *biznisman*,' he'd snarled, 'he would insist you sleep with him?'

Both knew it would be expected of her. There were thousands of women in Odessa wanting a job like this. Plenty who'd go the extra distance to get it.

'But anyway, it wouldn't be such a big thing,' she'd whispered. 'You just shut your mind. It's a small price to pay for a better life.'

'I accepted.'

At the breakfast table now, her words cut into his thoughts as if reading them.

'Accepted the job,' she repeated. 'I start on Monday.'

Suddenly he noticed her hair was different. Shorter, with a wave in it that hadn't been there before. When had it changed? Yesterday? A week ago? How would he know when he paid her so little attention?

He stared at her. Never would he have believed that his wife would defy him. Particularly that she should tell him so this very morning of all mornings.

'We'll see about that, Lena. We'll see about it . . .'

He couldn't spend time arguing with her now. Couldn't get involved in family issues when he faced the greatest crisis of principle that an officer could ever face. A crisis which he'd told her nothing about.

He pushed back the chair. He hadn't touched the *syrniki*. Without another word he stood up and put on the uniform jacket hanging in the hall. Lena stood by the front door as she always did to check over his appearance. She brushed an imaginary hair from his lapel, then leaned forward to be kissed. He pecked her cheek and walked out onto the landing to wait for the lift.

Once on the ground and outside, he strode across the grass to where their faded, rusting car was parked. If Lena was watching from the window above, she would be puzzled, maybe even alarmed, to see him get into the car instead of walking down the road to the administration building as he always did. She would know something unusual was happening and be wondering why he hadn't confided in her. But he hadn't been able to for one simple reason. If he'd told her what he was about to do she would have moved hell and high water to stop him.

The discovery a week ago that the drone spares request had been a forgery had thrown him into a deep quandary. An attempt to raise the matter again with Colonel Komarov had produced an uncharacteristic rebuff and an order, an *order*, to forget the whole matter. Yet his conscience wouldn't let him. Military equipment had been siphoned out of the system, its destination unknown. And worst of all his CO and long-time friend was clearly aware of the crime.

Such activities weren't new to the military of course. After the Soviet Union collapsed and Ukraine became independent in 1991 vast quantities of weaponry belonging to the new nation's armed forces had been sold off, both by the government and by individual officers. Huge personal fortunes had been made selling guns to foreign governments, terrorist organisations and criminal gangs. Now, however, it was his *own* unit and a personal friend of his that had become involved in such criminality. To him it was both shocking and unacceptable.

He'd brooded on the matter for days before deciding what to do. Then, on Tuesday of this week, he'd made an excuse to spend time alone with the driver who'd been assigned to the Ural truck that had driven the drone parts from the base. The lad would surely tell him where he'd taken them. To get the driver to himself, away from prying eyes, he'd decided to make a personal inspection by jeep of the Magerov runway, which was still supposed to be maintained in a usable condition, despite no aircraft having landed there for at least two years.

Private Reznik, a nineteen-year-old conscript, had steered the UAZ jeep slowly down the faded, rubber-scarred runway centreline while Pushkin scanned its surface for damage and for foreign objects that could be sucked into the engines of a jet. The youth had been stiff-backed with fear, knowing something was up. He was too junior to be assigned to driving senior officers around.

Thin-faced and shaven-headed, Reznik was grey from the malnutrition that was a conscript's lot. There would be bruises on his body, Pushkin knew, injuries from the bullying that was endemic in the armies of the former Soviet Union.

'You miss your home?' Pushkin had asked, knowing he must first break the ice.

'Of course, comrade Major.' The boy's tone had become almost dismissive. The question was absurd.

'You write to your mother often?'

'No, because my letters make her cry.'

Pushkin had looked away. If Lena had given him a son he would go to any lengths to pay the bribes that would secure a bogus medical certificate to spare the boy from military service.

'Where's home?'

'A small village. One hour west of Kiev.'

A peasant family, no doubt. No way for such sons of the soil to escape conscription.

'Any friends from home here with you?'

'No, comrade Major.'

Lonely then. Lonely and scared as they always were.

'Stop here a minute.' They'd reached the far end of the runway, the point furthest away from anyone who might see them. 'There's something I want to talk to you about.'

Reznik had blanched. He'd known what was coming.

'Last Friday you delivered a load in an eight-tonner.'

The boy had frowned as if trying to remember.

'Where did you go?'

'Where I was told to go, comrade Major.'

'But where was that?'

'Don't know, comrade Major. The officer said to follow their four-six-nine jeep, and I did.'

'But where to?'

'I wasn't looking, comrade Major,' he'd mumbled.

'Don't be ridiculous! Did they tell you not to say anything? Tell you not to say where you'd been?'

'Just said to follow the four-six-nine.'

'To a military base?'

'Don't kn—'

'Reznik!'

'There were gates, comrade Major. Then a yard. I wasn't concentrating.'

'In Odessa?'

'I think maybe.' Reznik had bitten his lip, realising the little he'd said was already too much.

Pushkin had offered a cigarette and lit it for him with a match.

'A yard, you said? There were soldiers in it?'

'I didn't see, comrade Major. Just kept my eyes on the four-six-nine like I was told. The officer gave me something to read while I waited for them to unload.'

'Pictures of girls in it?'

'Yes, comrade Major.' The boy had blushed slightly. '*Amerikanski.*'

'So instead of watching what was happening to the load on your truck you had your eyes full of spread legs!'

The boy had coloured beetroot.

Pushkin had known he would get no more from the youth and had ordered him to return him to the administration block. At the moment the jeep had driven up to the entrance, Colonel Komarov had emerged from it. He'd looked startled to see them together.

Pushkin switched on the ignition of his eight-year-old Zaporizhzhia. After an agony of churning, the rear-mounted engine spluttered into life. A cold drizzle smeared the windscreen, which the well-worn wiper blade did little to clear. He engaged the gear and the machine jerked down the road towards the main gates of the Magerov base. Set on a stone pedestal at the far end of the drive a corroding MiG-15 acted as a gate guardian and a reminder that the Magerov base had once had a more prominent role.

The railway station would take him just five minutes to reach.

Pushkin had blamed himself partly for what had happened to Reznik after that gentle interrogation. It had been downright careless to allow Komarov to see him with the youth.

The following morning he'd arrived at his usual time at the headquarters building, the Ukrainian flag flying from the staff on the roof. Top half azure, bottom half golden yellow, symbolising fields of corn under a blue sky. A salute from the guard, then upstairs to his office.

'The report on the accident, comrade Major.' One of his lieutenant clerks had met him at the top of the stairs. 'It's on top of the pile, Major. On your desk.'

Accident?

In his gloomy room with its smell of stale tobacco, he'd picked up the topmost sheet from his desk. A report from the Militsia traffic department. There'd been an explosion in a jeep last night, while the vehicle was being driven outside the base.

One occupant only. The driver – Private Ivan T. Reznik. Killed.

Deeply shocked, he'd sat staring at the poorly typed, misspelled report, simply not believing it. That it could *not* have been an accident was the one thing he was certain of. Jeeps did not explode of their own accord. No accident either that the victim was Reznik.

The boy had been murdered. A miserable young life cut short before any chance of happiness. A young man silenced because of what he could tell about the destination of the drone spares. *Could* tell, but *hadn't* in any significant way. And remembering Colonel Komarov's shock at seeing Reznik with him the previous afternoon, Pushkin had thought the unthinkable. That his commanding officer and close friend had had a hand in Reznik's death.

And yet he knew in his heart that Oleg Komarov was not a criminal. And most certainly not a murderer. If his daughter's godfather was involved in these criminal acts it was because forces beyond his control had compelled him to be.

Only at that point had Pushkin understood. The forces concerned would be Mafiya. Suddenly he'd become deeply afraid.

The Lieutenant from his outer office had knocked and entered, a fair-haired twenty-five-year-old with cool blue eyes.

'Bad about Reznik, comrade Major.'

'Yes. Very bad.'

'A fault with the jeep? Fuel leak perhaps?'

'Probably.'

'Should I question Vehicle Maintenance?'

'Yes. You'd better.'

'Odd though. You'd have thought he would have smelled something.'

'Yes. Yes you would.'

The Lieutenant had hovered over him. There was one more matter to be dealt with.

'It's the telegram, comrade Major. For the family. You usually put your name to them.'

For the Lieutenant the death or serious injury of conscripts was a routine matter that he dealt with repeatedly.

'Yes. Yes, of course.'

'Wondered if you wanted to say something special, since Reznik drove you only hours before the accident?'

'Ah. Perhaps I should.'

'It's the mothers, Major. Makes them feel their sons were treated like human beings here instead of dogs.' He'd spoken without irony.

Pushkin had sat for another hour at his desk, smoking cigarette after cigarette and pondering, stubbing out the butts in the shell-case ashtray his father had given him when he graduated. He was dealing with something of an unfathomable size and shape. It had puzzled him at first why Mafiya gangsters should want a drone. Their wars were fought at street level with Skorpions and Kalashnikovs, not on a battlefield where aerial reconnaissance had its use.

Then it had dawned on him.

All along his thinking had been confined within the tight parameters of his own military environment. He'd imagined that the spares misappropriation must be some *internal* army scandal – that the drone would be used for the purpose it had been designed for. But a machine built for one purpose could be easily adapted for another. Replace its camera sensor with a bomb of equivalent weight and the device became a guided missile. A fearsome weapon for some Mafiya gang – or a group of crazy foreigners bent on terrorism.

The more he'd thought about it, the more he'd realised that the consequences of what had happened here at Magerov might soon reverberate around the world. Hundreds, maybe thousands of lives might be lost as a result of the misuse of property belonging to the army of Ukraine. And apart from lives, *honour* was at stake here too. The honour of the Ukrainian armed forces.

The army was in his blood, as it had been in that of his ancestors. The son of one of the few Ukrainian heroes of the Great Patriotic War to survive the conflict, Mikhail Pushkin was a man to whom honour and duty mattered more than anything else. His duty, he'd realised, was to pursue the matter further. And first he would need to raise his concerns again with his commanding officer. Only if *that* action produced no satisfaction could he take it to a higher level.

Plucking up his courage, and after one more cigarette, he'd marched from his room to the rather more spacious one occupied by Colonel Komarov.

His daughter's godfather had been sitting behind his

desk, his round face in profile, staring through the window at the red-brown leaves of a large horse-chestnut tree on the grass outside.

'Comrade Colonel!' Pushkin had stood to attention with the Militsia report in his fist.

Komarov had swung round to face him, his normally warm, soft features looking drawn and tired, his eyes drained of life.

'I wish to report my concerns about the case of—'

'A tragic accident, Misha.' Komarov had cut him off sharply.

'But I wish to lodge a formal—'

'No, Misha. You do *not*.' The eyes had chilled, but behind their ice was fear. 'Accidents are events that none of us can do anything about. *None* of us, Misha. Remember that. For your sake. For my sake. And for the sake of my god-daughter, whose life I treasure very dearly.'

At the mention of Nadya, Pushkin's determination had faltered, but only for a moment.

'It is my duty to tell you, comrade Colonel, that I now have firm evidence that the spares for the VR-6—'

'Your duty, Major Pushkin, is to obey my orders!' Komarov had been white-faced with anger and fear. 'For God's sake, leave that matter alone, Misha. Return to your desk now and involve yourself in routine things. Do not give one more thought to the VR-6 business. Forget it. Because there is nothing to be done. I am telling you, Misha. *Nothing can be done*.'

There *was* something, however. And Pushkin was now doing it.

He parked the Zaporizhzhia on a patch of waste ground opposite the bleak, open platform that served as a railway station for the small town of Magerov. His appointment with General Major Orlov at the headquarters of the Odessa Military District was for midday but he wanted to be in the city in good time to leave nothing to chance.

The armed forces of Ukraine had become sick beasts since independence from Russia. Undernourished and with their post Cold War roles still undefined, corruption and opportunism had eaten away at the moral fibre of their officers. Giving in to that corruption could only make matters worse. Pushkin knew he had to make a stand. It was his *duty* to do so.

Going over the head of his commanding officer and friend had a secondary purpose too. Oleg Andrey'evich Komarov had become the Mafiya's tool, their prisoner.

General Orlov, he hoped, might have the power to free him from that grip.

23

14.30 hrs
Headquarters of the Odessa Military District

Pushkin stared blankly at the high, bare walls of the waiting room on the ground floor of the Odessa headquarters, his broad-brimmed cap on his knees. The pale-green room was in need of fresh paint, but it was light, with a large window overlooking an internal courtyard where rain fell in a steady drizzle. He'd been kept sitting on a metal-framed chair for more than two hours, while a stream of other visitors came and went. He'd begun to feel like a disobedient schoolchild left to sweat before his punishment, rather than an officer upholding the highest standards of the service.

At last a dark-haired woman in her late thirties appeared in the waiting room doorway and smiled at him. She wore a silky apricot blouse and a pleated skirt. He stood up and she apologised for the long wait, saying the General had been called away but was now back. Pushkin followed her into the lobby. They passed through a security turnstile and up two flights of stairs to the long, wide corridor where the generals had their offices.

The Odessa Military District was under the overall command of a General Colonel, an old tank commander reputed to be in despair at the decline of the army he'd served for thirty years. Beneath him were half a dozen generals major acting as department heads.

The secretary knocked at a pair of heavy doors decorated with elaborate mouldings. The name on a small engraved panel read General Major N. M. Orlov. Pushkin was more nervous than he'd ever been in his life. General Orlov was Colonel Komarov's direct superior, responsible for military supply. He'd met him only twice before, once on his appointment to the district and again during an inspection at the Magerov base three months ago.

A short, dark man with a brooding, Napoleonic air about him, Orlov waved him to a chair. He wore his uniform jacket, the lapels decorated with the insignia of special forces, his left breast marked by three lines of campaign ribbons. Orlov had distinguished himself in Afghanistan. His hands rested on a broad blotter where he'd scribbled notes about previous meetings. At the front edge of the desk was a gilded pen stand.

'Comrade Major. I must say right away that the terms under which you requested this meeting are extremely serious,' Orlov began, looking at Pushkin over the rim of a pair of half-moon reading glasses. 'I understand you've come here to make allegations against your commanding officer, is that correct?'

Orlov's bluntness threw him momentarily.

'Comrade General. I . . . well it's not exactly *against*. More in support, I would say. I mean, what I have to say to you, General, is that I have evidence that a substantial quantity of military equipment stored at Magerov—'

'Mikhail Ivanovich,' Orlov cut in, his voice a little softer. 'Before you make your allegations, which could have very serious consequences for many people, not least yourself, let me ask you this: have you really thought about what you're doing? It is a *very* serious step you're taking. Suppose your allegations were to prove unfounded. Your career – it would be over. You would have to resign. And without a pension worth anything. Your family . . . Lena, Nadya. Have you thought about them?'

A chill descended like dew. The General had done his homework.

But he couldn't stop now.

'Believe me comrade General, I have thought about it. The decision has been a painful one for me. Very painful.'

'Of course. Oleg Andrey'evich is your daughter's godfather.' Orlov pursed his mouth to emphasise the significance of this. 'You and he, you have *kym*. The bond, it's like family. And yet you are prepared to break it?'

The homework again. A voice at the back of Pushkin's mind told him to give up now. To back off. To shut up. To slink away to his desk at Magerov and carry on as if nothing had happened. But he couldn't. There was too much at stake.

'Comrade General, I believe a very serious crime has been committed and that—'

'Crime! Yes. It's all around us. We are *led* by criminals, Mikhail Ivanovich.' Orlov leaned forward on the desk as if imparting a confidence. 'In the government – in the army even, according to some. We all know it. Ukraine has become a criminal state.'

'But you're surely not saying we should accept it, General?'

'Accept? The choice is hardly ours, I think.'

'But comrade General, the crime that I'm talking about,' Pushkin continued, his confidence returning, 'I believe it could have very serious consequences outside Ukraine as well as within the army. This is why I have to report it, why I've had to ignore all matters of personal loyalty.'

The General sat back, his eyes as hard as coal.

'Well then, if your mind is made up. What is it you have to tell me, Mikhail Ivanovich?'

Pushkin began to talk. The General listened, poker-faced. When Pushkin had finished Orlov drummed his fingers on his blotter.

'You know exactly where these Yastreyo technical parts were taken?' he queried warily.

'No, comrade General. But with the resources you could call on it shouldn't be too—'

'These suspicions of yours,' he cut in gruffly. 'Who else have you told about them?'

'Nobody, General. Only Colonel Komarov.'

'Your wife knows?'

'No. I never discuss duty matters with Lena.'

'Quite correct. Quite correct.'

Elbows on the desk, Orlov leaned forward, pressing his hands together as if in prayer. He touched his finger tips against his lips.

'And you must *not* discuss it with anybody else. You were quite right to tell me about what you'd uncovered. Absolutely right. You've done your duty, Mikhail Ivanovich. You have upheld the honour of the army of Ukraine. I congratulate you on your determination and your strength. You are personally an honourable man.'

He paused, touching his fingers to his lips again as if he had a caveat to his praise. Then he seemed to think better of it.

'And you can be assured that I *will* take action as a result of what you've told me. I most certainly will.'

Pushkin allowed himself a smile of relief, a feeling, however, that was to be more short-lived than he could have ever imagined.

'At this stage, Major, there is nothing more you need to do. But the matter is extremely sensitive. There could be others involved. It would be dangerous to alert them to what you've uncovered. So it is better you put nothing in writing. Have you by any chance already . . . ?'

'No. I thought it best to speak to you first before writing my formal report.' He glowed with pride that the matter was being treated with such seriousness.

'Good. Good. In a week or two I may ask you to make a written statement, but do nothing until I tell you. I will contact you directly, in due course. In the meantime I will arrange an immediate transfer for you to another unit.'

Pushkin froze. That hadn't been his plan. To leave the apartment they'd been so lucky to get. To be shunted to some remoter part of the country where they might have to share a *kommunalka*.

'Comrade General, I don't . . .' he spluttered.

'But of course. It's impossible for you to remain at Magerov,' Orlov cut in. 'Regulations – if you make allegations against your commanding officer, you have to be relocated. For your sake and for the sake of Colonel Komarov, whose version of events I must also hear. He may perhaps have an explanation for all this which he may give to *me*, but which he didn't think appropriate for *your* ears. Your relationship with a commander – it has to be based on trust. That trust has broken down, has it not?'

'Well, yes.'

'Quite. Now, leave everything to me from this point on. You understand me? You have done your duty, for which the army will undoubtedly show its gratitude in time – assuming your allegations are proven. But you must keep silent from now on. That's the most important thing. Loose talk could destroy the detailed investigation which I shall now have to set in motion. The army needed your voice to reveal this crime. Now it needs your silence so the criminals can be uncovered and dealt with.'

'Yes, comrade General. I understand. You can rely on me.'

'I'm sure I can. I'm sure I can.'

The meeting was over. Pushkin stood to leave. General Orlov stood too. The two men were the same height. They shook hands.

'Goodbye, Mikhail Ivanovich.'

The secretary in the apricot blouse escorted Pushkin from the building.

As he walked slowly back to the railway station, Pushkin felt a great weight gone from his shoulders. He was infused by a new lightness of spirit. The painful delving into his conscience had produced the right result. He'd done his duty and been rewarded by the compliments of the General.

But the feeling of satisfaction was a bitter one. He'd betrayed a friend. For that, he would never be forgiven. By Oleg Andrey'evich Komarov or by himself.

The cloud blowing in off the Black Sea had thickened. The air was warm, almost muggy. No rain now, but Pushkin sensed it might thunder later. Traffic had built up to its end-of-working-day congestion, dilapidated buses vying for space with lines of Volgas and Zhigulis, and the sleeker, newer products from Germany and Japan.

He reached the end of a small park surrounding a statue of Taras Shevchenko, the Ukrainian hero poet, and crossed a broad avenue towards the gothic bulk of the railway station. Halfway across he paused to let a tram pass, its steel mass setting the ground vibrating beneath his feet. He checked his watch. Ten minutes past four. The *elektrychky* to Magerov didn't leave for another hour. He would ring Lena, who would be expecting him home before long.

He crossed the station yard, dodging taxis and private cars depositing passengers laden with overstuffed bags. Up the steps into the booking hall, he felt in his pocket for a telephone token. A line of phones to his right. The first three he tried didn't work, but with the fourth there was a tone. He dropped in the token and dialled. Lena answered just seconds after the number rang out.

'Misha?'

He'd not spoken a word but she had already guessed it was him.

'Yes. I'm in Odess—'

'Misha! Thank God!' she interrupted, her voice cracking. 'Misha, Misha . . .'

Pushkin felt ice slide down his spine.

'What's the matter? What's happened?'

He heard Lena trying to stifle her sobs.

'Nadya . . .' she gasped.

The ice encased him, freezing his voice.

'What's happened,' he gulped eventually. '*What's happened?*' His voice rose to a shout. A fat woman on the next phone turned to look, her broad peasant face wrinkled with alarm.

'An accident.' Lena's voice was reedy and thin.

Pushkin's throat cracked dry. The warnings – he'd heard them and ignored them. He felt himself sliding down, down.

24

By the time the delayed *elektrychky* dropped him at Magerov it was getting dark. On the phone Lena had told him little about the incident, except that it had happened while Nadya had been waiting for the bus home from school. The girl was hurt, but all right, she'd said. And Lena was scared. Petrified. Begging him to get home as soon as he could.

Half-walking, half-running from the platform, he propelled himself across the road to the waste ground where he'd left the car. But he couldn't see it. In the spot where he'd left it was an abandoned wreck which some vandal had sprayed with red graffiti. He stopped, staring angrily at the other cars, demanding to know why it was *his* that had been stolen. Then his heart sank. The vandalised machine, he realised, was a Zaporizhzhia. And beneath the red swirls of paint it was the same colour as his car.

It *was* his. The ice ran down his spine again. Devastated by the desecration of his most expensive possession, he examined it from one end to the other. This was no act of random hooliganism. Such things didn't happen in a dump like Magerov.

'Sons of whores!'

Bitter tears came to his eyes. Tears of indignation and of fear. He glanced round, imagining he was being watched. Then he looked again at his car, touching the red swirls that had defaced it. Hard lacquer. Bone dry.

Done soon after he'd parked there. As a warning. A warning from the criminals who'd murdered driver Reznik and corrupted Oleg Komarov.

The paintwork was ruined but no other damage was visible. He unlocked the door and sat in the driving seat. Paint on the windscreen too, but he could see past it. He started the engine. It worked. So did the lights. He crunched into first and swung the car onto the road, grateful that the dusk would help conceal his shame.

At the gates to the base a guard held up the flat of his hand and shook his head, not recognising the occupant. Pushkin opened the door and leaned out. When the guard saw him he saluted and reached with consternation for Pushkin's papers.

'*Hooligani,*' Pushkin explained.

'And the *Militsia* will do nothing, comrade Major,' the guard sympathised, handing Pushkin back his pass. 'They should round them all up and send them in here. *I'd* soon sort them out.'

Pushkin drove up the short avenue of pollarded plane trees that led to the administration building. At the junction in front of it he turned right, away from the pools of light cast by the few concrete standards that had working bulbs and swung the car onto the dark square of cracked tarmac in front of the officer accommodation blocks.

He switched everything off, then looked up anxiously. Lights were on in both rooms of his flat. Had Nadya been seen by a doctor? At the Magerov base there was only a first-aider. He locked the car door and hurried towards the entrance to the apartments.

Suddenly he heard something. The click of a cigarette lighter to his right. His heart turned over. He felt the presence of death. Had they come for *him* now? Here within the secure perimeter of the base? Another click, then a small flame visible in the midst of a clump of birch trees that had been planted to mark Independence Day.

'Misha!' Komarov's voice. 'Over here.'

No, he thought. The Colonel had every right to want to kill him after what he'd just done in Odessa. He turned, meaning to run for the apartments, but his legs felt rooted. Running away had always been hard for him. He was going to have to confront his Colonel sooner or later, he decided, so he walked over to the trees, bracing himself for whatever might come.

'Comrade Colonel,' he mumbled awkwardly. 'What . . . what're you doing here?'

'Trying to save your life, you idiot,' Komarov hissed. 'Though God knows why after what you've done in Odessa this afternoon.'

What you've done . . . He knew already. Knew where he'd been, whom he'd spoken to.

'You've had me followed,' he accused.

'Huh!' Komarov exclaimed dismissively. 'You think I have need for that? You are so naive, Misha.' His voice was saw-edged with emotion. 'You don't understand, do you? You simply do not understand.'

'I understand well enough, Oleg Andrey'evich,' Pushkin protested feebly. 'I understand what's right and what's wrong.'

In the darkness he saw Komarov shake his head with a heavy sadness.

'Nothing. You understand nothing. I did try to warn you. And now . . .' He gestured first towards Pushkin's vandalised car, then the apartment block. 'Poor Nadya . . .' When he said her name there was love in his voice. 'It's entirely your fault, you know. If you had understood what these people are like, what they would do if you got in their way . . .'

'They?' Pushkin interrupted. 'Who are *they* exactly?'

'Men whose power is greater than the state's.'

Komarov sighed. 'You cannot fight people like that Misha. I tried, but when they want something from you they will never let go.'

'We can fight them together, Oleg Andrey'evich.'

Komarov grabbed his arms and shook him.

'Listen, you ignoramus! I will tell you what happened to me, then perhaps you will understand.' He paused as if collecting his thoughts. 'I was approached by someone . . .'

'Who? Who are these people?'

'It is better you don't know. But, if you allow your simple brain to think about it you may guess. The man who came here knows me well. Knows you also. And knows the army's procedures for equipment supply.'

Pushkin frowned. In his confused, anxious state the clue wasn't clear enough for him.

'Who?'

'No. You must not ask. Suffice to say he was able to tell me in precise detail what he wanted me to provide for him. He offered a substantial sum in dollars in a foreign bank. But I refused.'

'Of course! I knew you would.'

'But I wish I hadn't, Misha, because I would have been in the same position I am now but a lot better off.'

'What d'you mean?'

'I mean that when I refused to co-operate voluntarily they forced me.'

'But how?'

'Through Vyra.'

'Your wife? I don't understand.'

'She was driving the car to Odessa one day. Suddenly the car in front of her stopped dead. She ran into the back of it. The Zhiguli was badly damaged, but that didn't matter. It was the other car – a BMW. Wrecked.'

Pushkin understood. There was no car insurance in Ukraine. Under the law damage must be paid for by the guilty party. And a car that runs into the back of another is automatically guilty.

'The BMW owner gave her a choice. Come up with six thousand *hryvna* within a week or he would get the Militsia involved. That means *prison*, Misha. I couldn't let that happen. And six thousand *hryvna* – it would take two years for me to earn so much, and leave nothing for food.'

'I'm beginning to understand.'

'The next day the man who'd approached me about the drone came back. If I agreed to co-operate they would forget the debt.'

'Yes. I knew it must have been something like that. I always believed in you Oleg Andrey'evich.' Then anger rose in him again. 'But Reznik. That was *murder*!'

'So let there be no more, Misha,' Komarov pleaded. 'Let there be no more.'

'What are you saying?'

'That you must get away from here, Misha. With Lena. With Nadya. Get away from here tonight.'

'But General Orlov – he's behind me. I told him you were involved against your will. Told him so this afternoon in Odessa. He will be taking action. He told me so.'

The Colonel closed his eyes and drew in a deep breath.

'Orlov is behind you?' he mocked. 'Then watch out. Yes. General Orlov will take action all right.' He shook his head again. 'You are so, *so* innocent, Misha. How can this be? Where have you been the last five years? Don't you read newspapers? Don't you know what happens to people who cross the Mafiya?'

Pushkin swallowed, unable to answer at first. 'But the army is stronger than them. General Orlov . . .' He gulped.

'*Orlov*? Misha, Misha. Remember what people call the Mafiya? *Sprut* – the octopus. Its tentacles are everywhere.

In the Militsia, in government. Even in your beloved army.'

Pushkin gaped at him stupidly, not believing what he was hearing.

'But you're not saying that General Orlov . . .' he croaked.

'You think generals can live on what they're paid any more than we can?' Komarov growled.

'But General *Orlov*!' he mouthed, sensing a great tidal wave closing over his head. He'd told the man everything. *Everything*. 'I can't believe . . .'

'You *must* believe it Misha. Because if you don't you're dead. You're a danger to them. They've seen now that warning you off isn't enough. Now they will kill you.' Komarov glanced round nervously. 'And don't think you'll be safe in this place.'

Pushkin's head span. The military edifice, the bulwark against the collapsing society that he saw all around him, was itself now crumbling.

'But where can I go?'

'Don't tell *me*. I can't be trusted either. Anywhere. Abroad if you can. In Ukraine you will *never* be safe.'

Pushkin quaked. How could he have been so naive? He cringed at the thought of how that very afternoon, against all common sense, he'd propelled himself into the jaws of death. Like a mindless toy soldier – that's how he'd behaved.

They stood in silence, listening to the wind moving the branches above their heads. Then in the distance they heard a car. Komarov backed away like a ghost fearing the approach of day.

'Goodbye, Misha. Forget honour. Forget your loyal oath. This is not the time for such thoughts. Do what you have to do for *them*.' He pointed up towards the apartments. 'That's where your duty lies now.'

Then he was gone, melting into the darkness, picking

his way back through the shadows towards the block where he had his own home.

As the headlights of the approaching car got nearer, fear tore at Pushkin's guts. He sprinted to the door of the apartments and flattened himself against the wall inside. The car passed by without stopping. Harmless? A jeep on security patrol? Probably. But he knew he could never be sure of such things again. He pressed the button for the elevator. Then, as he heard the winding machinery gather speed, he backed away. Better to walk. Nothing was as it seemed any more. Nothing could be trusted.

He reached the fifth floor, out of breath. There were four apartments on each landing. He heard a door close. Someone watching, waiting? He slipped his key into the lock and entered his flat, a broken man.

Three hours later at a quarter to ten the three of them squeezed into the defiled Zaporizhzhia together with two small suitcases and a polythene carrier bag filled with essentials and the clothes and possessions they treasured the most.

Nadya's face was badly grazed and her arm was in a sling. Lena had explained that a car had mounted the kerb as the child had walked to the bus stop. Only the fortuitous presence of a tree at that point in the pavement had prevented her from being crushed to death.

At the gate the guard had changed since his return to the base earlier. The new man peered into the vehicle, surprised at the Major driving out at this time of night in a car looking like a work from a modern art exhibition. Pushkin, dressed now in casual trousers and a pullover, pointed at the rear seat.

'The child. Taking her to a doctor.'

The guard noted Nadya's bandaged arm and grazed face.

'Good luck, comrade Major. Hope you find one who doesn't make you pay through the nose.'

Pushkin turned the car towards the centre of Magerov village. He kept a wary eye on the mirror, but no lights followed them. He put his foot down until they were within a hundred metres of the train station. Then he pulled into the kerb, switched off the engine and extinguished the lights.

'Five past ten, the last train,' he reminded Lena, helping her and Nadya from the car. The girl was wide awake but subdued. 'You have the money?'

They'd managed to save a few *hryvna* in the past year, keeping it inside a tin musical box hidden behind their winter stock of bottled fruit in a cupboard in the flat. Just enough money for the rail tickets to Kiev.

Lena patted the pocket of the long winter coat she was wearing, her face strained and tear-stained. It had been she who'd come up with the solution of seeking temporary refuge with his widowed sister in the capital.

'The Kiev train leaves Odessa at eleven-thirty. Get some seats. I'll find you on it.'

She kissed him with a fervour that betrayed her fear of never seeing him again.

'Be careful,' she whispered. Then, after a pause, 'I love you, Misha.'

Then they were gone, walking slowly towards the train station, Lena carrying a bag in each hand and Nadya with a small rucksack on her back.

Pushkin watched them for a moment, then took a deep breath to steady his nerves and restarted the engine.

Forty-five minutes later he had reached his destination, an area of marshland on the northern perimeter of Odessa, overlooked by the billowing flares of an oil refinery.

Although brought up in Kiev, he knew Odessa well. As

a child they'd come to visit their cousins here every summer. He turned off the ring-road, still moderately busy with traffic despite the lateness of the hour, and headed down a severely pitted lane that crossed the swamp on a man-made dyke. The headlights picked out tall, yellow-green reeds and then at last a clump of willows. He stopped the car beside the trees, got out and, using a hand torch, searched the ground for saplings. Finding some, he broke off a couple of lengths of bendy wood and threw them in the back of the car. Then he continued on his way.

At the end of this track he knew that the ground rose a few metres and there were houses – dachas set in vegetable gardens. But a few hundred metres before the houses, if he'd remembered correctly, the track would branch.

In the distance the lights of a house twinkled suddenly. He slowed. The car window was open and he screwed up his face at the smell from the sewage treatment plant whose effluent ended in the swamp.

Then he stopped. A mud path ran off to the left, just wide enough for a car, its surface rutted by the wheels of vehicles used by reed cutters. He turned down it. After a short distance the track ended in a ramp that dipped into the swamp. He halted the car with its lights pointing into the mire. Water glinted blackly. Recent rain had raised its level. The smell here was stronger than ever. By the edge of the sludge lay the skeletal remains of an old rowing boat.

He doused the headlights but left the sidelights on and the engine running. He got out, putting a leather briefcase on the ground beside him. Then he wound down all the windows and retrieved the two sticks of willow from the back seat. He wedged one of them between the accelerator pedal and the front seat base so that the engine note rose. The second stick was stouter.

Leaning in through the open driver's door, he jammed one end against the clutch pedal and pushed down. Then he made sure the handbrake was free, pushed the gear into first, and eased the stick's pressure on the clutch until the car began to move. He let go of the stick, jumped back and watched his cruelly abused jalopy jerk forward down the slope.

The stubby front of the car hit the sludge and slowed, but the rear engine powered the machine further into the mire. He watched the tail lights move steadily away from him. Then, suddenly, the engine spluttered and died as the vile-smelling slime penetrated the intakes. The lights shorted.

Pushkin waited a while, listening to the gurgle of the sinking car. Then, when the noises subsided, he shone a torch to confirm the gaily painted roof had dipped below the surface. Still visible beneath the water now, by the time daylight came he knew it would be gone.

Turning away from this destruction of the only thing of value he'd ever owned, he picked up his briefcase and began to walk, shielding the torch beam with his fingers.

Time was short. Very short. He began to run. He rejoined the main track and turned towards the light of the houses.

The first that he came to was ramshackle and decrepit, but the second was newly built of cinder blocks and timber. In front of it stood an elderly Toyota, almost certainly stolen a year or two back from somewhere in western Europe. The lights of the house blazed through open curtains.

Pushkin rapped at the door. He heard grunts of surprise from inside. He rapped again.

'Come on, come on,' he shouted. 'It's urgent.'

'Who is it? What do you want?' A slurred male voice from beyond the door.

'I need help. My car's broken down,' Pushkin shouted, praying they would make it easy for him.

'Go away!'

'I can pay you,' he lied. 'Dollars.'

At the magic word, the door opened a few centimetres, held by a chain. A bleary-eyed, middle-aged man dressed in old cords and a moth-eaten cardigan scrutinised him.

'All right, then,' he wheezed, convinced by Pushkin's clean, square looks.

The chain was slipped and the door swung open, the householder staggering back with it.

'Come on in, comrade.'

The house consisted of one main room combining living, sleeping and cooking areas. A fat woman dressed in thick woollens lay dozing on a couch. A television was on.

'If it's a telephone you want, comrade, you're out of luck,' the man muttered, eyeing him cautiously.

'That's not what I want, comrade. I have to get to the railway station in Odessa. The Kiev train in half an hour.'

The ruddy-faced dacha owner looked blank.

'You have a car. Will you drive me there?' Pushkin asked gruffly.

The other man's face creased with astonishment. 'No chance, brother. The Militsia, they'd put me in jail.' He held up a vodka bottle in explanation. 'Unless . . . *Dollars*, you said?'

'That was a lie. I'm sorry. I have no money,' Pushkin admitted.

'What are you saying? Why are you troubling me? Get out of my house!'

Pushkin knew he had no choice now. He bent down and clicked the locks on his briefcase, the dacha owner's eyes following his movements as if still expecting bank-notes.

'No money,' Pushkin repeated, 'but I do have this.' He pushed the muzzle of a Makarov 9mm pistol at the dacha owner's face. 'Give me the car keys, comrade,' he demanded apologetically. 'Immediately.'

The man's face crumpled with shock and incomprehension.

'The keys,' snapped Pushkin, clicking back the hammer of the pistol.

At the sound of ratcheting metal, the old man dipped a trembling hand into his trouser pocket and pulled them out.

'I'm sorry,' Pushkin mumbled, snatching them from him. 'I will leave it outside the station. Keys under the seat. Door unlocked.'

The householder gaped. Pushkin had no idea whether he'd understood or not.

He would need to drive like a madman. There were just fifteen minutes until the departure of the Kiev train, and to reach the station from these northern outskirts would normally take twenty.

On the hair-raising drive through the dawdling late-evening traffic his mind kept darting back to what Komarov had said – that the Mafiya monster who'd initiated this trail of horror was known to both of them. Until this moment it was a riddle he'd been unable to crack, but suddenly he could. Suddenly he knew who Komarov meant.

A year ago there'd been a Captain First Rank, seconded like the rest of them to a job below his station at Magerov, who'd unexpectedly resigned his commission. A former Spetznaz commander, he'd left to sell his skills to Ukraine's new criminal aristocracy. The man was an animal, a man he despised. But a creature who, when his silver-capped teeth were into you, would never let go. And Pushkin was convinced this was the man who was now out to kill him.

The car screeched to a halt outside the station one minute before 11.30. He sprinted across the forecourt where, despite the late hour, old babushkas still sat holding yellowing squares of paper advertising rooms to let. Up the steps into the ticket hall, he ran straight through, barging onto the platforms past the stalls selling pasties. In the background he heard the romantic Black Sea Song that blared from the station loudspeakers whenever a long-distance train departed.

Head craning for the platform number on the destination board, he crashed through relatives waving off loved ones just as the Kiev train began to move. Lungs burning, he squeezed more speed into his stride and grabbed the door rail of the final carriage. Leaping onto the step, he unlatched the door and swung it open.

He'd made it. His life, his future was a void. A black hole, a bottomless pit. Only one thing mattered now. Survival for him and his family.

25

Saturday, 5 October, 11.10 hrs
Mortlake Crematorium, West London

The flight back from Cyprus in the RAF C-130 yesterday afternoon had taken seven hours, most of it spent strapped into an uncomfortable canvas seat at the side of the wide, grey-painted fuselage which was stacked with military hardware being returned to the UK for maintenance. They'd found space for Chrissie's plain coffin close by the ramp and secured it to the floor with thick straps more used to restraining heavy metal than frail flesh.

Weary from his lack of sleep during the previous twenty-four hours, Sam had stuffed foam plugs in place to deaden the machine's monotonous, ear-damaging noise and slept fitfully on the flight. In his waking moments the sight of Chrissie's corpse was ever present in his head, her waxen body and the tattoo that had defiled it.

By the time Duncan Waddell had met him at RAF Lyneham, Sam had marshalled his thoughts. He'd decided that for now he would keep all mention of the tattoo to himself. During the car journey up to London, he'd briefed his controller on everything else he'd learned.

The taxi driver half-turned his head. 'I'm to wait, sir?'

They were passing through the wrought-iron gates of the crematorium at Mortlake. Skinny silver birch trees lined the roadway.

'No. I'll walk back. Along the river.'

Sam paid and got out. Dressed in a dark suit, white shirt and black tie, he clutched a bouquet of yellow and white chrysanthemums encased in cellophane. The crematorium itself was of dark brick, solid and non-denominational in style. Well-trimmed lawns surrounded it, dotted with white-barked trees. He carried his flowers towards the chapel, but before he reached it was intercepted by an usher.

'For Mrs Kessler, is it, sir?'

'Yes.'

'Have to ask you to wait another five minutes. The previous funeral's running late.'

Sam nodded. He could hear the organ sounds from within. He turned away. A few seconds later a hearse appeared round the bend in the drive followed by two black Daimlers. The attendant signalled the convoy to wait. Sam stepped to one side into a small garden concealed by a laurel hedge, hoping to avoid any direct contact with the husband he'd helped Chrissie to cheat on for so long.

Within a couple of minutes the doors to the chapel had opened and a handful of elderly women supported by a pair of younger men emerged sombre-faced. Sam watched them progress into the courtyard behind the chapel where wreaths were laid out on the brick paving. Then the hearse drew up to the doors and Chrissie's coffin was borne inside.

Martin Kessler followed it closely. Six feet tall, straight-backed and dressed in a dark-blue suit and black tie, his spectacles seemed to have slid down his nose a little. His face was gaunt and tense. A man fighting to retain control. By his side, with her arm hooked through his, was an elegant, dark-haired woman in her late sixties, whose lips were puckered with barely controlled grief. Sam took her to be Chrissie's widowed mother.

He let them go in, then emerged from the side garden and followed, laying his flowers next to others in the chapel porch. About ten mourners had spread themselves through the front two rows of seats. Family, he thought. Nobody he recognised from the Firm. Sam slipped into an empty row at the back.

A thin, middle-aged priest emerged from a vestry and shook hands with Kessler. It was obvious they had never met before. The service began, its pace brisk, as if the cleric were making up for the tardiness of the previous funeral. An electric organ belted out hymns at a tempo more suited to a wedding.

Sam didn't hear the words, his eyes boring into the back of Kessler's head. *He* must know what that tattoo signified, he thought to himself. Must know why she'd had it done. Or perhaps he'd never seen it. Perhaps, as Chrissie had hinted, Kessler's inhibitions were so deep that nakedness was an embarrassment to him.

Sam glanced to his left. The pew on the other side of the aisle that had been empty when he entered was now occupied by a lone woman. Under a broad-brimmed black hat, her face was pert, but drawn, as if she were sucking in her cheeks. She sensed him staring at her and looked his way. Coal-dark eyes appraised him. Then her carmine lips parted in as much of a smile as seemed appropriate in the circumstances.

Ten minutes later the meaningless ceremony drew to a close. As the coffin rolled mechanically through a curtained hatch on its way to the furnace, Sam felt a compelling need to be away from there. He stood up and slipped as noiselessly as he could through the swing doors.

Once outside he began to walk briskly away. He needed to be alone.

Jutting out his chin, he took a path towards the river and didn't slow until he'd reached the small iron gateway onto the towpath. Autumn leaves had speckled the ground a yellow-red. He walked to the water's edge and stopped. To his left rowers were carrying skiffs from a boathouse, taking advantage of the slack water at high tide. With his sailor's eyes well used to squinting against the light, he watched a cormorant fly low and fast up river, while Canada geese honked noisily overhead.

'Excuse me . . .' A woman's voice startled him. 'Are you Sam by any chance?'

He turned. It was the woman with the broad-brimmed hat. Her eye makeup had been blurred by her tears.

'Yes. Have we met?' he asked awkwardly.

Her moist eyes bored into his.

'No. I'm Clare. I don't know if Chrissie ever mentioned . . .'

'Oh yes.' Shopping trips and visits to the gym. Endless alibis for her visits to his flat. 'You live in Fulham.'

The hollow-cheeked look was natural, he now realised. She was almost anorexic.

'You've got a good memory,' she replied.

They each pulled a forced smile.

'Grim, yes?' she checked.

'Very.'

'Martin looked shell-shocked, I thought.'

'Yes.' Sam felt uncomfortable talking about him. 'Was that . . . ?

'Chrissie's mum? Mmm. Must be hell to lose your only child, even one that didn't keep in touch.'

In the years he'd known Chrissie, she'd hardly ever mentioned family. It wasn't a subject they'd talked about. He frowned, trying to remember what they *had* discussed other than the latest twist in Chrissie's schizoid relationship with her husband. The periods they'd spent together were of necessity short and the logistics of adultery all too time-consuming.

'She loved you, you know,' Clare told him out of the blue. She took a handkerchief from her shiny black handbag and blew her nose.

'You think?'

'Oh yes. But you know that.' There was an accusing tone to her voice, which Sam didn't understand. Suddenly she took off her hat and shook her hair free. It was cut short to the nape of the neck and shone like a raven's feathers. 'I hate hats. Chrissie would've screamed to see me in one.'

Sam smiled politely and turned his gaze back to the river. The scullers were setting off upstream. From a boathouse on the opposite bank an eight was taking to the water. An outboard-powered dinghy scudded in impatient circles like a snarling dog. A coach at the tiller snapped at the rowers through a megaphone.

'Fancy a drink?' he asked, without thinking. Common sense told him it was bad security talking to this woman, but he felt a compulsion to do so, a need to open the lid on any part of Chrissie's life he didn't know about. 'I could do with one.'

'Yes. Brilliant.' She looked round as if expecting a bar waiter within hailing distance.

'Down there,' pointed Sam to their right. 'Beyond the road bridge. There's a pub.'

'Oh, yes. But just a minute. I think I'd better fix my face. Could you . . . ?' She handed him her hat then took out a compact from her bag and checked her mascara in the mirror, dabbing with a tissue at the streaks. 'That'll have to do. Short of plastic surgery . . .'

She took the hat back and they began to walk. Sam loosened his tie, then removed it, folding it carefully and putting it into his jacket pocket. He wondered whether Chrissie had confided in this woman about their work.

'You knew Chrissie a long time?' he asked.

'Yes. From boarding school onwards,' she replied proprietorially. 'Best friends for *twenty* years.' She bit her lip as tears threatened again. 'Can't believe it,' she choked, putting a hand to her mouth. 'Can't believe she's really dead and that, that *performance* we've just been through was *it*.'

'I know what you mean.'

They walked in silence under the wide Portland stone road bridge that carried one of the main trunk roads out of central London.

'You've been friends since school then,' he prompted.

'Yes. There've been gaps of course. She went to university, I didn't. Nearly lost touch then. But when she graduated and settled in London working for the Foreign Office, we resumed where we'd left off.'

'And you? What were you doing by then?'

'Human Resources for a big retailer. What they used to call personnel. But she and I, we never talked about our jobs. Chrissie insisted on it. She said all the stuff she dealt with was highly confidential and she couldn't, so it was best we didn't discuss my work either. I wondered once if she was bullshitting me – you know, covering up the fact that in reality she was just some lowly clerk.'

They stepped from the path onto a narrow roadway lined with expensively renovated Victorian villas protected from the high tide by walls and steps.

'But I should have known better,' Clare continued meaningfully.

They stepped to one side to allow a milk-float to hum past.

'Chrissie had always been ambitious. A natural high-flyer. Unlike me. She was always fast stream. So were the men she dated – most of them. Not you, of course.' She stopped and grabbed his arm. 'God, that sounded awful. Didn't mean it like that. Will you forgive me?'

'Don't worry about it,' he bristled, suspecting she *had* meant it cuttingly. There was a bitchiness in the way she spoke.

'The point I was meaning to make was that she hankered after men like that, but at the same time was rather intimidated by them. And often she found them boring and self-centred. That's why she liked you so much. For your directness. Your down-to-earthness.'

'Thanks.' Directness was a quality this woman also seemed blessed with.

'Well, of course, she needed *ordinary* people around her sometimes. People like you and me. So she could feel comfortable. So she could be her true self.' The last sentence was spoken with feeling.

They'd reached the pub. Wooden tables and benches crowded a terrace that overlooked the river, but the first spots of rain were splatting noisily around them, so they went inside. He stood at the bar ordering drinks while Clare bagged an isolated table by the window. Sam had a feeling he was being ambushed. That the woman had some purpose in talking to him.

'Large Gordon's,' he murmured, placing the ice-filled glass and a tonic bottle in front of her on the varnished mahogany table. 'You don't smoke, do you?' he checked, moving a brimming ashtray to another table. She shook her head. He sat down and took a deep draught of his pint.

'Thanks for this,' she said, emptying half of the tonic into the glass. Then she raised it. 'To Chrissie,' she whispered. 'Happy memories.'

They sat without speaking for at least a minute, staring through the window as a squat Port of London Authority vessel scooped up driftwood and plastic bottles from the soupy brown water of the Thames.

'What will you remember best about her, Sam?'

Clare's eyes showed a sisterly determination, as if wanting to discover if he'd *really* cared for Chrissie, rather than just taking advantage of her.

'The enigma,' Sam answered without a second thought. 'The mystery of what made her tick. Because I have to confess I never really worked her out.'

'Ah, yes.' Clare smiled smugly. 'A woman's *mystery*. The cheese in the mousetrap.' She sounded cynical.

'Are you married?' he checked, suspecting a divorce.

She shook her head. 'Not my scene. But tell me about the enigma of Chrissie. What was it exactly that you didn't understand about her?'

A formal interview question. The woman was beginning to annoy him.

'Well, for starters,' he said, uncomfortable about where this was leading, 'how could she go on for the best part of five years deceiving her husband?'

Clare pooh-poohed his question. 'The French do it all the time. And anyway, your part in the deception wasn't exactly honourable, was it? Didn't you feel just the teensiest bit of guilt?'

'Frequently,' he admitted defensively. 'But you know how it is; it felt right. And I told myself that one day she would leave him and—'

'And you two would live happily ever after like the Flopsy Bunnies,' she mocked.

'I don't know. Maybe, yes.' He felt himself reddening.

She shook her head. 'She would never have married you. Never. You know why? You were too self-sufficient. You didn't *need* her in your life, you see. Apart from . . . for physical reasons.'

Her words shocked him. What did *she* know about his needs? What had *Chrissie* known . . .

A babble erupted around the bar. He looked towards the noise, glad of a distraction and a chance to let his anger subside. A rugby crowd in pullovers and scarves were priming themselves for Twickenham or the Old Deer Park.

Suddenly he felt her touch his hand.

'Sorry. Wasn't trying to be mean just then.' She pulled her hand back quickly. 'Wasn't getting at you.'

'Forget it.' He looked away again, determining to end the conversation quickly and leave.

'Shall I solve the enigma for you?' she asked, her elegant, tapered nose raised condescendingly.

'I have the feeling you're going to, whatever I say,' he told her brittlely.

'It's not hard really, Sam. You see, there wasn't really much mystery about Chrissie. She was the way she was because she wanted too much. That's all. Simple as that. The poor girl simply never learned when enough was enough.'

She pushed her slim fingers through the ends of her shiny black hair, letting the strands slip through them. Her dark eyes watched for his reaction.

'*Too* simple,' he retorted, folding his arms.

'Too simple for you, you mean. Because you want it to be more complicated than that. You *want* the mystery. Because without it, you'd have lost interest in her.'

He took a deep gulp of his beer in preparation to leave.

Clare crossed her arms as if hugging herself and teased at the lobe of one ear. Her nail gloss matched her lips.

'I'm *so* glad to have met you,' she preened. 'You're just as Chrissie described.'

'Really?' he snarled.

'She'd got you to a tee. She knew instinctively that divorcing Martin and moving in with you would be a disaster.'

Sam wanted to strangle her. He'd had quite enough of this woman telling him what was right and wrong with his relationship with Chrissie.

'The other thing she knew,' she added, determinedly twisting the knife, 'was that on your own, *you* would never be enough for *her*.'

'Look, I think you really have said quite enough,' Sam snapped.

'But listen,' she rejoined bitterly, 'that one wasn't personal to just you, Sam. It applied to all of us. *None* of us was enough for her. Don't you see? Not Martin, not you, not me . . .'

Sam narrowed his eyes. There was innuendo here. For some reason he still didn't understand, the woman was going for his throat.

'She wanted it *all*, Sam. And all at the same time. The financial and social security of a husband, but her lovers too.'

Lovers. The plural was like a knife. He didn't believe her. He simply didn't believe what she was implying.

'Designer clothes,' Clare enumerated, tapping fingers against the palm of her hand, 'always the top hairstylists, that brand-new BMW coupé . . .'

Sam frowned. He knew nothing about the car.

'And some of her jewellery was exquisite. She said there'd been some inheritances. And of course her husband earns a bob or two. Rather more than you, I should imagine. A mandarin in the Treasury, isn't he?'

'Something like that.' He'd had enough of her bitchiness. 'You sound as jealous as hell, Clare.'

'No *way* was I jealous of *Chrissie*,' she retorted, her face colouring. '*I* didn't want what she had. No, Sam dear. You've not understood. But then it's blindingly obvious you never *have* understood about Chrissie.'

He tensed, ready to stand up and leave.

'Not jealous of *Chrissie*, Sam.' Clare leaned forward, entwining her hands. 'Jealous of *you*.' She let the words sink in. 'And of Martin of course. Because you two *men* were each getting a share of something that I wanted for me alone.'

Sam felt the blood drain from his face. 'What are you talking about?'

Clare's eyes were triumphant. She gave a little laugh. 'I'm telling you Chrissie was bisexual, dummy.'

'Bollocks!'

'It's true, my *dear*,' she answered matter-of-factly. 'Chrissie and I had sex together at school when we were both seventeen. A crush that *I* never grew out of. She didn't either really, but as I said before, no one thing was ever enough for her. For some inexplicable reason she acquired the taste for men's bodies as well as women's.'

Sam gaped. This simply could *not* be true.

'She had a busy schedule did Chrissie, managing her . . . her little stable of partners.'

Sam was dumbstruck. He would have known, surely. Some sign. Some hint. Some coldness. But there'd been none. No indication to suggest their sex wasn't as satisfying for her as it was for him.

'Why are you telling me this?' His eyes were like lasers. 'Why does it matter so much to you that I know?'

For a long time she didn't answer, letting her eyes fill with tears.

'Because,' she whispered finally. 'Because I wanted you to feel what *I* have felt for God knows how long. To feel the pain of knowing that you are not enough for someone. And that you never ever will be.'

Sam pushed back the chair and stood up. He couldn't breathe. He felt the dark, soul-crushing confines of the cell in Baghdad again. He turned away, the panelled walls of the pub, the hunting prints, the brass lamps all now a blur.

Legs moving for the door, he reached the fresh air and sucked it in. The ground shook as Concorde flew overhead on its way into Heathrow. Brakes squealed and a car stopped inches from his knees. He'd stumbled straight into the road.

'Piss artist!' yelled the driver.

Sam reached the river path and turned right. The track dipped onto a boat-launching ramp, slippery with mud and strewn with tree branches and litter left by the tide. Beyond it, the path would take him back to Barnes. He marched ahead, oblivious of the filth spattering his shoes and dark trousers. All that mattered to him was to get away from there. From the satanic woman who'd poisoned his mind, and from the furnace that would soon be turning Chrissie's remains to vapour.

26

a.m.
Kiev, Ukraine

Block 16 of the Krystal residential complex in the sprawling Leningrads'kyi district of the Ukrainian capital was identical to the fifteen others that lined the broad highway leading westwards out of the city. Sixteen floors of dilapidated two-and three-roomed flats with walls so thin that residents learned intimate details of their neighbours' lives without the need to hold their breath.

Oksana Ivanovna Koslova stepped out onto the paved area between the blocks, glad to be free of the disinfectant smell that clung to the stairwell and lifts in the tower that had been her home for fifteen years. She had a broad, open face, and dark hair that was almost black. Small gold hoops hung from her ear lobes. Lines at the sides of her lipsticked mouth and around her surprisingly blue eyes belonged to a woman older than her thirty-eight years. Since her husband's lingering death some five years earlier she'd lived alone here with her daughter Luba, a troublesome fifteen-year-old who took a far stronger interest in pop icons than homework.

Oksana Ivanovna felt the first spots of rain and extracted a flower-patterned scarf from her shopping bag to cover her head. Overnight her life had changed. It was as if a hurricane had blown into the tedious monotony of her daily existence. Instead of being a woman of no consequence except to herself and marginally to her daughter, she now had three terrified people depending on her to save their lives.

She tightened the belt of her chocolate-brown raincoat and took the path that ran parallel with the highway. Horse-chestnut trees, planted when the tower blocks were built in an attempt to brighten up the harsh concrete, cast off their yellow leaves like the worn-out soles of boots. The Metro station was a five-minute walk away.

This morning the inside of her head was like a cavern of twittering bats. She felt desperately frightened by what she was about to do, but also guiltily excited by the drama that had burst into her life. It had been a shock seeing her bruised and bandaged niece when Lena and Misha had turned up with Nadya at seven that morning, all of them ashen-faced after a sleepless night on the train from Odessa. Nadya had big grey smudges under her eyes and fell asleep the moment they'd cleaned her grazed face with fresh disinfectant and settled her in her own daughter's bed. Luba had grumbled fiercely at being turned out of her blankets so early on a Saturday.

Their arrival was expected, because Lena had phoned from Odessa late last night, but it had been impossible to prepare for. What do you do for a family fleeing for its life? Shelter them, of course, because they were flesh and blood, but also make every effort to get them out of your home again as soon as possible in case the taint to their lives threatened yours. Moving them on was what she was now trying to organise.

It had shocked her that it should be Misha who'd fallen foul of the Mafiya, always the steadiest of her two brothers and herself, never stepping out of line, never doing anything to offend. And now here he was, under threat of death from gangsters. He'd refused to explain why, saying it would be safer for her if she didn't know.

All he'd revealed was that secret information had come into his possession which could be of considerable importance both to Ukraine and to the rest of the world. He'd told her that their own government's authorities were too corrupt to be trusted with it and he had no choice but to pass on what he knew to a western nation. In return he hoped for a visa and asylum. And since Oksana worked as a receptionist and telephonist at the British Embassy in Kiev, it was the British authorities he'd decided to approach, counting on her to furnish him with the contacts he needed.

At the head of the steps down to the Metro, two old country women in knitted cardigans sat on wooden boxes displaying a meagre spread of vegetables to sell.

'*Pajalsta*,' one of them begged as Oksana passed.

'Not today, babushka,' she answered. Not *any* day for her, because with the family dacha an hour's bus ride away, and she the only able-bodied family member still living in Kiev, she had all the fruit and vegetables she and Luba could possibly need.

She splashed down the steps into the station avoiding the worst of the puddles on the landings and entered the grim, concrete ticket hall. Then she held out her monthly travel pass for inspection and passed through.

The escalator to the platforms stretched into the earth like a sloping mine-shaft, its cavernous roof glazed with off-white tiles and the flat space between the up and down sides sporting lamps in the shape of flaming torches. Oksana idly watched the defeated faces on the up-staircase, knowing that their numbed misery matched her own.

Except not today, perhaps. Because today she had hope. Just a glimmer of it, something as frail as a sickly child, but hope nonetheless. Just what it was she was hoping for she wouldn't have been able to say if asked, except that it could involve a change to her life, a life that had stagnated for years.

She reached the bottom of the escalator and directed a friendly smile at the *dezhurnaya* in her glass-fronted box whose day-long job was to stare upwards at the moving stairs, her hand on the stop button ready for trouble. The girl was in her twenties, with a lifeless, pointy-nosed face, its skin the pallor of a creature that never sees daylight. Still, thought Oksana, it was a job. Enough to pay for food for herself and her child if she had one.

The wide platform had a huge arched roof covered with mosaics, its grandeur a monument to the time when the Soviet Union had been something to be proud of. The train, when it came in a few moments later, was almost full. Oksana squeezed in between the bodies, trying to keep beyond the reach of any slob who might try to take advantage of the crush. She had a shape she was quite proud of, but since the death of her husband had not let any man touch her sexually. The doors closed and the train moved on, the silent, uncurious faces waiting patiently for their destinations to arrive.

It had been eleven o'clock when she'd left the apartment. She knew from past experience that First Secretary Mr Gerald Figgis dropped into the embassy every Saturday morning at around midday to pick up messages from London. And she knew, because everybody in the small embassy knew, that Mr Figgis was the representative in Ukraine of the British Secret Intelligence Service.

She left the Metro at Universytet and walked a block and a half along the wide boulevard Tarasa Shevchenka keeping the Botanical Gardens to her right, until she reached the junction with Volodymyrs'ka. In front of her loomed the classical red bulk of the Shevchenko University. She sighed as she always did, reaching this point in her journey to work, because it had been during her student days at this very university that she'd met the man who became her husband. She in the final year of an English language course and Sergeyi a bright spark in the university's physics department, they'd been married after she graduated. Their daughter had been five years old when the Chernobyl reactor exploded in 1987 casting a pall of death over their country. As a physicist, Sergeyi had been enlisted for the clean-up team. He'd spent twenty-five days breathing the radioactive dust, then another four years waiting for the cancer to kill him.

She turned her back on the academic buildings and crossed the boulevard at the traffic lights. She could easily have walked the rest of the way to the embassy, but the bunion on her left foot was painful this morning and there was a tram drawing up at the stop on the corner opposite. She ran the few metres to reach it, her not entirely sensible heels clacking on the cobbles.

In front of her on the tram's steps was a young couple eating imported ice-creams out of bright foil wrappers. The girl, who was pretty with long brown hair, held a baby of about nine months in her arms. All the seats on the conveyance were taken but Oksana found a handrail to grab. The tram doors hissed shut and the elderly machine lumbered up the hill towards the old town, its steel wheels clunking over the joints in the track.

An elderly woman with an official badge pinned to a woollen jacket worn over pullover and skirt was making her way back through the tram checking tickets. Oksana dug her pass out from her bag in readiness.

'And yours?' the woman demanded of the couple with the baby. 'Why no tickets?'

'Because it's more than three months since we've been paid any wages, old woman,' the young man protested. 'It's the law. When the government won't pay our salary we travel free,' he reminded her defiantly.

'Oh yes? Too bad,' the inspector snapped. 'If you can

afford those ice-creams you can afford a tram ticket. You'll have to get off.'

The tram had reached its next stop and she pushed them towards the door.

'That's not fair,' the long-haired girl protested.

'Fair? Whoever said life was fair, child?'

The couple stumbled onto the pavement, still protesting.

As the tram moved on again the inspector nodded at Oksana's travel pass and muttered, 'Something for nothing, that's what they want.'

Yes, thought Oksana, but it was hard for Ukrainians to feel responsibility towards the state when the state no longer showed any towards them.

At the Mykhailivs'ka Square she got off the tram in front of the elegant façade of a nineteenth-century school. Kiev was a fine city; she knew that in some ways she would be sad to leave it. *Leave* it? Leave Kiev? Leave Ukraine? She was crazy. Crazy as a bird trapped in a room that sees daylight through a window and hurls itself against the glass. And yet escaping the hell of life here was what she, like so many people she knew, dreamed of. And if there was a chance that her brother with his military secrets could be given sanctuary abroad, then wasn't it possible, *just* possible, the same could be done for her?

Her watch said ten to twelve. She was as nervous as a kitten today, walking up this road that she walked up every working day. She rehearsed in her head the script she'd discussed with Misha.

The British Embassy appeared in front of her. A former nobleman's town house, the doors were locked, but she gave her name on the speaker-phone and stood back so that the guard could see her face on the security camera. The electric latch clicked and she let herself in, closing the door firmly behind her.

The small entrance hall, decorated with old prints of English hunting scenes, contained a row of chairs for waiting visitors, opposite which was a full-length mirror concealing a video camera so the guests could be studied before being let in. At the far end of the narrow hall was a thick armoured-glass window behind which she herself sat on weekdays. This morning it framed the surly face of the British security guard, who observed her approach with surprise and suspicion.

'What's up, Oksana?' he asked through the intercom. 'Leave your handbag behind or somefink?'

'No. I must speak with Mr Figgis,' she replied, trying to sound as if it were an audience she was used to. 'Is he in yet?'

'No. But soon, if he's on schedule. Expecting you, is he?'

'In fact not.'

'Hmm. Well, I suppose it's all right. But if I let you in to wait for him you'd better sit here where I can see you. Don't go wandering about, now.'

'Of course not.'

She bristled at his patronising manner, but pulled her bright red lips into a smile as he let her in through the steel-lined security gate. She sat in her usual chair behind the desk while the guard pottered about and told her things she already knew – that his tour of duty in Kiev was almost over and he was dearly looking forward to returning to Essex. It was a part of England Oksana had never heard of but which she began to think of as somewhere close to heaven.

She tried to think ahead to her forthcoming conversation with Mr Figgis, rehearsing her words and anticipating his responses. The man didn't look like a spy; indeed, spying wasn't really what an intelligence officer did these days, it had been explained to her once. His presence in Kiev was official and open, and he apparently spent much of his time in conversation with Ukrainian intelligence men at the SBU.

Occasionally Mr Figgis had visitors from England however, and some of *them* she'd had her suspicions about. A year ago there'd been a woman out from London whose presence in the embassy had never been explained. At the same time a man with a nice smile and a handsome face had called in three or four times and had chatted her up in a jokey sort of way while waiting for the woman upstairs to send down for him. She remembered him as being rather attractive, the sort of man who made life happen *for* him rather than *to* him. If circumstances had been different he was a type she might have shown interest in.

Another half an hour passed before Gerald Figgis walked in through the door from the street. Tall and thin with slicked-back hair, he wore jeans, trainers and a blue and red sweatshirt. When the guard let him in through the security door, he passed by the reception alcove without noticing the woman sitting there.

'Mr Figgis.' She rose to her feet, quaking. Her voice was husky, like a singer with a sore throat.

He stopped and half-turned. 'Oksana. Hello. Don't normally see you here on a Saturday.' Then he moved forward again, heading for the stairs.

'Mr Figgis, I . . .'

Figgis paused with one foot on the bottom tread.

'Yes? There's a message for me?'

'Could I speak with you please?' she asked, trembling.

'Of course.' He waited for her to start, then when she didn't the penny dropped. 'Well you'd better come up to my office. It'll have to be quick. I'm due on a tennis court in fifteen minutes.'

Figgis's room was at the back of the embassy, overlooking a garden of well-trimmed lawns and a row of garages for official cars.

'Won't you sit down?' Three modern armchairs in blue-grey leather surrounded a low round table. 'Please.' He pointed to one of the chairs, and waited for her to sit before lowering himself into one opposite her.

Oksana had never seen him in casual clothes before. She found it disconcerting, as if the lack of a suit deprived him of his authority.

'Now, what is it you want to tell me?' Figgis asked crisply.

Oksana suppressed her nerves and took in a deep breath.

'I have brother,' she began abruptly. She spoke English quite well, but with a strong accent. 'He is Major in army of Ukraine. But he has run away. You see, he discover something corrupt in army. When he report it to his General, they try to kill his child.'

Figgis's eyebrows shot up.

'I *beg* your pardon? *Who* did?'

'As warning,' she continued. 'To make him not talk about what he know. Now he think they try to kill him also. So he has come here to Kiev with his wife and with Nadya his daughter. They are at my home now. They arrive this morning.'

'Golly! This is pretty dramatic stuff,' Figgis exclaimed, unsure how seriously he should be taking this. 'But hang on a minute. I'm not getting this. *Who* tried to kill his child? The army?'

'Not exactly. He says it is Mafiya,' Oksana shrugged, as if it were obvious. 'He is very afraid of Mafiya in Odessa.'

'*Mafiya*? I see.' Figgis leaned forward, poker-faced. Everyone in Ukraine feared the Mafiya. Criminals controlled the country. But he could see already this wasn't a matter for him. The tennis court beckoned. 'Well, look, I certainly sympathise with your brother, but I really don't think—'

'Please! Listen to me.' There was desperation in her voice.

'Well of course I'll listen,' he said, taken aback by her vehemence. 'But I really think this is more a matter for your own SBU—'

'No! Militsia, SBU,' she protested. 'They cannot be trusted. Please let me tell you something more. Then you understand.'

'Go on then.'

'My brother he says it very important what he finds out, not for Ukraine but for countries like UK. He discover there are some corrupt officers in army in Odessa who sell military equipment to Mafiya. He knows about just one weapon, but very special weapon. Something like missile, he say.'

'A *missile*?' Suddenly she had Figgis's total attention.

'Like rocket, he say me. And he think Mafiya they send this outside of Ukraine. He think they sell to terrorists.'

What she was saying made alarming sense to Figgis. There'd been recent intelligence of IRA men sniffing around for surplus arms in the Trans-Dniestr area of Moldova, which wasn't far from Odessa.

'Does he have any idea *which* terrorists in particular?' he asked carefully.

'No.'

'I see.'

Figgis leaned back in the chair. His tennis partners were going to have to play without him.

'Now let me get this absolutely right, Oksana. Your brother believes that the army command in the Odessa Military District is directly involved in this illegal weapons sale, yes? And that because your brother's found out about it they're trying to silence him?'

'Yes.'

Figgis bored into Oksana's frightened blue eyes, trying to decide if she really knew what she was saying. The drift of it wasn't entirely surprising. Vast quantities of military hardware had been sold by corrupt military men in the chaos following the break-up of the old Red Army, but in recent years the problem had appeared to ease. Either the military's internal security people had got a grip on the corruption as they claimed, or, more likely in his view, all the stuff with a ready market had already been sold.

From memory he recalled what it said about Oksana in the personal file which he kept on all the locally employed embassy staff. A reasonable fluency in English. A good manner with visitors and on the switchboard. But something negative too, he remembered. A tendency towards emotional instability. There'd been a husband who'd died. A Chernobyl connection. She'd been known to spout tears when things got a bit hectic downstairs. But the key point was that there'd been no hint of any connection with a Ukrainian or Russian security agency.

Figgis was suspicious, however, because he was paid to be. Suspicious and cautious. There was the potential for trouble here. Relations between Britain and Ukraine were sweet just now, both at the diplomatic and the intelligence level, the result of years of effort. If he personally got involved in the handling of a defector from the Ukrainian army it could be highly damaging. There was also the possibility he was being set up. That somebody in the highly corrupt hierarchy of Ukraine had a reason for wanting to sour relations with Britain.

And yet from the little she'd told him already, he knew he needed to know more.

'You know, this really isn't a matter the British authorities can get involved in, Oksana,' he told her cautiously. 'But you've certainly aroused my curiosity. D'you by any chance know exactly where all this happened? And when? And this, er, this missile – d'you know the exact type your brother was talking about?'

'No. I cannot tell you this. But my brother he can tell you, of course.'

'Yes . . .' Figgis clasped his hands together. But there was no way *he* could risk compromising himself by talking to her brother. 'And how do you propose he does that?'

'I'm sorry?' She hadn't understood him.

'You led me to believe he wants to tell *us* about it, rather than the SBU,' Figgis explained noncommittally.

'Oh *yes*. In *England*. He will tell everything in England when you give him visa for him and his family.'

Her red mouth set in a tight line. The gold ear hoops trembled. Figgis understood how terrifying it would be for a quiet, unassuming person like her to be thrust forward by such circumstances. She was an attractive woman. And he could see now that there was fire there, something he'd not noticed before. He rocked back in his chair.

'What you're asking is not—'

'You see, it is not safe for him in Ukraine any more,' she insisted, ignoring him. 'They will find him – army, Mafiya. And, I think maybe it is dangerous too for me and for my daughter,' she added opportunistically. 'These criminals – they take away your life without second thought.'

'I understand your concerns,' he assured her. 'But it's not that easy.'

This brother of hers might have done something criminal for all he knew. It could be he was on the run from legitimate law enforcement agencies rather than from some criminal gang.

'Tell me, Oksana, has he spoken about this with the SBU at all?'

'Pschh! I tell you, they still all like KGB,' she hissed. 'He does not trust. You know this. Nobody in Ukraine trust Militsia or SBU.'

'I could give you a namc, you know. A man at SBU headquarters on vulitsya Volodymyrs'ka – someone I've got to know quite well. A man I believe to be straight.'

'No, Mr Figgis. My brother will not give information to SBU, because even if you know one honest man in SBU, he will tell it to other men who are not honest. Then they will kill my brother. No. He ask me to say to you he *will* tell everything that he knows, but only if you give visa for him and wife and daughter to stay in England. Because after he tell you everything, he can never return to Ukraine.'

'You're saying he wants to betray his country in exchange for asylum in Britain, yes?' Figgis checked, deliberately stressing the political nature of what was involved. 'That's a very serious step, you know.'

'Betray *country*? What means that?' Oksana protested. 'This is not betray country. Mafiya. Criminals. It is *they* who betray Ukraine. And our government that does nothing to stop them. No. My brother he want to give this information to countries outside Ukraine because he afraid some foreign terrorists do something very bad with what Mafiya sell them.'

Figgis tapped his fingers together again. Oksana's terms could never be acceptable as they stood. Before any visas could be offered they'd need to know in great detail what her brother had to tell them.

He studied her. There was desperation in those eyes. Like so many women in Ukraine, life had ground her to a low ebb. He would have liked to help, but it just wasn't going to work. Too many *ifs* in this. Her brother would have to talk to the SBU.

And yet. Before turning her down it would probably be wise to refer it to London.

'Can you give me a few moments, Oksana?' he asked suddenly. 'Perhaps you'd like to wait downstairs. There's someone I'd like to talk to about this.'

'Someone at SBU?' she whispered, heart in mouth.

'No. Not SBU, I promise. A colleague in London. At the Foreign Office. Would you mind?'

He stood up and opened the door for her.

'Won't be long. About ten or fifteen minutes, then I'll come back down for you. Okay?'

'Yes. Okay.'

He escorted her down to the reception desk, locking his door behind him. He explained to the security man that he would be talking to her again shortly. Then he returned to his office and crossed to the far side of the room to another door fitted with a coded lock. He tapped in a six-digit figure and stepped into a small, air-conditioned chamber containing racks of communications equipment. He squatted in front of the Automatic Telegram Handling System terminal and logged on, pressing his palm against the screen so the system could identify him.

There was a message waiting for him. He read it quickly.

'Bloody hell!'

He read it again, hardly able to believe the coincidence. Oksana Koslova's story had suddenly acquired an alarming relevance.

> SECURITY CODE ALPHA
>
> TO: STATION OFFICER KIEV.
>
> EX: DEPUTY CONTROLLER GLOBAL RISKS.
>
> URGENT CONFIRMATION NEEDED WHETHER VIKTOR RYBKIN IS STILL EMPLOYED BY SBU. ALSO ASCERTAIN WHY HE HAS BEEN IN CYPRUS WITH ANOTHER MAN (UNIDENTIFIED, BUT PHOTO APPENDED). BOTH SUSPECTED OF MURDER OF BRITISH AGENT. MAY ALSO BE INVOLVED FINANCIALLY OR ORGANISATIONALLY IN AN IMMINENT IRAQI TERRORIST ATTACK USING BIOLOGICAL WEAPONS.
>
> PLEASE TREAT AS MOST URGENT.

'My God!' he mouthed.

He already knew the answer to the first question. Rybkin had been sacked from the SBU three months ago. And as to a BW attack – Oksana's brother was talking about a missile which could easily carry such a warhead.

He accessed the photograph London had transmitted, copied it to disk then transferred the floppy to another PC for transmission on the link to the SBU headquarters that had been set up in recent months for the exchange of data on transnational crime. But he telephoned the SBU first. Courtesy calls were all important when dealing with an organisation still trying to slough off half a century's suspicions about the West.

The duty officer was a man he'd come to know well. After a few gibes about Dinamo's lamentable performance in its last match, he requested a registry check on the silver-toothed face in the picture that he was sending on the link, and any information they happened to have about the current activities of Viktor Rybkin.

Then he placed himself back at the ATHS keyboard and composed his response to London. Clearly Oksana's brother would need to be seen with all speed, but SIS would have to send a deep-cover officer to handle it, so he could keep his own hands clean. He sent the telegram and left the communications room.

Oksana Koslova had begun to despair by the time Figgis emerged from upstairs. Sitting by the reception desk she'd concluded that she'd failed her brother, failed his wife and daughter and failed herself.

Figgis stood on the bottom stair and beckoned her to follow him. His face betrayed nothing of what he'd just learned.

'It's possible something can be done,' Figgis told her cagily, once they were sitting in the leather chairs again. 'You'll be contacted within the next few hours. Not by me, you understand. Even if the voice on the phone sounds like me, it won't be – you get me?'

'Yes.' Her heart felt as if it would explode. 'I understand. Thank you.'

'Because I can't be involved. This conversation we're having now isn't taking place. You understand?'

'I understand. You can trust me.'

Figgis hoped to God that he could.

'Good. You'll be contacted to arrange a meeting with your brother. It'll be someone from London.'

'A familiar face?' she asked on the spur of the moment.

Her question surprised him. Who could she possibly have seen out of the handful of deep-cover agents who'd been to Kiev?

'I doubt it,' he told her. Then he remembered the drugs episode a year ago. 'Well, I suppose it's not impossible.'

27

Sunday, 6 October, early a.m.
London

The phone rang, cutting through what was left of his troubled sleep. Sam rolled onto his side and put the pillow over his head. His gut churned with acid, there was a brick-fight going on in his skull. He'd gone on a bender after the funeral yesterday, an attempt at obliteration which had failed. What Clare had revealed about the woman he'd loved was still like a lump in his chest.

And now the ringing of the phone was chiselling at his temples.

He decided to ignore it. There was nobody in the world he wanted to talk to. The one conversation he *did* want to have required a partner who was no longer reachable.

'Fuck!'

The damned phone wouldn't stop. Some sadist at the other end. Probably that raven-haired woman wanting to come round and hammer a stake through his heart.

He rolled from the bed and stumbled towards the door.

'Shi-it!' he yelled, stubbing his toes against the base of a chest of drawers.

Head thundering, he hopped into the hall and made it to the kitchen. As he reached for the phone on the wall he resolved that if the caller was someone trying to sell double-glazing, he would track the bastard down and stalk him or her to an early grave.

'Yes?'

'Sam!' The voice bore the Ulster twang of Duncan Waddell. 'We need to meet.'

'Wha—? Isn't it Sunday?' Sam's tongue filled his mouth like a gag.

'Don't care if it's King Billy's birthday, I need you at the Lodge this afternoon. Two o'clock sharp.'

'What? What's happened?'

'That's what the meeting's for. To tell you.'

'Yeah, but there's one small problem,' Sam mumbled, brain trying to catch on. 'My car – it's down at the Hamble.'

'Then we'll send someone to pick you up,' Waddell snapped, exasperated. 'Let's say one o'clock. And could you please try to sober up by then?'

The line went dead.

Hell. Something serious must have happened. Thousands dead from an anthrax attack? Packer felt like a child this morning, needing someone to tell him what to do.

The wall clock said five to nine. He filled the kettle to make some tea to clear his head. The 'Lodge' that Waddell had referred to was in the Banstead hills just south of London, a safe house less convenient than the flat over the launderette in Isleworth, but more secluded.

News. There'd be some on somewhere. He prodded the switch on the radio, switching bands and spinning the dial until he found a twenty-four-hour news station.

Nothing. A report on some food scare or other. He left the radio on. There'd be headlines in a few minutes.

His brain throbbing, he poured hot water onto a teabag then clasped the mug, letting the heat scorch his palms in an act of purgation. Stupid to get so plastered.

Stupid to allow himself to get so wound up over a woman.

He shook his head, still unable to believe that he'd never guessed at Chrissie's catholic taste in sex. Even with hindsight, he could think of nothing she'd ever said or done that should have given him a clue. She'd seemed the most heterosexual creature he'd ever met.

He'd been hurt yesterday by Clare's revelation, as she'd intended him to be – no man likes to discover he hasn't been satisfying a woman's sexual needs. This morning, however, he felt no anger at the fact that Chrissie had deceived him. After all, their affair had been *based* on deception. What worried him more was the fear there were other revelations to come. Viktor Rybkin's warning, the strange tattoo – there was a lot about her life that Chrissie had hidden from him.

The Greenwich pips signal jabbed him alert. The news headlines were about storms in the West Country. There'd been no anthrax attack. No massacre of the innocents.

He reached into the cupboard over the sink for the paracetamol bottle. If he gave the pills an hour to work and dosed himself with repeat brews of tea, he might pull through. Then, if he managed to hold down some breakfast and take a walk on the common in the chill easterly that was blowing outside, his head might even clear enough for him to work out what this meeting with Waddell was all about.

The Lodge that Waddell had referred to was a mock-Tudor pile just off the Purley–Epsom road south of London, built in a sooty brown brick and set at the end of a leaf-strewn gravel drive that ran for some fifty metres between high banks of bolting rhododendrons.

When FBI Special Agent Dean Burgess had arrived there, diverted on his way back to Washington from

Bahrain via London, he'd had the impression the six-bedroom house was deserted, its dark lead-lattice windows reflecting the slate-grey of the overcast sky. The car that SIS had sent to collect him from the hotel near the US Embassy in Grosvenor Square dropped him at the front of the Lodge where three other vehicles were already parked. A short man with a close crop of fair hair and wearing a check shirt emerged from a path at the side of the mansion.

'You'll be Dean.' The accent was Irish or Scots, Burgess couldn't tell which.

'That's right.'

'Duncan Waddell. Welcome to the Lodge. There's coffee inside, although your taste buds may not recognise it as such.'

Waddell led the American round to the rear entrance which faced an overgrown kitchen garden and a corroding aluminium greenhouse with cracked panes. The semi-glazed back door was pushed open and they walked inside.

'Good afternoon, sir.'

From a chair beside a scrubbed pine table in the middle of the cork-floored kitchen a grey-haired woman in her sixties stood up to greet Burgess.

'This is Beryl,' Waddell announced. 'She and her husband look after this place for us. They both used to be staffers with SIS.'

'Hi.' Burgess shook the offered hand.

'Will you take your coffee in with you, sir?' Beryl asked politely. 'The others have already got theirs.'

'Sounds a great idea.'

She turned towards the Aga stove on which an enamelled pot was keeping warm. She lifted it and filled a bone china cup with what Burgess could smell was a bitter, stewed brew. He already knew he wasn't going to drink it.

'Milk? Sugar?'

'Don't bother. Thanks.'

The hall of the house was panelled in dark wood and had been hung with bleak oil paintings. The place reminded Burgess of the studio set for *The Addams Family*.

Waddell pushed open a heavy door into a boardroom furnished with a long oak refectory table and a set of tubular-framed chairs that looked unsuitably modern. On one end of the table a laptop PC with a good-sized screen had been set up.

'Some introductions first . . .' Waddell offered.

Two men and a woman were already in the room.

'Jennifer Price you know already.'

'Sure. Hi Jen.'

The woman's public title was Political Counsellor at the US Embassy in Grosvenor Square, but she was one of the representatives of the Central Intelligence Agency in London. In her thirties, she had short, dark hair and a no-nonsense face, and wore a formal grey business suit.

'Hi Dean.'

'Opposite you've got the rest of our team. Martin Kessler, deputy controller of Global Risks . . .'

'How d'you do, sir.' Burgess leaned forward and shook the proffered hand. Jennifer had told him earlier that it was this pale man's wife who'd been murdered in Cyprus.

'. . . and Sam Packer, who I suppose is the man we ought to blame for all of this,' Waddell concluded, smiling at his own joke to cue the others to do the same.

'Nice to meet you, Sam. Must've been pretty rough in Baghdad. Glad to know you're okay.'

Okay wasn't exactly how Sam would have described himself at that moment. Apart from the hangover, the shock of coming face to face with Martin Kessler for the first time in his life had been considerable. When he'd arrived, the aloof grey eyes had fixed him with a look that seemed to embody both contempt and fear. They were framed today by smart new spectacles with oval lenses, very different from the smudged pebbles through which he'd watched his wife bid adieu to her lover in the open space of Barnes Common three months ago.

Their brief and awkward conversation on his arrival was the first time he'd ever heard Kessler speak. The voice was reedy and undistinguished.

'If you'd like to pitch camp next to Jennifer, Dean,' Waddell suggested.

Burgess placed his coffee cup on the table.

'I advise you not to touch that,' Jennifer cautioned. 'It contains undiluted hydrochloric acid.'

'I'd worked that one out already,' Burgess smiled.

'I'm afraid the lady who brewed it only drinks herb tea herself,' Kessler explained apologetically.

'No problem,' said Burgess.

The quality of the coffee was the least of his worries. He'd flown out of Iraq with the rest of the UNSCOM team on Friday after the Iraqis had refused further co-operation. After some intense message traffic with Washington, he'd flown from Bahrain to London, arriving late last night, and was due to fly on home in a few hours' time. Still dressed in the casual clothes he'd taken with him to Baghdad, he was suffering time zone fatigue again.

'Shall we start?' Waddell deferred momentarily to Kessler, who indicated quickly that he should carry on.

'You all know the background,' Waddell began, drawing this small nest of spies together with a sweep of his eyes, 'but the story's moved on in the last twenty-four hours. Moved a hell of a long way forward.'

Sam was totally alert all of a sudden. This was a different Waddell speaking. A man with no doubts whatsoever about the seriousness of what they were engaged in.

'The first thing I want to give you is this.'

Waddell clicked a key on the computer. The face of Saladin flashed on the screen, the picture Sam had produced on Sophie's PC in Cyprus.

'This man – sorry about the blurry image – was photographed in Cyprus on the night Christine Taylor was murdered there.' Sam noted Waddell's tactful use of Chrissie's operational surname in front of Kessler. 'He was standing a few feet away from Christine Taylor, apparently somewhat perturbed by the conversation she was having with two Ukrainians. Sam believes this man was also the leader of the group that took him prisoner in Baghdad, right?'

'I'm certain of it.'

'Were they Mukhabarat?' the CIA woman checked. 'I don't recollect what was said in the report filed at Langley.'

'I never knew who—' Sam began.

'Actually the answer's no,' Waddell cut in. He tapped the computer screen. 'You see, we've now got an ID on this fellow from one of our émigré sources. His name apparently is Naif Hamdan, a colonel in the Iraqi army. During the war with Iran, he held the rank of major and commanded a detachment of chemical troops on the southern front.'

'Now you're talking . . .' breathed Sam.

'There's more. Colonel Hamdan had a wife. I say *had* because she's dead now. You remember the Amiriyah shelter in Baghdad? Bombed in error in the Gulf War with three to four hundred civilians killed? Well, apparently Mrs Hamdan was one of those brought out inside several polythene bags.'

'Oh God,' whispered the woman from the CIA.

'But here's what's really interesting,' Waddell continued, holding up his hands for silence. 'Before she married the Colonel, Mrs Hamdan's family name was *Shenassi*.'

'Oh boy! This gets good.' This time it was Dean Burgess who spoke.

'I don't understand,' said Sam. The name meant nothing to him.

'Shenassi, Sam, was also the name of the Baghdad animal feed plant boss who committed suicide last Wednesday after UNSCOM found he'd been brewing up anthrax. Doctor Shenassi and Colonel Hamdan's wife were brother and sister.'

'Good Lord,' Sam breathed.

Waddell passed a hand over his thistle-like hair.

'So let's try and make sense of all this. We're into speculation of course, but we can try it for size. First, let's say that Hamdan and Shenassi conspire for reasons we don't yet know to produce an anthrax weapon. They need money to fund their plan for using the stuff, so they kidnap Sam Packer. Somehow – and we still don't know how – they knew that Sam worked for SIS.'

Not appearing to accuse *him* any more at least, thought Sam, exhilarated to hear Waddell endorse what he himself had concluded in Cyprus.

'They knew, therefore, that if they moved fast and acted discreetly there was a good chance we'd agree to send them Salah Khalil in exchange,' Waddell went on. 'And Khalil was loaded with money. Next. Colonel Hamdan turns up in Cyprus, escorting Khalil presumably, to make sure he gets his hands on that cash. And there was a *lot* of it involved. Enough to fund a whole string of terrorist operations.

'Now, the movement of that money is something we *are* sure about. Salah Khalil, as far as we can tell, is the sole shareholder of a Cyprus-based offshore trading company. I say that with a proviso, because the Central

Bank of Cyprus files show the shares being held by a nominee. But the nominee, surprise, surprise, happens to be the lawyer whom Khalil went to see last Monday.'

Burgess nodded. He knew a lot about shell companies. Tracking money movements had formed a good part of his duties at the New York field office he'd recently left.

'At midday on Monday Cyprus time, one hour after Khalil visited his lawyer, a bank account in Lugano in the name of the same Cyprus-based offshore company transferred five million dollars to an account in Jersey which belongs to yet another company registered in Cyprus. That money transfer was nominally against an invoice for a cargo of oil. We've not yet been able to identify the owners of the company that received the money, because yet again it's in nominee names.

'But, and we're still speculating like mad here, Cyprus is, of course, a favourite offshore business centre for criminal organisations from the former Soviet Union. So it's entirely possible the money was paid to an FSU Mafiya gang. Another pointer to that is the strong Ukrainian link we've uncovered in the murder of our agent Christine Taylor.'

He hit a couple of keys on the computer and the photo Sam had stolen from the Mondiale Hotel came up full frame.

'The full image, with Hamdan just a blur in the background, was taken in the bar of the Mondiale Hotel, Limassol on the eve of Christine's death.'

Burgess glanced at Kessler. Tough for the man to keep up such a cool front when it was his wife they were talking about.

'That's Chrissie, with her back to camera. Next to her in the green jacket is a former KGB officer called Viktor Rybkin. He's someone she'd met on a number of previous occasions and was friendly with. At first we thought Rybkin was in Cyprus on SBU business, but we've now learned he was kicked out of the Ukrainian intelligence service a few months ago. Like many of his colleagues in the military and security field, he'd succumbed to the lure of crime.'

'I thought as much,' Sam breathed. 'So it's confirmed.'

'Yes. And what's also just been confirmed is that he now works for the man you see sitting opposite him, the one with the interesting line in cosmetic dentistry. *His* name is Vladimir Filipovich Grimov, known as Dima. According to an Odessa police file which our Kiev station officer got access to this morning, he's a former army officer who now virtually runs the Odessa arm of a *biznis* empire believed to be headed by an ex-communist factory boss called Voronin. Like many of the new Mafiya godfathers, Voronin has ring-fenced his position as a gang leader by getting himself elected to the Rada – the parliament – which gives him automatic immunity from prosecution in Ukraine.

'Now, that covers the who's who. But what's going on? Well, we believe that Christine Taylor had made an important discovery, namely that the Iraqis she was shadowing *were* doing business with these two Ukrainian hoods. We believe she was trying to exploit her old friendship with Viktor Rybkin to find out what that business was. And we imagine she got close to succeeding, which was why they killed her.'

Sam's eyes were on Martin Kessler now. The only movement on the grey face was a quick, nervous licking of the lips.

'Chrissie died before she could report in, unfortunately. All we know, or rather *suspect*, about the business relationship is that five million dollars may have passed from Hamdan to Grimov. As I said before, a lot of money. And if it was money for help in launching an anthrax attack, then we could be talking about something pretty sophisticated,' he warned.

‘Can we get some background clear here?’ Jennifer asked. ‘I have to admit an ignorance on technical matters. I had legal training, not science. What exactly are we talking about here? The warning Sam was given was about an anthrax *warhead*, right? Now, is that a bomb or what?’

‘Good question,’ Waddell conceded. ‘We’d all benefit from an explanation of the technicalities. Dean – you’re hot from the front and you’ve spent the past few days with Andrew Hardcastle. Any of his expertise rubbed off?’

‘Some. I’ll tell you as much as *I’ve* understood,’ Burgess answered, leaning back in his chair. He smoothed his moustache. ‘Let me begin with the conclusion that we in the UNSCOM team came to at the end of our mission. We’re pretty darn sure that with the help of specialised equipment smuggled in and then out of the Haji factory on the weekend of the thirteenth of September several kilograms of freeze-dried, finely milled anthrax spores *were* produced. Enough for a weapons test and to fill a warhead or two as well.

‘The warheads, or whatever you want to call them, can be any sort of device able to release the anthrax in a controlled way. You see, to use anthrax as a weapon of mass murder, the powdered spores need to be released in a dust that’s fine enough to remain airborne long enough to be inhaled by the victims. And to reach those victims the device has to spread the stuff in a controlled way so that it gets into the victims’ air supply. It could be something real simple, like a ducted fan mounted on the back of a truck driven down a crowded city street or backed up against the intake for a subway ventilation system. Or it could be an explosive shell or ballistic missile warhead, though there’s a risk that much of the agent would be destroyed by the detonation of the weapon itself. Finally, the gizmo could be a simple canister that sprays the agent from a plane like a crop duster, or maybe even from a cruise missile or some other type of unmanned air vehicle. All the canister needs to have is a nozzle to control the flow and something to push the powder out, like a fan. Or just some holes opening in a controlled way at the front to let in the slipstream.'

'Surely anthrax can be in liquid form too, can't it?' enquired Martin Kessler, determined on clarity.

'Sure, sir. The spores can be in solution. But the dried version is easier to transport and handle and has a longer shelf life. Ideally the stuff needs to be kept cool and away from sunlight. If we're talking about a weapon being smuggled out of the country then powder is what makes sense.'

'I understand.'

'Okay, and I pretty much followed all of that too,' cut in Jennifer. 'But do you know what type of device was being tested this time?'

'No, we do not. If we'd been able to continue digging at the site in the desert we might have found some technical parts that would have given us the answer.'

'And this weapon you're envisaging,' Sam intervened, 'this canister or whatever – it would be easily portable? One man could carry it?'

'Absolutely. It could weigh just a few pounds. You'd probably need to wear a mask when handling it tactically, that's all.'

Silence fell round the table as they considered what Burgess had just told them.

'Five million dollars – phew,' Sam whistled. 'You could buy most things with that. A light aircraft, a cruise missile . . .'

'Exactly,' said Waddell. He and Kessler glanced at one another, as if they knew something more but weren't revealing it. 'Now, if all our speculation about Naif

Hamdan's plans is correct, the next and most important question of all is *why*? Is he planning an act of terrorism independently or is somebody else controlling him?'

'Saddam, of course,' Jennifer stated firmly. 'Listen. No little Iraqi splinter group could produce a stock of anthrax, test a warhead and get it out of the country without Saddam's intelligence set-up finding out about it way before it got anywhere. So if there *is* an anthrax attack being planned, it has to be Saddam who's behind it.'

'Don't be too sure of that, Jen,' Burgess chipped in, dabbing at his moustache again, as he always did when he was about to take a stand on something. 'The Amn al Aman security guys were real taken aback by what we were uncovering,' he told her, pulling himself up straight in the chair. 'Not once, but twice. They just were not expecting us to find anything sensitive either out in the desert or at the Haji plant. Those guys were out of the information loop. And in the opinion of people on the UNSCOM team who weren't greenhorns like me, that simply has never happened before.'

The CIA woman cleared her throat and straightened the sleeves of her grey jacket.

'Dean, you know as well as I do that folks in Washington are going to be real sceptical about the idea of any Iraqis freelancing with anthrax. The view in DC is that's just not possible. Look, Saddam's already had to give away much more about his BW programme to the UN than he wanted to. So, to keep what's left of it secret, he's had to set up a cell system, keeping the organisations that produce the stuff secret even from his own security people. I have to say, guys, that that's the line *I* favour. I'm of the school of thought that says *nothing* of importance can happen in Iraq without Saddam's say-so.'

'And normally we would agree with you, Jennifer,' Martin Kessler stated, his glasses having slipped down his nose a little, giving him an oddly *distrait* look. 'But the oddities of this particular case do go on and on.' He gestured to Waddell to continue.

'We had a signal this morning from our man in Amman. Sources there are saying there's been a handful of arrests in Baghdad and some deaths. Not deaths at the hands of the Mukhabarat, you understand, but *suicides*. People biting into cyanide capsules to avoid interrogation.'

'Like Shenassi,' Burgess exclaimed. 'You're saying there's a link?'

'We don't know.' Waddell turned to face Sam. 'Perhaps *you* can enlighten us.'

'Me? What d'you mean?'

'Take a look at this.' Waddell hit the computer keys again and a new image appeared on the screen.

'Jesus Christ!' Sam gasped. '*Sandhurst!* My interrogator in Baghdad,' he explained. 'I gave him that nickname because he sounded so British. The guy was also in charge of the swap at the border.'

'He negotiated the deal with us,' Waddell added for the benefit of the Americans, beaming with satisfaction. 'He called himself a Colonel. Real name's Major Omar Hasan. He's an officer in a chemical weapons regiment. And he killed himself to avoid being interrogated by the Mukhabarat.' He let his words sink in. 'Why? Why would he need to do that? And why did Shenassi also top himself, if what he was up to had the full backing and approval of the president?'

Jennifer folded her arms, trying to think of an alternative scenario.

'So what we seem to have is a small cell of dedicated men,' Waddell insisted. 'Colonel Naif Hamdan, his brother-in-law Doctor Husayn Shenassi and Captain Omar Hasan, who may well have served with Hamdan at some point. Then there was the older man who gave Sam the warning in Baghdad, who seems to have had a sudden attack of conscience and tried to sabotage his co-conspirators' plans by telling us about them. Then there were a few others not yet identified. Three of that group are now dead, two by their own hand. Why? Our suspicion is it was because Saddam had finally found out what they were up to and didn't much like what he saw. In fact, it put him into such a panic he decided to close the shutters on the UN and kick them out until he'd cleared up the mess.' He leaned forward on his hands. 'It *does* have a ring of logic to it, Jennifer.'

The CIA woman shifted uncomfortably. 'I'll agree it has to be considered.'

Martin Kessler pushed the glasses back up his nose, deciding it was time to take charge of the meeting.

'Let's focus on intentions now. If all this speculation is correct, and Hamdan is acting independently of the Iraqi leadership, what is it that he wants? Could it be connected with an attempt to overthrow Saddam Hussein? Any guesses on that one, Jennifer?'

'It doesn't match anything *we* know about. The only opposition group we thought stood a breath of a chance against Saddam was the Iraqi National Accord, a link-up between exiled politicians overseas and rebel officers inside Iraq. But as you know, the coup they were trying to stage fell to pieces a few months back. The Mukhabarat had the whole set-up infiltrated from top to bottom. Hundreds were tortured and shot and we had to stage an emergency airlift from the Kurdish zone to get out our own people and as many of the INA as we could rescue. Nope. Colonel Hamdan hasn't featured on any list of names that *I've* ever seen. And if he's hoping to use anthrax to kill Saddam he'll need to get it into the guy's bedroom rather than smuggle it out of the country.'

'Quite,' Kessler answered. 'So we're back to guesswork. Does Hamdan have some bizarre personal motive perhaps? Revenge against the US for blowing his wife to bits in the Amiriyah shelter? A remarkably elaborate and costly scheme if that *were* the case. Or, might he be a pan-arabist or Islamic fundamentalist set on clobbering the Israelis?'

He looked around the table for comments, but received none.

'Any of that's possible,' said Burgess sombrely.

'Without some new intelligence all we can do is distribute the file on Hamdan to any nation that's a potential target – the Israelis, Kuwaitis and Saudis – and also crank Interpol into action, though it'd be a bloody miracle if any border guard managed to pick him up from that blurry photograph.'

'My God! This is a nightmare!' Jennifer tapped on the table with her pen. 'The potential for some major incident with a massive loss of life . . . it's, it's just huge.' She turned to Burgess and put a hand on his arm. 'Dean, your guys back home'll have to make darned sure it isn't *us* that gets hit.'

Burgess nodded. 'I have to make some calls,' he declared, looking at his watch.

There were wheels to be set in motion before he caught the flight. He thought of Carole and the kids. When he'd called her last night she'd told him of a Pledge for the Family rally in Washington next weekend, which she wanted them all to go on. Needed to ring her again to say he wouldn't be able to make it.

'Let me just tell you what else we're doing,' Waddell continued, 'SIS has strong contacts with the SBU and we're working on them to dig up everything they can about Mr Voronin's organisation and the activities of Dima Grimov in Odessa. But we have to be realistic. Mafiya gangs like the Voroninskaya have tremendous power in Ukraine. The SBU does not have the clout of the old KGB and the Ukrainian Militsia are heavily corrupted. We may not be able to get hold of the information we need that way. So any other leads anybody can come up with – it could make all the difference.'

The meeting broke up. Burgess was running short of time. The plane to Washington was in three hours.

Kessler stood up to bid the Americans goodbye. As he shook their hands he said, 'Whatever these monsters are planning, we've got to stop them.' There was almost a touch of passion in his voice.

'Amen to that,' mouthed Burgess.

As Jennifer slipped on a long black raincoat, with a helping hand from Kessler, Waddell took Sam by the arm. 'Don't you leave just yet.'

Burgess reached back to shake Sam's hand.

'A privilege to meet you.' He held on to it as if to show his respect. 'I sure admire your guts.'

'Well, thank you.' Sam felt himself colouring with embarrassment. 'But really it wasn't—'

'No. Don't get all British about it. Keep well. So long now.'

The Americans were gone. Kessler and Waddell sat back at the table and indicated Sam should do the same.

'We've another mission for you, Sam,' Kessler announced without further ado. 'Needed the cousins out of the way first. The thing is we don't know if it's connected with the Hamdan business or not.'

Another mission? What Sam had been through in the past few weeks had been enough trauma for one life.

'What are you talking about?' he demanded.

'There's somebody who wants to come across to us,' Waddell intoned, sounding like an old cold warrior.

'What d'you mean "come across"? Where?' Sam asked uneasily.

'Kiev. He's a major in the Ukrainian army. Claims to have information about some sophisticated weapon or other that's been acquired by the Mafiya from his own military.'

'Christ! But that's exactly what—'

'I know. It sounds highly relevant, but we haven't been able to talk direct to the man yet. Defections are tricky diplomatically. That's why we need to send someone from here to question him. He's scared to death of going to his own security people because he thinks they're all involved with the Mafiya. Sounds a little paranoid between you and me. Even seems to think there's a contract out to kill him.

'The Major's holed up with his sister who happens to work at the British Embassy. As a receptionist. She would have been there at the time of your last visit to Kiev a year ago.'

Sam had a vague memory of a woman with dark hair and blue eyes.

Kiev. Where he'd first encountered Rybkin. Once he'd established whether the Major was relevant to the Iraqis' anthrax plan, he would track the former SBU man down, a man with a lot to answer for.

'When?' he asked.

'Tomorrow. You'll need to get a visa sorted in the morning. It'll be a quick trip. Straight in and out. Damn . . .' Waddell snapped his fingers. 'To get your visa you need an invitation to go to Kiev from a Ukrainian business. We've set up a paper company over there for just that purpose. I've got the letter for you, but it's in my car.' He stood up feeling in his trouser pocket for the keys. 'Back in a minute.'

Alone with Kessler, Sam felt acutely uncomfortable. But not for long, because Kessler took the initiative.

'I'm glad for a moment alone, Sam,' he began. 'Something I wanted to say.' He held up his hands as if in surrender. 'Forget the past. Forget our . . . conflict. We have a common interest now, do we not?'

Sam watched the man's discomfort, reminded unkindly of the squirming of a worm. How much had *he* known about Chrissie's life, he wondered? Could it be that he'd tacitly condoned her other relationships as the price for keeping her?

'There's a smell, Sam,' said Kessler, cutting through his thoughts. 'A nasty one, and it's sticking to Chrissie.' Sam saw fear in his eyes now. 'It's because of the way she died. The circumstances. Too much that hasn't been explained.' Kessler's hands squeezed together until the knuckles went white. 'It's a question of what the record will say. In the Firm. I'm sure you would share my wish that Chrissie's file should be blemish-free.'

'Of course,' Sam mouthed, taken aback at this appeal.

'It's why I wanted it to be *you* who went to Cyprus,' Kessler explained, crushed-faced. 'And to Kiev. Wanted someone on the case who had Chrissie's interests at heart. You *do*, don't you?'

'But of course—'

'Yes. So, if there's anything you can think of that'll make things smell a little sweeter . . .'

Sam felt pegged to the chair, convinced suddenly that Kessler wasn't so much concerned about his dead wife's reputation as his own. Worried the smell could spread *his* way.

'I . . .'

They heard Waddell returning.

'That's all, Sam,' Kessler mumbled in conclusion, 'all I wanted to say. Just that. That it would be best if Chrissie were remembered well.'

The eyes were as humble as a beggar's.

Kessler knows something, thought Sam. Some dark secret, darker than all the others. And suspects that *I* might know it too.

28

Late Afternoon
Haifa, Israel

A weary Israeli official stepped from the customs house on the main quay of Haifa Port and climbed into his car. Onto the seat beside him, he smacked down the clip-board on which he'd fixed a cargo manifest provided by the agents of the ship that had just arrived from Limassol. He'd been on shift since six that morning. He'd had enough for one day. He started up and pointed the wheels towards the container jetties.

An engine problem had delayed the vessel's departure from Limassol by a day, and further problems on the voyage had made its arrival here even later than expected. That in turn was delaying his own journey home and the chance to watch the football game his son had taped for him off the satellite sports channel – unless the kid had forgotten.

There was only one container from the ship that he needed to spot check, a forty footer whose documents listed the contents as vegetable juice. The box had been shipped out of this very port just over two weeks earlier but had been returned by the customer because the goods inside it were defective. That, however, was not the reason for his decision to inspect the box – the return of unsatisfactory goods was a regular enough occurrence.

What had caught his attention was simply that the container had begun its return journey in Ukraine, and cargoes from that part of the former Soviet Union were infrequent to say the least. After all, the country had precious little worth exporting.

Ukraine was a place he'd learned about from a neighbour in the street where he lived halfway up the slopes of Mount Carmel. The man had emigrated from the country three years ago and never stopped telling him to watch out for anything that originated from there because the place was controlled by organised crime.

He'd had no intelligence to go on. No tip-offs. It was curiosity more than anything else that was drawing him to this particular pier.

He flicked the wheel to avoid running the tyres into the rail tracks embedded in the road surface, then turned down through a standing area where containers waiting to be stuffed with cargoes for onward movement were stacked three high. Two lifts were working the ship, their massive gantries humping the containers from the deck to the quayside. Tractors and trailers queued up to remove those boxes that were authorised for immediate departure.

The customs official parked his car well clear of the activity on the quay and strolled over to the dock officer who was checking the container numbers against the manifest.

'You're in luck. The one you want to look at is next off,' she told him.

He watched the rust-red box swing to the shore suspended by steel cables. Once on the dockside a forklift moved it clear of the roadway so the trailer trucks could continue their work. He inspected the wire seal put on by the Ukrainian customs in Odessa, then broke it while the dock officer looked on.

'What're you expecting?' she asked.

'Something that don't smell too good.'

He unhitched the clasp and swung back the door. The stink was enough to make them flinch. Both of them.

They stared at the cartons of juice bulging out of their shrink-wrap of polythene. Some had already ruptured. The container floor was wet and sticky. The packs were stacked to within ten centimetres of the container's roof, leaving just enough space for a torch beam to reach down the gap. Holding his breath, he stepped on the edge of the pallet and aimed the light to the rear of the container. The line of cartons stretched all the way – as far as he could tell.

He stepped back. There was only one way to be sure that contraband *wasn't* hidden in the load and that was to order the removal of every single pallet.

But it was late. He was tired. And the football game was waiting.

'Enough,' he said. 'Shut the stink up again.'

Ninety minutes later the container was driven through the dock gates. The truck turned right onto the Sederot Ha-Hagana and headed for the main road south which led to Tel Aviv, the largest Jewish city that has ever existed.

29

Monday, 7 October, a.m.
London

Straight-backed and stiff-legged like an old soldier much older than his forty-two years, Naif Hamdan pressed the door button on the blue and white commuter train standing at platform seventeen of Waterloo station and stepped inside. He was making an effort to create the impression that he did this every day, despite not having been in London since the warmer climate of the 1980s when Britain had been perfectly happy to sell his country the materials it needed to make chemical and biological weapons.

He chose a window seat and looked round as casually as he could manage to check there were no signs of his being followed. The British visa stamped into his Jordanian passport had secured him easy entry for what he'd declared to be a three-day 'business' trip. He was certain that with his almost European looks he had avoided attracting the suspicion of the authorities, but dropping his guard could be fatal.

Under normal circumstances a gun would be the most suitable tool for the business he had in mind in this country, but it was a difficult object to travel with. Instead, in his heavy Samsonite briefcase were two nine-inch Sabatier kitchen knives still wrapped in the green and gold bag of the Knightsbridge store where he'd bought them an hour ago.

He'd been shaken by what had happened in Iraq since he left. Shaken, but heartened too by the knowledge that two of his closest co-conspirators had honoured the pledges they'd all made some three months ago. Since learning of their deaths he'd thought constantly of that evening when the four of them at the heart of the affair had sat together in the untidy kitchen of his Baghdad apartment. Curtains tightly closed, a candle in a jam jar for light and a photograph of his dead wife on the fat-spattered wall above the cooker, they'd each placed a bunched fist down on the cheap plastic-laminate surface of the table, knuckles touching, and sworn to die by their own hands if they had to rather than reveal what they'd agreed that night to undertake. After taking the oath they'd raised up their fists, still pressed together like the hub of a wheel, and held them over the candle so the flame would forge their resolve with its fire.

And now two of the others *were* dead: his late wife's brother Dr Husayn Shenassi, a brilliant scientist and a paragon of kindness, and Major Omar Hasan, his adjutant during the 1991 war, who'd been at his side as they'd picked through their regiment's corpses west of Basra after a decimating raid by B-52s. Dead now, lives taken by their own hands to preserve the secrecy of their conspiracy. But in the choice of who was to die from that original quartet, God had been kind. Husayn and Omar and the handful of men involved with them back in Baghdad had had roles essential only to the development of the plan they'd hatched. The two survivors of that inner council, himself and Sadoun, another major from his regiment, were the ones who'd reserved for themselves the responsibility for its final implementation.

Hamdan remembered again the resolve they'd all felt

at that candle-lit session in his flat. The resolve to rid their nation of its psychopathic leader.

During the early years of Saddam's rule, all of them had taken pride in seeing their country grow in prosperity and stature under his tutelage. All had condoned his brutal methods as being little worse than those of men who'd preceded him. But then, as Saddam's war with Iran dragged on, they'd despaired of the waste in wealth and young men that their leader's megalomania was bringing about.

Then finally, with that ill-judged gamble in Kuwait, they'd watched the devastation of their country being made total.

Hamdan remembered their anguish in the spring of 1991 as he and his defeated fellow officers waited with hope in their hearts for the Americans to sweep up from the south and eradicate their leader. *They* would not have resisted. Few Iraqis would have done. But the Americans never came, declaring it was for the Iraqi people themselves to remove Saddam Hussein, not them.

And the Iraqi people had tried. Tens of thousands of corpses bore witness to how *hard* they'd tried. For their sake, and for the sake of generations to come, it was time for desperate measures to make their sacrifice bear fruit. To think the unthinkable.

A warning bleeped and the commuter train's doors slid shut. Hamdan's heart was pounding. He had no clearly thought-out plan today, just the goal of preserving his secret at any price. With so much blood already shed, a little more would be no burden on his conscience.

As the train clattered over the points on its way from the terminus, he looked out over the bleak south London landscape of sooty brick terraces and drab office towers. There was little beauty surrounding the people living here, he thought to himself, but there *was* freedom.

Freedom from fear and from tyranny. Only those who were deprived of that freedom could know its true value.

The culmination of his scheme was still some days away, days of risk in which his desperate plan could be brought to nothing by men who knew too much.

There were two in London who posed just such a risk. The first he'd tracked down yesterday – a fellow countryman who'd been involved in their plans in a minor role, but who'd feared the very fate Hamdan had in mind for him and had fled to London where he thought he would be safe. He'd found this man too easily yesterday, stumbling across him by accident in a crowded west London street. The man had seen him, recognised him and escaped. But he wouldn't for long.

Now it was the turn of the second target, a man who'd looked him in the eye just once. Someone who'd pretended not to know his secret but *had* known it. A person he'd wanted to eliminate then, but couldn't if he was to secure the return of Salah Khalil. But now Sam Packer had to die – because he'd seen the face of Naif Hamdan. One man among the ranks of the intelligence agencies massing against him able to pick him out from a crowd was one man too many. And Packer, he'd learned in a discomfiting warning from the Ukrainians, had come dangerously close to the truth in Cyprus. He was a man with a terrier mind, Rybkin had said, a man who lacked caution. A man without the sense to leave things alone that didn't concern him.

The Iraqi stared through the window as the streets beside the track became leafier on their journey west. His eyes were unblinking and determined. Doubt and compassion had become unwanted baggage in his life. He knew all about feelings, but knew too they couldn't be allowed to stand in the way of an action that would change the course of history. If only the men he was seeking could see things from his point of view they would well understand why their lives must end.

Determined as he was, it worried him that he would have to do it with a knife. Killing that way was a skill he'd never had to practise. Using his pistol to finish off the half-dead Iranian boys who'd tried to storm his regiment's berms in 1987, their eyes and tongues bursting with mustard blisters – that had been easy enough. And ending the agony of some of his own soldiers in the spring of 1991, their flesh shredded by shrapnel and hanging from their bones – that had been an act of brotherhood made almost simple by the distancing mechanism of a trigger and black powder. But to plunge in a knife, to feel its point break skin and bone and slice down through muscle in its search for an artery, was an act he dreaded.

The train slowed for a station. He read the sign.

Barnes.

He got out. The mournful moustache was gone from his face. With his newly clean-shaven upper lip, a mid-weight, grey worsted suit under a light raincoat and a Samsonite briefcase in his hand, he could have passed for a salesman.

He'd studied an *A-Z of London* and had memorised the route from the station to the address Rybkin had supplied him with.

Ten minutes' walk should see him there.

Monday morning had passed quickly for Sam. To the bank for a wad of dollars, to a travel agent for the air ticket and to the Ukrainian Embassy for his visa. Now, at midday, the black taxi that had brought him from Kensington dropped him outside the front door to the mansion block. He hurried inside, not looking left or right, concentrating totally on the task ahead. Whatever outrage was being planned by Colonel Hamdan and his

Ukrainian helpers, the time they had in which to prevent it was fast running out.

There was another good reason for his single-minded concentration on his mission: it stopped him thinking about Chrissie.

He slung a suitcase on the bed and put in clothes for three or four days. A quick in and out was how Waddell had described the mission, but life was only that simple in the never-never land of desk men.

There'd been one phone message on the machine yesterday evening after he'd returned from the Banstead Lodge – from Tom Wallace, checking that he had returned *Backgammon* to the Hamble. He'd rung his co-owner and spun some yarn as to why the boat was in Guernsey. Wallace had called him a 'walking disaster area'.

The flight was at two. One of the Firm's cars was due any minute. He dressed in a light check suit, chose an Italian silk tie, then made sure of his ticket, money and passport for the umpteenth time.

The door buzzer sounded. Everything electrical off, he grabbed the grey raincoat from the hook in the hall, locked the front door and descended to the road.

The driver reached for his case. 'Take that for you, sir?'

'Thanks.' Sam had the briefcase in his other hand and the coat over his free arm.

The car was parked in a road at the side of the mansion block. He opened the rear door and slung his briefcase and raincoat onto the seat. Then, as he watched the driver put the suitcase in the boot, he removed his jacket so it wouldn't crease.

He became conscious of quickening footsteps to his left. A glance revealed a tall raincoated man approaching, incongruously wearing dark glasses despite the greyness of the day and with a Kangol cap pulled down hard on his head. The man bore down on him with increasing speed, gripping a large manila envelope.

Sam froze, certain the man had some desperate purpose and it was to do with *him*. He stared at the leathery face with its hair and eyes so carefully concealed. The man was clean-shaven. A prominent chin.

Fear took hold of him. The figure was five paces away and closing fast. His chin jutted forward as if in an involuntary spasm.

Seen that before, thought Sam. Bloody seen it before!

The hand holding the envelope jerked up, its fingers gripping the corner like they would a dagger.

'Hey!' The yell dried in Sam's throat. He knew who this was now. Christ, he knew!

Right arm up to protect himself, he balled his left hand into a fist.

Suddenly, from somewhere close, came the whoop of a police siren. Startled, the assailant faltered. Sam began to step back. The envelope slashed down in a sweeping arc, its corner catching his sleeve. Then his heel caught on a paving stone. He lost his balance and fell.

'Shit!'

The man hovered over him, raising his arm to slash again, but the siren wail alarmed him. He shot a glance back up the road as a police car darted past at the junction. Sam scuttled back. Cursing, the assailant began to run off.

'*Hamdan!*' Sam yelled after him, his heart racing.

The driver slammed the boot shut. 'What's up, sir?' The lid had obscured his view of what had happened.

'Bastard's got a knife,' Sam hissed, picking himself up. He sprinted off in pursuit.

Hamdan turned at the corner of a short alley leading to the high street. He saw Sam closing the gap and hurled his heavy briefcase at him. It spun through the air like a discus. Unable to swerve in time, the bag caught Sam on the shins.

'Fuck!' he howled, buckling with the pain shooting through his barely healing legs. He tripped over the case and fell heavily to the ground. 'Fucking bastard!'

'You all right sir?' The SIS driver had caught up with him.

'Get down the alley. After him!'

As the driver jogged off, Sam staggered to his feet. The pain in his damaged shins was excruciating. He hobbled to the corner of the footpath and saw the driver at the far end looking both ways along the high street, scratching his head.

'Fuck!'

It *was* Hamdan. No moustache now, but the same dog-like face that had watched his torture in Baghdad. The same nervous tic. Hamdan was here. In London. He grabbed the briefcase and opened it. Empty.

He needed to alert his people. As he hurried back to the car with its secure phone, he looked down at his sleeve. There was a small nick in the shirt stained with blood where the knife had caught him. He undid the cuff to look. It was just a scratch.

Waddell wasn't around when he rang Vauxhall Cross. He spoke to a duty officer, giving as good a description of the Iraqi as he could muster.

'Get the police in on it. This man's dangerous. Very dangerous,' Sam insisted, his heart still thumping.

As he hung up, the driver slipped back behind the wheel.

'Lost him, sir. Sorry. There's a mass of people on the high street. Want we go look in the car?'

'Yes.'

The high street was narrow and blocked by slow-moving traffic. They moved along it scanning the pavements, but it was pointless. Hamdan could have hopped into a taxi, darted down a side road or buried himself in a shop.

'Fuck this. Get me back to the flat,' Sam ordered, angry with himself for letting Hamdan outwit him. 'I need to clean up and get another shirt.'

Gingerly he fingered his shins, hoping they weren't bleeding again. He could only spare a few minutes to get straight or he'd be late for the flight.

But *why* was Hamdan in London? Why risk so much to try to kill him?

Because he was getting close, that was why – far too close to the heart of the matter for Hamdan to be confident his plot could still be carried out.

30

Evening
Kiev

The night-time city stretched out beneath him as the Airbus made its final approach to Kiev's Boryspil airport. Its web of orange street lamps was dissected by the broad, black snake of the river Dnipro. He caught a glint of gold from the onion domes of the floodlit Lavra monastery perched high above the water, and the occasional sparking flash from ill-connecting tram poles. The old town of Kiev was a fine-looking city, he remembered from a year ago. But the organisation that had tried to kill him in London – would they be one jump ahead of him? Waiting for him here?

The wheels touched and the aircraft taxied in past a row of engineless Aeroflot jets cannibalised for spares. The airport building was dimly lit, several of its neon tubes malfunctioning. The two booths where border guards checked passports glowed brightly, however, their glare luring the arriving passengers as if they were fish. Beyond, in the small baggage hall with its single working belt, nervous Ukrainians from a previous flight queued at customs, struggling with cardboard boxes of electrical goods they'd bought abroad, pale-faced with anxiety about the duties or bribes they would have to pay to get them into the country.

When the baggage from the London flight appeared Sam's small suitcase was one of the first off. He made for the green lane, his grey raincoat over his arm. Gerald Figgis, the SIS resident in Kiev whom he'd met briefly a year ago, was sending a driver for him. He scanned the names scrawled on scraps of cardboard held up outside the customs hall and was relieved when he saw his own.

'*Dobriden,*' said a short man with a moustache like a Tartar. '*Meester Packer?*'

'*Tak.*'

He'd picked up only a handful of Ukrainian during his last visit, and his Russian, never very strong, was creaky through lack of practice.

The driver took his bag and led him through the crowd of Slav faces out into the sparsely lit car park, turning briefly to check that Sam was following. He stopped beside an elderly brown Audi and lifted the boot lid. The driver indicated Sam should get into the car.

'*Bood' Laska.*'

The interior of the car was dark. In the far corner sat a shadowy figure. Sam started back, fearing it was Rybkin.

'Welcome.' The voice was Figgis's.

'God! Wasn't expecting you.' They shook hands. 'Thought you were someone else.'

'Good flight?'

'Good enough.'

'Fine. Now look, I'm ninety-nine per cent certain this driver doesn't speak English, but be careful. Fortunately the car's got a blown silencer, so once we get going he won't hear a word, *whatever* the language.'

The driver started up.

'I see what you mean,' Sam commented.

'Hotel Ukraina,' Figgis shouted above the racket.

The driver raised a hand in acknowledgement. He propelled the car towards the exit barrier, paid the parking fee then showed his papers to the police.

'Has to prove he's the vehicle's owner,' Figgis explained. 'Most western cars in Kiev have been stolen in Germany and illegally imported.'

Out on the broad but empty six-lane highway that led to the city centre, the machine roared like a torpedo boat. Figgis leaned across until his mouth was just inches from Sam's ear.

'I've fixed you a rendezvous with the renegade Major's sister at ten tonight. You would have seen her when you were last here. Receptionist at the embassy. Remember what she looks like? She certainly remembers you.'

'Blue eyes, that's all. I only spoke to her a couple of times as far as I recall.'

'I've got a photo of her for you.' He passed Sam a small Polaroid taken for a security pass.

'Thanks.' It was too dark to see, so he put it in his jacket pocket.

Through the window he could make out the black shapes of trees and remembered that Kiev was surrounded by woods which filled up with picnickers on weekends in the summer.

'What d'you know about the brother?' he shouted, turning back to face Figgis.

'Very little. I'm having to keep a low profile on this one. Can't even be sure he's legit. Our defence attaché's gone down to Odessa this week – there's a port visit there by NATO warships, including a British frigate. While in the area he'll see if he gets wind of anything to do with what the brother's talking about, but I don't expect him to. In a situation as diplomatically delicate as this we can't risk making open enquiries.'

The broad highway ended and they entered the eastern half of Kiev. Bleak high rises lined the road, interspersed by concrete monuments to heroes of organised labour. On the far side of the river Dnipro the wooded hills and onion domes of old Kiev were dominated by a massive stainless steel statue of a woman with sword and shield. Its construction had been ordered by Moscow when Ukraine was part of the Soviet Union, Sam remembered.

'The locals call her She Who Must Be Obeyed,' Figgis reminded him.

The traffic halted. Up ahead they saw a trolleybus with one of its power poles swinging wildly. The driver struggled to reattach it to the overhead cable. He eventually succeeded and they began to move again.

'Any leads on Grimov and Rybkin?' Sam asked.

'Not yet. The SBU's "K" Directorate which deals with economic crime have very little info on Voronin's gang. They know that his business interests in Odessa include import–export and transport as well as the usuals like protection and the sex trade. But unless we can give them something specific to investigate, there's little they can do. Just saying we suspect Dima Grimov of supplying some sort of logistical support to Iraqi terrorists is too damn vague for them. That's why Major Pushkin could be crucial.'

'Or useless,' Sam warned.

'Well, precisely. This whole jaunt of yours may be a waste of time.' Figgis leaned closer again. 'The sister's extremely nervous,' he warned. 'Really believes her brother's in danger and that she is too. She's got him out of her flat now. Hidden him somewhere, but won't say where. And she won't meet you at your hotel either. Too many spies around, she says. She's afraid of everybody. Military. Police. Mafiya, you name it.'

'So where *am* I to meet her?'

'There's a bookshop about fifty metres up Khreshchatyk from the Bessarabsky Market end. Left-hand side of the road. It'll be closed but she'll meet you in the doorway at ten. She insists you be on your own.'

The taxi burbled along through light traffic, aiming for one of the bridges across the Dnipro.

'I'm going to bail out in a moment. Ring me from a phone box after the meeting. I'll be at home. Be circumspect about what you say. My phone's bound to be bugged. If it's important, just say let's meet and I'll drive down to your hotel. Here.' He gave Sam a handful of brown plastic tokens and a card. 'There aren't many public phones that work – you can usually recognise the ones that do by the queues. Sometimes they work for free, but have these things just in case.'

'Thanks.'

Figgis leaned forward.

'*Mozhna?*' he said, touching the driver's shoulder. '*Dozvol'te.*' He pointed to a metro station coming up on their right.

'Good luck,' he said, pushing open the door when the car had stopped. 'You don't need to worry about the driver. He's paid for.'

'Thanks.'

The Hotel Ukraina was different from the Intourist-type chicken box he'd stayed in a year earlier, still retaining some of its pre-revolutionary charm. By the time he'd checked into his room and hung up his clothes it was after nine-thirty. The high-ceilinged room overlooked a small yard at the back. Rain beat steadily against the glass.

He opened his briefcase and pulled out the half litre of scotch that he'd bought duty free on the plane. He poured a modest measure into the glass he found on the desk, and added some filtered water from the jug next to it. Kiev's tap supply had a heavy-metal kick that left a tingle in the mouth.

He downed the drink while glancing at the Polaroid that Figgis had given him. Oksana Koslova was a nice looker, he remembered now. He'd not known her name when he'd chatted with her a year ago. Slightly shy, slightly reticent, he recalled, with a smile that took some effort to extract but was worth it when it came. He decided he'd better make a move. He draped the raincoat over his shoulders, removed a telescopic umbrella from his briefcase and took the lift to the ground floor.

The Khreshchatyk boulevard where he was to meet Oksana Koslova was a block away. He was there in minutes. A scattering of people ambled up and down the broad avenue despite the rain, young couples mostly. He crossed the dual carriageway at the traffic lights and walked up on the opposite side from where Figgis had said the bookshop was, remembering that it was from this very same street a year ago that Viktor Rybkin had taken him to sight-see the Mafiya hangouts.

Oksana Koslova emerged from the Teatral'na Metro station feeling that at any moment now she might die of fright. She was here to meet a foreign agent. Here to help her brother flee his own country. If the Militsia or SBU knew what she was doing they would lock her up. If the Mafiya knew, they would kill her.

There was a second reason for her nervousness however, caused by the fact that the foreign agent she was about to meet was a certain Mr Sam Packer. She'd only spoken to him twice and very briefly, and that was a year ago. But his smile and the interest he'd appeared to take in her while waiting at the embassy reception desk for Mrs Taylor to come out to collect him was something she'd not forgotten. Emotionally she'd been fragile since her husband died, prone to tears. Most Ukrainian men she knew wanted women as unpaid housekeepers and prostitutes, but Mr Packer had shown her kindness. In the weeks that had followed his return to London, she'd spun fantasies about him, even to the extent of imagining a relationship. The prospect of meeting him again therefore was unsettling.

Taking deep breaths to steady her heartbeat, she raised

the collar of her coat and tied a scarf over her hair which had been newly set that morning. She started up Khreshchatyk, quickly passing the doorway where they were to meet. No one there yet. Five minutes to go to the appointed hour. She didn't like being here alone at night. She'd heard stories of women being taken from the streets and pressed into the sex trade or worse. Snuff movies, they were called, she'd been told. Rape, torture and death on video for the gratification of sick minds and the financial enrichment of sub-humans.

She'd thought long and hard about how best to handle the situation she was facing this evening, resisting the urge to drench herself in perfume. The man had come here to see her brother, not her. He'd do the deal with Mikhail then fly straight back – to his own wife and children probably. In the end she'd decided on pearl-drop earrings, a light touch of make-up and clothes that were more tidy than alluring.

She bowed her head to keep the rain from her eyes, embarrassed by her own foolishness at having conjured up a whole world of fantasy from a foreigner's smile.

'*Dobriden. Oksana?*'

She stopped with a jerk and gasped. It was him. He'd been coming the other way down Khreshchatyk and had recognised her.

'Hello.'

She felt her face turn scarlet. She pushed the scarf back a little from her forehead.

'Shall we go somewhere out of this rain,' Sam said without further preamble. 'A bar? Café?'

'Oh yes. Where you like,' she said huskily.

'You say where. I don't remember my way around.'

'Of course, of course.' She stared round, trying to think. 'Truth is I don't know such place here. For normal people here in centre of Kiev is too expensive.'

'I'll pay, don't worry,' he reassured her.

'Sorry. I . . .' She noticed he was nervous. He kept looking past her and glancing over his shoulder. 'I didn't mean . . .'

'No, of course not,' he said, gently. 'Let's go any place you like that isn't soaking wet.' He was holding his umbrella over her now, but the wind blew the rain straight under it.

'I know somewhere . . .' She'd remembered a place that had just opened. 'At Independence Square.'

'Back this way, yes?'

'Yes.'

He turned round and she fell in beside him.

'Look, I do need to meet your brother very soon.'

She heard the urgency in his voice.

'Yes, but first we must talk,' she insisted. Misha had warned her to get the terms settled before anything else. He'd been showing signs of backtracking.

'Well we're talking now. There's not much time, Oksana,' Sam warned.

She felt a little afraid of him.

'Tomorrow. Tomorrow morning you can talk with Mikhail. As long as you agree to help him.'

'Yes, but we can't agree anything until we know what he's offering,' he cautioned.

Oksana felt she was on a downhill tram with failed brakes. They walked on in silence, soon reaching the square that was the social hub of the city. The fountains and their floodlights had been turned off and the gaunt, Stalin-era blocks that ringed it on three sides were darkly sinister. Two single men stood separately by a small monument, waiting for friends. On benches under the almost bare trees, couples huddled beneath umbrellas.

'The rain,' Oksana explained, trying to lighten things. 'It is reason not so many people here tonight.' She pointed across the square. 'I think there is new bar over there. Every month there is new, then close when Mafiya make them pay too much.'

Sam groaned as they entered the place. It was a plastic clone of an Irish pub. Abbey Theatre posters plastered the nicotine-coloured walls. Was *nowhere* in the world safe from the spread of stout bars, he wondered? The air was thick with smoke. Darkly varnished chairs and tables filled the floor space, occupied by young people in jeans and pullovers.

They hung their coats on a bent wooden stand and found a free table. As they sat down, Sam looked Oksana over. She wore a knee-length brown skirt and a cerise pullover. She had good-sized breasts although their shape was concealed by a pointy bra. The smooth, pale skin over her high Slavic cheekbones glistened from the rain and her wavy hair had been flattened a little by the scarf. Her eyes were very blue and very frightened.

'It's nice to see you again,' he beamed, leaning forward on his elbows. She seemed to melt before his eyes. For a moment he thought she was going to cry.

'I didn't expect you to remember me.'

'Never forget a pretty face,' he smiled.

A young waiter spotted Sam's western-cut suit and homed in on them, hungry for tips.

'*Dobriden*.'

'What would you like?'

'*Yablouchniy*,' she said.

'*Pivo*.'

The waiter slid away.

'They are learning about service now in Ukraine,' Oksana told him. 'Slowly.'

'So I see.'

He folded his hands. He felt somewhat uncomfortable here. With his suit on he stood out like a dog in a cattery. Should have dressed down.

'Look, I've got to have some more details on your

brother,' he told her, determined to waste no more time. 'What *exactly* is it he wants to tell us?'

'You see, he has told me almost nothing about it,' she answered with a shrug of her shoulders. 'All he tell me is what I tell Mr Figgis, that corrupt officers have sold kind of missile to Mafiya.'

'Yes, but what sort of missile? And who's it been sold to? I need names, Oksana, and details.'

'You see, *I* cannot tell you that. Misha says it is safer when I don't know such things. *He* will tell it – tomorrow, when you meet him.'

'Oksana, what he has to tell us could be extremely important,' Sam whispered, exasperated by her delaying tactics. 'Why not tonight? Take me to him now.'

She felt flustered. The Englishman was every bit as handsome as she'd remembered, but rather more aggressive.

'Because first I must know what you will do to help him. Tomorrow at eight o'clock I can take, if you have visas for Misha, Lena and Nadya. Visa for England for all of them.'

'Oksana, you know the ropes. It doesn't work that way.'

She glanced down at her hands. Yes, she knew it, but her brother had told her to be tough, so she was.

'You may call me Ksucha, if you like.' The words had popped out. 'It is more friendly I think,' she added quickly. 'It short for Oksana in Ukrainian. Like nickname, you say?'

'Fine.'

He'd call her anything she wanted so long as she got a move on.

'And what I call you?'

'Sam. Sam is fine. Look. This visa thing. We have to evaluate what your brother has to say. If it's as significant to the outside world as you suggested to Gerald Figgis and we're convinced that there *is* a threat to Misha's life and to his family, then yes, a visa can be issued rapidly, together with a permit to reside in England. If everything stands up, they could be on their way to London tomorrow evening. That's why I want to see him tonight, so I can get things moving.'

She put a hand up to an ear and fiddled with the pendant.

'Understand please how afraid we all are. Maybe Mafiya – Militsia – maybe they *know* you are here. Maybe they watching us now. We must be very careful. So tomorrow morning is safer.'

He glanced round. Several of the other drinkers were looking their way, but it didn't mean anything. Foreigners always attracted stares.

'Specially we afraid for our children. You . . . you have children?'

'No.'

'Why not? Your wife she not like?'

'Never mind that.' There was something insidious about her question. 'Tell me things about your brother. How long has he been in the army?'

She told him their family history, how they'd been brought up initially in the western town of Ivano-Frankivsk, where in the Great Patriotic War Ukrainian partisans had fought off the Germans and then the Russians. Their father had been a hero of that conflict, she told him.

'My brother Mikhail he want to join army because my father was great soldier,' she explained. 'But also, in nineteen-seventies, army officer was good career for boy. Misha he *so* proud of being officer, he wear uniform always, even when he home on leave. We live in Kiev by then. For him it was honour to be in army. And in those days they paid good money and much possibility to travel.

'But then in Soviet Union we get Gorbachev. And then end of Soviet Union and we have independent Ukraine. Everything change. Is chaos in our country, but *really* chaos, Sam. Misha he try so hard to keep things how they were. But soon he find that army changes very much. Nothing working any more and persons he does not respect become in control.'

'So he became an outsider?' Was this the real reason for the Major's wish to defect?

'Well, yes. I suppose,' she replied, puzzled by his drift.

'And now he wants to get his own back.' Embitterment. And in a bitter man, truth seldom survived intact.

'Please?'

'Misha wants revenge. Is that it? Revenge on all those people in the army he didn't like.'

Her mouth dropped open. 'You don't believe . . .' Her blue eyes clouded. 'No. You cannot believe . . .'

Suddenly the waiter arrived with his tray and off-loaded an apple juice and a beer.

'*Spaseeba*,' said Sam, handing the man a five-*hryvna* note. The waiter beamed and moved off.

Oksana looked utterly perplexed.

'We have to be very careful, Ksucha,' he soothed, realising he'd been less than diplomatic. 'You must understand that. It's why I want to talk to your brother as soon as possible. To make sure his story is genuine.'

And, more importantly, *relevant*.

Her glass of apple juice had been decorated with a slice of orange which she fished out with the swizzle stick. Her neck glowed with perspiration. She picked up a drinks menu and fanned herself with it.

How old was she, Sam wondered? She had lines on her face that put her in her mid-forties, but she was probably less than that. The last decade in Ukraine had been hard. And there'd been a husband who'd died, he recollected.

'You have a daughter. Have I remembered that right?'

'Yes. She is name Luba. It short for Lubova, which mean love.' Her expression suggested that as far as she was concerned the name was a joke. 'Luba is, how you say, a daddy's girl. So when Sergeyi die, she take it very bad. She think he die because I don't look after him right. Which is ridiculous, because it was Chernobyl, you know?'

'Yes I know. I'm sorry.'

'Luba is very difficult girl for me. She want so much things that I can't give . . .' She stopped herself. No man wanted to hear a woman moan. And yet she needed to say *something*. 'I am afraid for us too, Sam. Afraid that if Mafiya come for Misha maybe they try kill us also.'

'I'm sure it won't come to that.' He could see a demand for more visas coming. 'Let's talk about tomorrow. Eight o'clock, you said?'

'Yes.' She stood up and reached for her coat pocket. 'I have map for you.' She unfolded it as she sat down again and pointed out the Metro station where they were to meet. 'I see you there eight o'clock next to barrier. We walk from there. Just five minutes.'

'Okay.'

'But you will bring visas, yes?' she insisted, edgily.

Sam sighed. He wasn't getting through to her. Her mind didn't seem to be grasping the complexities of what she was involved in.

'No, I can't do that,' he explained again, gently. 'But they can be quickly arranged. It depends on what he tells me. You know this, surely.'

She nodded. She understood well enough, but her brother wouldn't. And she would have to answer his accusations of not pushing hard enough on his behalf.

'I must warn, if you do not promise visa, he will not talk to you,' she stated flatly.

'We'll sort it out when we meet. Don't worry.'

There was nothing more he could achieve with her. They were like two bit players waiting for the star to deliver his lines. And hanging around in this public place was unnerving him. He drained his beer.

'Until tomorrow then.'

She looked down at her hands. It was clear to him that she didn't want their meeting to end yet.

'You tired?' she asked. 'Or maybe you must telephone to your wife.'

That was twice she'd probed in that direction. Idle female curiosity, or something more complicated?

'No wife,' he answered flatly.

Her brightening eyes gave her away.

'That is sad for you,' she mouthed.

She was a lonely woman, he realised. The former Soviet Union was full of them – widows, divorcees, or those who'd despaired of finding a man who could stay sober. All of them day-dreaming of some foreigner to rescue them from the shambles they lived in. She might even have an alluring photo with an agency on the Internet like so many of them did.

He felt sorry for her. Women like her were vulnerable. But dangerous too. Oksana was the key to everything that mattered just now. Without her, he couldn't reach the brother. Without his testimony – if it *did* prove relevant – there would be no uncovering of what Colonel Naif Hamdan and his Ukrainian cronies were engaged in.

He worried he'd been too brusque with her this evening. Acted too much like the NATO bully that forty years of Soviet propaganda had drummed into people's imaginations here. He would need to go gently tomorrow.

'Tomorrow morning then,' he told her, getting to his feet.

'Oh. You going?' She made no effort to conceal her

disappointment. 'I hope maybe you tell me about England. Because if Misha and Lena go there, I visit them perhaps.'

Should he stay a little longer? To soften her up a bit? No. He wasn't in the mood.

'I've had a long day. Eight o'clock, we said.'

'Yes. Eight o'clock.'

He helped her on with her coat. When they got outside the rain had stopped.

'Goodnight Ksucha.' He took both her hands in his for a moment.

'You have such nice smile,' she stated simply.

He produced one for her, then strode off to find a telephone.

31

Tuesday, 8 October, 07.55 hrs
Kiev

The next morning Sam arrived early at the rendezvous after switching trains several times and doubling back to check he wasn't being followed. He hung around by the machine that changed coins into plastic Metro jettons, watching the barrier. He'd dressed in jeans and a windcheater that morning, hoping to pass as a local. Success in that was, he knew, unlikely. Foreigners stood out a mile here, not so much for their clothes as for their look of well-nourished contentment.

He had a tickle at the back of the throat that morning. All visitors to Kiev suffered from it, he'd been told. An effect of the endemic pollution. Or the after-effects of Chernobyl, some said.

He watched the press of bodies surging through the exit barriers and guessed from their large number that two trains had arrived simultaneously down below. The soft-featured faces bore the resigned look of a people well used to being trampled underfoot.

Sam felt in low spirits this morning. A scepticism had taken hold of him, a fatalistic conviction that Oksana's brother would have nothing of significance to tell them.

Oksana appeared at the top of the escalator, her fearful eyes already searching for him. She wore beige trousers under the brown raincoat this morning and had gone to town on her make-up. Her bright-eyed look reminded him of a startled deer.

'*Dobriden.*'

'*Dobriden,*' she replied, smiling fleetingly. She hooked her hand through his arm as they walked up the steps into the daylight. From the deliberateness of the act, he guessed she'd planned it.

'You don't mind?' she checked, whispering so others wouldn't hear their English. 'I think it look more natural. Then people don't think you foreign.'

'Good idea,' he mumbled, wondering whether her voice was always husky or whether the pollution had got to her too.

The Metro station exit was on the edge of a park dotted with trees that glowed with the tints of autumn. A path cut through it, its surface still wet from the overnight rain, despite the morning sky being clear and bright.

The skin prickled on the back of his neck. He felt exposed.

'Where are we going?' he asked tensely, looking round. There was no obvious sign they were being followed.

'Not far.' She pointed through the trees. 'See? Over there is Technical University.'

He saw a complex of brown brick buildings which had a nineteenth-century elegance. As they drew nearer he saw that its glory was all in the past. Walls were stained by leaks from rusty downpipes and most buildings appeared dark and deserted. One door had timbers nailed across to prevent entry. Of students there was no sign.

'Why are we—'

'You see,' she interrupted, 'in Soviet times this was very famous place for physic, for electronic, computer – all these things. Much work for military. But today is nothing happening here, because no money. Our science it stopped in nineteen-eighties. We are like prehistoric compared with West. So now we cannot compete. So nobody want.'

'But what's this place got to do with your brother?'

'Misha is here!' she whispered. 'Of course! Why you think otherwise we come? He staying at home of our uncle who was professor.'

They reached the far side of the park and entered the overgrown campus. Tall silvery poplars stood like sentries over the buildings and the patches of scrub and saplings that surrounded them.

'You see, university is my uncle's home for last twenty years. They gave him apartment for his life. He have to stay here even if there are no students, because there is nowhere else for him to live.'

'I see.'

'He does not live well. You will be shocked, I think.'

They turned a corner. Set back among the trees was a line of accommodation halls built in the same style as the academic blocks. The first was a ruin. Girders supported the end wall and half the windows were boarded up. The block beyond looked occupied, with old blankets draped across windows.

'You know about *kommunalka*?' she asked.

'Communal flats. Khrushchev's solution to the housing problem.'

'Exactly.'

They entered a lobby that smelled of damp and disinfectant. A panel on the dark green wall listed the occupants' names. Beneath it hung a rack of letterboxes, most with their locks broken.

'Five families in each apartment, just one room each family,' she explained, preparing him. 'All must share just one bathroom and one kitchen. Our uncle he live here alone now. His wife die long time ago and his son – my cousin – was killed in Afghanistan. He has pension –

maybe thirty-five *hryvna* each month, when they pay it. About twenty dollar. I bring him fruit and vegetable from dacha, otherwise he only eat bread and pasta.'

They climbed two flights of stairs, then passed through an open door into the flat. A long, dark corridor reached into it, half blocked with junk. An old bedstead and a mirror stood propped against the wall. Cardboard boxes full of yellowing papers were stacked from floor to ceiling. Every few paces there was a door, each with an electricity meter beside it.

'One small room for each family,' she repeated in a whisper.

The third door they came to was open.

'And here is kitchen.' She pointed in. 'Wonderful, no?'

Five identical gas cookers. Five small tables cluttered with crockery and cooking utensils. Five small refrigerators that had seen better days. The blue walls were shiny with grease and the place stank of gas.

They reached the end of the corridor and Oksana tapped on the final door. From inside a thin voice asked who it was.

'Ksucha.'

They heard something heavy being moved aside, then the door opened a crack, restrained by a chain. Recognising his niece, an elderly man in jacket and tie swung the door wide, standing aside to let them in. He eyed Sam with a deep suspicion.

The room was smaller than Sam's bedroom back in Barnes. Two single couches pushed against the right-hand wall were draped with rugs. Above them a dark oil painting hung from a picture rail. Against the opposite wall, bookshelves stood from floor to ceiling. At the far end a window was partly obscured by the short, sinewy figure of a man.

Major Mikhail Pushkin felt consumed by shame. Never had he imagined it could come to this. To be face to face with an agent of a power that had been his motherland's *enemy* until just a few short years ago . . .

He watched his sister introduce the foreigner to his uncle, knowing that now the moment of truth had come he couldn't go through with bending his knee to this foreigner, begging him to save his life.

'And this is Misha, my brother. My uncle he speak some English, but Misha not.'

Sam offered Pushkin his hand, but the Major wouldn't take it. Oksana scolded him for his rudeness, blushing with embarrassment.

'I understand how difficult this must be for you, Major,' Sam told him. 'I was a naval officer myself for many years.'

He glanced at Oksana and she translated.

Pushkin grunted noncommittally, then strode over to the door and wheeled the armchair barricade back in place. When he turned to face them again, he found he couldn't look them in the eye. His heart and his head were in turmoil. He felt ashamed at the ineptitude he'd demonstrated in the past ten days. It had been pure arrogance to question that spares order after his commander had ordered him to turn a blind eye. And, when the whole issue blew up in his face, it had been cowardly to run away. He blamed himself primarily for his string of misjudgements, but blamed Lena too. If she hadn't been constantly pressuring him, always demanding more . . .

'Misha?' Oksana stared at him in horror. She could see what was going through his head.

Pushkin met his sister's gaze, searching for a way to explain that he wasn't going through with this after all the arrangements she'd made. And he definitely wasn't. He'd made up his mind. He simply couldn't. Couldn't flee to an alien culture, couldn't struggle with a language he knew he would never master. Couldn't live as a stranger for the rest of his life.

'*Nyet,*' he growled.

Oksana knew this pigheaded look. She'd known it all her life. She wanted to scream at him as she had when they were children, but no sound came.

Sam understood enough to realise his worst fears were being confirmed. That his journey would be a waste of bloody time.

'Shall we sit down?' he suggested, exasperated.

The professor, who'd been watching the silent drama like a scarecrow, unfroze suddenly.

'Sorry Mister Englishman . . .'

He removed a stack of jigsaw puzzle boxes from the small, square table in the middle of the room, dumping them on one of the few areas of floor that weren't already taken up with junk. The table was covered with a white cloth embroidered in red cross-stitching.

Pushkin remained by the door, his eyes cast down.

'Like you some tea?' the old man asked his guest.

'What a good idea,' said Sam. A good old cuppa to break the tension.

The professor whispered to Pushkin to let him out of the room. Sam watched as the Major wheeled the chair stolidly to one side, then shoved it back in place. His face could have been carved from wood, his eyes dull pebbles. A man on the edge. Sam knew well enough how that felt.

Suddenly Oksana let rip with a torrent of Ukrainian. Pushkin folded his arms and ignored the tirade. He'd started to make up his mind a few hours ago, during the sleepless hours before dawn. For much of the earlier part of the night he'd even been considering suicide – shutting himself in the communal kitchen along the corridor and opening the taps on the five cookers. But that, he'd concluded, would be the ultimate act of cowardice, for which Lena and Nadya would never forgive him.

Having excluded death by his own hand, and having ruled out flight to England, a new way out had come to him just as the first birds began to sing in the trees outside the window. He would take his family back to the area where he'd spent his childhood in Ivano-Frankivsk. He had family there still. Uncles, aunts, cousins. They would find a deserted dacha to hide in and they'd live off the soil. They'd change their names. Cease to exist as far as the authorities were concerned. And if the Mafiya ever caught up with them, he would by then have demonstrated beyond any doubt that he had no intention of betraying their secrets. And they would spare him.

'*Misha!*'

Her eyes like ice picks, Oksana lashed at him with the flat of her hand. The smack to the face shook Pushkin to the core. His own sister. Never, ever had she dared . . .

'Please. Friends.' Sam pointed to the table. 'Let's all sit down and talk it through in a calm, rational—'

'Huh! You think you can make my brother *rational*?' Oksana snorted.

Sam pulled out one of the two straight-backed wooden chairs and indicated Pushkin should take the other. The Major stepped forward one pace then stopped at attention and began to speak. His voice was a slow monotone.

Sam understood enough to know he was apologising for the trouble he'd caused, but not the reasons why. He needed a translation.

'Oksana?'

She stood with her hands on her hips, her upper body canted forward.

'My brother very stupid man,' she spat.

Pushkin stared over Sam's head towards the light.

'He say he will not talk with you.' Oksana began looking for something heavy. 'I think I knock some sense into him.' She snatched up one of the professor's bulkier tomes from a stack on the floor.

'Hang on a minute. Tell your brother to sit down. I want to explain something to him.'

Reluctantly Pushkin pulled out the chair and sat on it. The man's eyes were like brick. This bastard would have been a tough nut to crack if they'd ever gone to war, thought Sam.

'Major Pushkin. My name is Commander Packer.' He would try the old one-officer-to-another trick. 'I understand you have information you intended to pass to the British government. I've no idea whether it's important or not, but it *may* be, for reasons you are unaware of. In fact it may be *so* important that thousands of people could lose their lives if you keep it to yourself.'

He paused for Oksana to translate. Her eyes widened as she spoke.

'I could be shot for treason for doing what I'm about to do,' Sam declared, exaggerating wildly. 'Because what I'm going to tell you has been classified ultra top secret by the intelligence agencies of Britain and America. But I'm quite prepared to risk being shot, if it means that *you* understand the importance of my mission here.'

Oksana translated again, her voice breathy and tense. Pushkin was now listening attentively, but with suspicion.

'Major Pushkin.' Sam leaned forward and lowered his voice. 'In the next few days, the West expects Iraqi terrorists to launch a biological weapons attack. The Iraqis have paid five million dollars to Ukrainian criminals to help them carry out that attack.'

Sam watched the blood drain from Pushkin's face and realised his journey mightn't be wasted after all.

'Major Pushkin,' he continued, more urgently. 'You wanted to tell us about a missile I believe. Sold to the Mafiya a few days ago. If that weapon is capable of delivering anthrax, tens of thousands of people may die. Do I make myself clear?'

In Pushkin's mind a light had appeared in the fog.

'If you have information that can prevent that attack and you decide to keep it to yourself, then *you* would share responsibility for those deaths. Get it?'

Obsessed by his own safety and that of his family, Misha had almost forgotten the dangers to the outside world. And now he knew those dangers were real . . .

His back straightened and his chin rose. Perhaps he *could* take pride in what he had done. He opened his mouth to speak, but then the doubts flooded back. What if the British took his information then refused to help him escape? What if they *did* give him the visas but he was arrested trying to leave Ukraine? For communicating military information to a foreign power the state would kill him just as surely as the Mafiya.

'*Misha!*' Oksana was on her feet again, her voice a rasp and her right hand balling into a fist.

'*Da.*'

He nodded. Yes. He would talk. He told himself that the man sitting opposite him was *not* a NATO vulture here to pick over his country's corpse. It *wasn't* dishonourable what he was doing. The oath of loyalty he'd sworn all those years ago was to a culture, a set of principles, not to a body of corruptible men.

'We don't have much time with this, Major,' Sam warned.

Pushkin began to talk. He spoke in short, clipped sentences, pausing between them for Oksana to translate. He told his story from the beginning – his job at Magerov, his initial suspicion about the orders for VR-6 spares and the murder of the driver who'd delivered them to a warehouse in Odessa. He explained about the shock of realising that his own commander was involved in the illegal sale, and his nearly fatal decision to take the matter to a higher authority.

As the translations fired out, Sam's pulse quickened.

They *were* onto something. The man was talking about the sort of unmanned air vehicle Dean Burgess had described at the Lodge on Sunday. How big? That was the key issue; some drones were very small. Before he could ask, there was a tapping at the door followed by the uncle's thin voice.

Not now, thought Sam. Fuck the ruddy tea.

Pushkin stood up and wheeled the heavy armchair aside. The old man entered, carrying a wooden tray laid with gilded porcelain cups and saucers and a matching teapot. A tin mug would have done Sam just as well, but he mumbled some compliment about how elegant it all was.

Pushkin took the tray and set it on the table. Then, with due deference to his uncle's age and status, he asked very courteously for the old man to leave them alone again. As the door closed and the armchair slid back in place, Sam finally asked the vital question.

'This VR-6, Major. What's its range and what could it carry?'

Pushkin quoted what he'd memorised from the technical manuals.

'He call the VR-6 Yastreyo. In English you say "hawk", I think.' Oksana translated. 'He says is like cruise missile but carries a camera. Length seven metres. Short wings.'

'And how's it fired, this Hawk?'

'Launched by rocket, he says. From . . .' She hesitated, searching for a word. 'From *lorry*. Eight wheels.'

Plenty big enough to carry a canister of anthrax in its nose instead of a camera.

'After launch by rocket there is jet engine,' she went on, fired up by Sam's interest. 'Some computer in it for guiding. Misha say radio control also. He say it fly maximum ninety kilometres. Fuel for fifteen minutes flight, no more.'

Fast, Sam calculated. Damned fast. He knew exactly what this thing would do. He felt the skin crawl on the back of his neck.

'So, where did they go, these spares?' he demanded. 'Who's got them now?'

Pushkin shrugged.

'You said the Mafiya, Major. But which gang? There's over six hundred in Ukraine.'

Pushkin was clamming up again. The man knew all right, but he wasn't bloody saying. He'd turned to face his sister and was talking earnestly, in Ukrainian this time so Sam wouldn't understand.

Oksana sighed. 'It like I tell you. He want to know about visa for him and for Lena and for Nadya.'

'Not now, Ksucha. In a minute.'

'He say now,' she insisted.

Sam looked from one face to the other. He could see the family likeness. The broad, flat forehead, the blue eyes that looked benign enough but were bloody stubborn when the chips were down.

'He say he must know if you give visa for all of them.'

'Yes.' He tapped his fingers together. No more prevarication. He had to commit. 'Of course they'll get their visas.'

Pushkin whipped three passports from the back pocket of his trousers and laid them on the table.

'Misha he ask *when*?'

'When he's told me everything. You'll have to trust me, Ksucha.'

Pushkin's face had set like cement. He'd been cheated once too often. The names Sam sought were the only cards he had left.

'He ask is it sure they will be allowed to *stay* in England?' Oksana whispered.

'Yes,' Sam growled. No way he could promise that, but he needed the names.

Pushkin stuck out his chin. For a moment Sam thought he was digging in still further. Demanding an audience with the bloody Queen, perhaps.

'Voroninskaya.'

Sam held his breath.

'*Anatoly* Voronin,' he added.

This was it. He'd struck gold.

'And? Some other names,' Sam demanded. 'Who runs Voronin's businesses in Odessa? Who was it who actually bought the drone?'

Pushkin's eyes filled with a bitter hatred for the former Spetznaz Captain First Rank who'd brought such devastation into his life and into that of one of his closest friends.

'Grimov,' he hissed. 'Dima Filipovich Grimov.'

32

The British Embassy, Kiev

'We've got to get 'em out tonight, Gerald,' Sam insisted, slapping the three passports down on the desk of the SIS station chief. 'They're in huge danger. Grimov's a man who kills as easily as he farts.'

'Point taken. We'll do our best.' Figgis gathered up the passports and placed them to one side. He opened his desk diary. 'When did Pushkin say this all happened?'

'It was on Friday twenty-seventh September that the spares were delivered to some warehouse or other in Odessa. He doesn't know where exactly. But he thinks there's a yard there owned by a shipping company called Hretzky Transport which is controlled by the Voronin group.'

'And how easy would it have been to turn these spare parts into a working missile?'

'Pushkin says the Hawk parts were all subassemblies. Reckoned that with the right skills they could plug the bits together in a matter of hours. It's not a very complex piece of equipment. And there's no shortage of unemployed ex-military men around who'd be ready to deliver those skills if the price was right.'

'The most likely way out of the country would be in a shipping container,' Figgis concluded, half to himself. 'So the first thing we need is a list of sailings from the Odessa region from the twenty-seventh onwards. Shouldn't be hard. Ukrainian Customs must have a record of exports. There won't have been many. Most of the containers go back empty to the place where they came from.'

Sam fretted that Figgis's enquiries might pose a risk to the Pushkins.

'How will you handle this without revealing to the Ukrainians where we got the tip-off from?'

'No problem. We'll do it through the drugs team. We've a man in Warsaw who liaises on narcotics issues with all the agencies of the former eastern bloc countries. It's a well-oiled machine. We'll get him to say we're trying to identify a container shipped out of the Odessa region with heroin in it.'

'How long to get an answer?'

'Could be a day or two. The customs service is new and small in Ukraine. Depends on how much of a squeeze the SBU can put on them.'

'Meanwhile the Pushkin family *will* be on their way to London tonight?'

'On the eight o'clock British Airways. Shouldn't be a problem. Unless, that is, the army's already reported him as AWOL. If they've alerted the border guards, that'll be tough titties. For him and for us, because they'll want to know why *we* gave the family visas.'

Figgis did a quick tot-up in his diary. 'God! It's eleven days since the VR-6 went to that warehouse! That Hawk could be almost anywhere on the planet by now.'

He scribbled a few notes.

'Right,' he breathed. 'Time I talked to London.' He disappeared into the secure communications chamber.

Sam stood by the window with his hands in his pockets. A Land Rover Discovery had just driven into the courtyard at the back of the embassy, pulling up in one of the marked spaces. When the driver got out, he saw that it was the ambassador. The man didn't know it yet but he was about to walk into a storm.

A day or two, Figgis had said. *Two days* to get to first base on the question of where the VR-6 was shipped to. Official channels were slow channels. *Too* damned slow. Thousands of people might have gone down with the early flu-like symptoms of a pulmonary anthrax infection by then, with death following within days. There *had* to be a quicker way.

Dima Filipovich Grimov had the answers they needed, of course. Engraved in Sam's mind was that heavy, lecherous face in the Mondiale Hotel photo. If the world were a just place, that man's head would be squeezed in a vice until he talked. But not in Ukraine. Here officialdom protected him, because officialdom had been bought.

And Viktor Rybkin? Rybkin too would know the current location of the VR-6. Sam thought back to his first mistrustful acquaintance with the former KGB man here in Kiev a year ago. There *had* been something likeable about him then. *A rogue with a soul*, Chrissie had called him, words she must bitterly have regretted in the moments before she died.

Sam remembered how in Cyprus Rybkin had distanced himself from her death, insisting he wasn't involved in it, as if it were an act he was ashamed of. But did that mean Rybkin had a conscience? Was it just possible that the thought of thousands dying from anthrax was causing him sleepless nights? Speculation ran riot in his head. Rybkin could have killed him in Cyprus, but he hadn't. Could it be that he'd *wanted* Sam alive – to have a fighting chance of preventing the massacre from taking place?

Figgis re-emerged from the communications 'box'.

'All squared,' he announced, flopping into one of the leather easy chairs. 'Visa clearances will be through by telegram within the hour. And they're booking the flights. Three seats in the name of Pushkin and one for you.'

'Me?' Sam spluttered.

'Yes. They want you to nanny the Pushkins back to Blighty. Orders from on high. A three line whip.'

It was after midday by the time Sam met up with Oksana back at the Metro station by the Technical University. She'd been waiting for him on the edge of the park and he noticed a puffiness around her eyes as if she'd been crying. They set off through the trees to deliver the news about the visas to her brother. He told her about the flight that evening. This time she made no attempt to link arms with him.

'So,' she sighed, 'your visit to Ukraine will be very short. Even shorter than last.'

'Yes.' In theory.

'Pity. I would like so much to talk with you. Last time we had such nice little chats, remember? You even pay me big compliment about how I look – but you don't remember that,' she laughed throatily.

'Yes I do. And I meant it,' he answered, not remembering at all, but knowing that he would have done. It was hard to understand why a woman like her should have failed to find a partner to replace the husband who'd died.

'Well, I don't think so. But one question you can answer me.' She looked at him coyly. 'I very curious. What about Essex?'

'Essex? Why on earth do you ask about Essex?'

'Because I hear it very nice place.'

He laughed briefly. 'Depends on your tastes. Lots of good-time girls. Some fine sailing in the estuaries. And Constable country.'

Why the hell was she interested in Essex?

'Constable?'

'English landscape painter. Very famous.'

'Ah yes. There is picture by him in entrance to embassy. Copy, of course.' She began to wonder which of these aspects of Essex life so appealed to the security man there.

The university campus came in sight through the trees. At the edge of the woods was a children's playground, which Sam hadn't noticed before. Three infants were being pushed on a roundabout by a weary-looking young mother in jeans and an anorak.

Oksana stopped him with a hand on the arm. 'I think maybe you hungry, yes?'

Food was the last thing on his mind.

'We stop here. Just few minutes.' She pointed to a bench. 'This morning six o'clock I make some sandwich for you.' She dug into her black nylon shopping bag and pulled out a package in grease-proof paper.

'I hardly think there's time . . .'

'Oh yes. Enough time. Misha can wait few more minutes.'

There was a look on her face that said, *Just do this for me please*. Lonely and vulnerable, he reminded himself. They sat down, briefly attracting the bored attention of the woman minding the children. This is bad, thought Sam. Bad to be sitting here in the open where he could be picked off. For one paranoid moment he wondered if he was being set up.

Oksana handed him two slices of pale brown bread with something white wedged between.

'Fresh cheese from dacha,' she explained. 'Neighbour at country house has cow.'

He bit into it. 'Very nice indeed.' He wasn't going to make the running in conversation. Leave it to her to say whatever it was she wanted to say.

They ate in silence for a few moments, then Oksana asked, 'You also, you have country house in England?'

'No. It's not that common with us. Just a small flat in London.'

'And live alone?'

'Yes, Ksucha,' he said, swallowing. 'I live alone.'

She sighed. 'But, you not sad to be alone? No child even . . . I have daughter at least. Though sometime I think it better not to have,' she snorted.

'What does Luba plan to do with her life?' he asked, steering the talk away from himself.

Oksana laughed. 'She want to be New Russian and have money.' She bit hard into her sandwich as if trying to decapitate a nightmare.

Neither of them spoke for a while. Then suddenly she broke the silence.

'I think maybe she want become prostitute.'

Her words dropped out as if it was nothing unusual.

Sam jerked his head round. 'She can't *want* to become a prostitute. That's not a career you choose. *It* chooses you.'

'Here, yes. You choose,' she replied matter-of-factly. 'Is same for many girls here. To be *putanky* is quick way to earn dollar. And with dollar get nice clothes, learn speak English, maybe work Europe or America. Find rich husband. What else they can do? Study five years at university then get job in office that pay less money than you need for living? How can I say, as mother, that go to university is *right* way and being prostitute is wrong?'

'But come on, Ksucha . . .'

'For young people only future is to leave Ukraine,' she insisted sadly. 'Because our country is . . . is disaster.'

'Now, yes. But it'll get better,' he said unconvincingly.

'Huh! Easy for you,' she derided. 'Easy for you to say, when you go away on plane tonight.'

There was a new bitterness in her voice.

'Tell you what. Maybe I come with you. You like to have woman who do *anything* for you in England?' Her low voice and mocking smile said she was joking, but her eyes were half serious. 'No. Better you don't answer me that.'

He smiled dumbly, trying to think of something he could say that would be kind but would put an end to this distraction.

'I think we better go to my brother now,' she announced, cutting short his embarrassment. She took from him the paper that his sandwich had been wrapped in and replaced it in the shopping bag so it could be used again.

'Thank you for lunch,' he mumbled.

It was so unfair. What had she done, what had *any* of them done, to deserve the mess their country had sunk into?

'And I'm sorry, Ksucha. Sorry that life's so bloody for you.'

Major Mikhail Pushkin was as tense as a caged rat when they returned to the communal flat with the passports. When he examined the visas he smiled with relief. His heart was heavy though. Starting life again in a foreign culture felt like a prison sentence.

'*Spaseeba*,' he whispered, pocketing the travel documents.

'The flight is at eight and they'd best be at Boryspil airport two hours before,' Sam explained for Oksana to translate. 'The tickets have been paid for by the British Foreign Office and can be collected at the airport.'

Pushkin nodded. Then he asked Oksana in Russian how they would get there. She explained she had a trustworthy friend with a car who could drive them.

'And Misha ask, you will be on same airplane?' she checked, turning to Sam.

Would he? Could he leave this country without doing his damnedest to prise the truth from Rybkin?

'Well, if I'm not, they mustn't worry. There'll be someone meeting them in London who'll look after them.'

Oksana gaped at his answer.

'Ksucha, I have one more question for your brother.'

'Yes? Tell me.'

'Does he have any idea where in Odessa I would find Dima Grimov?'

Thirty minutes later Sam was striding back through the woods towards the Metro with Oksana struggling to keep up with him. She could see he'd made up his mind, but just before they reached the main road, she grabbed his arm and made him stop.

'I think you crazy person,' she panted, her face screwed up with anguish. 'You crazy, crazy man. You get killed.'

'What are you talking about?'

'All this questions about Mafiya man Dima Filipovich Grimov – what you going to do? You go to Odessa to look for? You mad person.'

'It doesn't concern you, Ksucha,' he snapped, trying to pull away, but she'd locked onto his arm like an anchor.

'Yes, *does* concern,' she insisted. 'Why? Because I like you is why. I like you very much Sam. Don't worry, that is problem for me not for you,' she added quickly, noting his stony reaction. 'But these Mafiya, I know what they are like. They kill without second thought. Don't go Odessa. Please. I ask you this. Do this one thing for me.'

She was right about the danger of course. He'd be like a mouse walking into a cage of cats, but he'd convinced himself he had to try it. If there was a chance that Viktor Rybkin would reveal where the attack was to take place in order to salve his conscience, then he had to grab it.

And there was another reason he needed to pin down Rybkin. A reason called Chrissie. If he was ever to know peace again he had to learn the truth about her.

Oksana saw the stubbornness in his eyes and knew that inside he was just like her brother. She would not be able to dissuade him.

'Then . . . then if you must go Odessa, I will go with you.' The words spilled out without her thinking about them.

Sam turned to face her.

'Ksucha, listen. That's the daffiest suggestion I ever—'

'Shh! *You* listen.' She felt euphoric suddenly, out of control. '*I* know Odessa. I can be your guide and translator. I have cousin who live there. We can stay at his home.' She astonished herself by the brisk, business-like way she was saying this.

'You're crazy,' Sam growled. 'It's far too dangerous, you said so yourself.'

'Not crazy. I think it important for *you* that I go with you. Because alone you will be stranger there. And alone is more danger for you.'

She was right of course. He would stand out like a sore thumb.

'But your daughter . . .'

'Is easy. She will stay with friend. No problem.'

'It's too risky . . .'

But he was wavering. Without a translator he would be lost. His Russian was crap. She could smooth his path while he was finding his way around and keep her out of the way when things got hairy. And there was no one else.

She let go of his arm and stood back a pace, pushing her fingers through her freshly washed hair. Her face was as open as a book suddenly, and when she spoke again it was as a woman who was resigned to her fate.

'You see, I not afraid, Sam. Not afraid of Mafiya.' Her voice tugged like a newly rosined bow on a cello string. 'You see, if they kill me I really don't worry. Because here in Ukraine, to tell truth, *absolute* truth, I don't want to go on living.'

33

Wednesday, 9 October, 07.36 hrs
Odessa, Ukraine

It was a long step down from the train that had brought them overnight from Kiev. As Sam gave Oksana a helping hand, he noticed her mascara had smudged. The crush of half-awake bodies spilling from the carriages swept them up the platform towards the terminus with the same irresistible force as the quest for answers that had driven him to this Black Sea port.

Dawn had broken an hour ago, casting its veiled light over the endless steppe. The window blind in their second-class *kupe* sleeper compartment had been up throughout the journey because it was stuck. For much of the night Sam had lain awake on his top bunk, tortured by the itching skin of his healing shins and glancing through the glass whenever the flicker of lights outside denoted the passing of a town or village. Beneath him on the lower bunk lay Oksana, equally sleepless, or so he'd guessed. Across the compartment, just an arm's length away, two more berths were occupied by men.

Last night he'd gone to Boryspil airport to check that Pushkin and his family passed through the barriers unstopped. Then, once the British Airways jet had taken off for London Gatwick with them on board, he'd phoned Figgis at home and asked him to let Waddell know that he wasn't on the flight. His explanation that he was heading for Odessa had received a muted reaction from Figgis, followed by an insistence that Sam should meet him before he caught the train because 'I have something for you which may prove useful'.

When they'd met in the station concourse, Figgis had been startled to see Oksana with him. He'd dutifully passed on Waddell's displeasure at Sam's failure to return to London, but made no attempt to dissuade him from going after Viktor Rybkin. He'd merely handed over a plastic shopping bag and wished him luck. Inside there was something heavy wrapped in newspaper. After the train began to roll, Sam had taken it to the toilet to examine it, but had already guessed what it was.

The pistol was of small calibre and a size that would be easy to conceal. Feeling its heavy metal grip in the palm of his hand had again brought home the risks he was running. Yet it hadn't deterred him. If there was a chance of preventing a massacre by playing on Rybkin's conscience, these were risks he had to take.

They reached the station concourse, the crowd swollen by the arrival of commuter trains. Tempting smells from pastry stalls reminded Sam he was damned hungry, but Oksana wrinkled her nose saying station food was expensive and unhygienic.

'Taras will have some breakfast for us,' she assured him, her face grey with tension this morning. 'But I hope we find taxi. Or *chastnik*. Private driver.'

They paused on the front steps of the station, scanning the cars on the forecourt. An old woman in a thick woollen coat and shawl seized Oksana's hand, begging them to rent a room from her. They pushed on down the steps but the babushka hung on. Oksana had to sharpen her tongue to get rid of her.

'You spoke Russian to her,' Sam commented. It was the first time he'd been to this Black Sea town.

'Yes. People in Odessa they don't speak Ukrainian, even if it is official language. They not so nationalist here.'

Oksana ran a comb through the dark waves of her hair and checked her face in a mirror from her bag. Then, with her raincoat draped loosely over her shoulders, she stepped forward to the kerb. Sam looked about him tensely, aware that somewhere not far from here were the men who'd killed Chrissie.

In a few minutes a privately owned Zhiguli pulled up, its engine misfiring and its owner looking for ways to raise money for a mechanic. Oksana leaned in through the opened door and negotiated a price. Then, putting a finger to her lips to warn Sam not to speak lest the sound of a foreign tongue turned the fare from *hryvna* to dollars, they climbed in. Sam placed his suitcase on the front seat next to the driver.

They passed the vast Privoz farmers' food market, then turned up one of the tree-lined boulevards which formed the town's central grid. The town was a surprise for Sam with its air of Mediterranean elegance.

Oksana sat rigidly beside him, her knees together and the small holdall that comprised her luggage hugged tightly to her lap. Although trying hard to appear calm and composed, inside she was a mess. It had been pure impulse deciding to accompany him on this suicidal mission. During the night, rocking from side to side in that bunk on the train, she'd tried to analyse why she'd done it. Part of it was simple: she liked him and wanted as much time as possible with him before he disappeared from her life again. But she'd realised there was a more serious reason too – a compelling need to ensure he didn't get himself killed.

The Zhiguli took a left, away from the city centre. There was a relaxed confidence in the people Sam saw on the pavements. It was as if they had more hope here than in the capital.

They were heading now for the run-down district of Moldovanka, home to whores and junkies, Oksana had told him. Her cousin Taras had been reduced to living there after his restaurant business collapsed. Seedy today, Moldovanka had once been fashionable, and as they entered the district he saw signs of its former elegance. They drove along wide avenues shaded by plane trees. The house where Taras lived had crumbling but ornate balconies and a porch supported by Doric columns.

Oksana paid the driver with money that Sam gave her. The man sped off, leaving them on the kerb.

'We go in quick before someone see you are foreigner and steal your suitcase,' she urged in a hoarse whisper. 'Someone watching here. Always watching,' She jabbed her finger on a bell push beside the entrance to a walled yard at the side of the house. 'Every day people dying in Moldovanka,' she whispered again. 'Because making own drug here, called *vink*. Brown like soup.' She shuddered. 'Hope Taras not sleeping now.'

There was no response to her ringing.

She pressed the bell again. This time there was a shout from beyond the wall, then shuffling footsteps. The gate opened. Taras was a wreck of a man. Of medium height, with dark hair in need of a trim and several days' growth of beard, he wore a crumpled once-white shirt over black underpants. There were livid scars down one leg.

He let them in, breathing heavily. He reeked of alcohol. They stood in a small courtyard which was covered by strings with a vine clinging to them. Taras led them to a low building that appeared to have once been the stables to the main house. Inside its single room was a rumpled bed, a small, sticky-looking table, a couple of wooden chairs and a sofa. The place looked as if a hurricane had swept through it.

Taras pointed to a door leading to a kitchen, then fell onto the bed, giving every appearance of intending to go back to sleep.

Oksana gulped. This was worse than she'd feared. She put her bag on the sofa and suggested Sam did the same, then peered into the kitchen, wrinkling her nose.

'Bathroom,' she whispered, pointing past the grease-blackened cooker to a cement-floored corner. The loo was a hole in the ground and next to it was a porcelain sink. 'Maybe better for you in hotel,' she suggested, flustered by the state of the place. 'But at least I think we safe. No one will know you are here.'

That's for sure, thought Sam, wondering where the hell they would sleep if they were still here tonight.

'Now, I make some breakfast.'

She opened the fridge, then let out a groan of despair. Empty apart from spirit bottles.

'Taras,' she whimpered, 'maybe he have bread somewhere.' She leaned her head round the door. 'Taras?' No reply from the bed. She cursed him roundly, then checked a cupboard, but it contained crockery, not food.

'I am sorry.' She was red with embarrassment by now. 'My cousin said he would make everything ready . . .' She shrugged. 'I must go to shop, I think.'

Sam gave her a twenty-*hryvna* note.

After she'd gone Sam stared at the facces-spattered toilet and decided to keep as far from it as possible. Back in the main room Taras was snoring by now. An empty wine bottle lay on its side on the floor beside the bed. Drips from it had stained the well-soiled sheet that he'd pulled over himself.

This was not what he'd expected. Yesterday afternoon in response to his question about where to find Dima Grimov, Mikhail Pushkin had told him of a restaurant in Odessa used by the Voroninskaya as a base for their *gangstery*. It hadn't been much to go on but it was all there was.

'But Taras will know more,' Oksana had assured him. 'Taras know everything about Mafiya in Odessa.'

Sam's faith in Taras, however, had evaporated along with the promise of breakfast. He loathed this place. He wanted to douse it with disinfectant. Or petrol. For a few minutes he watched the almost imperceptible rise and fall of the bed-sheet and tried to tell himself that if *he* had suffered in the way Taras had then he too would probably seek oblivion from the bottle.

Oksana had filled him in on Taras's downfall while waiting for the train last night. A respected engineer under communism, when the economy collapsed the machine-tool factory where he'd worked had closed. For a few years he'd lived on the earnings of his wife who was employed by the port administration. Then, when Odessa began to sprout imported cars, smart boutiques and the other signs of New Russian money, he'd started a restaurant business in order to get his hands on some of it. He'd taken the right first step, signing on for 'a roof' from the Mafiya boss who controlled protection in the district where the restaurant was to be situated. Twenty per cent of his takings went for the *krysha*. Despite that leaching of his profits, the business had succeeded. And succeeded well, according to Oksana. But then the revenue men had got stuck in, demanding outlandish tax payments. Finally a gang war had erupted in the neighbourhood and the restaurant had burned down. With no insurance, Taras had lost everything, including his wife a few weeks later when she moved in with one of the *gangstery* who'd burned him out.

There was a grunt from the bed. The body rolled over, then resumed its snoring. Sam looked round the room. Off-white walls speckled with damp, a tacky electric candelabra hanging from the ceiling, clothes dumped on the floor. Against one wall stood a shiny veneered bookcase unit with cupboards in its base. Perched on it was a television and video recorder. Next to the machine lay a VHS tape without a box. Out of idle curiosity, he pushed it into the player and switched on the TV, muting the sound so as not to disturb Taras.

A picture appeared, but what it was exactly he couldn't at first make out. The tape was poor quality and damaged. Then it dawned on him that the pale shapes moving about on the screen were the limbs of several bodies locked in a complicated clinch.

Yes, thought Sam, if *he* were Taras, he too might find solace in porn videos.

He left the tape playing, idly speculating on which limbs belonged to which face. Then, before he could resolve the conundrum, the scene cut abruptly to something much simpler. A naked blonde girl was kneeling before a man whose penis was the size of a cucumber. The camera cut to a close-up as her mouth enveloped it, before rising up to give the man's view of her increasingly active lips. In a slow caress, the camera panned over her blonde curls, then down her glistening back, coming to rest on her neat butt and the heavy metal shackles that secured her wrists to her ankles.

Sam's hand hovered by the stop button. He'd always felt uncomfortable at finding this stuff stimulating. There'd been plenty of it in the Navy, the best tapes to be found in the chief petty officers' mess.

The camera cut back to the girl's face, her eyes closing in feigned ecstasy as the man shot his load. When he pulled back, she let his ejaculate dribble from her lips, then hooked it back in with her tongue.

Enough, thought Sam. Quite enough. He reached for the stop button.

But he didn't press it. Because the scene had changed again and what he saw now sent a shiver down his spine.

The girl was on her back this time, writhing on a bed, with the man kneeling in the fork of her widely spread legs. There was a mark on her stomach. A mark that looked alarmingly familiar.

'Shit,' Sam breathed, remembering.

The man thrust into her, supporting himself so the camera could linger on her breasts which were shiny with oil. She rubbed them with her hands, fingering the nipples. Thrusting buttocks, close-ups of faces, hers and his; the camera changed angles every few seconds. Then to a side view as the man withdrew for the cum shot.

'Shit . . .'

The eye-line of the man now – looking down at her scut of pubic hair as he jerked off onto her belly.

A belly with a mark on it.

A mark that was a tattoo.

The camera zoomed in. He hit pause.

Suddenly his world fell apart. The tattoo filled a corner of the screen.

It was a globe. A blue globe with a blob of red for land, and beneath it the letter B.

The same damned mark in almost the same damned place that he'd seen on Chrissie's yellowing body in that miserable mortuary at Akrotiri.

34

By the time Oksana rang on the bell to be let back in, Sam was starting to get his head straight again.

He went into the yard and opened the front gate. Oksana bustled in, laden with two brown paper bags full of supplies. He didn't want conversation at this point and encouraged her into the kitchen to make coffee.

Rybkin's warning rang in his ears like a dinner gong. *The more questions you ask about her, the more you will hear things you don't like*. But he *had* to ask. Particularly now. Had to know what the fuck this was all about.

The smell of brewing coffee caused a stirring in the bed. Taras raised himself on an elbow and frowned, trying to recall who the stranger was sitting on his sofa.

Sam stood up, grabbed the video-cassette from the player and took it across to the bed.

'Where'd this come from?' he demanded in the best Russian he could muster.

The Ukrainian's frown darkened as he recognised the tape, then he waved a dismissive hand and lay down again.

Oksana emerged from the kitchen carrying a plastic mug of coffee and a plate of bread and sausage with a pickled cucumber on the side.

'What's that?' she asked, nodding at the video-cassette.

'A tape,' he replied evasively. 'I need Taras to tell me where it came from.'

She rattled off the query but Taras remained dismissive.

'Why you want to know?' she asked Sam, her curiosity aroused. 'What is this tape?'

'It's pornography, Ksucha. Sex . . .'

Her eyebrows arched as if seeing him in a new light. 'You boys having some fun while I out shopping, yes?'

'Fun?' he croaked. 'Not exactly, Ksucha.' He was struggling to think of a way to explain his interest in it without showing it to her. 'There's a girl on the tape . . .'

'Well, I hope so,' she answered, her voice heavy with irony. 'If it just picture of boy then I begin worry about my cousin.'

'Look. Ksucha. This woman on the tape, she has a mark on her body. A tattoo. You know what I mean by that?'

Oksana nodded, the humour draining from her eyes. 'Of course. Many men have tattoo. And now become fashion for young girls, so Luba tell me.'

'Yes, but this one's an unusual tattoo,' he went on. 'I've seen it before. On the body of a woman who was murdered.'

Oksana recoiled. Something of Sam's past was emerging and it scared her.

'I think better you show me,' she told him. 'And show Taras – maybe he know what it mean.'

'I'm not sure you should be seeing this sort of stuff.'

'Oh Sam, you so *gentleman*,' she mocked, to conceal her unease. 'Is all right. I promise not be shocked. Taras . . .' She explained to her cousin what this was about. He protested, but she overrode him. 'Put tape in machine,' she said to Sam.

Before he'd removed it from the player, the VCR had spooled back a few seconds. When he pressed play now, the picture was of the man masturbating.

'Oh!' Oksana stifled a gasp. 'Oh, that *too* big, I think,'

she added, trying to sound worldly. 'Not comfortable for woman.' She flushed bright red.

Sam froze the picture on the close-up of the tattoo. Taras had pulled on some black trousers by now and stood in front of the screen, clutching the coffee that Oksana had brought in for Sam.

'You see that globe and the letter B under it?' Sam touched the screen. 'It has to mean *something*.'

Taras turned away. He flopped onto the sofa, coughing like a miner. He put the coffee mug on the bare wooden floor between his feet and rubbed his temples, then began feeling down the sides of the upholstery for a cigarette packet. Oksana rounded on him, demanding that he reveal whether or not he knew what the tattoo meant.

'*Nyet*,' he coughed. He found the half-smoked butt of a cigarette on the floor and lit it with a plastic gas lighter.

Sam didn't believe his denial. 'Ask him if the tape was made in Odessa.'

She did. Taras chewed the tobacco smoke as if it were stringy meat. When he spoke, his words had the texture of wet gravel.

'Yes. He think so,' said Oksana. 'He say Odessa has big film studio, but now no money for normal work so they make sex video.'

'And who owns the studio? Who's making these tapes? Mafiya?'

'Of course. All such *biznis* is Mafiya,' Oksana confirmed.

'Yes, but ask Taras. Which Mafiya? I need names.'

Taras ignored his cousin's query.

'He not want to talk about this,' she explained. 'Because of what happen to him. You understand?'

'Tell him he *has to* talk,' Sam snapped. 'Tell him thousands of innocent people are about to be murdered. Explaining this damned tattoo might even save them!'

Oksana gaped. 'What you talking about?'

It was nonsense. The answer he sought was to solve a personal riddle, not the anthrax case. But if it kicked Taras out of his stupor, all well and good.

'It's connected with the VR-6 being sold to Dima Grimov. Tell him.'

She looked extremely doubtful as to how that could be, but did as he asked. Suddenly Taras rose up from the sofa, spreading his feet wide to steady himself. He prodded at Sam's chest, growling out a string of questions.

'You understand what he ask?' Oksana whispered.

'Wants to know who I am and what I'm doing in Odessa?'

'Yes. What I tell him?'

'Whatever you *have* to tell him to persuade him to talk.'

He snatched up the plate of food that she'd prepared for him and took it back into the kitchen, leaving her to sort her cousin out. There were two more mugs of coffee already poured. He grabbed one and drank it. The liquid was thick and strong. He wolfed down the bread and garlicky sausage. Twelve hours since his last meal. The dialogue in the main room was hard for him to follow, half in Russian and half in Ukrainian.

When he'd finished the food and the coffee he waited for a while until the silences lengthened before stepping back in there. He offered a mug to Oksana.

'Thought you could do with this.'

'Yes. Thank you.'

Taras looked away from her but she prodded him.

'Okay,' he said eventually, in English, staring at the floor.

Oksana sighed.

'He will tell you all he know about Mafiya in Odessa,' she announced simply. 'He say maybe he not have to be afraid of them any more, because they already do everything bad to him. Only new thing they can do is kill him and he say he don't care about that.'

This readiness to die, Sam wondered – a family affectation or a national one?

Taras began to talk in a low, weary monotone. Oksana let him ramble on, assuming he would pause for her to translate. When he didn't, she began to interrupt.

'In Odessa, Taras explain, big new crime gangs first appear in about nineteen-eighty,' she translated, 'at time when private business starting in Soviet Union, but still illegal. In Odessa, because of port, many businesses trade with foreign currency – dollar, German mark – but hard currency was forbidden here then. Very strict law. So, some criminals they realise they can make money from this. They say to businessmen, pay us some dollar, otherwise we tell Militsia and KGB what you doing with foreign currency.'

'Blackmail,' Sam prompted.

'Yes. Blackmail. And businessmen they can do nothing, because if they complain to police about what criminals do to them, then they get labour camp.'

'Easy money.'

'Of course.'

She prompted Taras to continue.

'He say Odessa criminals became into two strong gangs. Big enemy each other. One called "Repin" gang because leader was very good artist. You know of Russian painter Ilya Efimovich Repin?'

'No.'

'Nineteenth century. Great realist painter before revolution,' Oksana explained, 'Friend Tolstoy and Mussorgski. Maybe like your painter Constable from Essex.'

Taras continued his history.

'At end of nineteen-eighties was big gang fight in Odessa. Like war. All big boss men in Repin group were killed.'

Taras suddenly spat out the name Gorbachev, following it with a torrent of abuse.

'Taras talk about what Gorbachev do to economy of Soviet Union. Gorbachev call it reform, but it more like robbery. He allow criminals to take *everything*. Oil, chemical, metal, machine – Ukraine was rich in such things. But criminals and party bosses they buy all this from state for *nothing*, then sell to foreign country for much, much money.'

'I know all that, Ksucha,' Sam nudged. 'But what of today? What's that damned tattoo mean?'

'Sure. Sure. I ask Taras.' She prompted her cousin to speed up.

'Okay,' she went on, after another torrent of slurred and monotonous Russian, 'He talk about situation today. Taras say now maybe there are fifteen gangs in Odessa that they call Mafiya. All leaders are survivors of that gang war six, seven years ago. Mafiya now control everything which make money in Odessa. One gang control petrol. Each time you fill car, you pay money to Mafiya. Other gang control bank, casino, restaurant, selling vodka, cigarette, car – anything people need and can pay for. Much fighting between gangs. Many *schpana* and *gangstery* get killed. And journalists too are shot dead if they write truth about Mafiya.

'And Militsia do little to stop them. Why? First reason. Officer in Militsia get paid very little. So, many police take bribe from gangs. Second reason. Mafiya have more guns than Militsia, faster car, better radio – *and* . . .' She paused for effect. '*Blat*. Connections with government. You see, many gang leader they member parliament now, and law in Ukraine say if you are in Rada you cannot be prosecute. So they have protection from top. Right at top of government. Understand?'

'Totally.' He knew most of this stuff. 'But what about

the gang making these porn videos? Who the hell are they?'

Oksana pressed the question on Taras. Her cousin sighed and replied with a slight shake of the head.

'He not absolute sure,' she explained. 'He say tattoos are tradition with all gangs. Many gang, many design. But this tattoo he think belong to Mafiya which have strong connection in Russia, America, Israel – many countries in world. That why tattoo is look like world.'

'But that damned letter B? What does that stand for?'

She checked with Taras. As he answered her jaw dropped.

'Sam! You see, that letter you call B . . .' She shook her head.

'Oh God . . .'

He knew what she was about to say. How stupid. How incredibly bloody stupid of him.

'Not Roman alphabet,' she whispered.

'No . . .'

Of course it bloody wasn't.

'Is Russian Cyrillic alphabet. Letter is like V.'

'Yes,' he wheezed.

'And Taras think it stand for Voroninskaya.'

He turned away from her, covering his mouth with his hands. The hurricane was back in his head. Chrissie had borne the stamp of Grimov's gang. Branded like a steer, a mark to show who owned her. The suspicions lurking in the darkest corners of his mind now came thundering out.

'No!' he croaked. It simply wasn't possible. He tried to beat the suspicions back.

Oksana saw how shaken he was and her heart went out to him. She had no understanding of what this was about, except to believe that the tattoo was a personal matter, nothing to do with the VR-6 drone. She got to her feet and put a hand on his arm.

'Sam?'

His mind was back in Cyprus. When had they tattooed her? On the night they killed her? All part of some sado-sexual ritual demanded by Dima Grimov, which she'd gone along with in the hope it would enable her to extract secrets from him?

'Please Sam,' Oksana begged, cutting through to him. 'Can you explain me? Why this tattoo it matter so much to you?'

He turned round. Her eyes were almost turquoise now, moist eyes full of concern. Her mouth had become a red bud. He shook his head. He couldn't possibly tell her about Chrissie.

The danger of what lay ahead hit him anew. He'd brought Oksana this far but it would be criminal to involve her further. And yet what else could he do? He needed her still, needed her language and her knowledge. Needed her company so he wouldn't stand out.

He was so close now. So close to the answers he sought. He knew what he had to do next. Knew too that he couldn't do it alone.

'Ksucha,' he whispered, taking her hands in his. 'There's something I want you to do for me . . .'

This was wrong, he told himself. Wrong, wrong, wrong. But there was no other way.

35

Shortly before midday

The bus that took them to the centre of Odessa was packed solid. Oksana stood pressed against the man into whose hands she'd as good as entrusted her life, close enough to smell the animal tang of his body. She'd decided to shut her mind to the potential consequences of what was happening.

Throughout the journey she'd watched him staring through the window, knowing that those brooding eyes of his were seeing nothing of what they passed. She'd tried to concentrate her own mind in an effort to see into his, and to understand why he had such extraordinary faith. In her country no man would have the courage or the foolhardiness to confront the Mafiya in the way he was planning.

She felt mesmerised by this Englishman. He was an agent for the esteemed MI6 of James Bond, a man, she imagined, whose courage and judgement must have been honed by brushes with danger all over the globe. To have been enlisted by such a person, a man who believed in a concept of justice that Ukrainian people could only dream of, had brought a trace of purposefulness into her life where there'd been none before. And if it proved to be brief or illusory, then so be it. But while it was there she would cling to it, because to be on this man's side against the forces of evil was irresistible, however terrifying.

She knew she was being absurdly fanciful. But why not? Her life had become a drudge. She felt a euphoria being with him – even if in reality it was hysteria. She imagined it might even have been this way for the disciples of Christ. A belief that no harm would come to her, because no harm could come to him.

She kept her eyes on his face, drawing on the strength of it, fired up by its power. The feelings she was experiencing from his presence were increasingly sexual and she knew why. Back in that revolting room in Moldovanka, Taras had gone out for nearly an hour to track down a friend who knew more about the Voroninskaya organisation than he did, and Sam Packer had lain on the sofa with his eyes closed. Before long he'd been snoring and she'd taken her chance to play the videotape again, watching it from the beginning. She'd never seen such explicit images of submissive sexuality before and had found them disturbingly exciting.

The bus lurched to a halt a block away from the Opera. The early mist had fully cleared, leaving a blue sky and bright sunshine which bathed them in a warmth more appropriate to late summer than autumn.

Sam eyed the bustling crowds warily, subconsciously searching for the scarred face of Viktor Rybkin. When he found the man – as he felt sure he would – it was important that he was alone, not with Dima Grimov, if there were to be any chance at all of tweaking his conscience. From everything he'd learned about Grimov himself, that man had none.

Taras had served him well in the end, pulling himself together enough to find out the address from which the Voroninskaya ran their businesses – a renovated block on the vulitsya Artema. Dima Grimov was definitely known to operate from there, and wherever Grimov lodged so, Sam assumed, would Viktor Rybkin.

Sam had put on the light check suit and an open-necked blue shirt for the 'business' meeting he was planning, but the air was so warm he took the jacket off and slung it over his shoulder. Oksana had changed into a pink cotton blouse embroidered with a relief of flowers and a smooth, slate-grey skirt that ended just above her knees, in order to look like the personal assistant she was pretending to be. She'd brushed a shine into her hair and sprayed herself with an *eau de parfum* that smelled appealingly of rose petals. From a thin strap over her shoulder hung a small bag in artificial leather. She hooked her hand through his arm again, her extra-firm grip on his biceps the only sign of her nervousness.

Whatever personal reasons Oksana might have for helping him, they were irrelevant to Sam now. All that mattered was that he *needed* her at this moment, and she was here. He admired her courage. Admired her determination to stick with him. He'd also grown to quite like it when she put her arm through his.

They crossed a small square of trimmed lawns in front of the baroque Opera house, and entered the elegant Prymorsky boulevard whose neo-classical homes had once belonged to the nobility. Set on a sandstone cliff, it overlooked the port and had the feel of a resort. Crowds of proud-breasted young girls in thin T-shirts strolled beneath the planes and chestnuts, some with boyfriends.

'I think this some public holiday,' Oksana said, pointing out the stage being set up in front of the white-columned town hall at the end of the boulevard. 'Maybe some concert tonight.'

She sighed.

'I love Ode-ssa.' She lengthened the middle syllable as if caressing the word. 'When I was child, we come here every summer.' She squeezed his arm. 'They say Odessa girls most beautiful girls in Ukraine. Maybe you notice already.'

Sam's eye, however, had been caught by a group of sailors ambling through the throng, bunched together like geese. Their uniform, he realised suddenly, was extraordinarily familiar. As they drew closer, he read what was written on the bands of their hats.

HMS *Devonshire*.

He remembered the NATO visit that Figgis had told him about – the British defence attaché was here in Odessa for the occasion. He turned around and realised the promenade was full of foreign sailors eyeing up Odessa's talent. Black Americans in gleaming white. Olive-skinned faces from some Mediterranean navy or other. And cocky-looking Brits, all ashore on their best behaviour.

'Look down there in port,' Oksana exclaimed, pointing through a gap in the laurel hedge that lined the promenade. 'Navy ships. See American flag? They looking so new. That's how you can be sure they not Ukrainian,' she added with irony.

They stopped in the middle of the boulevard at the head of a broad sweep of stone steps leading down to the port.

'You know these steps? You ever see famous film *Battleship Potemkin*?' Oksana asked.

Sam nodded, remembering the massacre scene in Eisenstein's 1920s classic. 'The pram . . .'

'Nearly two hundred steps.'

At the foot of them the port spread like an ugly stain, its cranes mostly motionless and its wharves less than a quarter full. The visiting naval fleet was in the inner harbour. He counted half a dozen warships, among them the familiar profile of a British Duke Class frigate.

'We're wasting time,' he whispered, urging her on. 'How much further to this vulitsya Artema?'

'Five minutes. No more.'

She began to feel heavy on his arm, as if trying to hold him back.

His plan for getting through what Taras had described as a heavily guarded entrance to the Voroninskaya fortress was to pose as a British wholesaler in adult videos wanting to purchase tapes. Not much of a scheme, but once inside he hoped that bluff would get him to Viktor Rybkin.

They left the boulevard, passing an old palace undergoing renovation, and crossed a footbridge over a gorge. In a small park at the far end a wedding couple posed for photographs in front of a fountain.

Oksana kept clearing her throat. Her nerve was going.

'You know about Odessa catacomb?' she asked, desperate to interest him in something that would delay the moment of truth.

'No,' he said flatly, not wanting to know.

'Yes. When they build Odessa they dig stone from underground. Make tunnels. Some people say one thousand kilometre altogether underneath Odessa. Like honeycomb. During Great Patriotic War partisans hide there from Germans. Taras father – my uncle – he was partisan in Odessa,' she burbled.

He looked at her and forced a smile. Not easy, because he was as tense as she was.

'Nearly there, Oksana?'

'Nearly there.' Then she stopped dead and turned to confront him. 'Don't you think maybe this bad idea?' she pleaded, her pale cheeks hollow with fear.

'Probably,' he said, giving her shoulders an encouraging squeeze. 'But it's the only damn idea I've got.'

The building Taras had directed them to was a recently restored corner house on four floors with a buttressed roof decorated with rococo mouldings. Its windows were capped by finely arched lintels and hung with blinds to obscure the interior. Parked outside was a large black Mercedes being guarded by two watchful men in black roll-necks and black trousers.

'*Sam* . . .' Oksana whimpered, her throat dust-dry with terror. '*Gangstery*!'

'Stick close, Ksucha,' he breathed, trying to exude a confidence he didn't feel. As they aimed for the entrance, the two heavies scrutinised them with a drill-like gaze.

The outer door was of armoured glass. Oksana spoke into a wall-mounted speakerphone, saying a Mr Molloy from England wanted to buy porn videos.

This'll never work, thought Sam, feeling the thugs' eyes scorching his back. Miraculously the door clicked open and they entered a small lobby, the door snapping shut behind them. They were in an airlock of mirrored glass. There'd be a camera watching their every blink, he realised. He turned his face towards the street in the hope of avoiding its scrutiny.

After a minute, a second buzzer clicked and they were admitted to the inner sanctum that resembled the reception area to any small and prosperous business. A young woman in a turquoise silk blouse and pearl necklace eyed them from behind a desk, her face frozen with suspicion.

Oksana filled her lungs and told the woman that Mr Molloy was one of the UK's most prominent dealers in adult videos, and that he'd been advised it was Viktor Rybkin that he needed to see here.

Sam heard '*nyet*' in the reply, but understood nothing else.

'She says is not possible,' Oksana explained, her face taut with the strain.

'Well tell her we'll wait here until it *is* possible.' He pointed to the long black leather sofa lining one wall. Oksana shook her head, her eyes pleading with him to let them get out of here while they still had legs to walk on.

As he sat down he noticed the receptionist lean back

and slide her knee forward under the desk as if nudging a buzzer. Not long now, he guessed. He felt strangely calm.

Oksana sank onto the sofa beside him, her breathing jerky and spasmodic. She clasped her hands on her lap, their knuckles turning white.

The reception area was a windowless box with reinforced doors at each end that were fitted with coded locks. The place was indeed a fortress. In the corners of the high corniced ceiling two cameras swivelled on their mounts. Sam looked down at his shoes and counted the lace holes.

It was the right-hand door that opened. A short, slim man in his twenties wearing an oversized jacket stood there with a smile that looked as if it had been painted on.

'Please,' he said in English.

'You wait here, Ksucha,' Sam whispered.

'No. Both of you,' the man insisted. He stood to one side to let them pass. Beyond the door was a carpeted hallway and a regal staircase rising upwards, its walls adorned with oil paintings. The door closed behind them.

Suddenly two more men stepped from a side-room, dressed in track-suits, their hair clipped to within millimetres of their scalps. Sam clenched his stomach expecting a punch. Instead, hands like claws seized each arm and frogmarched him towards the stairs. Heart racing, he felt cold metal press into the bone behind his right ear. Behind him Oksana screamed, her muffled shouts revealing that she too was being manhandled.

'Leave her alone!'

Jesus . . . What had he done, bringing her into this?

He stumbled up the steps, carried forward by the powerful grip of his handlers. Behind him, Oksana's commotion was silenced by a sharp double slap.

'Leave her alone, arsehole!' he barked, craning his neck to see.

A few steps from the top his eyes locked onto a pair of legs standing on the landing. Shoes in fine, black calf. Grey trousers, well-pressed. He looked up. Blue shirt, gold tie kept neat by a jewel-encrusted clip – and above it the lopsided jaw of Viktor Rybkin.

Clearly shocked to see him here, the former KGB officer spun on his heel. Sam was bundled after him into a small bare-walled room, furnished with a table and two chairs. The men in track-suits frisked Sam for a weapon. When they found none Rybkin waved them out of the room.

'What the hell are you doing here, stupid *cunt*,' he spat. 'In Cyprus I told you I didn't want to see you again.'

'Fuck what you told me! You're in trouble, Viktor, and I've come to help you.'

Rybkin's eyes registered disbelief.

'*You*? Help *me*?'

'Yes. And, that woman who was with me, you leave her alone, understand?'

'You've got a damned nerve telling me what to do. Whatever game you think you're playing with us, just remember we don't play cricket in Ukraine,' Rybkin cracked.

He took a pack of Marlboro Lights from his pocket, pulled one out for himself and tossed the pack to Sam.

'You're crazy coming here,' he said. Softening his tone. 'You know that?' The American accent seemed to be broadening by the minute, an accent honed on Tarantino movies. 'Who is she anyway?'

'Works at the British Embassy in Kiev. A translator. So treat her with respect.'

'Respect!' Rybkin laughed. 'We always treat our women with *respect*, Sam. You've seen the videos . . .'

Sam pushed the cigarette packet back to him.

'Hell! I should have shot you in Cyprus,' Rybkin fumed. 'Now, tell me what the fuck this is all about.'

'They know about the VR-6, Viktor,' Sam growled, hunching forward. 'MI6, the CIA, the whole western intelligence apparatus – they know about your deal with Naif Hamdan.'

Rybkin flinched. Sam knew he'd hit home.

'And if the Iraqi anthrax attack does take place, then you and your lunatic boss are going to be nailed to the wall. Understand?'

Rybkin blew smoke at him.

'Even if you've got half the Ukrainian government in your pocket, they won't be able to save you. The pressure from the rest of the world will be so goddamned great, nothing will prevent you from being taken out.'

'You don't know what you're talking about,' Rybkin snapped.

'No? Your only chance of getting out of this crazy affair still able to walk is to make sure the attack never happens. You understand me?'

Rybkin's jaw had set solid.

'As a *friend*,' Sam added sarcastically. 'I'm telling you this as a friend, Viktor.'

Slowly, Rybkin leaned back in the chair and folded his arms. His eyes narrowed, as if trying to work out how much Sam really knew.

'Hamdan?' mouthed Rybkin, frowning. 'I don't know anybody of that name.'

Sam's heart flipped. The man was so convincing with his lies that for a second he believed him. Just like he'd believed him in Cyprus when he'd said he still worked for the SBU. And that he didn't know how Chrissie had died.

'They also know what a liar you are,' Sam added.

There was a sharp rap at thc door and the young man in the oversized jacket entered. He leaned past Sam and handed Rybkin a wad of papers. Oksana's ID documents, Sam guessed. Rybkin perused them then gave them back, snapping out an order in Russian.

'I tell him to be nice to your friend Oksana Ivanovna Koslova,' Rybkin explained after the younger man had gone. 'To be *respect*ful.' He smiled like a cat that had eaten a sparrow. 'Where is *Mister* Koslova, by the way? You up to your old tricks with married women?'

'He's dead. Chernobyl.'

'Ah. That is sad for her, of course.' His eyes flashed with malice. 'So you and she have both lost people that you loved. I guess that should give you plenty to talk about.'

Sam didn't react. 'Where's the attack to be, Viktor?'

Rybkin feigned mystification. 'What attack?'

'The anthrax attack with the VR-6 drone.' The brown eyes blinked back at him. 'With luck you can still stop it. It'll save your skin.'

The Ukrainian fingered the scar on his cheek, as if considering the offer. Then he leaned forward and pointed his finger at him, the thumb cocked like a gun.

'Go home, Sam. Go home while you're still breathing.'

Sam glared icily at Rybkin. He'd been wrong. There *was* no conscience here. The rogue with a soul that Chrissie had liked a year ago had sold out to the devil.

And yet . . . The man was fidgety. Something, some doubt might have taken root inside that lopsided skull.

Rybkin stood up suddenly. He smoothed his trousers.

'Now, we will say goodbye for the very last time,' he growled. 'And I mean the last time.'

'Not saying goodbye yet, Viktor.' Sam remained seated. 'I haven't finished with you.' There was *one* answer he was not going to leave without.

'*You!* Finished with *me* . . .'

'Why the tattoo, Viktor?'

Rybkin froze on his way towards the door.

'Why was Chrissie marked with that goddamned Voroninskaya tattoo?'

'You don't know?'

Rybkin didn't move. Then, slowly, he turned back to face Sam, mouth half open as if with the intention of enlightening him. But he changed his mind, opened the door, and beckoned Sam out onto the landing.

'*Why*, Viktor?' Sam snapped.

The thugs in track-suits grabbed hold of him.

'Why?'

Rybkin turned on him with a supercilious leer.

'You know something? They taught us poems when I learned English in Moscow,' he said. 'One of them I can remember. It ends with the words "Where ignorance is bliss, 'tis folly to be wise." Stay ignorant, dummy.'

Sam bunched his fists.

'Bye bye Sam. My men are going to make sure you leave Odessa today. Both you and your lady friend. Next time I see you, if there *is* a next time, you'll be in a box with a lid on it.'

He spun on his heel and walked away along the landing.

Five minutes later Sam and Oksana were being raced through Odessa in a black-windowed Mercedes, wedged between the two men in track-suits. They'd not spoken since being pushed into the car, but he could feel Oksana trembling. The side of her face nearest him glowed from the slaps she'd been given.

The machine wove through the traffic like a police car, eventually pulling up at the station. One of the heavies nudged them to get out, grunting an instruction in Russian.

'He say we must be on Kiev train which leave in five minute,' Oksana croaked.

They were pushed towards the ticket hall, then through

the swing doors to the platforms. The departure music was playing, but they scrambled on board the train. The *gangstery* scowled into the carriage from the platform, prompting two other passengers to pick up their bags and move to another compartment.

Sam seethed. He'd achieved nothing in Odessa except to frighten the wits out of Oksana. She was sobbing now, a handkerchief pressed to her face.

The train began to move. He looked at his watch. It was two-fifteen. He waved two fingers at the thug outside. Rybkin was not going to get away with this.

Oksana blew her nose loudly.

'You all right, Ksucha?' Her cheek was still glowing.

'I thought they will kill me,' she whispered, sniffing.

'I'm sorry, Ksucha. I should never have—'

'But you *learn* something?' she interrupted, her eyes brightening. 'It was worthwhile for you?'

What should he tell her? The truth.

'No. I learned nothing, Ksucha. Except something about myself. Namely that one can still be a trifle naive, even at the ripe old age of thirty-six!'

'*I* learned something.' She gave a little smile of triumph.

'Yes?'

'Yes. I learn that I don't want to die!'

'Ah. Now *that's* something.'

The smile widened and stayed on her lips as the train gathered speed through the bleak concrete landscape of Odessa's outskirts.

As the town disappeared behind them and the view became steppe, Sam put his mind back to work. If Viktor Rybkin couldn't be reasoned with, then he must be *forced* into talking.

'Oh! Our luggage!' Oksana gasped. 'We leave it at Taras house.'

Exactly, thought Sam. And there was something in it that he needed.

'I have idea. When we arrive Kiev, I telephone my cousin and ask him to bring it to us tomorrow. You will pay his ticket?'

'To *Kiev*?' Sam frowned.

He would be on his own from now on, he decided. It was between him and Rybkin. One on one.

'Yes of course, Kiev.'

She was puzzled by his tone. Then she saw the stubborn jaw and dogged eyes. He was going back. Back to Odessa. Back to the nightmare they'd just escaped from. Her insides somersaulted. How could he be so foolish – or so brave?

'Oksana . . .'

'I know,' she said. 'And I am coming with you.'

36

Darkness was falling by the time they returned to Moldovanka, both of them dead with exhaustion, both driven by compulsions they couldn't control.

He'd tried to persuade Oksana to continue on the train to Kiev but she'd told him that if he had the courage to go back then so did she. They'd got off at the first halt, a fifty-minute ride north of Odessa, and sat in a smelly shelter for two and a half hours until a train stopped on its journey south to take them back to the Black Sea. The weather had changed for the worse, with clouds scudding in from the north, bringing a drop in temperature. Still in their light clothes, she'd huddled against him for warmth and with a little gentle prompting had told him the story of her life with Sergeyi – a contented partnership cut short by the biggest man-made disaster the world had ever seen. She'd cried a little at the end of her story and he'd held her, happy to let their closeness give her whatever strength she could draw from him.

They stood outside the gate to the stable yard where Taras lived. The street was dark except for the lights of passing cars. Oksana had a key that her cousin had lent her. She opened the gate. There was no light coming from the old stables and they had to feel their way to the door.

For Oksana, telling Sam about Sergeyi in that railway station shelter had been an essential unburdening. It was, she'd decided, important that he knew how she'd loved her husband. Only if he understood what she'd felt for

Sergeyi could she desire him without guilt. She'd built a bridge now between her past and her future, whatever it might be. She'd not expected Sam to respond to her outpourings by revealing things about himself. She'd understood by now that the fence surrounding his private life was of the thickest barbed wire. To cut through it would take time, more time probably than she would have with him. But there was something about the way he'd listened that had convinced her that he too had suffered loss. Sensed too that whereas her loss was history now, his own grief was still continuing.

She opened the door.

'Taras?'

No reply, and the place was in darkness. She fumbled for a light switch, but it didn't work. She turned to look back over the top of the wall that surrounded the yard. Darkness everywhere.

'Power cut,' she sighed. 'In Odessa it happen most day. Maybe Taras have candle.'

She groped her way to the kitchen while Sam aimed for where he remembered the sofa to be. His suitcase should be on it, and inside that a torch.

They both produced light at the same instant.

'See? We make good team,' said Oksana with a brittle laugh.

Nervously Sam illuminated Taras's bed, fearing irrationally that Rybkin's men had been here and murdered the man. But the bed was empty, its soiled sheet and blanket rolled into a ball.

'I think he go find friend who make *samogon*,' Oksana ventured, setting down the candleholder next to the television. She hugged herself for warmth. 'You hungry?'

Sam was so tired he had to think about it. He sank down onto the sofa.

'Yes, Ksucha. I do believe I am.'

'I see if Taras leave any of food which I buy this

morning,' she said, returning to the kitchen. Then after a few seconds she called out, 'Oh yes. We soon have dinner.'

Sam rested his head on the sofa back and let his eyelids droop. He *had* to sleep if he was going to be able to function tonight, yet his keyed-up nerves weren't going to let him. The plan he'd worked out was shaky at best, and more dangerous than ever. Oksana could not under any circumstances be a part of it. Yet her determination to share his every risk seemed absolute. Somehow he would have to extract himself from her grip.

To corner Rybkin he would need luck more than anything else. He had no clue where the man lived nor whether he ever moved about without a phalanx of bodyguards. Sam had one lead and one lead only: the name of the restaurant given him by Major Pushkin, the nocturnal operating base of the Voroninskaya gang. He checked his watch. It was seven-thirty. In about three hours' time he would need to be back in the centre of Odessa, alone.

Oksana busied herself laying out food on a tray, forcing herself not to look at the filth of her surroundings and more importantly to resist the feeling of dread that had overcome her since returning to this flat. It was a feeling much greater than fear and yet lesser too, because she was powerless to do anything about it. She could be here in Odessa, could be with this Englishman that she adored, but there was nothing she could do to prevent him walking into the jaws of his fate.

She returned to the main room with bread, sliced sausage and cheese, and a dish of tomatoes and pickled cucumbers.

'Sorry not more exciting,' she told him. 'But this kitchen is not place which make me want to cook. Soon I make some tea for us – when water boiling.'

Sam smiled as she sat beside him. There was a body

smell about her now, her rose petal scent tainted by the tensions of the day. A woman's smell, an animal odour that triggered him like a switch.

As she balanced the tray on her knees, she looked at him with a watchful steadiness. To Sam it was the look of someone who'd seen the future and was waiting for it to come to pass. A look with the fateful knowledge of a tarot card. It startled him. He glanced away.

'Thanks for the food, Ksucha,' he whispered. 'I always seem to be saying that.'

He loaded a plate from the tray and began to eat. Oksana continued to watch him.

'Aren't you going to eat?' he asked.

'Not now.'

He'd decided what he would do to get away from her. She might hate him for it later, but not, he hoped, at the time.

'What you going to do, Sam?'

Her huskiness drew him like a velvet vortex. In the dull light of the candle her eyes were almost grey-green.

'I'm going to try again.'

'But how?'

'I'll think of something. I'll wait until the morning,' he lied.

He put the plate down on the floor. She was still looking at him, her gaze unwavering, cutting through, trying to see the truth he was hiding. He took hold of her hands. They were small and had a smooth softness that surprised him.

'You have beautiful eyes,' he told her.

They didn't move from his, but her lips parted into a smile.

'That what you told me a year ago, only you don't remember,' she teased.

He pulled her to him and kissed her. She held her

breath, one hand against his chest as if uncertain whether to allow this. Then the hand went to the back of his neck.

Oksana sniffed in his smell and tried to imprint it in her memory before it went away. She didn't know why she felt so strongly that Sam's life had only a few more hours to run. Such certainties were never easy to explain. But the same dread feeling had come to her the night when Sergeyi died. The doctors had told her it would be months before the cancer killed him, but she'd known as she lay down beside him in the bed that when she awoke in the morning he would be gone.

She pulled back from him. His eyes were half closed as if locked on some far horizon.

'Why you do this?'

'Because I want to.' He kissed her again but she pushed him back.

'Let me look, you very beautiful man.' He was like a sleep walker, she thought. Heading for a precipice.

She took one of his hands and put it on her breast. As he felt its shape a shiver rose up from her womb.

'I very afraid for you, Sam,' she whispered.

From the kitchen came the sound of water boiling. And suddenly the lights came on. They blinked at the unaccustomed brightness.

'I'll switch it off again,' he suggested.

'I think is better.'

As he crossed over to the wall switch she slipped into the kitchen to turn off the gas.

The television came on. News headlines on some English language satellite channel. He watched the screen, fearful suddenly that the anthrax attack might already have happened.

Oksana came up behind him and slipped her arms round his waist.

They watched the screen. A car bomb in Jerusalem – tension over Jewish settlements on the West Bank. A truck drivers' strike in France. Political sniping from the election trail in the USA.

He turned it off again.

Oksana held onto him.

'You very dear man to me,' she murmured. Her hands were on his chest. 'I feel your heart beating.'

She kept her hands there, feeling his life force, determined to have of it what she could.

'Please love me,' she breathed. 'Love me now.'

He turned round. Her eyes had a melting softness. She pressed her hips against his groin and lifted up her mouth. He teased at her lips while feeling for the buttons of her embroidered blouse. He undid them slowly, then reached behind her back for the clip to her bra.

Suddenly she turned away from him and looked towards the bed. As one, they decided without the need to voice it that to lie where Taras had lain night after night, week after week, masturbating over his porn tapes was not an option.

'Sofa,' she whispered. 'Come. I show.'

She took their bags off it and put them onto the floor, then began heaving at the seat cushions. With a creaking of unoiled springs a bed unfolded, its mattress covered with a linen protector that looked passably clean.

He held her again, their breath faster now after the exertion with the sofa. A smile crossed her face like the beat of a butterfly, her eyes full of longing, but a little afraid. He slipped the blouse and bra from her shoulders. Her breasts were round like a young girl's, their nipples as hard as orange pips.

'Sam . . .' she breathed, her mouth caressing his ear as he bent his head to kiss them. 'I want you to tell me something.'

He stood up straight and put a finger against her lips. 'There's nothing you need to know.'

'Yes,' she insisted. 'This is important to me.'

'Nothing's important,' he croaked. 'Nothing except this.' He felt for the zip of her skirt.

'Yes,' she insisted again, pulling back from him and holding him by the waist at arm's length. 'Tell me.'

'What then?'

'I want to know if you love someone, Sam.'

Love? He didn't know what it meant any more.

'No,' he breathed eventually.

She didn't know whether to believe him or not. But it freed her, what he'd said. She placed her palms on the hard muscles of his behind and pressed him to her, fearing the lump in his trousers that she'd felt against her belly might have been softened by her prevaricating. It wasn't. She began unbuttoning his shirt.

They undressed quickly and stood naked in the flickering candle light, her eyes clouding at the sight of the burn marks on his chest. Before she could ask, he kissed her hard on the mouth and then her neck. Her heat enveloped him as their bodies touched. She tasted of salt. Her fingers clasped the back of his head and he felt her opening up to him like a crocus in sunlight.

Then she did something he wasn't expecting. She detached herself from his embrace, knelt in front of him on the bed and hooked her hands behind her back as if they were shackled to her ankles.

'I very happy you not like man in video,' she smiled. Then she took his penis in her mouth.

Sam gasped. He held her head, gently stroking behind her ears as she sucked. But he quickly realised she'd not done this before. Her movements were frenetic and uncertain. A desire to please but without knowing how.

'Hey,' he breathed, pulling back and crouching in front of her. 'You don't have to do that.' He kissed her lips, tasting his own salt on them, and cupped her breasts with his hands.

'I want to . . .' she moaned, throatily.

'No you don't.'

He lay her back on the bed and kissed her down the length of her body. The touch of his hands and tongue felt like fire to her.

'I love you, love you, Sam,' she mouthed, stretching wide her legs so she could take all of him into her, every last piece of him and hold him there, hold him so tight and so firm that he would never be able to leave her. And so that the volcano that had been dormant inside her for years could finally erupt.

37

He awoke with a start, his heart kicking into life like a motorbike engine as he remembered what he now had to do.

The candle had burned down, but light from the bare bulb in the kitchen was bright enough for him to read his watch by. After eleven. He'd slept for far longer than he'd intended. Oksana lay by his side breathing heavily and evenly. After making love they'd lain with just a scratchy blanket for cover and fallen asleep like babies.

Moving slowly so as not to wake her, he swung his feet to the floor and stood up. He thanked God that Taras hadn't returned.

He gathered his scattered clothes, dressed, then carried his suitcase to the kitchen. He dug into it until his fingers found the package Figgis had given him in Kiev. He unwrapped the pistol, and checked it over. Figgis had called it a PSM, a Russian version of the Walther Polizei Pistol he'd once had instruction on. He checked the location of the safety, finding it at the rear of the slide instead of the side. The gun was slimmer and easier to conceal than a Walther. He unclipped the magazine to check it was full, then, after replacing it, tucked the barrel of the weapon into the sock on his left foot and bound the grip to the inside of his calf with a necktie. He straightened the trouser leg over the weapon and took a few paces to ensure he could walk with it.

His passport and cash he stuffed into a money belt and

secured it round his waist next to his skin. Then he pulled a thick sweater over his shirt. It was cold in this house and it would be colder outside. Pocketing his torch and the street map that he'd bought from a kiosk at the station on their return to Odessa, he checked he'd left nothing in the suitcase that he needed, then said goodbye to it, because he didn't expect to be seeing it again.

He tiptoed back into the bedroom. Oksana's breathing was steady and full. She lay on her back, her legs apart like a sated creature and with one hand on the pillow. He decided he must leave her a note. There was some scrap paper and a ball pen by the video. He scribbled a message saying that she should catch the first train to Kiev in the morning and he would contact her there soon. He left it on the pillow then stepped over to Taras's bed, picking up one of the empty vodka bottles lying on the floor beside it and stuffing it under his sweater. Finally, with a last look at Oksana, he slipped out into the night.

He walked quickly though the broad, ochre streets of Moldovanka, concerned that the lateness of the hour meant he'd missed his chance. The feeble street lighting of the neighbourhood concealed the terrible disrepair of its graceful buildings. He avoided doorways and patches of shadow where there were shapes that moved. A short-skirted whore, stoned out of her head, who was exposing her bony crotch to any car that passed, made a lurch towards him, then spat abuse when he ignored her. From time to time cars sped by at lunatic speeds as if escaping the scene of some crime. From inside a house he heard a woman scream, though whether from ecstasy, from a beating, or from the effects of *vink* he couldn't tell.

He shivered, partly from cold and partly through fear. He'd never felt more alone or more full of doubt. He knew that the prospect of persuading Rybkin to tell him about the anthrax plot had the flight potential of a brick, but that wasn't the only issue he needed the man to resolve.

The night sky was clear and pricked with stars. He'd been walking for more than twenty minutes by the time he reached the street he was aiming for, a street very different from the slums he'd left behind. White fairy lights twinkled in the lower branches of the lush trees lining its broad, cobbled carriageway. Beneath the canopy of leaves, plastic tables and chairs clustered under parasols marked Marlboro and Pall Mall. This was vulitsya Deribasovska, the centre of Odessa's night-life.

Despite the chilly air, hundreds of twenty and thirty-somethings thronged the pedestrianised zone in jeans and bomber jackets, or smart suits, dresses and long coats. They were socialising with the vivacity of Romans. Sam slipped among them, slackening his pace to match that of the ambling crowd. As his eyes adjusted, he caught the occasional flash of white or navy. The NATO sailors were still in town. On a corner opposite, shiny helmets glinted above the watchful eyes of a US Military Police patrol.

The street was dotted with cafés and bars. Doing good business for a nation on its knees, thought Sam wryly. New Russians, new money. And somewhere here was the restaurant the renegade Major had identified as the nocturnal haunt of Dima Filipovich Grimov and his friends.

He'd memorised the tourist map of the centre. He was in the grid of the old town, little altered since it was laid out by architects from France and Italy in the nineteenth century. Roads intersected every hundred metres. The restaurant used by Grimov's gang should have been to his left at the fourth junction down, but when he looked into that particular side street it was in darkness. None of the garish neon that adorned every night-spot he'd seen so far.

He was about to check out the next street when he saw something. He slipped into the turning, losing himself in shadow while his eyes attuned to the dark. After a few seconds he could make out a large car parked about thirty paces down whose bodywork had the square bulk of a Mercedes.

Too dark to see if there were men inside or standing by it, but fearing his presence had been noted, he pulled the empty vodka bottle from under his sweater, raised it shakily and as visibly as possible to his lips, then lurched down the street like a drunk. Once he'd drawn level with the car on the opposite side of the road, he halted, swaying like a willow in a gale, and opened his fly to urinate.

He could see now that there *were* two men on the far pavement and they were watching him. Suddenly they turned back towards the building behind them as if responding to a noise. A shaft of light beamed up from a basement, accompanied by coarse laughter. One of the men shouted at Sam who took the words to mean *fuck off out of it.* The thug began moving towards him so he quickly zipped his fly and shuffled away. He heard the click of a gun being cocked and lurched away faster, terrified these hoods might be in the habit of using drunks for target practice.

After twenty paces he risked a look back. Next to the Mercedes several men were now gathered, talking in low voices. Some ducked into the car. Doors closed and the engine roared. As the machine pulled from the kerb, its headlamps ablaze, Sam leaned drunkenly against a tree.

The Merc's tyres slapped thickly at the cobbles as it passed him. The glow of the tail lights revealed a man on the opposite pavement. Sam cowered, fearful it was a gunman coming looking for him. But the man walked briskly on, his head bowed.

A burly man. A man with the same build as Viktor Rybkin.

Sam abandoned his empty vodka bottle and kept pace with the dark-coated figure, praying he'd got lucky. As they headed towards Prymorsky Boulevard, he heard beat music and remembered the concert platform they'd seen earlier being set up in front of the town hall.

Was this Rybkin? The dull street lighting showed the man had thick hair, but he needed to see the face. He quickened his pace to get closer.

Suddenly a massive explosion shook the town. High above the rooftops fireballs burst into huge floral circles. The man stopped to look up. There was less than ten metres between them now. In the light from the flares the shape of the jaw and the scar on the cheek were unmistakable.

Sam smiled. The gods were being good to him. Then he flung himself behind a tree, as Rybkin looked round. The pistol nagged against his ankle.

Rybkin cut left across the cobbles. Sam waited for him to turn the corner into the boulevard, then sprinted forward.

The square at the head of the Potemkin steps was a mass of craning necks as the fireworks detonated above. He looked left, right, straight ahead.

'Damn!' he breathed.

He'd lost him. He elbowed through the throng, searching for the thick head of hair that was his moving target. At the far side of the square the crowd thinned to nothing. He swung right. Then left. Then he saw him. Turning into an alley, looking back, checking. But checking for what? For an assassin from a rival mob? Or to make sure Sam was following . . .

Had they recognised him outside the restaurant? Was Rybkin leading him by the nose to that coffin he'd been so keen to nail the lid to? The coward in him wanted to turn back, but he couldn't. He had to know now. Had to bloody know what Rybkin knew.

He reached the corner where he'd seen Rybkin, half-expecting a bullet. The alley passed through a small courtyard lit by a single lamp high on a wall. Dark, iron-railed balconies overlooked cobbles and a dry fountain. At the far side the lane continued beneath an archway linking two halves of a mansion. A shadow moved.

Deliberate. Drawing him like a lure.

He glanced behind, fearing he himself was being tailed. But there was no one else. Just him here. Him and Viktor Rybkin. A trap, almost certainly. But he had a gun, and if walking into it was the only way to achieve his end, so be it.

He sprinted across the courtyard to the side of the arch. A few paces further on, the alley seemed to end in a void. He tried to visualise where he was. Odessa was built on a plateau whose edge sloped sharply to the sea. Maybe he'd reached it.

Moving forward, hugging the alley wall, he discovered steps leading down. At the bottom was another yard, lit by a single lamp high on the wall of one of the apartment houses surrounding it. Beyond the roofs he saw the sharp pricks of light from arc lamps in the harbour.

He ran down the steps. His skin prickled. The lower yard was a paved pen, overlooked by windows from all sides. He heard water dripping from a broken pipe and, back in the direction of Prymorsky Boulevard, rock music competing with the crackle of rockets.

No sign of Rybkin.

He saw doorways, four of them. Each was open, each appearing to access stairwells to the flats above. Did Rybkin live here? Hugging walls again he reached the first entrance, stopped and listened. A woman's keening echoed down the stairwell.

He held his breath, sensing Rybkin here somewhere, listening too.

Silently he moved to the next entrance and listened again. The third doorway was different. Steps up yes, but down too. Down to a lower landing. He smelled alcohol suddenly, a lingering in the air like the exhalations of a man who'd spent the evening drinking. From below he heard a door creak.

Sam dropped to a crouch, his hands scrabbling for the knot binding the gun to his leg. Then he checked himself, something telling him to keep the pistol hidden. He felt a sudden compulsion to shout Rybkin's name, to end this unbearable tension by revealing himself and demanding that they talk.

He breathed deeply to steady his pounding heart, then edged down the stairs. Too dark to see, he pulled the Maglite from his pocket and twisted the cap, narrowing its beam with his fingers. At the bottom was another door, painted green and scratched with graffiti. It was half ajar. Heart in mouth, he put his hand on the latch and jerked it open, shining the full beam inside. Two more steps down. And the smell of booze again, stronger now.

His fear was intense. He wanted to run, but couldn't. The torch lit up a cellar a few paces wide and maybe ten long. Empty but for a row of locked, steel cabinets, each the height of a small man. Their green paint was streaked with rust. Lockups, he decided. For the flats above. To keep their wine cool. Hence the drink smell. Not Rybkin's breath at all.

'Shit!'

The skin crawled on the back of his neck. He spun round to the stairs he'd just descended but there was nothing. Nobody. No sign of life. This was a blind alley. The bottom of the trap.

He let out the breath he'd been holding. Then he

listened. Listened and listened, but there was nothing. Not a bloody thing apart from the crack of fireworks. Rybkin had shaken him off.

Shaken him off? The man had *tempted* him down here with the creaking door. So where the fuck had he gone?

He looked again at the line of cabinets. They had doors. Each and every one had a door big enough for a man to pass through. He moved along the line, rattling them. All locked, all with the tinniness he would expect.

Except for the last one which was as solid as stone.

He stood back. The cabinet looked identical to the others, but wasn't. He pointed the torch down. The cellar floor was dusty, littered with scraps of cardboard and leaves blown in by autumn gales – except here, in front of *this* one, where instead of dust there was an arc of clear floor.

He gripped the front of the cabinet and tried to swing it, but couldn't. He felt at the sides for a catch, but there was none. It *would* open though, he was certain of that. Because it was the only way Viktor Rybkin could have got away from him.

He stared at it. The doors were double. A single keyhole surrounded by a heavy brass escutcheon. He touched it to see if it would move sideways. It seemed firm. Then he tried a twist.

From inside the cabinet came a whirring sound. It swung forward revealing a hole in the concrete wall high enough for a man to pass through at a crouch. A light current of air came from the hole, fresher than that in the cellar and with the dry texture of air conditioning.

His throat tightening with terror, Sam ducked through, his torch picking out a narrow downward sloping passage. He took a few steps, then threw himself against the rough stone wall as the steel cabinet hummed shut behind him. He flashed the torch on it. No handle. No escutcheon to twist on this side. No way he could see to get the damned thing open again.

The passage stretched into the distance. He felt the walls. Sandstone. Suddenly he realised that he'd entered the catacombs Oksana had told him about, the tunnels formed when the city's builders cut the stone to create their Little Paris on the Black Sea.

As he moved forward, the ceiling lowered until he was forced to stoop. His breath thundered in his ears. The gun hurt his battered shin as if it had slipped round his leg when he'd fiddled with it. He crouched to straighten it and to loosen the tie so it wouldn't snag when he needed it.

A score of paces further on, the tunnel forked, the left-hand path blocked by a fallen roof. Sam swung the torch to the right. The beam hit a steel door with a speaker grille in it.

He stared for a moment, mesmerised. Was this a secret entrance to the Voroninskaya's lair? A way for the gang's leaders to escape if their fortress came under siege above ground? Rybkin had led him here for one reason. To get him through that door and never let him out again.

He gulped. Beyond here was the point of no return.

His hand went for the buzzer. As it touched, a floodlight blazed on from above, dazzling him. The door swung inwards and Viktor Rybkin stood there, a Skorpion machine pistol in his hands, its muzzle aimed at Sam's heart.

38

I should have shot you in Cyprus,' Rybkin spat, his deep-set eyes hooded by the overhead glare. 'The first ideas are always the best. You're like a dog, Packer. Kick you and you come back for more. Put your hands on your head.'

Shaking, Sam did as he was told. From behind Rybkin the track-suited *shpana* who'd stood on Odessa station to watch them off sprang forward on rubber-soled shoes to search him.

He'll find the sodding gun, thought Sam. Still, if he'd been holding it in his hand when they'd opened the door he'd be dead by now.

The hands groped under his arms, then at his thighs and crotch, but a frisk downwards ended at his knees after an impatient shout from Rybkin. Sam felt a rush of astonished relief. Sweat was dripping from his armpits. The thug shoved him inside and Rybkin swung a kick as he passed.

'That's right,' snarled Sam. 'Enjoy yourself. You won't be able to for long.'

'Shut your mouth, idiot. If I had my way I'd finish you now. But my boss wants to show you something – to make sure you die hurting.'

The boss was Grimov. The huge door closed behind them with a clunk of heavy bolts.

The passageway ahead was well lit by ceiling lights every ten metres. Warm air wafted from chambers on each side. In some of them stood barred safes that would do justice to a bank. In others, tables were topped by computers and calculators. Incongruously, on one desk there was an abacus.

'Quite a business you have here, Viktor.' Keep him talking, thought Sam. Keep the bugger talking.

'So now you understand what you're dealing with,' Rybkin answered.

No people around, Sam noted. No night shift.

'It'd be sad to lose it, my friend,' he goaded.

The Ukrainian snorted contemptuously. 'In these caves? We do not lose, *my friend*. When partisans hid here in the Great Patriotic War, the whole German army couldn't get them out.'

'I'm telling you, Viktor, if that anthrax is used, *nothing* will keep you safe. The Americans will come with earth penetrator bombs. This lot'll be vaporised. And if by some miracle you survive, they'll string you up in the name of the thousands who died. Hang you from the streetlights as a lesson to the other hoodlums.'

He was on a desperation-induced high, unable to stop his insane tongue.

'Shut up, idiot!' Rybkin jabbed him in the back with his gun. 'In here!'

The shaven-headed escort shoved him to the right, pushing him through a steel-framed doorway into a small, square chamber. On a table against the far wall, television monitors, tape players and a control console were set up – a video editing suite. And in front of them all, watching pictures of a naked woman being trussed like an oven-roast, sat a heavy-set man with hair like a wire brush, dressed in a blue and white shell suit.

Sam was held in the middle of the room. For several seconds no one moved and no one spoke.

Then Dima Grimov froze the video and swivelled his chair. His rubber-mouthed face was unsmiling, his button-hard eyes, one out of line with the other, were angry and curious.

Face to face with the man who'd killed Chrissie, Sam felt icy cold. He itched to pull the gun from his sock and punch holes in the bastard's head.

'*Da!*' said Grimov. '*Viy gavareetyeh pa-rooski?*'

He was being asked if he spoke Russian.

'*Nyet.*'

'Then it is lucky for you that they teach me English when they train me in Soviet army to invade England,' Grimov laughed uproariously. 'But nowadays we don't invade your country by force,' he added, mocking. 'No need, when you British can be bought.'

'You can't buy *me*, Vladimir Filipovich,' Sam answered reactively.

'No? Anyway *you* are not worth buying. But in London there are good businesses. Property, restaurants. And nice houses. Holland Park – you know it?'

'I know it.'

'In six weeks I will have house there,' he declared proudly, snapping his fingers for Rybkin to wheel up a chair behind Sam.

'Sit,' he growled.

Grimov himself stood up. Not a tall man, Sam saw, but muscular.

'Why you come back?' he demanded, hunching forward and crossing his arms like some Hollywood villain. 'We're going to kill you. You know that.'

'I came back to warn you.'

'*You* warn *me*?' he guffawed.

'Yes. In case your buffoon of a guard-dog here forgot to tell you that your time's running out. Western intelligence agencies know all about your deal with the Iraqis. If the anthrax attack takes place, you and your organisation will be wiped out by the international community.'

'Ha! *International community!* You come back to tell me this *joke*?' he squealed, jabbing out a finger, its tip ending inches from Sam's nose. 'You come here to tell me how to run my business? Ha! You and she – you *so* alike.'

She meant Chrissie. So she *had* cracked it. Had tried to stop the deal with the Iraqis.

'You are ridiculous person.' Grimov stepped back and perched his backside against the editing table. He appeared puzzled. 'But that is *all*? You come here to tell me *that*?'

He knew it wasn't all. Knew Sam had another reason for coming back. He was playing with him. Patting him with his claws like a cat pats a bird with a broken wing.

'With thousands of lives at stake, what else could I do,' Sam said grimly.

'But you lie. That is *not* only reason.' Grimov's smile was like a torturer's.

'No?'

'You want to know about Christine. *That's* why you come back. You want to know how she died, because you love her.' Grimov licked his lips as if preparing for the kill. 'Well, I'm going to show you how.'

He turned to the machines, ejecting a cassette from the player and inserting another.

Sam's stomach turned over. He couldn't breathe.

'I *like* videos,' Grimov purred.

Two monitors behind Grimov's head – two identical pictures appeared on them. A room, shot in wide-angle from a camera high on the wall. A man and a woman on a bed. Fucking.

'Jesus . . .'

Sam's chest was bursting. He couldn't watch this. Not Chrissie doing it with this *arsehole* . . .

The picture zoomed. Her face was turned to one side so he couldn't see her eyes, but there was no mistaking the strands of chestnut hair gummed to the perspiration on her cheek. Her slender legs were hooked round Grimov's tanned back, his comically white buttocks thrusting with a dogged rhythm.

'Shit . . .'

Sam's stomach clenched. He put a hand over his mouth to catch the vomit if it came up. For the job, he told himself. She'd been doing this for the job. To save innocent lives. No other reason.

'Want to listen?' Grimov pushed a fader to bring up the sound. 'Directional microphone,' he murmured proudly.

Male grunts, then Chrissie's voice, throaty and insistent.

'*Dima, Dima . . .*'

Sam tensed. Any second now he would hurl himself at the machinery and smash it with his bare hands. Chrissie – mouthing that slimeball's name. Mouthing it in the same hungry, pre-orgasmic gasps that he'd thought of as being for him and him alone.

Grimov laughed. 'What you think now? What you think of your girlfriend?'

'I think *you* are a shit. A murdering little shit.'

'No. *Her*. What you think of her? What word is right word for her in your language? Look this video. See what she doing?' he gloated. 'So professional, yes? Come on. I want to hear you say right word.'

He stood over Sam, glowering down at him, his slash of a grin glinting with silver.

'*Whore!*' he screamed. 'That is word in English. You say for me now! *My girlfriend is whore!*' His good eye gleamed maniacally.

Sam balled his fists. A sharp upper cut would be so satisfying . . .

'And you know all about whores,' he snarled, his words spilling out like bile. 'Something of an expert . . .'

Grimov backed off, stung by Sam's defiance. Eyes blazing in two directions at once, he turned angrily to the tape player and jabbed at fast forward.

The picture broke up. The scene changed. A flickering, jumpy image, but enough to show Chrissie alone on the bed, kneeling with a towel round her shoulders. Talking. Mickey Mouse sound, but talking as if in an argument.

'I show you,' Grimov fumed. 'I show what we do with English whores.'

Sam heard a soft tongue click from Rybkin, standing to his right, as if he disapproved of what was happening here.

The picture went dark. Grimov pressed play again then spun round to savour Sam's pain.

The image was grainy and yellow. Outdoors, indoors, impossible to tell at first. The light flickered, as if it came from a guttering candle. Chrissie was sitting on a wooden chair, her ankles bound to its legs. Behind her were railings, and her hands were tied to them. Then Sam recognised the blurred twinkle of the distant lights. Limassol. The balcony of the half-built house in the hills.

He wanted to leap up, to stop this re-enactment of her death to assuage his lingering guilt for failing to prevent it.

Chrissie's face was puffy and bloated, her mouth a ring of sores. She fought for breath, her eyes bursting with terror.

'No!' Sam howled, springing forward. 'No! Turn the fucking thing off!'

Grimov knocked him back with the strength of an ox, then the *shpana* pinned him back on the chair.

Sam wanted to look away but some terrible compulsion made him watch. Grimov appeared in shot, his hands grabbing Chrissie's lank hair and swollen jaw. He yanked her mouth wide open.

Sam felt the blood drain from his brain.

A second pair of hands held a funnel over her, of the size used for pouring petrol into a car. On one of the thumbs on the hand that held it the end joint was missing. Rybkin's hands, and they rammed the funnel into Chrissie's mouth.

Sam's mind exploded. There was a roaring in his head. He felt he was outside his own body, looking down on the room noting where everyone stood. On his left, the shaven-haired thug, eyes glued to the screen. On his right Rybkin, long-jawed and guilt-ridden, looking away. Ahead of him Grimov, unrepentant, revelling in his home-made snuff movie. Non-humans the lot of them.

From the corner of his eye he saw the Skorpion machine pistol dangling from Rybkin's hand. It was the only weapon in the room, except his own.

Sam reached for his ankle. The pistol fused with his palm and slid from its binding like a greased sword from a sheath. An extension of his arm, a part of him now, it rose up in front of him. His left hand came up to join the right. Thumb slipping safety, finger on trigger, eyes on tunnel vision, Grimov turning towards him in consternation.

The pistol kicked silently. Then kicked again. No sound but the buzz in his head. Two red rings stamped on Grimov's temple. The monster slumped forward.

Sam sensed movement to his right. He kicked against the floor, skidding the swivel chair back on its castors. The Skorpion swung towards him. Two more silent kicks from Figgis's PSM sent the machine pistol clattering to the floor and Rybkin staggering against the wall, clutching his shoulder.

Movement to the left now, the *shpana* diving for the Skorpion. Again Sam fired. Again some supernatural force gave him an accuracy he'd never acquired through training. The thug jerked and choked as the bullets hit his middle, blood spurting from his side.

Sam scrabbled to his feet, the blur clearing from his brain. Sharp sounds pierced his ears now. Rybkin yelling in pain, his hand pressed against his shoulder.

Sam stared around him in disbelief. Grimov was lifeless, the man on the floor moaning and still. He himself was trembling, the pistol shaking like jelly. Had *he* done this?

But mingled with Rybkin's yells, there was another, far more dreadful sound hammering at his ears. A gagging and choking that was cutting his heart out. He lunged at the edit bench to stop the tape.

Then he rounded on Rybkin, bent on killing him too.

'You shitbag! You are dead! *Dead!* Understand? Down on your fucking knees, animal!' He scooped the Skorpion off the floor and held it in his left fist.

'Listen, listen to me,' Rybkin pleaded. 'All what you see – it was Grimov. His idea. Everything. Killing . . . making video . . . He's crazy for such things. Me, I just do—'

'What he tells you. Don't fucking come that one! You murdered her. Both of you. It's on the fucking tape.' He aimed the pistol between Rybkin's eyes and took up first pressure on the trigger.

'Don't shoot. I can tell you things . . .'

'Then fucking talk!'

'Yes. I will tell you . . .'

Suddenly the full impact of what he'd done hit Sam with a terrifying force. He backed away, looking about him. He'd killed the Odessa commander of the Voroninskaya gang. He'd done serious damage to one of his hoods, and he was stuck in the bowels of the gang's headquarters which must have echoed like a base drum to the crack of his shots. The door was still ajar. He listened for footsteps or shouts.

'First. Who else is here?' he demanded. 'How many others of you?'

Rybkin blinked as if trying to decide how little he needed to reveal. Sam prompted him with a pistol jab against the old scar on the side of his head.

'Three,' Rybkin fumed, flinching. 'But they are up. Above ground – in the office where you came earlier.'

'How do they get down here?'

'Elevator.'

'And will they?'

'Only if I call them.'

Was he lying? Sam couldn't tell.

'Just remember, arsehole, if they turn up at that door, I blow a hole in your head. Understand?'

'Understand. I'm telling you the truth.'

'Now tell me the truth about the anthrax. Where's it to be used? And when?'

Rybkin froze, then tried a shrug, but the pain shot through his shoulder again. 'I don't know,' he coughed.

'You're a fucking liar!' Sam clubbed his head with the Skorpion. 'Now, fucking tell me or you're dead!'

Rybkin regained his balance. The scar tissue on his cheek had split and begun to bleed.

'I'll tell you, I'll tell you,' he puffed. He looked down as if with shame, his chest heaving with the enormity of the betrayal he was about to commit. 'I'm not sure, but I think it's Israel.'

'What d'you mean you're not sure? You arranged transport for the drone – where the fuck did it go?'

Rybkin looked up, his brown eyes feigning harmlessness. 'All of this – it was Dima Filipovich. You understand? Not me. I just—'

'Obeying orders. Shut up and tell me where the VR-6 was shipped to.'

'Haifa,' he whispered. 'Container went to Haifa . . .'

'God Almighty!' Sam flared. 'You realise what you idiots have done? If the Israelis get hit by Iraqi anthrax, they'll nuke Baghdad. You're mad. You know that? Totally fucking mad.'

'Grimov – he decide these things.' Rybkin mouthed, pointing at his dead boss.

Jesus, thought Sam, he had to get out of there fast. To warn the Israelis.

'But when?' he demanded. 'When's the attack to happen? And why? What's the reason for this lunacy?'

Rybkin shook his head. 'I don't know. *Truly*,' he pleaded, as Sam raised the Skorpion, ready to hit him again.

For some reason Sam believed him this time.

'Look, I'm bleeding pretty bad,' Rybkin pleaded. 'I need doctor. And for Sasha . . .' He indicated the man sprawled on the floor.

'A doctor?' Sam wheezed, incredulous. 'Like the one you so generously provided for Chrissie? No. The next time a doctor looks at you, chum, you'll be on a marble slab.'

There was one more question. One vital one he needed an answer to before he got the hell out of there. A question he was almost afraid to ask.

'Why the fucking tattoo, Viktor?' he croaked. 'Why was Chrissie marked with the Voroninskaya logo?'

Rybkin's face lit up with surprise. 'You still don't know?'

'No.'

'Then you must look at the tape,' Rybkin murmured, a glint of triumph on his face.

'I just did.'

'No. The rest of it.' Cruelty crept back into Rybkin's gaze. 'The part Dima Filipovich spooled through.'

The shots of Chrissie by herself. Talking . . . Rybkin's eyes cut him like lasers. *The more questions you ask . . .* The Ukrainian's warning sounded in his ears yet again, but he had to go on. The answers were here, inside that damned machine.

'Show me,' he croaked, prodding Rybkin towards the equipment. His heart felt as if it were clamped in a vice.

Rybkin hovered over Grimov, clicking his tongue.

'Get on with it,' Sam snapped, putting the pistol in his trouser pocket.

Rybkin leaned forward and operated the player awkwardly with his left hand. He spooled back, then touched play.

The towel over Chrissie's shoulders almost covered her breasts, but it failed to conceal a livid red love bite on one of them. She'd put some briefs on.

When her voice rang from the speakers, as clear and true as if she were here in this room, Sam's eyes began to blur with tears.

She was shouting.

'*Look Dima, you damn well have to, and tha's it.*'

He didn't take in her words at first, except to notice they were slurred.

'*It's not enough. Not for what I've done.*'

Not enough? Sam didn't follow.

'*It is all you get.*' Grimov's voice. Distant. Off mike. But hard and dismissive. '*It is the price. It is what you are worth to me.*'

Worth? Price? What was this to do with her extracting secrets from the villain?

'*Jesus, Di-ima. How can you say that?*'

She was very drunk, her tongue, her face muscles all going slow. Sam's eyes locked on to her lips, which were raw from the sex.

'*Not only is it me that gives you the most crucial piece of information for your lunatic scheme,*' she snapped, '*you get to fuck me all over, you dirty little weasel.*'

Information? The word reached out from the speakers

like a hand clutching at his throat. The nightmare he'd tried to suppress was coming true.

'*Weasel?*' Grimov's voice this time, annoyed and off camera. Sounds of running water, as if he were in a bathroom. '*What you say?*' Louder now, as if he'd re-entered the room. Louder and angry.

'*A weasel's a little furry animal,*' she answered timidly, her slate-grey eyes suddenly meek and scared. '*Quite sweet, really . . .*'

'*Don't make mistake, Chrissie . . .*' Grimov moved into shot, naked except for a towel round his waist. '*Don't make mistake to think we need you.*'

Need? Sam prayed he was misunderstanding, that this was some crazy, perverted piece of virtual reality.

'*You* did *need me, Dima,*' she persisted. '*Couldn't have got started without my help.*'

God Almighty. What had she done?

'*And you have been paid,*' Grimov retorted. '*So it is finish. Understand?*'

Chrissie pulled herself up straight. '*I'll have to talk to Voronin.*'

'You begin to understand?' Rybkin was watching Sam like a hovering hawk.

He didn't answer. Couldn't. He'd slumped onto the swivel chair, the Skorpion across his knees.

On the screen Grimov slapped her face, knocking her sideways.

'*How dare you!*' she protested, picking herself up. '*If you think that what Voronin paid me entitles you to treat me like dirt . . . I've had to betray people. Friends, Dima, friends! Not that you'd know the meaning of the word . . .*'

Grimov's arms hung at his sides like an ape's.

'*A hundred thousand is not enough,*' she insisted, drunkenly oblivious to the pit she was digging herself. '*Half a million is what I want.*'

'You are mad. You agree fifty thousand this time,' Grimov snapped. *'Already you have fifty thousand last year.'*

Sam curled up with pain. 'Oh God . . .' he mouthed.

'I agreed to that before I knew what this was all about, Dima. Before I knew how much you stood to make from the deal. And before I realised just what an insanely dangerous game you were playing. Jesus, Dima . . . Anthrax. You never said anything about anthrax when I agreed to help. You realise this could lead to World War Three?'

Sam looked into her eyes searching for some sign of shame, but there was none to be seen.

Grimov didn't answer her.

'Listen to me, Dima. You'd bloody better pay me what I want.' Her threat was unspoken, but quite explicit.

Sam put his head in his hands. There were no more words to be heard now. Just the sickening smack of punches, the razor cut of Chrissie's screams and the animal grunts of Grimov's breathing.

Rybkin switched off the machine.

'So now you know.' He flinched as fresh pain stabbed through his shoulder. 'Chrissie belonged to Voronin, since a year ago when you and she were in Kiev. The tattoo is Voronin's way with women. When they take his money they have to wear it. Like a receipt. She wouldn't have it at first, but she agreed back in June, when she got wind there was another fifty grand on offer.'

June. The month in which she'd ended their relationship. Ended it so she wouldn't have to explain to him where the tattoo came from.

Sam forced himself to his feet, clutching the Skorpion in his left hand. He couldn't breathe in this place. Still couldn't grasp what Chrissie had done to him.

'It was *she* who told you I was being assigned to Baghdad?' he heard himself ask.

'Yes.'

'And then you told Naif Hamdan, so he could set me up.'

'Yes.'

'And she also told you where I live in London, so that Hamdan knew where to come when he tried to kill me?'

Rybkin sighed. 'I didn't know he planned to kill you.'

Another lie, thought Sam. The habit of a lifetime. He pressed the eject button on the VCR and pulled out the tape.

'Get me out of here, arsehole,' he grunted. He stuffed the tape into the waistband of his trousers.

Why had she done it? For the money? So she could have that goddamned gingerbread cottage by the river? Have the new BMW Clare had told him about? She'd risked his life for *that*?

He remembered that tiny bedroom in Amman, her concern for him after his release from Iraq. That loving concern that he now knew had one purpose and one purpose only, to learn if he'd tumbled to the fact that it was *she* who'd betrayed him. He remembered too her questions about the anthrax. Not idle questions as they'd seemed at the time, but to discover how much of the plan had been blown.

'Move,' he snapped, pointing the Skorpion at Rybkin's stomach. 'Get me out the way I came in.'

Rybkin caught his breath. 'I need to go to hospital,' he gulped. 'And Sasha.' Sam glanced at the man on the floor. No sign of breathing. Probably too late for him.

'Move it!'

The passageway was empty and eerily quiet. Sam pushed the Ukrainian towards the heavy steel door.

'Open it and then get me into the cellar with the lockers.'

Rybkin spun the heavy handle that withdrew the bolts

and the door swung back. They passed through and the door closed shut behind them. Sam clicked on the torch.

He was having to force himself to think ahead, to put behind him what he'd just seen and done. To turn Chrissie into history. A history that should never have happened.

If this had been a sane country he would have taken Rybkin at gunpoint to the police, but this was Ukraine and Rybkin would have friends in the Militsia. Friends who could block Sam's escape from the country. And escaping was what he had to do – and fast.

Suddenly he thought of a way.

His torch lit up the tunnel until their path was blocked by the plain metal back of the fake storage cabinet.

'Open it.'

Rybkin was too weak to prevaricate. He reached with his left hand to a patch of wall above the opening and, pressing on some invisible switch, the metal panel swung back.

'This is where we say goodbye, Viktor,' Sam growled, stepping through the gap. 'I should kill you too, but I have a sneaking feeling Mr Voronin will soon do the job for me.'

Rybkin scowled. The cabinet swung shut with Rybkin still behind it in the pitch black of the tunnel.

'Don't get lost, now,' Sam chided.

He shone the torch round the cellar to check he was alone, then he removed the magazine from the Skorpion and pocketed it. He hid the machine pistol on top of one of the cabinets. With the PSM weighing heavily in his other trouser pocket, he moved up the steps into the courtyard, then on towards the lights of the town.

When he reached the Prymorsky boulevard the crowd had dwindled to a handful of lovers and a scattering of sailors heading back to the port. As he began to make his way down the broad sweep of the Potemkin steps, he heard not far off the wail of a police siren – and it was getting closer.

He panicked and began to run. Rybkin had had five minutes. Enough time to get onto his pals.

Two hundred steps, he remembered Oksana saying. Two hundred chances to miss his footing. As his feet hammered down them, his mind was spinning again. There was something not right. Something wrong with what he'd been told, something that didn't add up.

How *could* Chrissie have known? How could she *possibly* have known that he was being assigned to Baghdad – unless her husband had told her? Martin Kessler giving her information that was top secret. Had Kessler been bought too? A rotten apple in the hierarchy of SIS? Was this the smell he'd wanted Sam to conceal?

He reached the last flight of steps. Suddenly he stopped. There was a road to cross to reach the entrance of the port, and parked in the middle of it was a police car. Beside him a trio of sailors was zigzagging down the last of the steps, clinging to one another for support. They were singing.

'. . . *never walk alone* . . .'

Sam slung an arm round the one on the end and began to sing with them.

'Eh . . . 'oo are you, wack?'

'What a night, eh?' Sam muttered. 'Fucking wiped out, I am.'

They reached the road and began to cross, the police car just feet away.

'Yeah. But 'oo are you? Youse not with us.'

'Cracking talent, eh? Odessa girls, w'hay!' Sam turned his face away from the Militsia car.

'The one I 'ad wasn't,' the sailor lamented. 'Ugly as a fuckin' robber's dog.'

'*Never walk alone* . . .' Sam howled.

On the far pavement they began lurching up the ramp

to the port, two armed policemen looking over them as they passed, their eyes weary from a night of watching drunks.

'What ship you from?' the sailor asked.

'Yours.'

'No you're not. 'Ere,' he shouted, turning to his mates. 'This bloke's not from the *Devonshire*, is he?'

'Give it a rest, mate,' Sam growled, trying to hurry them. 'I'm a techie, sent out from UK to fix the radar.'

'Oh, right.'

A footbridge led down to the inner harbour where the NATO warships were berthed. Sam let go of his new friends, now they were in sight of the ship. The sailors unlinked their arms and fell silent, trying to appear sober. Sam watched as they stomped up the gangway and saluted the officer checking names against a crew list. Then he followed.

'Sorry, sir, you can't come on here,' the lieutenant declared, putting a hand on Sam's chest.

Sam took in a deep breath.

'My name is Lieutenant Commander Packer. I work for British intelligence. I need to speak with your captain immediately.'

39

Thursday, 10 October
The Black Sea

The Sea King helicopter dipped its whirling tail rotor and descended like a predator onto the demarcated landing area at Istanbul's Atatürk airport. Sam twisted his helmeted head against the hard webbing seat back in the cramped interior, straining to see out of the small, spray-smeared window to his left. He was relieved at having escaped from Odessa, very relieved. But what he'd seen and done in the last few hours had left him stunned.

His arrival on the brow of the British warship last night had caused more ructions than he'd expected. He'd imagined there'd be *somebody* among the ship's seventeen officers who would know him from years back – the Navy was like an extended family – but he'd been out of luck. Most were of the next generation to him, well under thirty years of age, and four of the officers were women.

At first the captain hadn't believed his story of working for SIS, depriving him of his pistol and keeping him under guard in the wardroom while checks were made through the ship's secure satellite link with the Ministry of Defence. It was four in the morning before the dust had settled and a circuit was patched through to the duty officer at Vauxhall Cross.

This morning HMS *Devonshire* had sailed from

Odessa with the rest of the NATO flotilla at six a.m. The joint exercise with the Ukrainians was over. Once the frigate was well clear of the harbour, Sam had made his way to the quarterdeck at the stern and stood beside the sonar winch, holding Figgis's PSM pistol in his fist. He'd found it hard to grasp the fact that he'd actually used this gun. Killed one man, injured another, possibly fatally. Without the gun he himself would be dead by now, of that he was certain. But he didn't need it any longer, and it would be best for him and for Gerald Figgis if it were never found. He'd tossed the weapon into the scar of foam the *Devonshire* was carving into the smooth grey surface of the Black Sea.

Then, for several minutes, he'd remained there by the rail, clutching the cassette of Dima Grimov's horrific home video. It was evidence. The only proof that existed of Chrissie's treachery. Yet what it contained was vile, scenes more obscene than the worst pornography. Above all it had shown a Chrissie he'd never known, one that he wanted no one else to see. With a wide swing of his arm he'd sent the tape spinning into the foam.

Two hours later, well beyond Ukraine's territorial waters, HMS *Devonshire*'s captain had obtained clearance for her helicopter to fly the two hundred miles to the Turkish metropolis, claiming that its passenger was in need of urgent medical attention back in England.

The helicopter settled firmly onto the landing pad of Istanbul airport and shut down. Sam undid his straps and the crewman directed him out. Once on the tarmac he removed his bone dome, dry-suit and life-jacket and looked across the field to the airport passenger terminal. His onward flight to London was in two hours' time, just before midday. Supposed to be a car to take him over there, but it wasn't here yet.

He'd found it hard talking to the anonymous duty officer in London a few hours ago. Particularly hard to tell the British Secret Intelligence Service that one of its agents had betrayed friends and country for a bag of cash, when the agent in question had been his own lover. Hard, too, to explain with cold detachment how he'd found himself killing the man who'd murdered her.

He'd kept it as clinical as he could and to the point. Just the bare facts. The issue of whether MI6's own Deputy Controller of Global Risks had been the source of Chrissie's knowledge about his being dispatched to Baghdad could wait. Of more immediate concern to him had been the fate of Oksana Koslova. Rybkin had her name and address. If the Voroninskaya sought revenge for the death of Dima Grimov, it was conceivable *she* might become a victim. He'd asked that Figgis make plans to get her out – if that's what she wanted. From everything she'd said to him he guessed it would be.

It was adrenalin that had kept him going through the night, but by now it had burned off. He was dropping with exhaustion. During the helicopter flight across the Black Sea he'd kept nodding off, but the image of Chrissie's terrified face being impaled by the funnel kept jerking him awake again. The shock of seeing her death and of discovering her base nature had been fermenting in his gut. He burned with anger now, anger at Grimov and Rybkin for their grotesque cruelty, at *her* for being so contemptuous of all those who'd trusted her, and at *himself* for having been so totally taken in.

The crewman touched him on the arm and pointed off to their left. A fuelling bowser was drawing up to replenish the tanks of the helicopter and in its wake was the car that was to take him to the passenger terminal.

London, 4.30 p.m.

Duncan Waddell listened, his face devoid of expression.

'Didn't bring the videotape back with you, I suppose?' he asked when Sam had finished.

'No.' Despite Waddell's reproachful look he was glad he'd dumped it.

They were meeting in the Isleworth flat.

'Totally and utterly fucking horrific,' Waddell growled, shaking his head. 'To tell the truth it's hard to believe that such a good-looking woman could be so diabolically devious.' Then he smacked himself on the forehead. 'What am I saying? She only deceived her own bloody husband for five long years!'

He looked quizzically at Sam, slightly embarrassed by what he'd just said. After all, she'd fooled *him* too.

'Has it occurred to you to think about how she knew?' Sam asked acidly.

'About you being in Baghdad, you mean?'

'Yes.'

'First question that came into my head when I heard about your report to the duty officer.'

'And?'

'I began to wonder when it was that you last saw her.'

'What the hell does *that* mean?'

'It's just that Martin Kessler thinks it was rather more recently than either you or she made out. Thinks it was well after your relationship with her was officially over. A few days before you went to Baghdad, in fact.'

'*What?* Kessler thinks *I* told her? What a load of bollocks!'

'Well he's quite adamant it wasn't him.'

'He bloody would be.'

Waddell looked thoughtful.

'For the record, when *did* you last see her before Baghdad?'

'June.'

The terrier face had a closed look about it now. 'Leave it with me, will you?'

Sam felt under suspicion again. 'As long as you understand that she didn't hear about Baghdad from me.'

'I hear what you say,' Waddell mouthed. 'It *is* a pity you didn't bring that tape back . . . Anyway, let's move on to other things. We've arranged a visa for this Oksana Koslova woman – if she wants to take it up when she gets back to Kiev. Her brother will certainly be glad of her company here. He speaks no English. Nor does his wife.'

'Are they miserable?'

'He is. But his wife and daughter spend most of their time wandering round the shops with their mouths open.'

'What about the Hawk drone?' Sam asked. 'Where is it?'

'We don't know. But it looks as if what Rybkin told you could be right. The SBU got onto us a couple of hours ago. We'd asked them for a list of container movements out of ports in the Odessa region. There weren't many shipments on the dates in question and they've all been verified except for one box, a container of fruit and vegetable juice – supposedly – being sent back to Haifa because its contents had gone off. It left Ilychevsk twelve days ago for Piraeus. Has to be in Israel by now, according to the shippers. Shin Beth are peddling like billy-oh to track it down. They're considering putting the civilian population in gas masks. And the defence forces are drawing up plans for an air-strike on Baghdad.'

Sam narrowed his eyes. There was a niggle in the back of his mind, a suspicion they were being duped. He couldn't explain why, other than that every time he'd met Rybkin he'd been deceived. Just because he'd been holding a gun to the man's head this time didn't mean he'd turned straight.

'Rybkin is not to be trusted,' he cautioned.

'Dead right,' Waddell concurred, 'but as I said, there's other evidence to support his line. We're hopeful the Israelis will come up with the goods, but in the meantime we're keeping an open mind. The attack could be anywhere. Riyadh, New York, London even. I think for the next few days it's best you keep out of sight, just in case Hamdan is still around – we've found no trace unfortunately. You can stay here. There's a divan in the room next door and we've stocked the fridge with food.'

'Very thoughtful of you. But no. Home is where I want to be now. I like my own bed. There's a police station down the road – you can tell them to keep an eye open around my place.'

Waddell looked disappointed but not entirely surprised.

Sam stood up. 'If you *do* get word from Israel, one way or the other, I wouldn't mind a call. Just to set my mind at rest.'

'Of course.' Waddell stood up too. 'You'll want to be on your way. Must be exhausted. I told the car to wait, just in case you refused our hospitality.'

On the drive back to Barnes sleep began to engulf him. The debrief with Waddell had been something of a watershed, a lifting of responsibility from his shoulders. The grownups had taken over again.

There was, however, one issue that he was going to have to resolve before long. Because it was clear the SIS establishment was closing ranks around one of its own.

Martin Kessler.

12 noon EST
Washington DC

Dean Burgess picked his way through the open-plan general office of the Counter-Terrorism Center, up on the top floor of the FBI headquarters on Pennsylvania Avenue.

'Going out?' The question came from the pushy, raven-haired woman who occupied the pen next to his.

'Just for a half hour.'

'Like some company?'

'I got things to do, Jess. But thanks for the offer.'

She beamed a smile that said *any time*, and waved him on his way. Jess Bissett was one of the more attractive of his fellow special agents in the Counter-Terrorism Center, a nuclear weapons specialist. But she was a voracious divorcee and she scared the hell out of him.

He took the elevator to the ground floor, sharing it as far as the second with his immediate boss in the department, Ive Stobal, a long-server in the FBI with the physique of a basketball player. Burgess left the building by the Pennsylvania Avenue entrance, heading for the deli he'd discovered soon after his move from New York and which suited his needs for a bag lunch.

Since his return to Washington from Iraq at the beginning of the week he'd been urging Stobal and the other seniors in the department to treat the threat of an anthrax attack with deadly seriousness, but he'd come up against an insularity he hadn't realised existed before. A feeling that since the threat had not been detected and processed by an *American* intelligence agency it shouldn't be given total credence. It wasn't until Tuesday morning, when the British revealed that a Ukrainian UAV had been procured as the attack platform, that the department began reacting seriously.

The line at the deli was six deep – a five-minute wait, no more. Burgess was conservative in his lunch-time tastes. Chicken and mayo on rye, every time. It was a warm October day. The slash of sky that appeared between the blocks down here by the Federal Triangle was a hazy blue.

News about the VR-6 Hawk on Tuesday had prompted a special conference at the FBI chaired by its hands-on director. A recent presidential directive had given the Bureau lead role in investigating terrorism in the USA, but the counter-terrorism team was still being built up. Suddenly they seemed to be facing a real threat, an anthrax attack that could be directed anywhere in the USA.

If the terrorists were importing the drone in a shipping container it could enter the country through any one of half a dozen Atlantic ports between Houston and New York. No more than five per cent of arriving containers were spot-checked by US Customs in normal circumstances, Burgess had learned. Spreading the net wide would devour manpower. And if the Iraqis were being helped in the USA by Russian-émigré organised crime, *that* was a beast the FBI had been finding even tougher to crack than the Cosa Nostra. Some 350,000 former citizens of the Soviet Union now lived in the USA. Efforts to discover which of them might have links with the Voroninskaya Mafiya in Odessa had made little progress.

This morning, however, the feeling that the crisis they faced might develop the unstoppability of a tornado had been eased by the reports suggesting it was Israel that was the intended target. Hence Burgess felt it okay to lunch outside the J. Edgar Hoover building today. It was the first time he'd done so that week. He was a natural 'brown bagger', preferring to eat on the move rather than line up for a table in the eighth-floor cafeteria.

'Black pepper?' He'd reached the head of the line. The

Hispanic behind the counter had her thick black hair covered by a white baseball cap labelled 'Bett's Eats'.

'Sure.'

He paid for the sandwich and a can of soda then set off down 9th Street towards the open spaces of the Mall. He *needed* this break from the office. Needed room to think, so he could try to straighten his life out.

He'd not been home to Westchester County since returning to the USA – one more misdemeanour for Carole to put on her list. Burgess well understood how hard it was for wives when husbands couldn't explain their reasons for ignoring them. But what concerned him was not the marital chafing every FBI agent faced, but the fact that Carole seemed bent on turning a little bit of friction into outright war.

Yes, she would come to Washington soon, she'd told him, but not to find a home and schools for the family to move to, which is what he wanted. She would be here on Saturday, along with tens of thousands of other American wives, children and their *husbands*, to attend the Pledge for the Family gathering that would end with a candlelit vigil in front of the Washington Monument. She wanted Dean there too, pledging himself in front of God and a host of witnesses to the care of her, Patty and Dean Jr. She wanted him to make the same commitment to his family that he'd made to the Bureau. Not more of a commitment – she wasn't being unrealistic – but certainly not less.

When he'd explained he couldn't make it to the Pledge rally because a crisis had blown up, she'd begun yelling down the phone. Watch out, she'd said. On Saturday morning before the rally, she would be on that pavement outside the J. Edgar Hoover Building, holding a placard saying *Give me back my husband, FBI.*

And Burgess knew she meant it. He knew too that with her Jamie Lee Curtis looks and feisty manner, she'd soon get attention from media crews looking for early coverage. She could well end up on the evening news shows, while he became the butt of jokes. A game for her in which she would have won a round, but a coffin nail for his career and for their marriage.

Burgess crossed over Constitution Avenue when the lights turned green, glancing at the dome of the National Museum of Natural History to his right, then walked on down 9th Street until he reached the grass of the Mall. He'd been hoping to find some place to sit, but all the benches were taken and the grass was damp because there'd been a heavy shower an hour ago. He unwrapped his sandwich and began to eat while turning to his left and walking towards the Capitol.

It had become clear to him in the last couple of days that either he or Carole was going to have to give way, or their marriage would be over. Either *she* must agree to move south to DC, or else *he* was going to have to ask to be reassigned to his old New York posting on compassionate grounds. But that would wrap his career in a concrete vest, which was something he couldn't take.

So, logically, it was Carole who was going to have to knuckle down and move her butt. The trouble was he was far from sure she would.

Everywhere he looked on the broad lawns running between here and the Capitol he saw couples. Kids fresh from campus in crisply pressed shirts, locking into their first relationships funded by salary checks, and couples in their thirties and forties who'd never made it to the altar, or who were starting again – or cheating. All of them bonding because their hormones and their instincts told them to.

Sometimes Burgess wondered if he had a deficiency in that department. He'd found Carole when he was sixteen and that had been it. She was exactly what he wanted. No teenage expectation of finding something better round the corner, no compulsion after marriage to bolster his ego with casual conquests. No overpowering sex need that couldn't be discreetly satisfied on his own if Carole wasn't around. Yes, he wanted her and the kids to be there for him, needed them to be there like he needed all four walls of his house to stay in place. But he wasn't sure he had the fire in his guts to fight for it if it couldn't be on his own terms.

He stopped in his tracks, shocked by the conclusion he'd just reached. Was he *truly* telling himself he was ready to sacrifice his marriage for his job?

'Aw, heck!'

That wasn't right. He didn't *have* to choose. Marriage and career could both be made to work.

He began to climb the steps leading up to the west face of the Senate. A kite was being flown by a tall thin man with long black hair standing halfway up. Nearer the top were three or four oddballs holding VHF radios to their ears, monitoring the air traffic talk-back of flights passing by on their way into National airport.

Burgess turned and looked back down the length of the Mall. Carole would be here on Saturday – and Patty and Dean Jr – hallelujah-ing with a bunch of born-again Jesus freaks in front of the Washington Monument. And she wanted *him* in among them.

'Okay, hon,' he mouthed.

Now that the anthrax was heading for Israel and not the USA, maybe he *could* find the time for it. If it bought him some peace, then a little hypocrisy was a price he was happy to pay.

He checked his watch. Time to get back to the Bureau. He cast a last curious glance at the plane spotters with the scanners, wondering what sort of vicarious pleasure they got from it. Most were young, but one guy was a little older than the others. He wore a long raincoat.

Odd, thought Burgess. Must be cooking inside it on a day as warm as this.

The man noticed him looking and turned away.

A craggy face, Burgess noted. Like the head of a big dog, the top of which was covered by an English-looking cap.

40

Friday, 11 October
London

Sam awoke suddenly from a deep sleep. He stared up at the plain white ceiling for several seconds before grasping that he was in his own bed in his own flat in Barnes.

The phone was ringing. It was that which had woken him. He stumbled to the kitchen to answer it, glancing at the wall clock. Ten minutes to ten. Hadn't slept this late for an age.

'Hello.'

'Sam?' Duncan Waddell's voice.

'Yes.'

'I'm in west Ealing. I want you to get your skates on and come over here.'

'What's up?' Sam asked groggily.

'Something for you to look at. A body.'

'Shit.' Sam was instantly wide awake. 'Anyone we know?'

'No. But connected. Very much connected.'

'I'll call a cab. Give me the address.'

When he'd written it down and rung off, he grabbed an apple to eat in the car.

Thirty minutes later the black taxi dropped him in a narrow lane of two-up-two-downs in an Asian quarter of west London. Outside the pebble-dashed house a police car was parked. He murmured who he was to a constable standing guard at the red-painted front door and was let inside. Waddell was waiting for him in the tiny hallway which had a decades-old smell of curry.

'Forensic are in there at the moment,' he said, pointing to a half-open door behind him. Sam saw a camera flash go off beyond it. 'When they let us in, I want you to see if you recognise the bloke.'

'Explain.'

'He's an Iraqi national, name of Sadiq Abbas – mean anything to you?'

'Not a thing.'

'Anyway, he was an ex-pat, settled in Jordan. Must've had good connections back home because he was still allowed in and out, from what I gather. For about a year he'd been driving one of those big GMC things between Amman and Baghdad as a taxi. I imagine he smuggled stuff for high-ups in the regime. Then something went wrong. His brother was killed in Baghdad and he seemed to think that whoever did it was after him too.'

'When?' Sam prodded, sensing the connection. 'When was this brother killed?'

'Middle of September.'

'Ah.' The pieces were beginning to fit.

'That was about a week before Sadiq Abbas arrived here. He entered UK on a tourist visa, lodged a claim for asylum and made contact with a support group for refugees. It was they who found him this place to stay. The woman who runs the group has filled us in on the little she knows about him. Anyway – here's the nub of it. Three days ago he gave her a letter. Told her it should only be opened if something happened to him.'

'And now it has.'

'Exactly. Abbas missed an appointment with her and she got worried. So she opened the letter, nearly had a heart attack when she read it, and gave it to the police. When they saw what was in it, Special Branch contacted us and then broke into his room. Here.'

Waddell handed Sam two lined pages torn from an exercise book. They were covered with a spidery script.

'His English wasn't great . . . and the handwriting's crap.'

Dear Freda, Sam read.

'Freda's the woman at the support group,' Waddell explained unnecessarily.

If you reading this letter it becouse something bad happen me. I see him on Sunday so I think I will be kill. He very clever very shure of what he do. He was here in London. I see in his eye he want to kill me but I run away.

'The first part's confusing,' Waddell prompted.

'Who's the *him*?' Sam queried.

'Read on.'

I must to tell about this man call Colonel Naif Hamdan . . .

'Fuck!'

'Yes. You see now?'

I very afraid him becouse he very danger man. He is reason I come England. Already he kill my brother Haji. He try kill me in Amman becouse he afraid I know some thing about his plan. Now he follow me here.

Sam shuddered, remembering how close Hamdan's knife had come to ending his own life.

Colonel Hamdan want Saddam dead. But he know it impoussible for Iraqi soldier kill him. Many try already and are kill by Saddam. Hamdan say only America can do it. They have army can invade Iraq and destroy Saddam. In 1991 they do not do it becouse they say they have no reason. So Colonel Hamdan decide this time he will give America very big reason for to kill Saddam Hussein.

'Shit! It's *America*? Not Israel?' Sam growled. 'He's trying to bomb Washington into another war?'

'Apparently,' Waddell answered, cautioning him with his eyes not to be specific in front of two police officers emerging from the back room.

'He's fucking mad.'

'Or extremely clever,' Waddell added.

Sam skimmed forward, searching for the clue they so badly needed – the precise where and when of the attack. But it wasn't there.

He re-read from near the beginning.

My brother Haji was army major in same corps as Colonel Hamdan. He retire on pension in 1992 but stay close friend Naif Hamdan. In July he tell me secret thing about Colonel Hamdan. He say Hamdan was one of army officer who try to make coup against Saddam in summer this year with help from CIA. In June Saddam find out and kill many them. Hamdan very lucky to still alive. Soon he make new plan. He decide to keep it just very small group this time because safer. Have few people very close to him in inner consil. Few others to helping, who not so close. Friends like my brother. It was group like egg. If you are in yellow part you know everything. In white part only know what yellow part tell you. Haji was in white part. He tell me Hamdan want to attack US President with anthrax bomb.

'Fucking mad,' Sam repeated. 'Washington knows about this?'

'We've just told them. But it's six in the morning over there. They haven't had time to panic yet.'

Sam continued to read.

Naif Hamdan says Americans will belief it is Saddam who do this and send soldiers to destroy him. Haji think it is bad plan. Many Americans be kill. But he is loyal to Hamdan and he agree to take bomb to Jordan for him. Him and me we take it in my car. There was big place in gas tank for hiding such thing. But when Haji return to Baghdad, Hamdan kill him to stop him say what he do.

Not quite, thought Sam. The man had been killed because he'd *already* talked.

I do not know how Hamdan make his attack or when he do it. But Haji think the weapon go to Cyprus from Jordan.

'Shit! Cyprus. Why?' Sam mouthed.

He'd reached the final paragraphs.

Dear Freda. You are good friend to me. These things I was afraid to tell to anyone while I am alive becouse of Hamdan, but if you read this letter it is becouse Hamdan has found me and killed me. He is very danger man. He think what he do is for good of Iraqi people. But he is like Saddam. He does not understand ordinary people. I feel very guilt that I knew this bad secret and not tell anyone. But if Naif Hamdan will kill me, I feel better when I meet my God and my brother if I have told it to someone. Your faithful, Sadiq Abbas.

'Incredible,' Sam breathed.

A uniformed policeman of senior rank emerged from the back room.

'All done, gents,' he told them. 'You can come in now. But I should cover your noses if I were you.'

'Thanks.' Waddell moved first. 'Abbas was stabbed,' he warned.

'I guessed.'

'Done with a kitchen knife bought at Harrods. Hamdan left the bag behind.'

Inside the room the stench of decaying flesh had combined with something equally vile. The dead man's bowels had evacuated at some point during his last minutes of life. With a hand to his face, Sam looked down at the thin, not very tall man lying on a floor rug that was caked with blood and excreta. The earnest, sallow face bore a strong family likeness to the man who'd whispered the anthrax warning to him in the Rashid Hotel lobby nearly three weeks ago.

'Yes,' he confirmed, gagging on the stench. 'He's a dead ringer for his brother.'

Two siblings dead. One beaten to pulp with clubs while suspended from a ceiling hook, the other slashed by a kitchen knife. Both lives terminated to conceal the terrible secret of a man Sam had dignified with the nickname Saladin.

Waddell's mobile phone trilled.

'Seen enough?' he asked, before answering it, backing from the room.

'Plenty,' breathed Sam, following him out into the hall.

Waddell hovered just inside the closed front door, listening intently to what was being told to him on the phone. He said 'I see' a number of times and ended with a 'Keep me posted'.

He beckoned to Sam. 'Let's go sit in my car. Things are moving fast.'

The small blue Rover was parked under a lamp post a little way down the road. Next to it a gaggle of Asian men watched their approach with curiosity. They'd been standing there for a while by the look of them, idly observing the comings and goings of the police.

'Get in,' Waddell mouthed to Sam. 'We'll drive round the corner and find somewhere less conspicuous.'

A couple of minutes later they were parked up in a quiet side street.

'Bloody Cyprus!' Waddell snapped. 'That sweaty little tax haven's got a lot to answer for.'

'Tell me.'

'Okay. The first development is that the Israelis have got two cast-iron witnesses who swear blind that when the container from Ukraine was unstuffed at a warehouse on the outskirts of Tel Aviv last Monday, it contained packs of rotting vegetable juice and nothing else. They're totally certain. No Hawk drone. No anthrax.

'Second. They've also discovered that the container from Ukraine did *not* come direct from Ilychevsk to Haifa but was transshipped. Not once, but twice. First at Piraeus where it went straight from one vessel to another, then at Limassol where – and get this – it spent three days in a sodding bonded warehouse!'

'God . . . Just at the time when Grimov, Rybkin and Hamdan were all there!'

'Correct. The buggers did a switch. That VR-6 drone arrived in the container from Ukraine. They took it out, mated it with the anthrax warhead they'd smuggled in from Jordan, then refilled the box with rotting fruit juice which they'd managed to dig up from somewhere and sent it on its way to Israel. A bluff, Sam, a mime show which tied in precisely with what that arsehole Viktor Rybkin *confessed* to you in Odessa.'

'I should have killed the bastard,' Sam spat.

'And now, that drone and its horribly lethal warhead are in some *other* damned container, which we know nothing whatsoever about – except that it's heading for America.'

41

19.30 hrs EST
Chesapeake Bay, USA

The MV *Karen Star* was a giant of the seas. The length of three football pitches and as wide as a major highway, she tramped the Atlantic in the furtherance of international trade. In her hold and stacked high on her deck were 3,274 shipping containers – below her capacity, but she'd already made three port calls to offload cargo this side of the pond.

The thirty-four-year-old Danish First Officer stood on the starboard bridge wing, studying the eastern shore of Chesapeake Bay through gimbals-mounted binoculars. One half of his family had migrated to America a century ago and he had a second-cousin living near to the very shore they were passing. In Easton, Maryland.

They were abeam of Tilghman Island now, about a mile and a half to starboard, but despite the power of the lenses and the clarity of the air, the unspoilt waterman's village that he'd visited a year ago was just so much white clapboard. He remembered the anchorage on the far side of the island, home to a small fleet of heavy timber-masted skipjacks. Working boats. When he'd been there last summer they'd been moored up, waiting for the oyster season to start, but they'd be busy this time of year. He looked in vain for their big white sails, then remembered that the beds they worked were on the other side of the island, along the mainland shore.

The *Karen Star* had slowed to twelve knots, just half the maximum she clocked up on the regular run from Algeciras. The wide waters of the bay were broken by flecks of foam, flicked up by the brisk easterly. A sailing breeze, and a few miles ahead the Dane saw a speckle of sails where a class race was under way.

In a couple of hours the *Karen Star* would pass beneath the high US-50 bridge and point her bow to Baltimore, in order to be alongside the Seagirt Terminal at 23.00 hours. The First Officer did a quick check of the chart to assure himself they'd be on time – the Karen Line prided itself on punctuality. Once alongside, there'd be an hour or so of berthing formalities, then he'd get his head down while the longshoremen lugged at the 450 boxes due off at this stop.

He stepped back inside the bridge, a tranquil haven after the breeziness of the wing. A hundred feet below, the ship's twelve-cylinder diesel rumbled its monotonous but comforting rhythm. The only other sound was the hiss of ventilation and the faint whistle from the tubes of the radar sets.

He walked forward to the front windows and looked down onto the neat lines of brightly coloured containers stacked on the deck. He wondered sometimes what was really inside these boxes. They could have *anything* in them. Anything at all. If the paperwork was done right and the authorities had received no tip-off that prompted a spot check, even a nuclear bomb could be smuggled into the USA without much problem. Ports like Baltimore were hungry for business. Speed and throughput were what mattered to them, not the verification of manifests.

He moved away from the windows to check the radar. It was a fact, he'd decided long ago, that with so many voyages like this every year, so many thousands of containers being transported, one day, unwittingly, he could be party to some great evil. But it didn't concern him greatly, because there was nothing to be done about it.

The J. Edgar Hoover Building, Washington DC

Dean Burgess picked up a coffee from the machine in the fifth-floor elevator lobby. Since first thing that morning when word had come through that Israel was *not* the target for the anthrax attack, the Counter-Terrorism Center had been frenetic. Now, at the end of the working day, things had begun to settle.

He stirred the coffee with a plastic straw then carried it down the drab, cream-walled corridor towards the heavy steel hatches of the FBI's Strategic Information Operations Center. Known throughout the building as SIOC, this screened and bombproof cell stuffed with monitors and communications panels was like the inside of a submarine according to those in the know. Manned twenty-four hours a day on a stand-by basis, the staff had nearly doubled since the place went fully operational a few hours ago.

Burgess passed through into the small room at the back of the SIOC, where a briefing had been called to report on the day's limited progress. Already present were some thirty men and women, each a terrorism specialist. He'd met a dozen or so during the few weeks he'd been in post, but to only a handful of them could he put names. In addition to the Bureau's own specialists there were representatives here from the CIA, the Pentagon and the National Security Agency.

He sat down. A few seconds later the shirt-sleeved FBI Director marched in, accompanied by his Assistant Director for National Security and by Burgess's own giant of a section chief, Ive Stobal. Completing the quartet on the podium was a US Air Force Brigadier.

The Director began by stressing the weakness of the intelligence that had come their way so far and the difficulty they had in interpreting it. 'But somewhere out there, gentlemen and ladies, is a most lethal box of tricks and we have to assume it's coming here,' he told them sombrely. The mood of the room was alert and tense. Managing a crisis this big was something they'd trained for, but never done for real.

'We've given this operation that we're now engaged in the codename Fire Hawk, ladies and gentlemen. And we have to assume the UAV with its anthrax warhead could already be in the United States some place,' the Director went on. 'Boxed up and probably all ready to launch from a standard forty-foot shipping container like you'll see in any freight yard in any state in the USA. The container's serial number we don't have, nor any shipping details. It's a needle in a haystack, folks.

'The VR-6 Hawk UAV is a battlefield reconnaissance drone that's standard issue in the forces of the former Soviet Union. Normally it's launched from a canister on the back of an eight-wheeled vehicle. Converting a shipping container to perform the same function would pose few problems to military technicians who knew what they were doing. And we have to believe these guys *do* know what's what. There's a stake of five million dollars behind this single act of terrorism.'

Somebody gave a low whistle.

'Sure. That's a lot of backing. Now, whether this crazy scheme is the brainchild of Saddam Hussein or of some maverick is more a concern for the NSA and the Joint Chiefs than for us. As lead agency in response to a terrorist attack, the FBI has two fundamental issues to address. How to prevent that attack, and if we can't, how to deal with it when it happens.

'As I just said, we have to assume the container with the missile could already be in its launch position. Where would that be? Well, just about any place within fifty miles of the target. And where's the target? We don't know. The terrorists *may* be going after the President, but we can't assume that. Anthrax sprayed from a missile is not the most sensible way to assassinate one extremely well-protected individual.

'Fortunately this weekend the President is staying in the White House most of the time. The exception is on Saturday night when he makes an election appearance at the Veterans Stadium in Philadelphia. The Eagles have a bye week. The meeting's being networked live on TV, which the terrorists would see as an advantage, of course. A decision on whether the President goes ahead with that event will be taken nearer the time.

'Our first priority has got to be to find that container before it can be used. The terrorists probably have to work on the missile before it can be fired – it's come a long way – so they'll want some place to do that without being disturbed. An old barn or disused warehouse would do just fine. Police in east coast states from New Hampshire to Florida have been tasked to check out all such sites.

'Priority two is for all agencies to be ready if that goddamned missile *is* fired. The VR-6 has inertial guidance which needs to be programmed and stabilised before launch, a process that takes about twenty minutes, so I'm told. It gets kicked into the air by a solid-fuel rocket booster, then a gas turbine takes over for the cruise. In the brief period between launch and the release of the agent – say ten minutes – there *is* a chance it can be shot down. The DoD has already set up full airborne radar coverage of the eastern sector of the United States. E-2s and E-3s.'

He turned to the military man to check he'd got his designations correct. The Air Force Brigadier nodded solemnly, then held up a hand to speak.

'Go ahead Brad,' said the Director.

'I just wanted to set the record straight on this,' the flyer cautioned. 'The practicality of shooting down a UAV depends on a whole host of factors. The VR-6 *moves*. Up to five hundred miles an hour. Getting an interceptor on to it in time won't be easy. And firing missiles and cannon over a densely populated area doesn't make a lot of sense. The Joint Chiefs are talking with the President right now to decide what rules of engagement would be acceptable. We might just end up killing as many people by intercepting it as by leaving it to reach its target. However, we have put up a CAP of F-15s and F-16s just in case. And the Army's Technical Escort Unit from the Chemical and Biological Defense Command at Aberdeen, Maryland is on stand-by to help the Bureau's own decontamination teams clean up after, if it *does* happen.'

He handed back to the Director.

'Thanks Brad. That brings me to the next phase. How we handle the anthrax release if we can't prevent it. The spores would most likely be sprayed in a line a few hundred feet above the ground upwind of the target, creating an invisible and lethal cloud that would drift onto the victims. In ideal conditions, just a few pounds of biological agent could infect tens of thousands of people this way. The spores, however, are easily damaged by heat and sunlight and can be dispersed by strong winds or rain. Met conditions are critical. The Iraqi terrorist commander is a military specialist, so he'll know all this. He'll know too that the weather forecast for the next few days is in his favour. Cool temperatures, light winds, no rain.

'Gentlemen and ladies. If the attack happens, we have to expect that thousands of people will die within a week. All available stocks of antibiotics will be flown from neighbouring states. We can reduce the death rate that way, but only partially. As you all know, pulmonary anthrax is usually fatal. In the days and months after the attack there'll be the risk of further infection from spores on the ground and in the air-con systems of public buildings. A massive decontamination programme will be required.

'The optimum time for any BW attack is around sundown, which is a perfect fit for the President's appearance in Philadelphia on Saturday. He's scheduled to speak at seven p.m. If it *is* the President the terrorists want to hit, Philadelphia's the best guess. If they just want to massacre a big crowd, there's no shortage of targets this weekend. There's a good half dozen major football games, both college and NFL. And tomorrow in Washington Pledge for the Family is holding a Sacred Assembly in the Mall.'

Burgess felt ice down his spine. It had crossed his mind, of course, what a fine target tens of thousands of praying Americans would make for a Godless fanatic, but to have it spelled out like this . . . He'd made Carole's day last evening by telling her that he *would* be in the Mall with her after all. Now he was going to have to tell her something very different.

'The President is fully engaged in all this, gentlemen and ladies,' the Director continued. 'I talked with him just over one hour ago. We discussed issuing a public warning. We talked about cancelling all open-air events. But in the end we agreed to delay that action in the hope we get new intelligence that narrows the focus. A nationwide announcement would cause real panic. The

Israelis can do it because their population's small and they've lived in a state of war for nearly fifty years. *And* they have good stocks of respirators. We don't. No way can we protect everybody who's at risk.

'So, no warnings at this stage. Just maximum preparedness of all relevant agencies. For now all we can do is hope. Hope for an intelligence breakthrough and pray this nightmare never becomes real.'

The meeting wrapped up and Burgess returned to the general office that he shared with a dozen others. The dark-haired nuclear specialist was clearing her desk for the weekend.

'Looks like biological's going to hit the jackpot,' she remarked as he passed her pen. 'No early night for *you*.'

'You sound almost *envious*, Jess,' he commented incredulously.

She had the grace to look a little embarrassed. 'Not exactly that, but this *is* what we train for, isn't it? So if you need any help, just let me know, okay?'

'I will.'

He sat back at his desk. On the work surface beside his PC he'd set up a small leather photo frame that contained a picture of Carole and the children. He picked it up. He didn't want them in Washington this weekend – because of the terrorist risk, however slight that might be in reality, and above all because their presence here would mean him having to face up to that collision between Carole and his career.

He put the picture down again. He had work to do chasing up US Customs who'd been tasked to search their records for any sign of a container from Ukraine or Cyprus in the past few days. Pointless, since the switched container would surely have originated from somewhere else, but a check that had to be made. He picked up the receiver, but hesitated. Then, instead of dialling customs, he rang home. No point in delaying the evil moment any longer.

'The Burgess residence.' Dean Junior's seven-year-old voice pretending to be grownup.

'Hiya kiddo!'

'Dad! You coming home tonight?'

'Not tonight, Dean. Didn't Mom tell you?'

'Sure, but I thought you might have changed your mind.'

'I'm sorry. It's just that I've got—'

'Too much work. I know.' The kid's voice was heavy with sarcasm. Not bad for a seven-year-old, thought Burgess. 'Mom's here.'

He heard the phone being passed across.

'Honey, you all right?' Suspicion in her voice. He'd told her not to expect him to ring that evening. 'We're still on for tomorrow, I hope.' They were coming on the train first thing. He'd arranged to meet them at Union Station.

'Carole . . .' He'd rung without first working out what to say.

'Oh boy . . . I can hear it in your voice. You're the pits Dean, you know that?'

'Carole listen to me. There's something going on that I can't tell you about.'

'What are you talking about, Dean?' Her voice had gone small, as if suspecting he was having an affair.

'You know what my work is here . . .'

'Well, no, honey,' she goaded. 'I don't. You never talk about it, remember?'

'Counter-terrorism. You know *that* much Carole,' he retorted.

'Oh sure. Two words. But that's all I know.'

Hell! He was handling this badly. Sliding straight into a spat.

'Carole listen! There's something going on right now

that's real serious. I don't want you to come to Washington tomorrow. It could be dangerous for you and for Patty and Dean. I want you and the kids to stay in Westchester tomorrow.'

There was a long silence at the other end.

'Carole?'

The line cut as she rang off.

'Shoot.'

He heard something being dropped on the floor outside his pen. He stood up to look over the partition and came face to face with Jess.

'Just wondered if you needed any help right now,' she explained awkwardly, picking up a ballpoint. 'Make some calls for you? I don't have anything fixed for tonight.'

'No thanks.' He could see from her blush that she'd overheard his call. 'I can manage.'

'Sure. See you Monday.' She handed him a business card. 'Home number's on the back. I'm around over the weekend if you change your mind or want company.'

She was as ready for it as a hooker, thought Burgess. If Carole didn't shape up he might even . . .

Oh no. That wasn't the way.

He dialled again. The number rang ten times before Carole answered.

'What?'

'Honey, listen to me, will you? This is serious.'

'Too damned right it's serious, Dean. You think I'm stupid? You think I'll believe anything you come out with? Any goddamn excuse you care to dream up? You've been trying everything to avoid the Pledge assembly. Well it won't work, Dean.'

'Carole, listen to me . . .'

'I've done with listening, Dean. And if you're not there at Union Station tomorrow morning, I'm done with you too.'

She rang off. When he dialled again, he found she'd left the phone off the hook.

19.45 hrs EST
Newark, NJ

The flight from Amman via Frankfurt had landed on time. The first few passengers were already emerging. Hanging back from the crowds waiting by the customs barrier in Newark airport's arrival terminal stood a tall, middle-aged man with sandy-grey hair. His large, Labrador eyes seemed like those of a man at his ease, but inside he was as tense as a coiled spring.

Naif Hamdan had been in the United States for two days now, just long enough to get over his jet lag and to recce the launch site and target zone. The man he'd come here to meet was the last piece in his jigsaw, a brother officer as dedicated as he was to the removal from power of Saddam Hussein. Major Sadoun's knowledge of the VR-6 reconnaissance drone was second to none. He'd been responsible for introducing the system into the Iraqi armed forces in 1990 after a stock had been bought from the Soviet Union.

At first he didn't recognise Sadoun without his moustache, shaved off for this mission like his own. A short, wiry man, he wore a smart grey suit and towed a small wheeled suitcase. Hamdan made a move towards him, just enough to catch his eye, then turned and headed for the car park, knowing Sadoun would follow.

They drove in the two cars which Hamdan had hired, heading south on the I-95 towards Baltimore. As each man looked about him at the mongrel mix of American faces in the cars and trucks they passed, his tension grew. In a few days' time, they knew, some of these people could be in the early stages of death.

22.45 hrs EST
Washington DC

By the time Dean Burgess returned to his small rented room in a red-brick lodging house in Alexandria his mind was pounding around like a carousel on speed. He'd tried continually to call Carole again, but the phone had stayed off the hook. He was pissed with her by now. She was behaving with selfish irresponsibility.

There'd been a couple of times during the evening when he'd taken from his pocket the card that Jess Bissett had given him. The address was Arlington, the same side of town as Alexandria. Serve Carole right if he had an affair with a woman who understood the importance to him of his work. Particularly one with a body that most men would give a lot to see unclothed.

But he knew damn well that any satisfaction he got from that would be short-lived. It would solve nothing. Particularly not the immediate problem of Carole being in Washington tomorrow with Patty and Dean, walking into unquantifiable danger like tens of thousands of other innocents. Their train from Manhattan was due in at twelve-thirty. Somehow he had to be there at Union Station to meet them – if only to make darned sure they caught the next train back to New York.

His room in Alexandria had a single bed, a wardrobe and a table and chair. A bathroom and shower out in the corridor was shared by one other room. For him it was a place to sleep, nothing else, its main advantage being its cheapness and its closeness to the Metro. And the landlady did good breakfast for her tenants. He'd chosen it as a temporary refuge until he moved the family down.

He sat on the edge of the bed and removed his shoes, wondering how the heck he was going to manage any sleep with his brain on such overdrive. He kept thinking of all the procedures set in motion by the Bureau that day, convinced they'd forgotten something. But then he always felt that way in the middle of a case.

He lay back on the covers, his eyes on the tasselled satin lampshade that hung from the corniced ceiling. Throughout the evening his mind had kept drifting back to Iraq and to the shock of seeing that Iraqi scientist convulsing on the ground outside the Haji plant. Fanaticism – that's what they were dealing with here. Men so ready to die for their cause they'd prepared themselves in advance. And some of those men must now be here in the USA. Two men at least. One to launch the drone, the other near the target with a command radio to trigger the release of the fatal pathogens.

Two men, one of whom would be Colonel Naif Hamdan.

And no one in America knew what Hamdan looked like. Not a soul. All they had was the hopelessly blurry photograph the British agent had got hold of in Cyprus.

Burgess sat up suddenly. Of course! *Sam Packer* had seen Hamdan in the flesh. And where was *he*? Four thousand miles away on the wrong side of the Atlantic.

Would SIS co-operate? They darned well *had* to.

He looked at his watch. Nearly midnight. Five o'clock Saturday morning in London.

'Sorry Mister Waddell,' he mouthed, digging into his briefcase for his contacts book. 'Breakfast's gonna be real early for you this morning.'

42

Saturday, 12 October
London

Sam woke early, pulled on jeans and a pullover, then walked briskly into Barnes village to buy a newspaper. He'd taken a decision overnight between bouts of sleep – to make an unannounced visit later that morning to his fellow Barnes resident Martin Kessler. He needed to know the truth about Baghdad.

Back in the flat he'd made himself some fresh coffee and had his nose buried in the *Telegraph* when the phone rang.

It was Waddell, ringing to say the Americans wanted him.

'They need your eyes. Think you might spot our Iraqi friend in a crowd. They've booked you on Concorde at ten-thirty from Terminal Four. Can you make it?'

Sam checked his watch again.

'Easily.'

'US Government's picking up the tab, thank God,' Waddell added dryly.

'Good for Uncle Sam. Do they have a fix on the switched container yet?'

'No. The Limassol police are holding the owner of the warehouse where the switch took place, but by late last night he hadn't talked. And, surprise, surprise, the customs files listing the containers stored in the warehouse have disappeared. Khalil's five million dollars have been spread nice and wide, that's obvious.'

'Can the warehouse owner be made to talk?'

'Probably. The police in Limassol have been known to dangle a suspect's head in a metal bucket which they beat with truncheons. Usually works.'

Sam rang off. A car was coming in half an hour. Just enough time to pack a flight bag.

Getting the truth out of Martin Kessler would have to wait.

Washington DC

Dean Burgess got back into FBI Headquarters shortly after eight a.m. He'd slept little after his call to Duncan Waddell's home in London. In the CTC he discovered that a fax had come in confirming Packer's flight details. Concorde would get him as far as JFK in New York, then a shuttle would bring him into Washington National at 11.59 a.m.

Burgess had been assigned a position in the SIOC from today. He checked into the Operations Center through the security doors and was immediately grabbed by Ive Stobal, who had a good three inches' height advantage over his own six-two.

'The Cypriots have just ID'd the container,' he told him in a voice that came up from his boots. 'It came from Haifa. Contents listed as a printing press. And the US port of entry is *Baltimore*.'

'My God! Do we have it?'

'We'll know in a couple of minutes. They're checking

the box number on the Automated Shipping Information System. The ship in question docked nine hours ago, but the port gates didn't open for truckers until seven. So there's a chance it's still there.'

'And we know exactly what's in the box?'

'Sure. The owner of the Limassol warehouse had his nuts squeezed and has talked. He's admitted doing a deal with a bunch of Ukrainians. He says a technical team flew in from Odessa and worked on the boxes overnight while the warehouse was unstaffed. The container that had arrived from Israel in transit for Baltimore was full of cartons of bad juice, not printing equipment. They took out those pallets and put them into the box from Ukraine bound for Haifa which had brought in the Hawk components. Then they welded launch rails into the empty Israeli box, assembled the drone and fitted it, then closed both boxes and replaced the customs seals. The next day they flew home again and let the shipping agent take over.'

'Neat. Real neat.'

They stepped over to a computer terminal where a dark-haired woman had a phone pressed to her ear. She turned her head and flashed a smile. It was Jess Bissett.

'I know she's nuclear, old buddy,' Stobal whispered, seeing Burgess's surprise. His mouth was right up close to Burgess's ear. 'But she was real hot to be in on this one. Called me up late last night.' He gave a *What could I do?* shrug.

Jess was typing notes straight into the system as she listened to customs. After a couple of minutes she was done.

'Okay. The good news is they found the container on the Baltimore computer. The bad news is it left Seagirt Terminal by truck at seven-thirty this morning.'

Their eyes turned to the digital clocks above the bank of monitors.

'Fuck! They've had nearly an hour already,' Stobal griped. 'Okay, we throw up a seventy-mile-radius road block centred on Baltimore port. You got the licence number of the truck?'

'Sure. And the names of the shipping company, the truckers, and the importers. It's all on the screen.'

'Good. Flash it to the FBI field offices and police in Maryland, Virginia and Pennsylvania.' Stobal took Burgess aside again. 'Dean, I want you to set up a video conference with the emergency services. This thing could happen a hell of a lot sooner than we thought. But make sure they don't give anything out to the media yet. Panic is one problem we can do without just now.'

Burgess concurred. But they both knew it wouldn't stay secret for long.

'Hey!' Stobal grinned, clapping him on the back. 'Why the long face? I've got a good feeling we're going to win this one!'

Burgess wished *he* had.

08.40 hrs
Lower Layton, Maryland

The small Maryland community of Lower Layton consisted of just three farmsteads, but the families that occupied them were expecting new neighbours. The plot of building land that old Matt Halcrow had put on the market a year ago had finally sold just four weeks earlier. Why anybody from Philadelphia would want to build a house in this isolated part of the tobacco and corn belt had mystified all concerned. It wasn't as if the place would have a view worth looking at this far from the creeks of the bay. However, the piece of land that presently supported an old timber barn for which Matt had no further use was to be turned into a country homestead for some well-off migrant from eastern Europe. The timber-frame house, Matt had told his two neighbours, was to be of a Canadian prefabricated type and would be delivered in sections inside a couple of huge shipping containers that were going to find it hard to get down the lanes.

The first of them had arrived a few minutes ago. Up at the Jones's place they'd seen it from the kitchen window as they finished their breakfast. A huge steel monster snapping a small branch from a dogwood as it passed. Then Mrs Whitman had caught a close-up of it lumbering past while she was picking up the mail from the box at the bottom of her drive. And finally old Matt Halcrow himself had phoned his friends and neighbours to apologise for the disturbance and to assure them there'd only be one more truck like it, and anyway not for another couple of days.

Twenty minutes later they saw the tractor half of the truck head back through the lanes at speed, its driver eager to get his wheels onto a highway again.

In an hour or so both Mrs Jones and Mrs Whitman would find some reason to take a drive past Matt's old barn – just to satisfy their curiosity. But they would see nothing, because the container had been tucked away inside the huge timber shed and the doors were closed.

09.20 hrs
John F. Kennedy Airport, New York

When Sam arrived in New York, the local time was an hour earlier than when he'd left London. As he stepped from the plane a steward pointed out a heavy-set man waiting for him in the pier to the terminal. Introducing himself as an agent from the FBI's New York field office he spirited Sam through immigration in minutes and delivered him to the gate for the 10.35 a.m. American Airlines shuttle to Washington National.

Sam found himself looking at faces, trying to visualise Hamdan. The Iraqi had changed his appearance once already by shaving off his moustache. Recognising him might not be easy, he realised.

10.30 hrs
The Executive Office Building, Washington DC

The President of the United States listened glumly to the intelligence summary being presented by the Director of the CIA. Also listening at the long table in the Old Executive Office Building next to the White House were the Secretaries of State and for Defense and the Chairman of the Joint Chiefs of Staff.

'The British still believe Colonel Hamdan is the primary instigator,' the CIA Director stated, 'with up to a dozen co-conspirators. They also still believe he's acting without the authority of Saddam Hussein. But they cannot be certain of that and nor can we, Mr President. In fact we're a lot less sure than the British are. One of our own sources has revealed that Hamdan *was* one of those military officers set up to act against Saddam back in June, although his name wasn't known to us at the time. Our source is surprised that Hamdan escaped the fate of the others when the coup plot collapsed. He thinks Hamdan may have agreed to work directly for Saddam as the price for being allowed to live.'

'Meaning?' the President prompted.

'Meaning that this *is* a plot by Saddam. An anthrax attack on the US being carried out under the guise of a maverick terrorist action. Something he can deny culpability for.'

'But you have no proof of this one way or the other.'

'No, sir.'

'May I put in a word here, Mr President?' The ever-polite but forceful Chairman of the Joint Chiefs leaned forward with his hand raised.

'Of course, General.'

'The attack that may be about to take place has to be characterised as a military one, not a terrorist action. The delivery vehicle for the anthrax is a military drone. The men directing it are, so far as we know, still serving members of the Iraqi army. If the attack happens, Mr President, this will be nothing less than an act of war, to which there's only one correct response. A military counter-strike that's extremely quick and extremely lethal.'

'Lethal to Saddam Hussein?'

'Ah . . . no. Unfortunately there's no guarantee of that,' the General conceded. 'Taking *him* out is going to be as hard as it's always been. But lethal against his armed forces, his military infrastructure – *and* his self-esteem. But we *have* to hit him, Mr President, both to show our national resolve and to deter further attacks on us.'

'Mmm. We all agree that?'

There was a murmuring of assent. Then the Secretary of State intervened.

'Before we get to that stage Mr President, I believe we should give Saddam a strong warning,' he stated firmly. 'Through his ambassador at the UN would be quickest. Spell it out to him in words of one syllable that we know about the drone and about Hamdan and that if this attack happens the consequences will be extremely serious.'

'That's wise,' the President nodded. 'We should do that right away.'

'Our own ambassador already has it in hand, Mr President. She's meeting the Iraqi in a half hour.'

'Good.'

There was a moment's pause while they all reflected on the enormity of what could be about to happen to their country.

'So, do I have your authority to prepare military contingency plans, Mr President?' the General checked eventually.

'You certainly do, General. Make us ready for the worst.'

11.00 hrs
The SIOC, FBI Headquarters

Dean Burgess took his seat in the conference room just as the Director arrived. Anxiety had taken hold in the SIOC. The investigation was making little progress.

'I have just spoken with the President,' the Director announced. 'He says if the attack takes place we'll be at war with Iraq. He's set a deadline for us of two p.m. If we're no nearer finding the missile by then, he'll cancel his engagement at the Vets stadium in Philadelphia and bring in the media. Ive, give us an update and for Christ's sake try to make it sound hopeful.'

'That won't be easy, sir. But we do have some new data on the container. The importation from Israel was arranged by a Philadelphia-registered printing company set up one month ago – specifically for this operation, we assume. The listed directors don't appear to exist. There are some indications of Russian-émigré organised crime being behind all this, but we don't have specific names yet.

'The container was picked up from the port by a regular trucking company this morning, but the driver was under instruction to rendezvous with the client at a truck drop-in on the I-95 just north of the Baltimore Beltway. A witness there saw him get into a white van. Soon after, the van drove north and another driver took over the truck. The original driver's not been seen again and his mobile phone's been switched off, so we can't get a trace on him.

'The traffic management cameras in the Baltimore area must have picked the truck up somewhere, but the tapes are still being checked. Unfortunately luck isn't with us today; the recordings for the *eastern* Beltway are incomplete because of a technical failure.'

Luck like that was all they needed, thought Burgess.

'We don't know whether the truck went north, south, east or west. And state police enquiries about disused barns or industrial sites large enough to conceal the container have yielded nothing so far.' Stobal turned to face his Director. 'In my opinion, sir, we should get the media involved right now. A public appeal for information could bring us the luck we need.'

'I agree,' said the Director immediately. 'Unfortunately the President doesn't. He's still hoping for a miracle. Two o'clock is what he said. No word to the media until then. For now, we're on our own, folks.'

12 noon

Burgess looked up from the computer screen, needing a break. He'd been scouring the registry files of known Russian-émigré criminals for some link that the automated search systems might have missed.

They called it ROC in the New York field office where he'd worked until a few weeks ago – Russian Organised Crime. An assembly of letters as deadly as LCN – La Cosa Nostra. Two acronyms spoken in the same respectful breath when crime-busting professionals talked of the transnational organisations they did battle with, organisations whose wealth and influence could turn them into a super-power if they ever managed to combine their criminal forces.

Dean Burgess wished he was back in New York, working on his sources in Brighton Beach. *Somebody* must know of a Russian-émigré organisation stupid enough to get mixed up in an act of war. Only a handful of the ROC gangs in the US operated on a grand scale like the Sicilian 'families' and the FBI had chopped the head off one of those in 1995 with the arrest of Vyacheslav Ivankov. Over two hundred of the thousands of Mafiya gangs in the former Soviet Union had operations in the USA however, but most used freelance hoodlums here instead of creating permanent gangs. It was their *lack* of a 'mob' structure that had made them so hard to corral.

He checked the wall clock. Ten after twelve. In twenty minutes Carole would step off the Amtrak from New York with Dean and Patty, expecting him to be there at Union Station. And he wouldn't be. It was impossible to leave the SIOC for the half hour to an hour it would take.

But hell! She'd surely understand why he'd let her down. When it all came out what he'd been involved in, no way was she going to finish with him like she'd threatened. They shouldn't be here at all, that was the trouble. Back home in the safety of Westchester was where he wanted them. Still, he told himself, if they'd been planning a day in Philadelphia he'd be worried a heck of a lot more.

He concentrated on the screen again. Then the phone rang. Security down at the E Street visitors' entrance, telling him Sam Packer had arrived. He asked for a messenger to bring him up to the fifth floor so he could meet him in the elevator lobby. Stobal had given enthusiastic approval to Burgess's overnight initiative, and had arranged a pass for the Englishman to enter the secure spaces of the SIOC.

Sam followed the wiry black security guard out of the elevator. The building, he noted, had that smell common to all American public buildings and motels. A dead, artificial smell, something to do with the air conditioning or with the stuff they used to clean the carpets.

'Hi! Good to see you!' Burgess was marching towards him along the blue carpeted corridor with his hand outstretched and an attempt at a smile. Sam had forgotten how tall he was. 'Flight okay?'

'Wouldn't dare say anything else after the Concorde treatment,' Sam grinned.

'Good. Can't tell you how glad we are to see you.'

He led the way into the SIOC.

'Coffee?' Burgess checked, once they were through the security hatches. 'Or maybe something to eat?'

'Coffee's fine.'

'Cream and sugar?'

'Black, thanks.'

As Burgess tapped menu codes into a drinks dispenser, Sam took in the banks of screens in the operations centre and the couple of dozen heads bent over them. It was like the citadel of a warship, and he felt instantly at home.

Burgess took him into a side room to brief him.

'Top guess is Philadelphia. The president's date at the Vets stadium tonight has been in the public domain for a couple of weeks at least.'

He spelled out what they knew about the container and the fact that it hadn't yet been found.

'Surely the President's going to cancel his rally?' Sam asserted.

'If we don't have that container by mid-afternoon, yes he will. Then we're back to guessing again. First question is will Colonel Hamdan know that the Philadelphia meeting's been terminated?'

'Yes,' Sam affirmed immediately. 'He'll find out. This man's thorough.'

'Our opinion also. So, next guess . . . Will he go for an alternative target?'

'Again, yes. He won't hang around.' Sam narrowed his eyes. 'What's going on in Washington today? I saw crowds converging on the Mall.'

'Pledge for the Family. A right-wing religious outfit. Thousands of born-again men committing themselves to spending more time with their kids,' Burgess explained uncomfortably.

Sam whistled. 'That's a tempting target,' he stated. 'Particularly if Hamdan wants to create a frenzy of hatred against Saddam Hussein.'

For a while Burgess just stared at him.

‘I sure as hell wish you hadn’t said that,’ he murmured eventually.

13.20 hrs
Lower Layton

The barn smelled of decayed animal excrement. In one corner lay the camping mats and sleeping bags the two Iraqis had used during the night, although sleep hadn’t come easily to either of them. A cardboard carton still held most of the food Hamdan had bought yesterday but which neither of them had had much stomach for.

They’d both felt greatly relieved at the arrival of the container. Relieved and anxious to get it over with, because the sudden appearance of the huge box in this gossipy corner of nowhere land was tantamount to putting a match to a beacon.

They’d begun work soon after the taciturn Russian-born trailer driver had left, checking first through a split in the barn’s walls that nobody was near enough to hear the noises they would soon be making. They’d opened the container doors with trepidation, half expecting it to contain rotting fruit juice or printing equipment. Seeing the dull grey paint of the drone’s nose cone, however, they’d smiled at one another and solemnly clashed their fists together in the way they’d done over the candle flame in Hamdan’s flat in Baghdad all those weeks ago.

There’d been checks to be made. They’d started up a small petrol-powered generator to produce the current needed for the VR-6 control system. First, Sadoun had tested the firing and guidance circuitry, programming in co-ordinates for the waypoints and for the target itself which Hamdan had acquired through the use of a handheld GPS plotter. Then Hamdan had walked a couple of hundred metres to a copse of poplars and tried out the disguised VHF transmitter that he would use in a few hours' time to vector the drone's final moments and to trigger the warhead's electro-magnetic shutters.

They'd discovered a glitch in the aileron controls, which Sadoun traced to a loose wire. Then, satisfied with the drone itself, they'd called each other up on their rented cell phones to check they could communicate.

Now they were ready for the final part of the preparation. They stood back from the rust-streaked container and, without looking each other in the eye, donned respirators, easing the rubber over their chins and sucking in air to check the seals were tight against their smoothly shaven skin.

Hamdan entered the container first, ducking under the stubby delta wings of the drone to reach the far end. There, secured against the container wall by an elastic strap, was a dustbin-sized insulated drum. Remarkably, when they lifted the thick polystyrene lid they found the inside still cool from the ice-packs that had been crammed into it in Cyprus. Reaching in with gloved hands Hamdan extracted a metal canister the size of a large vacuum flask. Weighing five kilos and wrapped in transparent polythene, the cylinder contained enough anthrax spores to wipe out the population of a small town.

First, Hamdan checked visually that there'd been no leak from the warhead's seals. Then, satisfied it was intact, he carried it forward to the front of the drone and cut away the plastic wrapping. Between them they installed it into the drone's empty camera bay.

Hamdan stepped down onto the floor of the barn to let Sadoun complete the wiring.

Finally, when the Major was satisfied, he joined Hamdan on the ground and removed his mask.

'It is done,' he whispered. 'The weapon is ready for firing, Colonel.'

14.55 hrs
FBI Headquarters

Dean Burgess watched Ive Stobal's heavily jowled face grow steadily longer as each minute passed with no breakthrough in the hunt for the container. Highway video cameras had detected the truck heading south from Baltimore, then lost it after it turned onto some smaller route. At this stage of the game they badly needed the help of the public – and needed it right now.

The President had cancelled his Philadelphia rally nearly an hour ago and was due to go live on TV and radio in a couple of minutes.

Sam had been assigned a spare terminal in the SIOC and had been reading computer files on Russian-émigré crime in the faint hope he might spot some link with Dima Grimov that Burgess had missed. The Odessa connection dated back to the seventies, Burgess had told him, when a Russian crook named Balagula had migrated from there to Brooklyn. He'd quickly grown rich on gasoline tax evasion and fraud, and spread his tentacles abroad to South Africa and Israel.

Most of the ROC criminals with FBI files had the ruthlessness to be acting for the Voroninskaya gang in America, but discovering which were actually doing so would take up more time than they had. Burgess was right. What they needed now was the intelligence of the streets – the eyes and ears of Joe Public.

Burgess nudged him. The President's face filled the monitors on the video wall. He was beginning his address to the nation.

'My fellow Americans . . .'

Never seen him so grim, thought Sam. The familiar face looked in shock, the eyes with none of their usual twinkle.

The country faced a grave threat, he announced solemnly. A terrorist attack with a biological weapon that could make the bomb in Oklahoma City look like a side-show. He was sparse on detail. No names given out, no nationalities identified. A cautious President holding back on public accusations until certain of who to blame and how to retaliate.

'Until this threat has passed, my security advisers have told me it's prudent if I cancel all my public appearances. My apologies therefore to the people of Philadelphia. We shall not be able to meet at the Vets stadium tonight as scheduled. They are also advising that all other open-air gatherings in Pennsylvania, Maryland and Virginia planned for today and tomorrow should be cancelled. Wherever possible people should remain indoors in their own homes where they will be perfectly safe.'

Up to a point, thought Sam. If the stuff were to get into the air-conditioning ducts of an apartment block . . .

The President kept it brief and to the point, winding up with a promise to keep the nation informed and with a plea for there to be no panic.

'Let me assure you, this is a situation that our national security agencies are trained to handle. Please co-operate with them to the full. With your help we can put an end to this threat before any harm is done.'

'Hope he fools some of them,' Burgess muttered, stroking his moustache.

The output of all the main TV networks had combined for the broadcast. Now all channels switched to a briefing room at the Pentagon.

'Uh-oh!' Burgess exclaimed. 'The guys in the green uniforms are pulling rank over us Big Bad Feds.' He shook his head. 'Means the President plans to go to war.'

The screen filled with a picture of a container truck, then dissolved to a map of the Baltimore/Washington area with an appeal for information about any similar vehicles that might have been seen off the main highways.

'Hey, Dean!'

Jess Bissett called him over. Burgess beckoned Sam to go with him.

'Jess, Sam. Sam, Jess.'

'Hi,' Jess smiled just for an instant. 'Dean, a highway patrol on Route Three, six miles south-west of the junction with ninety-seven, has just picked something up at a roadside eatery. They spoke with a trucker who saw a forty-foot container trailer turning off Route Three a couple of miles north of some place called Clifdene. Said it surprised him because the lane it turned into wasn't much wider than a farm track. They're sending six cars to box the area.'

'Great!' Burgess spun back to his own terminal to print off a map covering a five-mile radius from Clifdene.

'First time in Washington?' Jess asked Sam.

'No. But first time inside this place.'

She smiled and swung back to face her screen. 'Catch up with you later, okay?'

Sam joined Burgess by the laser printer, watching the map come off.

'Will you leave it to the state police to check this out?' he asked.

'Nope. There'll be a couple of special agents from the Washington field office heading out there right now,' he explained. 'Sure as hell hope this is the one.'

His eyes were back on the TV screens. Two of the channels had gone live to cameras at the Pledge for the Family rally in the Mall less than half a mile from where they stood.

Burgess felt strangely relieved. The rally was sure to be terminated now. Carole and the kids would soon be on their way home to safety.

Lower Layton

In the first of the farmsteads in the village of Lower Layton, Mrs Betsy Jones sat on the back veranda reading a biography of Eleanor Roosevelt while her husband took a nap. Neither of them listened to the radio much and they only watched TV in the evenings. The world could be about to end for all they knew and they'd never hear about it until it happened.

A quarter of a mile further down the lane the Whitman house was deserted, the couple having taken their kids for an afternoon in the powerboat they kept in a Chesapeake Bay creek just south of Annapolis. On this ordinary weekend day in the early fall, they'd gone fishing.

And in the house a hundred yards from the old barn that had been sold to the businessman from Philadelphia, old Matt Halcrow was bent over his accounts for the Inland Revenue Service, listening to a Sinatra CD his daughter had bought him for his birthday a couple of months ago.

Betsy Jones heard the scrunch of tyres on the gravel drive at the front of the white clapboard house and wondered who the heck that could be, coming a-calling.

She got up from the wicker easy chair and walked in through the lounge.

'Oh my!'

A patrol car was in the drive, its red light going.

'Oh my,' she repeated, clutching her chest. Something terrible must've happened to one of their grownup children.

She opened the front door. The fact that the police officer who faced her was a woman only served to heighten her fears.

FBI Headquarters

Dean Burgess stood in front of the TV monitors unable to believe his eyes. The networks were all focusing on the Pledge rally down in the Mall now. Because instead of dispersing as they'd been requested to do by their President and by the DC Police Department, the thirty thousand crowd stood calmly facing the podium set up in front of the Washington Monument, listening to their leaders praying for the Lord to stay the hand of the evil-doers.

'Get the fuck outta there!' Burgess's words came out as a strangled cry.

Startled at the emotion in the outburst, Sam guessed there was a personal element to Burgess's plea.

'What is it?' he asked.

'Carole – my wife – she's in there somewhere,' Burgess confided. 'Kids too.'

'Christ!'

Sam stared at the screens, the cameras panning wide now to reveal the size of the crowd. At its edges, over by the Smithsonian on the far side and up towards the steps of the Capitol, faint hearts were breaking away, some walking – mothers and fathers urging kids to hurry – others breaking into a run that was only just this side of panic. Maybe the rally leaders were right, thought Sam. Tell that lot to hurry on home and there'd be mayhem, with kids being trampled underfoot.

The cameras began to pick out faces. A crying child. A stressed and anxious father, a young, fair-haired mother biting her lip and glancing fearfully at the sky. Quick camera cuts, a new face every two seconds. Just time to register one expression before moving to the next. Two teenagers laughing, because – well, why not? Older faces, eyes closed in prayer.

And a man in dark glasses and a Kangol cap holding a radio to his ear.

'Jesus Christ!' Sam jabbed a finger at the screen.

'What did you see?'

'Are you taping this?'

'Sure.'

'Good. Because if I'm not mistaken I've just seen Colonel Naif Hamdan!'

43

Lower Layton

The launch rails were extended, the barn doors flung wide and Sadoun's anxiety had reached a point close to panic. Operating in the heart of enemy territory had never played a part in his previous military experience.

The generator worried him most. Easily heard. Every moment that passed increased the risk of some local coming round the corner for a look-see. If it happened he would be ready, but far from willing. Hamdan had left him a long sharp knife.

Sadoun knew nothing about the President's broadcast. Nothing of the police net that was closing in on him. Even if he'd had a radio or TV in the barn with him he would not have understood, because he spoke no English.

He checked the dials on the control panel again to ensure no faults had developed in the VR-6. The firing of the drone itself was automatic. All he had to do was trigger a two-minute countdown then make good his escape in the small Chevrolet parked behind the barn, out of sight.

The weather here was cool and overcast. If it was the same in Washington seventy kilometres away there'd be no need for them to wait for dusk for the attack. In the cool air the anthrax pathogens would settle in an even blanket, untroubled by upward air currents. Fire the drone and be done with it, escape while they still could – that's what he wanted. He was strongly tempted to call Hamdan on the cell-phone and tell him so. His hands were hovering over the buttons when the device startled him by ringing.

'Yes?'

'We must do it now!' Hamdan's voice in a coarse whisper. 'They know about us.'

'Damnation!'

Hamdan sounded agitated, out of breath as if from running. 'Start the countdown now. I am nearly in place.'

'I'm doing it,' Sadoun snapped back, flicking the switches for the start sequence.

'Firing in two minutes. God be with us.'

Washington DC

Dean Burgess was the fitter of the two. Sprinting down 9th Street he pulled slightly ahead of Sam. But as they passed the Natural History Museum they were forced to slow by the tide of bodies moving out from the Mall towards the Federal Triangle and Archives/Navy Memorial subway stations.

No panic among these people, just a determination to get the hell out of there.

Sam and Burgess crossed tree-lined Madison Drive. Once on the grass they slowed to a walk. The Washington Monument was half a mile to their right. A mass of bodies between here and there, most listening attentively to the evangelising from the platform, relayed on rock concert speakers.

Burgess pushed through the throng almost forgetting

Sam was with him. There was one face he was looking for and one face only: the pert, boyish looks that belonged to his wife. Carole was tall for a woman. Should make it easier to see her. But how the heck would he find *anybody* in this crush?

'Dean,' Sam panted. 'Stop a minute.'

Burgess swung round, a wild look in his eyes. He wore an earpiece connected to a communications set in the inside pocket of his light-grey jacket. Half his mind was listening to the feedback from the agents and police dispatched into this crowd to organise its dispersal.

'Hamdan's here because the Hawk needs terminal guidance, right?' snapped Sam. 'A radio signal to release the anthrax.'

'We guess, yes.'

'But unless he's suicidal, standing right here among the people he's trying to kill won't be his plan.'

'But the TV camera caught him with the Smithsonian behind him,' Burgess pointed out. They'd replayed the tape before leaving the SIOC.

'I know. But he won't be there when the missile comes over. He'll be well upwind of this place. Standing high up where he can see the thing coming.'

They turned as one towards the Capitol.

'Well,' Burgess shrugged, 'I guess that's the only hill in town.'

'C'mon!'

Lower Layton

Mrs Betsy Jones sat in the back of the patrol car pointing past the driver's ear as he motored as fast as he dared down the lane that ran through the spread-out hamlet.

'Two more bends, then we're at Matt's old barn,' she croaked, scared but excited by the drama. Above all she was relieved beyond measure that the arrival of the police had not meant bad news about her children.

Suddenly the driver hit the brake and swerved onto the verge. A small blue Chevvy had careered round the corner towards them.

'Hey up . . . who's that ma'am?' the woman officer asked, her eyes tracking the darkhaired driver as the economy car zipped past them.

'I've no idea. Certainly not anyone local.'

'Okay . . .' The officer grabbed the microphone and called in the car's description. 'There's a patrol back on the highway should pick that one up,' she explained when she'd finished.

The police driver swung back onto the carriageway and rounded the second bend.

'This it?' he asked, pointing at the barn.

'It sure is. Guess they must have put the trailer inside. There's plenty room for it. It's a big barn. Well, you can see . . .'

The patrol car stopped on the stony track that led up to it. Both officers got out, unbuttoning their pistol holsters and drawing their weapons.

'Stay in the car ma'am,' the woman officer ordered as Betsy made to follow.

'Hear something?' the driver asked.

'Sure do,' the woman replied. 'Pump or generator.'

Suddenly there was a roar like an earthquake. White smoke exploded from the barn door, then a long, grey dart burst into the air, streaking up into the sky, streaming fire.

'My God!' the woman officer screamed, pointlessly levelling her pistol at it.

The SIOC,
FBI Headquarters

Ive Stobal hunched over the central command console, his hand on the microphone that would link him live to the police, fire and public health departments.

The alert from the patrol in Lower Layton had come in just seconds ahead of a Pentagon report that the missile launch had been detected by a Navy E-2C Hawkeye and a pair of F-16 interceptors were being vectored onto its flight path. The Hawk was heading towards Washington.

'It's DC, folks.' Stobal's deep voice was deceptively calm as he spoke into the microphone. 'I guess the missile's heading for the Mall. For God's sake get those people outta there! And get all public buildings in downtown Washington to turn off their ventilation fans. And the subway – no more trains to enter the central area.'

Jess Bissett put down the phone from the Maryland state police. They'd just arrested a very frightened Arab in a small blue car. She turned to see how Burgess was getting on and noticed for the first time that his chair was empty.

She guessed where he'd gone. She knew more about his problems with Carole than he realised.

'Dean, you asshole! What're you *doing*?' she mouthed.

Sam's lungs burned as they pounded towards the Capitol. No way of knowing whether the Hill was where they needed to be, but where else could they go? Burgess was ahead again, one hand pressing the communications insert more firmly into his ear.

They'd reached the reflecting pool. Three hundred more lung-bursting yards to the Capitol steps. They were well beyond the crowds attending the Pledge rally now.

The steps looked empty as far as he could see. Burgess had radioed ahead for the Police Department to send officers out from the Capitol to check for a tall man carrying a radio.

At the foot of the steps, Burgess stopped and pressed the flat of his hand against his ear as a new message came in.

'F-16 pilot has the Hawk on radar but can't get missile lock,' he told Sam between gasps for breath. 'The drone's too small. Too close to the ground.'

Sam's shins thrummed with pain from the running. Both of them were out of breath.

'Jeez!' Burgess gasped. 'The pilot says the drone's just two minutes away.'

'Christ! Come on then!' Sam thundered on up the steps. When they reached the top an overweight black police officer waddled over, waving them back.

Burgess whipped out his FBI badge. 'Seen a big guy with a radio?' he panted desperately.

'None that matches the description that come over from headquarters,' the police officer drawled. 'We done cleared the place anyways.'

Sam spun round. The two stone staircases leading down from the Capitol were indeed empty, as was the Capitol terrace itself. His heart sank. Hamdan was going to win.

Burgess looked down at the Mall stretching away to the west; tens of thousands of people still gathered by the Washington Monument a mile away. He felt paralysed. Among that crowd was his own family. Carole was as stubborn as hell. No way was a terrorist going to stand between her and a pray-in that might yet get her husband back on track.

Suddenly Sam felt a cool breeze on his face, whistling up from the south, like a softly whispered message.

'This way,' he snapped, desperately pointing along the terrace. 'Hamdan's going to be upwind if he's here at all.'

They began running again, Sam in front now. A police barrier blocked the terrace, but they vaulted it.

'Missile's one mile east of the Capitol,' Burgess shouted, monitoring his radio.

As they reached the end of the terrace they both looked up at the sky to their left. One mile was ten seconds, Sam calculated.

'Shit!'

No sign of Hamdan here. He'd guessed wrong. The chance to avert a disaster was slipping from their hands. He stared across at the tall buildings on the south side of the Mall.

'Can people get up on top of those?'

'I don't know. I'm new in town.'

Too late anyway. Far too late. He put a hand on the stone balustrade to support himself, eyes scanning the sky for the small dot that would mean death for thousands.

Suddenly his eye was caught by a movement on the grass below them. A man was lying there. Grubby jeans; long, unkempt hair. Looked like a tramp, except that the big brown eyes were so steady, so concentrated in their scrutiny of the sky. And he was holding a radio. A radio with no sound coming from it . . .

'Dean!' Sam croaked, pointing. 'Down there!'

Burgess pulled out his pistol.

'It's him?' he hissed. 'You're sure?'

Sam froze. How could he be?

Suddenly the man sat up straight, the radio held out in front of him. A small grey dart appeared to their left and crossed above the trees. The man's chin jutted forward in an involuntary spasm of last-minute nerves.

'Hamdan!' Sam bellowed. The man flinched and half turned.

Burgess fired. Then fired again. In their regular range

training sessions agents were taught to kill. The bullets exploded the man's head, blowing off the wig of rats' tails that had covered his grey hair.

'Jesus!' Sam gasped.

He looked away, looked down the Mall. The Hawk flew straight and true, passing half a mile south of the crowd round the Monument. Then, as it reached the Potomac River, it made a slow turn left, followed a few seconds later by the F-16 fighter that was tailing it.

'Oh my God!' Burgess croaked.

The crowd in the Mall had seen the drone too. Cries of panic rolled towards the Capitol like a mist, a swelling ululation of terror as men, women and children fought to get away from the invisible cloud of pathogens they believed the drone had dumped on them. At its edges the crowd began to bleed into the neighbouring streets.

Burgess was transfixed. Somewhere in that mob down there were the three people who mattered more to him than anything else in the world. Much, much more than anything else. How the heck had he ever doubted it?

He pulled himself together. He had to report in. He bent his head to the microphone in his lapel and told SIOC what he'd done.

Sam ran back to the steps and down to the lawns. He needed to be certain. By the time he reached the slumped body two police officers were turning it face up, guns in their hands. Despite the mess the bullets had made, now that the ludicrous wig was gone the sand-blasted face of Naif Hamdan was unmistakable. Sam looked down at the man responsible for so much misery, unsure still whether he'd won or lost.

'You see him press anything on that radio?' Burgess asked, running up to Sam. 'No,' Sam answered, 'but that doesn't mean he didn't.'

The radio lying on the ground was spattered with blood – a compact black VHF receiver with a long aerial and preset tuning buttons that had a very different function from switching music channels.

'Maybe the technical guys'll be able to work out whether or not he transmitted,' Burgess muttered, his mind locked onto procedural matters to prevent it thinking of what could be happening a mile down the Mall.

They turned away and walked numbly for a few paces, unsure what to do next. The noise of the panicking crowd was drowned now by a cacophony of sirens.

'They're sending in the clean-up teams,' Burgess mouthed, repeating what he'd heard on his earpiece. His face crumpled.

Lines of military trucks appeared on Pennsylvania Avenue, disgorging soldiers dressed in protective suits and masks. Helicopters clattered overhead. An FBI scene-of-crime team from the Washington Field Office came running from behind the Capitol, carrying silver boxes of equipment. All wore gloves and respirators. They opened one of the boxes and handed masks to Burgess, Sam and to the two police officers.

'Put 'em on, quick!' said a muffled voice from behind one of them.

Burgess donned his, then quickly briefed the field office men on what had happened. He wanted to be away from here. He asked for the FBI car to drive them back to the Hoover Building.

'Jesus God!' he hissed as they walked towards it. 'This is a holocaust.' Then he touched a hand to his ear. 'Hold on.' He put out a hand to stop Sam. 'F-16 pilot saw no release of agent.' His voice rose in pitch. 'Says his FLIR should have picked it up if there had been any release. What the heck's a FLIR?'

'Forward-Looking Infra-Red,' Sam explained. 'Thermal imager. I imagine the anthrax spores would be a different temperature from the surrounding air, making them visible.'

They turned to one another.

'Does that mean we did it?' Burgess coughed.

'It's beginning to look that way,' Sam grinned.

'Hold on, there's more,' Burgess added. 'I don't believe this. The Hawk impacted in the grounds of the Pentagon when its fuel ran out. An army biological team landed by helicopter a couple of minutes later. They think the warhead's intact.'

The two men gripped each other by the arms.

'Hey! You beat the bastard!' Sam howled, whipping off his mask.

'Me? It was you that—'

'But you shot the guy,' Sam insisted.

'Asshole! You're going all British on me again.'

Five minutes later the FBI support car dropped them outside the entrance to the J. Edgar Hoover Building on Pennsylvania Avenue. As they walked towards the door Sam heard a stifled gulp from the man at his side and turned to see him fling his arms round a tall, dark-haired woman who reminded him of that stunner in *A Fish Called Wanda* whose name he could never remember. Her face was grubby with tears.

A girl and a boy, both looking to be less than ten years of age, clung to the legs of their parents.

44

Sunday, 13 October
London

Sam's departure from the United States had been as unheralded as his arrival there, but carried out with greater modesty. MI6 was funding his fare home and they'd booked him on a 747 in economy.

In Washington, after the US Army Technical Unit confirmed incontrovertibly that anthrax spores had *not* been released from the crashed VR-6 Hawk, Dean Burgess had wanted to lionise Sam for the part he'd played in averting a catastrophe. But Sam would have none of it. British he was and British was the way he was going to behave. The Intelligence Service he worked for was secret, he told them, like his involvement with it.

He arrived back in London at six a.m. after an unexpectedly good sleep in the crowded rear of the jumbo. His body clock had remained on British Summer Time since leaving England fewer than twenty-four hours earlier.

Duncan Waddell met him at Heathrow airport and personally drove him home, oozing satisfaction at the way things had turned out.

'Saddam Hussein's done an interview on CNN,' Waddell told him.

'*What?*'

'Denying all knowledge of the anthrax plot and branding Hamdan and his friends as traitors. Mowbray's picked up rumours in Amman that Saddam's arrested another two hundred army officers.'

'God! Night of the long knives.'

'Talking of which, you'll be interested to know that your old friend Viktor Rybkin has been taken out of circulation,' he confided dryly. 'The SBU assure us he'll never be seen again. We didn't ask for specifics, but word has it his body had seventeen holes in it when they dumped it in some swamp on the outskirts of Odessa.'

'Couldn't have happened to a nicer bloke.'

'And one other thing. And this may really surprise you.'

'What?'

'Oksana Koslova has said no to our visa offer.'

'Good Lord!'

'She told Figgis she thought she was safe enough in Kiev now and feared that if she did come to England, all her illusions would be shattered. In Ukraine at least she *has* none. It's what she said, Sam, honest!'

Sam smiled. He could imagine her saying it. He guessed too that a good few of those illusions would have been centred on him.

'There *is* something still troubling me about all this, Duncan,' Sam ventured. He knew what Waddell's reaction would be but felt compelled to raise it again.

'What's that?'

'Baghdad. The question of how Chrissie knew that I was on a mission there. It had to have been Martin Kessler who told her.'

Waddell hunched over the wheel as if troubled by an ulcer. 'Forget it Sam,' he cautioned. 'It's history, okay?'

He dropped Sam in the side street outside the mansion block by the river in Barnes, promising to ring him to fix lunch so they could have a proper chat about things.

Sam climbed the stairs to his flat and closed the door behind him, trying to think of it as an act of symbolism, a final back-turning on the recent past. But it didn't work, because he *wasn't* finished with the past and wouldn't be until the Kessler issue was resolved. There was an injustice here, one he had to deal with personally.

He removed his clothes, which felt sweatily uncomfortable after being in them for twenty-four hours. He looked down at his shins and noted that the scars were healing well at last. Then he took a shower, dried himself and shaved.

London was grey and rainy that morning. He padded to the kitchen, enjoying the liberating feel of his own nakedness, made some fresh coffee and some toast, then dressed in cord trousers and a shirt and pullover.

He *did* feel differently today. And he instantly knew why. For the first time in a long time Chrissie was no longer with him. Her aura which had lingered in the flat after their breakup in the summer had finally been exorcised. It felt as if he'd got his life back.

The answerphone had been bleeping since he got in and he could no longer ignore it. The message was from Tom, telling him he bloody well *had* to fetch the boat back to the Hamble, because *he* hadn't the time or the money to go to Guernsey to get her.

Yes. He would fetch the boat. Tomorrow maybe. First there was Martin Kessler to be dealt with.

Duncan Waddell's insistence that he consign the 'who told who' issue to history had convinced him that SIS must have accepted Kessler's suggestion that it was Sam himself who'd told Chrissie about going to Baghdad. Apart from any other considerations, *that* record had to be straightened.

It was nine a.m. by now. He pulled on a light Goretex jacket, then went downstairs to the street. The Sunday morning traffic was sporadic. He waited for a bus to pass, then crossed the main road to the towpath and began to walk along the bank downstream.

Five minutes later he turned away from the river, heading into the maze of leafy streets that made up the suburb of Barnes. He walked for a couple of hundred yards. Most of the cars that lined the kerbs had newish registrations. A grubby builder's van spoiled the otherwise pristine line of Audis, BMWs and Golfs.

He stopped outside a semi-detached, cream-stuccoed house which had a paved front garden and a white picket fence.

The home of Martin and the late Christine Kessler.

He'd never stood here before. No-go territory in his relationship with Chrissie. He felt like a trespasser.

He looked up at the windows of the main bedroom, still baffled by the bizarre relationship that had been conducted behind its lace curtains. A relationship of infinite deception.

A woman with a small grey dog emerged from the neighbouring house and stared at him with the hostility due a burglar. Sam stepped smartly up to the porch and rang the bell.

It was only a few seconds before Kessler opened the door. He was dressed in a blue track-suit and clean white trainers. He looked pale and drawn, and extremely startled.

'Sam! What d'you want? I can't see you here.'

He swung the door shut, as if repelling a duster salesman.

'Oh yes you can!'

Sam shouldered forward to prevent the latch clicking. He shoved hard, knocking Kessler aside.

'How *dare* you!' Kessler protested. 'This is private. My *home*.'

'Exactly. And we're neighbours. So I thought it time for a chat.'

The small entrance hall of the 1930s abode had a polished woodblock floor and smelled of lavender wax. Against one wall stood an oak side table with a silver bowl on it of the type in which people once left visiting cards.

Above it hung an oil painting.

The picture took Sam's breath away. It was a life-size portrait. The likeness was remarkable. He felt caught in a time warp as the vortex of Chrissie's cool grey eyes drew him in with the same look they'd had in life, a look of restless longing, of always wanting more from life than she'd already squeezed out.

He turned away. The picture's image was too strong for him.

'The artist was American. Quite in demand,' Kessler said, warily. As he spoke he circled round Sam and quickly pulled shut the door to the living room. 'Chrissie sat for him when we were stationed in Washington.' He pulled himself up straight. 'Now look. This is most improper your being here. You're as good as trespassing.'

'Yes,' said Sam, 'but I've got reason to.'

He shot a quick glance round the small entrance hall. Tucked to one side beside the front door was a large black suitcase.

'Going somewhere?' he demanded.

'A few days' break, that's all,' Kessler explained uncomfortably. 'A visit to some friends. It's been a hell of a shock, Chrissie's death. Only just catching up with me. Now look. I'm very busy. Go away before I call the police.'

'No.' Sam folded his arms. 'Aren't you going to ask me why I'm here?'

'What the hell does that mean? Look, you can't just come barging in. If you don't get the hell out of my house right now, I'll . . . I'll make damned sure you never work for SIS again.'

Sam fixed him with a look that would ignite paper.

'You had it done in Washington you said.' He pointed at the portrait of Chrissie. 'By an artist in demand. A fashionable artist. Expensive no doubt. Yes, it must have been a truly fascinating post, Washington. Chock-a-block with interesting people. People with money. Terrific for networking. For building contacts – contacts with men like Viktor Rybkin.'

Kessler blanched.

'Are you implying something?'

'Yes.'

Kessler remained in the living room doorway, one hand gripping each side of its frame.

'What are you hiding in there?' Sam snapped.

'Nothing.'

Sam moved towards him. 'In that case you won't mind showing me.'

'I certainly would mind. Who the hell do you think you are? Get out of here! This is my property.'

'And this is my *life* you've been buggering about with!' Sam's anger was erupting like magma. He grabbed Kessler's shoulders and tried to shove him aside, but the man clung to the door frame like an octopus.

'You bloody *will* move, you bastard,' Sam raged, bringing his knee up sharply.

Kessler buckled forward, air howling from his throat, hands hovering over his groin. Sam elbowed past him and pushed open the door.

It was in here, he told himself. He felt it. In this room somewhere. The proof he needed.

The furniture was antique Victorian, neat and attractive. Chrissie's taste. But the place was in chaos. On the floor lay a roll of plastic bubble wrap, sheets of brown paper, some string and sealing tape. Leaning against a glass-fronted cabinet of fine blue and white china were several hardwood frames with canvas stretched over them. Oil paintings.

Sam picked the first one up and turned it round. It was good. Very good. Reminded him of Hockney. He read the signature. God, it *was* a Hockney.

He heard movement behind him and spun on his heel. Kessler was bearing down on him, wielding a large crystal vase. He aimed a swinging blow, but Sam deflected it with his forearm. He staggered back, smarting from the pain.

'Fuck you, Kessler!' he spat, searching frantically for a weapon for himself. 'Is this what you spent all your payoffs on? Bloody oil paintings?'

The spymaster was advancing on him again, murder in his eyes this time and the vase raised above his head. Sam grabbed the Hockney as a shield.

'Careful Martin. Wouldn't want to wreck your investment, would you now?' He saw Kessler falter.

He couldn't believe this. The two of them, Chrissie and her husband, endorsing mass murder in order to surround themselves with valuables.

'Thousands of people were going to die so you could have these, Martin!' Sam yelled incredulously. 'Don't you understand? That's *insane*.'

'You don't know what you're talking about,' Kessler retorted self-righteously. 'We knew absolutely nothing about the anthrax. Nothing whatsoever.'

Sam gaped. An admission at last. An admission of Martin Kessler's total involvement.

'*Didn't know about the anthrax?* What the hell *did* you think it was all about?'

'A financial scam,' he answered dismissively, 'that's all. A scheme to get hold of some of Saddam's hidden cash.'

Sam searched for shame on Kessler's face but found none. The man was as free of conscience as his wife had been. Defiant even.

'Oh! That's okay then,' he mocked. 'If it was just for *money*. Perfectly all right to betray a few minor state secrets. Perfectly okay to send poor old Sam to hell and back, if it helped you on your way to a Rembrandt!'

Kessler lowered his head contemptuously. He looked like a bull ready to take out the matador. His glasses were askew and the eyes behind the oval lenses contrived to be both expressionless and calculating.

Sam edged to one side, still clutching the painting. Out of the corner of his eye he'd spotted a mahogany bureau with its flap open.

'Where were you taking these pictures, Martin?' he asked as a diversion.

'Not mine. Borrowed from a friend. Taking them back,' Kessler mumbled, moving sideways.

'You borrowed a *Hockney*,' Sam mocked, shaking the painting. 'Who from? The Saatchis?'

'Look, put it down will you. It's valuable.'

'I know it's fucking valuable. That's why I'm holding it.'

Sam had reached the desk. He'd spotted an air ticket on it. And a folder of travellers' cheques. And a passport. He rested the painting on the floor and made a grab for the ticket.

'Jamaica,' he read quickly. 'Oh, *very* nice.'

Suddenly Kessler lunged. The painting flew aside before Sam could restore his grip on it. He lost his balance, falling backwards, hands flailing the air as Kessler went for his throat. Thumbs fixed onto his windpipe like artery clamps. The floor came up behind him, his head cracking down on the parquet. The weight of Kessler on top of him burst air from his lungs, air that wouldn't come back.

No air.

No air for God's sake!

He was choking, with Kessler's smelly breath daubing his face like a sick-soiled flannel.

Panicking, he scrabbled for Kessler's own throat, but the man tucked his chin hard into his breastbone. He went for the eyes beneath the glasses, but Kessler pressed his face down onto Sam's chest. He tore at his hair, pushed against his shoulders, kicked up with his legs, but the man's weight pressed down on him with a strength that seemed to grow as his own consciousness began to ebb.

Jesus, thought Sam. He's going to kill me. After everything that's happened, the bastard's going to squeeze the life out of me.

Suddenly he heard a crash from the hallway. He felt Kessler flinch. Feet thudded on the floor. There was a shout, then the weight was lifted from him. Air roared back into his lungs.

'Sam? You all right?'

A face bending over him. A man's face with broad features. Familiar, probing eyes that didn't blink.

The name came back to him. It was Charles. The man who'd questioned him in the flat above the Isleworth launderette on his return from Baghdad. SIS internal security.

He felt himself being raised into a sitting position.

'Yes,' he coughed, sucking in air to the very depths of his lungs. 'Yes, I'm all right. Where the hell have you sprung from?'

'We were outside in a van, listening. We've been bugging this place.'

So much for his belief that Waddell and friends were protecting one of their own.

'Thank God you were.'

On the other side of the room Kessler was being restrained by two men with powerful physiques. He'd lost his glasses and looked like a mole caught in a shaft of sunlight.

Sam got back onto his feet.

'Thanks. That bugger tried to kill me,' he accused, shaking with shock.

'And he would have done, easily,' Charles told him bluntly. 'Kessler trains with weights twice a week. He's as strong as an ox.'

The security man took a cell-phone from his pocket and dialled. 'Police Special Branch,' he whispered to Sam as the number rang out. 'We have to get them involved. I don't have any power of arrest, you see.'

Sam looked around the room again, seeing its entirety for the first time. French windows overlooked a neat garden with a freshly mown lawn and a bed of dahlias that exploded with colour. Next to the window stood a grand piano, its lacquered black surface cluttered with photo frames. He picked one up. Then another. All the pictures were of Chrissie. He turned his head. Everywhere he looked in the room there were photographs. On the mantelpiece, on the bookcases. He picked up more of them. Chrissie as a small child and as a teenager. Chrissie at her wedding with Kessler. Chrissie on the beach, walking in the country, studio poses . . . The room was a shrine. A shrine to a woman who'd betrayed every damned friend she'd ever had.

The man called Charles stuffed the aerial back into his cell-phone. 'There'll be someone here in half an hour,' he told Sam. 'Sooner, more likely.' He picked up the canvas from the floor. There was a small tear in it now. 'Never liked his stuff much,' he murmured. 'But then I *am* old-fashioned.' He put the Hockney back with the other paintings. 'The Yard's Art Squad will need to take a look at this lot.'

He turned towards Kessler who now stood straight-backed and still, watching what was happening with a dispassion that suggested none of it concerned him.

'There is one thing I'm still curious about, Martin,' said Charles, standing squarely in front of him. 'Which of you was in the driving seat? You or Christine?'

He'll blame it on *her*, thought Sam.

'*I* was,' Kessler answered promptly. '*I* ran Chrissie. She needed me, you see. Couldn't run a *tea shop* on her own.' He turned to Sam with a look of triumph on his face. 'By the way,' he added, and there was a vindictive edge to his voice, 'I knew all along, you know.'

'Knew what?'

'About you and her. And about her and Clare.'

'*What?*' The man was lying, he felt sure of it.

'Yes. That's surprised you, hasn't it. It's true. Chrissie always told me absolutely everything. From the very beginning.'

Sam stared blankly at him. Whether this was true or not, Kessler seemed proud of the fact that he'd coped so manfully with his wife's serial adultery. Eager to show what an enlightened husband he'd been, a man ready to accept what his spouse got up to, just so long as she *talked* to him about it.

Charles grabbed Sam's arm and led him out to the hall.

'I think that's probably enough,' he cautioned. 'There's some sensitive stuff here and anyway it'll be best if you aren't around when the police come.' He tried the other two doors off the hall and, discovering one was the kitchen, ushered Sam inside for a moment. 'It makes things tidier for us if you're not here. I'm sure you understand.'

'Of course,' Sam nodded. His mind spun as he tried to fathom out what sort of world of sensory deprivation Kessler had been living in all these years.

He noticed Charles was waiting for him to leave.

'I . . . I still don't quite understand,' he stumbled. 'How long have you known about Kessler?'

'Not long. We had very strong suspicions, that's all,' the security man confessed, 'but what he said to you a few minutes ago made all the difference. It's all on tape.'

'Since when did you have these suspicions?'

'Well, actually, since the day you came back from Baghdad. All your protestations of innocence on the question of how the Iraqis knew about you – you convinced me, you see.'

'Could have fooled me . . .'

'Ah yes. But that's my job.' Charles allowed himself a smile. 'We did some checking – what the Kesslers spent their money on, that sort of thing. Cars, holidays . . . They had a package tour to Jamaica last year. But enquiries on the island revealed they hadn't been there most of the time. They'd travelled on to the Cayman Islands. To set up bank accounts.'

'Good grief!'

'But that's confidential, all right? It'll come out as evidence. Now, how do you feel? Okay to be on your way?'

'Absolutely,' Sam sighed. 'Never felt better.'

They shook hands, then Charles opened the front door for him. 'You can leave it all to us now,' he said on parting. 'Okay?'

'Willingly.'

Outside, the air smelled wonderfully fresh. Overhead the sky was clearing and a breeze was getting up.

As he walked towards the river Sam began to feel as if the past hour had been spent on the far side of some mirror. The fact that one of the characters who'd inhabited the world beyond it had taken such a hold on his own life for an embarrassing number of years troubled him somewhat.

But the more he thought about it, the more he realised

that all it did was confirm something he'd known about himself for a very long time. He was a lousy judge of women.

But at least Chrissie was history for him now. For Kessler, he guessed, she would never be. Chrissie would always be there in that world of his behind the looking-glass.

Sam was approaching the river by now. He began to think of the real world that was beckoning him, not one seen through a distorting lens and never felt, but one that roughened the skin, froze the fingers and quickened the pulse.

Yes, he thought, looking up at the sky again. Tomorrow had the makings of being a damned good day for a sail.